FOR RICHER, FOR POORER

"I don't find the lodgings poor at all. They're perfect," she murmured. Her eyes met his, softly highlighted by the glow of the firelight. "And you spent your last shilling on this luxury for me, didn't you?"

Marcus smiled gently. "You're a noblewoman."

She stepped close to him. "I'm a woman, with a woman's heart."

Despite his staunchest efforts, her words caused his mask to slip. His gaze connected deeply with hers, intense in the recognition of their mutual desire. His voice dropped almost to a whisper, his words deeply melancholy. "What have we gotten ourselves into?"

"I know not, except the hunger I feel for you."

Her words were sweet invitation, and Marcus drew on all his strength to resist. She was untouchable. He had to remember that, or the consequences could be horrendous for them both . . . .

Praise for *Only in Your Arms:*

"Only in Your Arms is a stunning tapestry of Elizabethan England, with enchanting characters. Don't miss it!"
—Deb Stover, author of *Stolen Wishes*

"Run, do not walk, to get this book . . . . A story that even the Bard would be proud of . . . Not only entertains but will keep you enthralled until the last page is turned. I laughed, I moaned, I cried right up to the amazing ending."

—*Scribesworld.com*

ONLY IN YOUR ARMS

Tracy Cozzens

Zebra Books
Kensington Publishing Corp.
http://www.zebrabooks.com

ZEBRA BOOKS are published by

Kensington Publishing Corp.
850 Third Avenue
New York, NY 10022

First Printing: March 2000
10 9 8 7 6 5 4 3 2 1

Printed in the United States of America

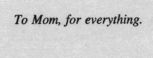

To Mom, for everything.

"A pair of star-cross'd lovers."
—*Romeo and Juliet,* Act 1, Prologue

ACT 1

"The course of true love never did run smooth."
—*A Midsummer Night's Dream*, Act 1, Scene 1

Chapter 1

England
April 1601

"Do you truly mean to kidnap the bride from her own wedding festival?"

Marcus Sinclair tore his gaze from the juggler performing in the center of the banquet hall and glanced at his acting partner.

Alan Tremaine's eyes were huge in his adolescent face. He tugged at the bodice of his gown, trying to get the oranges to settle properly against his flat chest. Marcus knocked his hands away and tugged the false bosom into a more natural arrangement. "Don't breathe a word of it, Alan," he said in a stage whisper. "Not in this crowd."

The youth nodded vigorously, making the brunette wig on his head jiggle. But still he whispered, "Lord Richard must be a great friend for you to risk your neck for him like this. I mean, look at all these nobles! If they so much as suspected your plans, they'd—"

"Alan," Marcus warned. He didn't want to think of the dangers ahead. Instead, he gathered his thoughts for the coming performance. Afterward, he would concentrate on finding a way to fulfill his promise to his best friend and rescue Lady Judith Ashton from the debauched viscount.

Beyond the archway where they stood, the vast hall at Viscount Mowbray's country estate played host to the cream of London society. The resplendently dressed courtiers were not a very forgiving audience. The juggler, garbed in belled cap and parti-colored clothing, received only scattered applause when he tossed six pewter plates into the air at once. He missed his catch, and a plate crashed to the floor. Jeers and catcalls filled the air.

Marcus ducked as a boy dressed in livery rushed past, carrying aloft a platter piled with venison. The aroma of roast meats mingled with smoke from the wall sconces and two iron chandeliers thick with candles.

Beside Marcus, thirteen-year-old Alan shifted nervously from foot to foot. This was his first performance in front of the nobility in such an intimate setting. Both of them preferred taking the stage with their acting company at the Globe Theater in London. Marcus never would have made the three-day journey from London to perform here if it weren't as a favor to a friend.

From where Marcus stood just outside the hall, he couldn't see the wedding party. He had hoped to catch a glimpse of the lady in question before he performed. He was more than a little curious what this paragon of beauty, this living Venus De Milo, this Helen of Troy incarnate, truly looked like. All he knew about Lady Judith Ashton was the color of her eyes and hair, facts he had needed to write Richard's love poems to her. He knew how easily a man could become foolishly besotted with a woman. He expected that was the case here, because no woman on earth could possibly be as fair and perfect as Richard described Judith to be.

And Richard's unbridled affections had led Marcus straight into this risky enterprise. He shook his head and sighed. Women were marvelous creatures, it was true. But falling in love was best left to the characters he played. Certainly no man should become so enamored with one that he actually risked his neck.

As if reading his mind, Alan prodded, ''Marcus, I still don't understand. If Richard wants her so badly, why doesn't he rescue her himself?''

Marcus kept his gaze fixed on the hall. "*Because*, Alan, if he misses his law school examinations one more time, the earl will cut him off for good."

"Still, it's an awfully big favor," Alan said. "Of course, he *is* a nobleman. Mayhap he'll be your patron someday. When he inherits, I mean. That is, if—"

"Shh!" Marcus cut Alan off with a chopping motion. The boy snapped his mouth closed. "We're almost on."

Several groups of people in the hall began to applaud as the juggler balanced five spinning plates on his nose and fingers while standing on one foot—until he lost his balance and juggler and plates came crashing down.

He scraped himself off the floor amid laughter and jeers. With hasty bows, he took his plates and shredded dignity, and he exited past Marcus and Alan. "They're all yours," he muttered to Marcus, "and they're out for blood tonight."

Marcus tugged on his elegant costume of blue shot through with gold, a nobleman's castoff the company had purchased at a bargain. Then he took a deep, preparatory breath and swept into the center of the hall, Alan following closely.

Once in position, Marcus faced the head table and waited for the viscount to give him leave to begin. The viscount was a small man, well past fifty, with a hooked nose, narrow eyes, and gray hair and goatee, which he stroked as he whispered into his betrothed's ear. Marcus sickened at the salacious expression on the man's face.

Marcus glanced at the lady in question. For the barest moment, his heart stopped. Golden hair fell in soft waves past her shoulders, held back by a rich headdress adorned in seed pearls. Her face was a perfect oval, with delicate cheekbones and tempting, well-shaped lips.

Richard had been telling the unadorned truth when he said Lady Judith could compete with the visages of the classics.

Marcus absorbed her features, noticed the slight tilt to her nose that lent her face so much charm, the sweet little cleft in her chin. Richard wasn't such a love-besotted fool after all,

Marcus reflected. He could swear her dark, soulful eyes told of ages of beautiful women and the tragedies they endured.

Then she looked up, and her gaze locked with his.

A shock coursed through Marcus, sparking to life an awareness, an innate knowledge of the woman who gazed at him. He understood instantly that the recognition was mutual, that she felt it, too, impossible though it must be. For he had never seen her before in his life. The moment stretched beyond eternity.

A well-placed elbow in his side yanked Marcus back to reality. "Sir," whispered Alan urgently. "The Master of Revels is signaling us to begin."

Reluctantly Marcus tore his gaze from Lady Judith and began his speech. "Good evening, Viscount, esteemed guests, lords and ladies," he said, projecting his stage voice throughout the huge hall. People began to fall silent.

Marcus introduced himself and Alan as members of Lord Chamberlain's Men of London. He was pleased with the enthusiastic response for the popular acting company from several nobles, who called out "Hear-yea! Hear-yea!" pounding the table with their pewter mugs, heedless of sloshing ale on the fine linen tablecloth.

Marcus grinned and bowed in acknowledgment. "For my lord's pleasure, and the pleasure of his betrothed and her family." He turned to the viscount, then to Judith's family, her father and various uncles, aunts and cousins. As he spoke, he covertly studied the man he guessed to be Judith's father. Heavy-set and with graying blond hair, the baron's well-formed features had probably made him quite handsome in his youth. Now he looked positively exhausted, as well as downcast.

"It is our pleasure to present to you tonight a scene from the uproarious comedy, *Taming of the Shrew*, newly returned to our repertoire," Marcus continued. "I invite you to attend the full performance at the Globe Theater in Southwark, outside of London." Marcus launched into a summary of the plot to bring the audience up to the moment of the scene he and Alan would perform.

Alan was ready in his place on a stool behind Marcus. Marcus retreated into the world beyond reality, becoming Petruchio trying his damnedest to tame the shrew Katherine.

A few minutes later, the nobles were laughing uproariously, just as Marcus had promised. Feeling victorious—as he always did upon capturing an unruly crowd—Marcus fed off the audience, growing bolder, his performance more energetic, pulling laughter even from the holdouts in the vast hall. He had them now, he thought with satisfaction as he neared the climax of the scene. The audience was his—every last one of them.

Exultant over his victory, Marcus finally cast his gaze toward Lady Judith once more, just as the scene reached its most hilarious. Her forlorn expression nearly caused him to break character. He was surprised and more than a little annoyed that she wasn't enjoying the performance that was so delighting the rest of the lords and ladies.

The scene ended. He clasped hands with Alan, his Kate, and bowed deeply to receive his thunderous accolades—and calls for more. Naturally, Marcus was prepared.

"The next scene we would like to perform for you is from the heart-rending love story that bewitched London theatergoers last fall—*Romeo and Juliet*, by William Shakespeare, favorite playwright of Her Majesty the Queen. The scene is Verona. Imagine if you will, a balcony, upon which the fair Juliet awaits, dreaming of her beloved Romeo." He gestured dramatically toward Alan, who was seated upon the same stool. But with a little imagination, it became for the audience a balcony.

As soon as the scene was over, and Romeo had bid farewell to Juliet, Marcus cast his gaze toward Judith to gauge her reaction. A tear spilled down her cheek, and she brushed it away with a slender hand.

The sight cut Marcus to the quick. He had the outrageous urge to personally console her. He was even more disturbed because the scene ended happily, even if the play itself did not. She was obviously a very unhappy lady.

His eyes slid to the older man at her left—her father—who had noticed his daughter's tears and tried not to show it. He looked downright guilty. Marcus itched to lay into the man for sacrificing his daughter to Viscount Mowbray.

Instead, he accepted the hearty cheers of the crowd and waited for Alan to pass him his lute. He cradled the smooth mahogany of the bent-necked instrument in his hands. Music had been his first love, and the lute was his most prized possession.

Hooking his foot around the stool, he slid it beneath his boot and supported the instrument on his knee. He plucked gently at the strings, bringing forth a joyous melody despite the newly awakened anger he was feeling. After all, this was a wedding feast. He had to continue with the farce of what a happy occasion was being celebrated.

As Marcus strummed his lute, he knew he was casting a magical harmony over the entire hall. But his energies were directed toward the unhappy bride. His gaze returned to her again and again to see how she fared. Each time, he found her luminous eyes riveted to him. Satisfaction surged through him. She was obviously captivated by his performance. He had finally won her over. Inspired anew, he spun out the melody, wove an intimate spell around her, pleasured her with song.

He kicked aside the stool and began to stroll up and down the tables, flattering a woman here, complimenting a man there as he sang. He paused before the head table, and to everyone's astonishment, a bouquet of flowers appeared in his hand, which he held out to the lady of honor.

Everyone applauded the sleight-of-hand except Judith. She lifted her gaze from the lavender and white bouquet, and their eyes locked. His breath caught. Time stood still. The noise in the hall faded away. He entered a dreamworld as he did when acting a part. But this time he was a spectator as well, and she was the one performing magic on him.

"Don't just stare at them, little pet, take the flowers," said Mowbray.

Despite the endearment, Marcus heard the viscount's irritation plainly. He cast a sideways glance at Mowbray and nodded in agreement. His gaze settled again on Judith. "Please. They're for you," he murmured for her ears only.

She reached out a slender hand and clasped the bouquet. For the barest instant, her soft hand touched Marcus', sending a tingle up his arm straight to his heart. A frisson of foreboding curled up Marcus' spine. He stepped away from Judith and back into his stage persona. He bid the hall *adieu,* acknowledging their applause with a wave and a bow before he and Alan departed.

Lady Judith Ashton watched the actor leave, wondering at the power of the spell he had cast on her. It was like nothing she had experienced before. Only when he was out of sight did she lower her gaze to the bouquet clutched in her lap. Almost immediately, she found a folded slip of paper hidden within the flowers. A note? A love letter? Judith caught her breath, then glanced furtively toward Mowbray on her right. He wasn't watching her, for once. She slipped the paper into her palm.

She burned to unfold it and read it, but there was no way she could without attracting the unwanted attention of one of the two conspirators on either side of her, her father and her future husband.

"Are you partaking of the masquerade ball, my little pet?" Viscount Mowbray asked as he leaned close to her. Many couples had left the banquet to prepare for the ball, which had begun in earnest in a nearby gallery.

Judith shuddered as Mowbray's greasy breath struck her face. "I—I'm feeling a touch ill, milord. I thought mayhap I would retire to my chambers."

The viscount's stiff smile revealed crooked, stained teeth with flecks of food imbedded between them. "You had best learn to enjoy the entertainment of an evening, dearest bride. I expect my wives to indulge in the revelries I offer."

Not wanting to stir Mowbray's ire, Judith nodded once. Her hand tightened over the mysterious message as she tried to steady her nerves. She squeezed so hard the folded scrap cut into her palm, but the pain reminded her she had something else to think on than the horror of her upcoming nuptials.

She had heard much about Viscount Mowbray's "entertainments" at Queen Elizabeth's Court. Here, all manner of debauchery and lewdness catered to the basest desires of the nobility. Even now, entertainments that would have been lauded at Court—such as the actors' marvelous performances—had given way to female dancers clad in bizarre animal costumes, prancing about as if seeking delicious prey.

Something brushed against her cleavage, and she jerked back. Mowbray's finger drifted toward her bare skin again, a wicked glint in his eye. "Soft, as I thought. Small, but adequate. I have a preference for voluptuous women, but you shall serve." He laughed deeply, his fingers now entwining in her hair. "You shall serve. My friend and I will see to it. You *do* recall what I said about my special friend? How I use it to train my young pets?"

She did, and the thought sickened her. She sent a pleading look toward her father, but he kept his gaze cast toward his plate, as if unwilling to recognize the fate he had damned her to.

Judith leaned toward him, her voice low, yet strained. "Father, I beg leave to retire. *Please.*"

"Hush, girl!" Baron Howard Ashton wouldn't even look at Judith as he whispered the command. "Depart if you must, just—*don't*—make a scene."

Judith blinked back a sudden rush of tears. Her father had been acting strangely for weeks—withdrawn, sullen, and not at all his jovial self. His moodiness had struck about the time of her unexpected betrothal. But he refused to explain it to her, which disturbed her even more than her impending nuptials to the most dissolute man at Court.

When she had pressed him, he became enraged and demanded she watch her tongue. His sudden anger had been uncharacteristic, and it frightened her. Usually he treated her as his most valued treasure.

In return, Judith had never disobeyed her father, never wished to upset him. She loved him dearly, for he was the only family she had. But she wished fervently that her father had not committed her to a marriage even he did not seem pleased with.

Not bothering to ask Mowbray's permission, Judith excused herself and fled the hall. She wasn't Mowbray's "pet" yet. For three short days, she belonged only to her father.

In a few minutes, she was alone in the chamber that had

been provided for her and her maid. With relief, she closed the door and threw the lock home.

Placing the bouquet on her dressing table, she lit a candle and sat on the four-poster bed, her fingers shaking as she unfolded the scrap of parchment. She read the words several times, hardly believing what they said.

After the banquet, Romeo will visit Juliet.

Her pulse sang with excitement, with fear. "What if he's caught?" she whispered urgently to the empty room.

In the hall, something magical had transpired between her and the dark, charismatic actor; of that she was certain. He must have prepared the note before his performance. Which meant he had seen her somewhere before. Yet Judith knew if she had seen him, she would never have forgotten him.

Certainly, she had never attended a play in her life. Her father believed the theaters corrupted the youth of the city and the crowds spread infection.

Instead, she had been pampered and watched carefully her entire seventeen years. There had been precious little opportunity for adventure, for spreading her wings, for tasting magic.

She rose and began to walk toward the balcony of her room, her pace picking up the closer she got, until she ran onto the balcony and peered over the side. She saw no sign of the author of the note, the only movement the shadows of trees swaying with the spring breeze. She lit the candles in the tall stands by the balcony door to serve as a beacon to him. The task was surprisingly difficult, her hands were shaking so hard.

Judith paused, amazed by her reaction. She had never felt this sort of excitement before—not for Richard, not for any of the lords at Court. And this was a man she didn't even know. On top of that, he was an *actor*, for goodness sake, what her father would call a vagrant. A titleless, landless commoner from the streets of London. Worse, she was betrothed to another man.

"God preserve me," Judith sighed, sinking onto the bed. Who was he, this incredible man who touched her soul and heart like no one ever had? What was he thinking to try to visit her in her private chamber? He must be utterly and completely mad. And so was she for even thinking of welcoming him. A proper daughter would alert her father, so her honor was not impugned. But when she had gazed on him in the hall, behaving properly was the last thing on her mind.

Judith heard a clatter outside her balcony. She forgot her father as a thrill surged through her. She rose and nervously smoothed her blue velvet dress. She glanced in the mirror hanging above the dressing table and tidied her hair, then almost pinched her cheeks to bring color into them. But her color was already high.

A deep voice startled her. "You don't need to primp. You look perfect as you are."

Chapter 2

Judith spun around to find the actor leaning against the balcony doorway. He was already inside the room, and she hadn't even heard him enter. Despite the climb, he didn't show the slightest sign of being out of breath.

Dressed all in black, he was potent, mysterious, a thief in the night. His face was obscured by a silver harlequin's mask, no doubt because of the evening's masquerade ball. But Judith recognized him. Her gaze played over his broad shoulders and slender hips, noting how his padded doublet emphasized his lean frame. Black hose outlined his lithe, muscular legs. His shoulder-length hair was as dark as the shadows cast by the flickering candles.

As she perused him, Judith became aware that he studied her just as intently. To her surprise, she felt not the least self-conscious.

"You don't seem nervous to have a strange man in your chamber." He moved closer and leaned against the dressing table. He was now merely a stride away.

He was no young maid's fantasy. His virile magnetism filled her chamber. Judith stepped slowly toward the bed to put dis-

tance between them. She faced him, her hand on the bedpost.
"Pray, do I have a reason to fear you?"

The corner of his mouth quirked up. "It depends on what
frightens you, milady."

The man was audacious, too bold for his own good. A delicious thrill warmed her, the sense of doing something outrage-
ously brazen for once in her sheltered life. A secret tryst with
a dark, enigmatic man. . . . "I don't even know who you are,
other than an actor, I mean."

"Marcus," he said softly, his husky voice sending goose
bumps up her arms. "My name is Marcus."

"Marcus." Her lips tingled with the forbidden familiarity
of his Christian name. By rights, she should be addressing him
with the title of "master," but she couldn't bring herself to do
so. "Marcus, do you believe in fate?"

His smile faded somewhat. "Fate?"

"Aye. The stars—they are aligned tonight. My astrologer
told me so."

"Aligned . . ." Marcus hesitated. "In what way?"

Judith smiled, her heart swelling with conviction. God had
seen fit to grant her one magical evening, one to savor for a
lifetime. . . . "The stars are perfectly aligned for transcendent,
all-consuming love that cannot be denied."

"And you believe this?" Marcus took a step closer to her.
Instinctively, Judith held out her hands toward him. Marcus
reached for them. Before touching her, he pulled back, his lips
curving in a mirthless smile. "I find little of worth in astrologer's prognostications, milady."

"Then, how do you explain—"

"Lord Richard sent me." His words were abrupt. "The Earl
of Langsforth's son. I'm going to rescue you from this place,
and from your father's mistake in betrothing you to Mowbray."

Judith's wild flight of fancy crashed to earth. "Lord Richard?" His name was barely a whisper on her lips. "*He* sent you?
I thought—" Judith stopped her words before she embarrassed
herself further. In the wake of her letdown, a wave of anger
came to her defense. "I see," she said coolly. "Surely you
jest. I can hardly just slip away from here. Do you think things

are that simple? Does Richard? I had no idea he was so lacking in sense," she finished dryly.

Marcus was clearly puzzled by her reaction. "Mayhap, milady, but it's all for love of you."

"I know it is." She sighed. She had first attracted Richard's notice two months ago, when she appeared as a shepherdess in a Court masque. Almost every day since, the young gentleman had shown himself to be thoroughly infatuated, sending her love notes, waxing poetic about her grace, her form, her looks, begging for a ribbon or small token of her affection. Judith had never received such worshipful attention from a man, and it had moved her. Richard himself was but a stranger to her. Yet he embodied the promise of a love match, a dream she had been forced to forsake when she had been betrothed to Mowbray.

Now this actor stood here, gazing at her, torturing her with thoughts of what could never be.

"Please remove that mask," she commanded. She narrowed her eyes. "I find it tiresome." She flipped her hand toward Marcus' face.

He peeled back the mask, and Judith instantly regretted her command, for she found herself staring at the actor as if she had never seen a man before. He was by far the most attractive man she had encountered.

In the hall she had noticed the startling power of his deep-set gray eyes, his voice, his presence. But he had been performing for everyone there. Now he was looking only at her. His magnetic gaze drew her to him as if she had no will. She explored every nuance of his face—straight nose, expressive mouth, high cheekbones.

"By the cross, if you don't stop looking at me thus . . ."

At his impassioned warning, Judith finally remembered just who—and what—she was. She struggled to hide her fascination and salvage her pride. "Excuse me. What is your name again?" she asked as if completely mystified.

He gave her a knowing smile. "Marcus Sinclair, at your service, milady." He swept into a deep bow. He righted himself and crossed his arms, his feet spread as if he commanded the room. "Richard has a plan to free you from your father's promise. All you need do is come with me. We'll escape and he'll handle the rest. Do you understand?''

Judith looked at him askance, irritated at his condescending tone. ''Your weak explanation hardly addresses the problem of how we're to assuage the viscount's anger. He might even seek vengeance—on my family, if not on me directly. Surely this isn't what Richard has in mind?''

To her surprise, her strong words made him smile with pleasure. Most men did not appreciate when she pointed out flaws in their logic. But then, she had never known an actor before. Perhaps they were a different breed. This one most definitely was.

''I regret that you troubled yourself so,'' she said, crossing to the balcony door in order to usher him through it. ''That you came all this way on a fool's errand. I hope Richard will compensate you for your trouble. If he does not, I will.''

He didn't budge. ''I don't need any compensation other than your presence by my side when we shake the dirt of this place from our feet. You are to be wed in three days. I want to be gone from here, with you, long before then. With the revelry going as strong as it is, tonight provides an excellent opportunity to escape—''

''Out of the question, kind sir,'' she interrupted. ''I can no more break my family's betrothal agreement than I can fly. Since, as you see, God did not equip me with wings, you know how unlikely that is. Thank Richard for me, but no thank you.'' Judith stepped to the bureau, wanting only to shut out the man and the foolish dreams with which he tempted her. She unclasped a gold, star-shaped pendant from around her throat and removed it, a sure signal to the actor that he should leave her to her privacy.

The man didn't take the hint. He stood behind her, hands on his hips, watching as she laid the expensive necklace carefully in its silk-lined box. His gaze met hers in the mirror. ''You're a fool not to take this chance. Mayhap you have not heard, but Mowbray's reputation as a husband leaves much to be desired.''

Judith spun on him, her hair cascading around her shoulders. ''Not heard! Not *heard*? Do you think I was born under a rock?

Which reminds me—I did not find your scene from that first play, that one with the shrew—"

"*Taming of the Shrew.*"

"As you say. I did not find it in the least humorous."

He frowned. "It seems you were alone in that assessment. Everyone else was picking themselves up off the floor."

"Everyone else isn't pledged to marry a man as wicked and sinful as Cain, either. Your, your Petronio—"

"Petruchio."

"Whoever. He was vile and mean, and I found the scene most offensive, the way he dragged her around by her hair and forced her to do his bidding."

His expression softened. "Perhaps," he said softly, "perhaps it was a poor choice of scenes. My apologies. It didn't occur to me—I didn't even think how you might see it. I beg your forgiveness."

Judith gazed at his honest expression. "I already forgave you. After the second scene."

He smiled. "The one from *Romeo and Juliet*?"

"Aye," she said on a breath.

"Mayhap I was . . . inspired." His voice was pitched low, almost a murmur. He looked at her intently, as if able to see the wealth of emotion, the impossible dreams, that she allowed no one to see. She found it difficult to tear her gaze from his.

"Marcus," Judith said, speaking his name slowly, savoring the sound of it.

He seemed to shake himself. Abruptly, a shutter fell across his eyes. "I'm here for Richard, milady, as his messenger. As his servant."

"Richard." Judith repeated, as if the name alone could conjure some feeling other than a fond memory of a kind admirer. "Aye. Well, I cannot be rescued, as you put it, for I am not a prisoner. I am marrying Lord Mowbray of my own free will."

Marcus closed the distance between them and gazed down into her face. Her heart was pounding so hard she was certain he could hear it.

"No woman in her right mind would elect to marry Viscount Mowbray. The debauched man has already rid himself of four wives—two through nasty annulments and two to various . . .

maladies. Tell me true, fair Judith. What was he whispering to you during the banquet?''

"He . . ." Embarrassment and shame flooded her. In defiance of her own feelings, she lifted her chin proudly. "He said he was looking forward to our wedding night."

"And?"

Judith could no longer face him as memory of the viscount's obscene suggestions echoed chillingly in her ears. She stepped to the bureau and toyed with the trinkets there. "Very well, I will tell you. He said he wants to introduce me to his . . . his . . . special friend."

"Friend?"

Judith swallowed hard. When she spoke again, her voice was remarkably steady. "I gathered he speaks of some sort of discipliner."

"He intends to *whip* you? My God. The bastard!"

Judith caught his expression in the mirror, saw his tightly clenched jaw, the valiant effort he was making to contain his fury. His reaction nourished her heart and warmed her soul. She had been right to tell him, stranger that he might be. For he was not a stranger to her. Never that.

"You don't have to marry him, Judith." His tender words assailed her defenses. "By God, don't do it."

Marcus slipped behind her and laid a hand on her partially bare shoulder. Judith trembled at his touch as he traced the edge of her gown with his thumb. In the mirror, their gazes connected. The vision of them together was intimate, yet somehow perfect, her fair-haired femininity contrasting with his dark, bold looks. His eyes light, hers dark. Yet both were slender, tall, her head reaching just above his jawline. As she gazed on their images, a strong sense of foreboding shook Judith, and she gasped.

He whispered seductively in her ear, "Sweet Judith, listen to your heart."

She lowered her eyes, frustrated by how he was making her hope. There *was* no hope. "Don't speak thus, I beg you! I *must* wed Mowbray. The betrothal papers have been signed."

"Nonsense. The agreement can be broken. Your father's

rich enough to pay Mowbray for his troubles. God knows, it's *his* concern.''

Judith tore away from him. She swung to face him. "*I* am an Ashton as well! He would lose face in front of the other lords! He would be appalled!" She paced before him. "Everything is so easy for you. You know naught about my situation! You are not a member of the nobility.''

Marcus' expression hardened. "Nay. I am not of the nobility. I'm a common man. But even a common man of common sense can see you would be a fool to wed Mowbray.''

Judith stared at him, amazed at his audacity in talking to her so boldly. He refused to recognize the difference in their stations. His every move toward her, his every word and action, showed he cared not a whit for her noble status. Instead of infuriating her, as it should have, it fascinated her to be so open and honest with a man.

Regardless, she had no intention of allowing him to sway her. "My happiness isn't the issue here. My father has every right to marry me to whomever he pleases. I have no say in the matter. My one duty is to provide a male heir to carry on the Ashton line, to inherit his title and estates. I'm his only child, and he needs me. He's counting on me to make a good match. I can't defy my father in this.''

Marcus' expressive lips quirked up. "I doubt the viscount can even sire a son—he's not done so yet as far as anyone knows, and he's long past seen his fiftieth year. They say when his wives fail to conceive, he finds ways to get rid of them and find new ones. Richard, on the other hand, is a mere four-and-twenty years." His tone took on a trace of bitterness. "He is of the nobility, the fourth son of an earl. He can help you fulfill your *duty* as you put it.''

His cool logic caused a fresh ache in Judith's chest. The thought of being disobedient filled her with anguish. She had never gone against her father, had always strived to be a dutiful daughter, especially since her mother's death. She certainly had never considered defying him in something so important as her marriage.

Until now. . . .

"Come away with me, Judith," Marcus urged. "Tonight.

You can be with Richard in a day. You'd be a fool to go
through with this marriage."

He has no idea of the torture he visits upon me! Judith cried
silently. In the past few weeks, she had come to accept her
fate. Now he dared to give her false dreams. She could stand
it no longer. "You know nothing of my life, sir!" she burst
out. "You are naught but an actor Richard hired. Leave me
alone and stay out of my life. I never asked for your help, and
I don't want it!" Before she could stalk away, a strong hand
caught her arm.

Marcus forced her to face him. "I'm not here because I want
anything to do with your life," he said through gritted teeth.
"Richard sent me to get you out of here. You tell me which
man you'd rather spend the rest of your life with—Richard,
or the viscount? You have less than three days to decide."

Judith's gaze locked with his, and she felt her knees go weak.
She knew she wasn't afraid of Marcus Sinclair, but the look
on his face, the anger—his passion—fascinated her.

"I *will* make you leave here with me, Judith. I swear it. If
I have to bodily carry you out of here, I'll do it."

He stared down at her a moment longer, his gaze traveling
over her face, as if absorbing every feature, every nuance of
expression. Then he was gone, striding toward the balcony
again and slipping over the side, disappearing into the shadows
beyond.

Judith pressed her back against the bedpost, forcing herself
not to run after him and watch his exit. She wouldn't do it,
couldn't let him see how he affected her. It was madness, pure
fantasy, an outrageous dream to imagine anything of a romantic
nature with this enigmatic stranger. Curse him, what on earth
had the man done to her?

It wasn't until she had slipped between the cool sheets of
her bed that she realized the actor had taken the indecent liberty
of using her Christian name.

Marcus returned to the masquerade ball, more determined
than ever to succeed at his task. He had a vague notion that if
he slipped into the right conversational circles, he might learn

something important about why Judith's father had seen fit to grant her hand to the debauched Lord Mowbray—something that could help him convince her to leave.

He haunted the ball for the next several hours, asking casual questions, listening in on conversations. Nothing valuable was forthcoming. No one understood why the wedding had been arranged so suddenly, or why Baron Ashton had agreed to give his precious daughter—a maiden with a reputation for exceeding virtue and gentleness—to the dissolute Mowbray.

Toward the end of the evening, Marcus struck gold.

Drawn by his host's familiar voice, he entered the small gaming room off the gallery. At the far end of the room, Baron Howard Ashton and Lord Mowbray were engaged in an intense discussion. Neither saw him.

Marcus thanked the stars for his well-timed entrance. He slipped behind a curtain a few steps from the door.

"I cannot wait that long, Ashton," Mowbray complained, his voice pitched low, yet menacing.

"Judith must become accustomed to the idea," Howard Ashton pleaded. "Give her more time."

"Accustomed! To what, pray tell? You think your daughter is a paragon of virtue, don't you? All fathers do. But when I make her mine, she'll learn soon enough what it takes to satisfy her husband."

"I'll not have you speaking of Judith in such a way," Howard shot back, his voice shaking with fury.

"You have no choice, Ashton. Unless you want a certain queen to learn something of great interest about one of her courtiers."

"Don't even mention it," Ashton replied in a harsh, worried whisper. "The walls may have ears."

Marcus smiled humorlessly to himself.

Mowbray didn't bother to lower his voice. "And you're concerned someone else will learn your dirty little secret."

"It's not dirty. You will not speak so degradingly of me. I am a man of honor."

"Does the word 'traitor' sound better? That's what Essex was, and that's what you are for backing Essex in his foolish rebellion. When the queen hears, at the very least she'll strip you of your honors, your title. Why, she may even fancy sending you to the block. Your head will decorate London Bridge so all may witness the fate of traitors. Then what will happen to your precious daughter? Marriage will certainly never enter into what I have planned.''

''You wouldn't dare!''

''I do not make idle threats. The wedding will be three days hence, as we arranged. I didn't think you truly meant to alter our agreement.''

Wearily, Lord Ashton finally responded, his voice quavering. ''Aye.''

Marcus held his breath as Mowbray passed by on his way out of the room. Ashton broke into sobs. Marcus was furious with the man, but, concerned about the safety of his own neck should he be discovered, he slipped out of the room and returned to the raucous celebration.

Ignoring the dancing and drinking of the noisy revelers, Marcus leaned against a wall and considered what he had learned. It lent an entirely new slant to this venture.

The Earl of Essex's doomed attempt to overthrow Queen Elizabeth two months ago was still the talk of London. Even Marcus had felt the heat of the rebellion. Two days before it occurred, several of Essex's followers went to the Globe Theater and bribed the players to perform Shakespeare's *Richard II*, so that people might see it was possible to depose a monarch. The play showed how King Richard lost his throne to Bolingbroke, who then became the fourth King Henry. Essex, a courtier who had fallen from favor, hoped the populace would take the hint and join him in unseating Elizabeth.

Along with William Shakespeare, Marcus opposed dragging out the old, retired work. But Essex's offer of forty shillings for each player was enough to convince the company to perform it for a theater packed with his supporters. In retaliation, the queen dragged each player in for questioning—not a pleasant experience.

Then she forced the company to perform for her the evening before Essex went to the block.

Playing before the queen ordinarily would have been a singu-

lar honor, but was in truth a ploy to shame the players. Thank
God that was as far as her ire went.

But Baron Howard Ashton had done much worse than the
players. Undoubtedly, he was among the nobles who had helped
finance the short-lived rebellion. Lord Mowbray had discovered
the truth and was blackmailing Ashton. Payment for Mowbray's
silence was Judith's hand.

What a fool! Marcus railed silently. What had possessed the
man to become involved in a rebellion? But then, few knew
how Essex himself could have been so foolish. Marcus cursed,
furious how people in power caused the innocent to pay the
price of their recklessness, as Judith now was.

But he knew he could never use this information to convince
Judith to leave here. He would convince her some other way,
for the knowledge would only draw her into the web of deceit
and possibly endanger her life.

"Why, lass! Are ye not takin' in the show?"

The gravelly voice startled Judith out of her reverie. She was
resting on a bench under a wall of climbing roses. Across the
path, a gardener weeded a bed of impatiens. She had vaguely
noticed the man making his way toward her with his wooden
toolbox.

Judith had escaped to the garden after the sumptuous break-
fast in the hall. She enjoyed the serenity of the knot garden,
the perfectly barbered boxwood and privet hedges imparting a
sense of order and discipline, something she lacked within
herself this morning.

All night, dreams had assailed her, restless, provocative
dreams of a dark man promising light, of a bright future painted
in vivid hues of joy and love. A future she had forced herself
to forsake. Throughout the hurried preparations for the wedding,
she had done her best to quash the desires of her girlish heart.
She intended to do the right thing—honor her father and his
wishes for her.

But the actor Richard sent had shaken her resolve. Worse,
she found herself captivated by a man she could never have,
a commoner who would be considered a more appalling match

for her than Viscount Mowbray. *Why* had Marcus Sinclair entered her life, only to torment her with unrequited desires?

She forced herself to respond to the gardener's question. "Nay, I have no desire to watch any more plays, or see any more actors."

The gardener wore simple brown clothes and a floppy hat. But the most notable thing about him was a prominent hunchback. So intent was he on his task, he kept his gaze on the ground where his hands worked as he spoke to Judith, his back partially turned to her.

"Eh? Ye have a right dislike of actors?"

Judith sighed, wishing the man would leave her to her thoughts. She did not feel energetic enough to engage in polite conversation. "I know naught about actors, except they can be a nuisance." She sighed to herself. "An astounding nuisance."

"Do ye like me garden?" The man gestured toward the flawless geometric curves and gravel paths surrounding flowerbeds and manicured shrubs. A topiary display and fountain graced the center of the garden. "Not a weed in it. I see to that. For the viscount."

"Aye, you do a very good job of it, too. It's a beautiful garden."

The gardener worked in silence a moment. Judith tried to ignore him. She pulled down a spray of damask roses from a cane above her head and inhaled their rich scent.

The gardener lowered his voice confidentially. "There's more 'n bushes and flowers planted in the lord's garden, y'know."

"What do you mean?" Judith asked, her curiosity piqued.

"Rumor 'as it that the lord's last two wives 're buried 'ere, as well. De-e-e-e-p underground," he said with great emphasis. His voice lowered to a whisper. "Buried in the dead o' night, they say."

Judith released the roses. The cane sprang up with a snap. "Why, that's horrible! I believe not a word of it. If it were thus, then whose bodies are in the family crypt?"

The gardener shrugged his hunchbacked shoulders. "The graves are empty. Lord Mowbray couldn't let anyone see what 'is wives looked like when they died, or he would've been accused of *murder*, they were in such *horrible* condition.''

Judith began to feel sick. It was true Lord Mowbray was rumored to beat his wives. But to beat them so badly they died from it? Mercy! And this was the man who would soon be her own husband?

'' 'E's brought a new un here now, another young beauty in the bloom of first womanhood, to be 'is wife. Ye would think 'e'd 'ad enough, after four of 'em, wouldn't ye?'' The gardener sighed. ''But nay, 'e's marrying 'nother un. Keeps tryin' to plow the fertile field, if ye grasp my meanin'. Rumor 'as it this new un's the most beautiful un yet. Eh? Wha'd'you think? 'Ave ye seen her?'' His eyes flicked over his shoulder, but didn't fall directly on Judith, his face still concealed by his hat.

Obviously the gardener had no idea to whom he was talking. ''I . . . well, yes, at the banquet. She was there.''

''Was the bride beautiful, as passin' fair as they say, sweet as a rose in the first 'eat of spring?''

''I suppose so. Adequate enough. As fair as any girl her age,'' Judith answered softly. The conversation had become so strange, she decided it was time to end it. ''Excuse me. I think I will go view that show after all.'' She rapidly walked away down the path.

Safely alone, Marcus shoved up the brim of his gardener's hat and grinned, his eyes following Judith's slender figure as she retreated. She was damned beautiful, in truth. But she was modest nonetheless. And, thank goodness, unsuspecting.

Marcus had concocted the story of the murders as a way to frighten her into leaving with him, for he was not about to tell her the truth about her father and Mowbray. Now he needed to see if the seeds of doubt he had planted had taken root.

He glanced around the garden. Only a few other guests strolled the crushed gravel paths on the far side. He decided it was time to become himself again and confront Judith with rational arguments. For despite her words, she had headed off in the opposite direction from the show and was still wandering the garden paths.

Marcus slipped behind a tall cypress and quickly removed his costume, wig, and the pillow he had used to form a hunched back. He stuffed them in his gardener's toolbox, then shoved the toolbox deep under a shrub, out of sight.

He returned to the path, clad now in his usual breeches and doublet. Unfortunately, he hadn't been fast enough. Judith was nowhere to be seen.

Judith wandered along the neat rows of trimmed boxwood in the viscount's elaborate hedge maze, trying not to dwell on the gardener's dire warning. Mowbray was unattractive and crude, but he couldn't be as horrible as people said. He would treat her right because she was his wife. Wouldn't he?

She rounded a corner and heard a maiden's giggle. She wasn't alone after all. Thinking it might be one of the young guests, Judith decided she should act like a proper hostess and greet the owner of the voice. The viscount's guests were hers, too, after all. She turned the next corner and froze.

The woman giggled again, but she didn't see Judith, because she was crouched on all fours. A man knelt behind her, whispering something to her, while his hands—they were somewhere up her skirt! The man—Judith stared in shock, her stomach knotting up—it was her own betrothed, the viscount! Judith stayed frozen until the viscount shoved the woman's skirts above her waist and began grappling with her.

Judith stumbled toward the exit, unable to prevent a gasp from escaping her lips.

"Ah! It's the bride to be, come to join us in our frolic. Stay."

At the viscount's lewd command, Judith forced herself to face him, wanting suddenly to have it out with the disgusting man. She turned on him, only to see his plump doxy lolling on the grass, an unrepentant smile on her pock-marked face.

"This is our *wedding* festival," she said, her words a harsh rasp. "How could you be so despicable as to—"

Mowbray leapt to his feet with surprising agility, his clawlike hand wrapping around her wrist. He yanked her close. "I see you have spirit after all. I approve of spirit." He twisted her arm behind her back, forcing her chest against his. His small potbelly pressed against her own stomach, his eyes on a level with hers. "It's much more enjoyable to tame a spirited bitch than a docile one."

Indignant, Judith slammed her heel into his foot. Her show of defiance wrought a change in Mowbray's demeanor. Threat—always simmering below the surface of his gentile facade—rose starkly to the surface. In a rage, he kicked Judith's feet out from under her, and she fell hard to the grass.

Shocked and winded, Judith looked up at Mowbray. Fury contorted his hawklike features, giving him a demonic appearance. No man had *ever* treated her thus. No man would *dare*. Once Judith's initial shock passed, panic surged through her. She scrambled on all fours toward the exit, trying to gain her footing on the slippery grass and put distance between them.

"Hold her."

The doxy instantly obeyed Mowbray's command, tackling Judith and pinning her to the ground. "High 'n mighty bitch," she whispered as she pressed her heavy body into Judith's. Judith choked as fresh spring grass and mud filled her nostrils.

"Bring her here, Avis," Mowbray commanded.

Avis began dragging Judith toward Mowbray. Judith wasn't about to take such treatment without a fight. She kicked at Avis and tried to wrench her arms from the doxy's grip. "Let go of me, you ill-mannered wench!"

Avis laughed, clearly certain of her own power in Mowbray's presence. She sat astride Judith and sneered down at her with a buck-toothed countenance. "Ya don't look so high 'n mighty now, princess, do ye?" Grass stains covered Judith's ornate buttercup gown; her hair hung in disarray. Mud clung to her cheek.

"Lock her arms in place," Mowbray commanded.

Judith struggled, but Avis' heavy, work-hardened hands pinned her wrists above her head, bringing the wench's garlic breath within inches of Judith's face.

"Let me go," Judith gasped. "I'll not interfere with your tryst. I promise. I never will. Whatever you want to do is fine, but leave me be!" She blinked to keep the tears at bay.

"Nay, you shan't interfere," Mowbray said. "You'll be part of my games, I'll warrant. The best part, once you're properly trained."

Judith couldn't see past Avis' huge body, but she felt air strike her legs through her silk stockings. She kicked out furiously, felt the satisfaction of hitting something, followed by a grunt.

"Bitch!" Mowbray had the advantage, since Judith couldn't see what he was doing. Sitting on her ankles, he began shoving her gown and petticoats past her knees. Nothing else protected her from his sight, and her skirts made poor barriers.

The walls of the hedge—previously so bright and friendly—closed in on Judith. She shuddered in terror as she felt hands slide along her shins and over her knees.

"Indeed—" he grunted. "Must see what I'm buying." Mowbray's raspy voice floated toward Judith, followed by thick panting as he forced her legs apart, undoubtedly looking on her most intimate female parts.

Judith cried out as Mowbray pinched the inside of her thigh, hard. "A little lover's mark, to remember this by," Mowbray panted.

She caught a glimpse of him fumbling with his trunk hose.

"Avis, cover her mouth." With a gleeful sneer, Avis leaned her great bosom forward and pressed it in Judith's face. Judith was certain she would pass out from the stench of the doxy's body, if not from lack of air.

"Lord Mowbray! Be ye about?" The deep Scottish brogue came from the other side of the hedge. "A messenger from the queen has arrived and seeks an audience with ye, milord!"

Mowbray scowled and struggled to his feet. "Who calls me thus?" He adjusted his clothing and approached the hedge opening.

The messenger remained out of sight, but he spoke with authority. "Master Duncan, milord, of Highsmythe House in Edinburgh. Yer chamberlain sent me to seek ye ou'."

Judith knew the Highsmythes were among the visiting nobility, and the messenger must be one of their retainers.

Mowbray swore thickly. "Leave her, Avis. She's all mine," he commanded, before vanishing from sight.

Judith hardly had a chance to thank the stars for the messenger's timely arrival before she realized Avis had no intention of obeying Mowbray's command. Instead, the woman kept

Judith imprisoned, pulling her arms up so high sharp pains shot through her shoulders.

Judith gasped in agony, but the doxy merely laughed. The more Judith struggled, the higher Avis pinned her arms.

"Lily-white bitch." Avis' rank breath and foul words struck at Judith. "Ye'll ne'er learn to please milord, e'en whoring all day and night. I'm the only one who can. I'm—ugh!" Avis lost her breath at the same moment Judith pulled free.

Judith sat up and cradled her sore arms, watching in blessed relief as Avis cowered on the ground before Marcus Sinclair.

"Crawl back into your hellhole, you filthy whore!" Marcus' handsome face had transformed into a mask of fury. He raised a booted foot, ready to kick Avis.

The doxy took the hint. She scrambled through the exit in a flurry of skirts and whimpers.

"I don't usually strike women, but by God, that one . . ." His gaze settled on Judith, who struggled to her feet.

Suddenly, the strength drained out of Judith. Her legs grew wobbly as a wave of nausea twisted in her abdomen.

"Steady, there."

The gentle words settled around her like a benediction. His strong arms enfolded her, caressed her back, soothed her like a frightened child. Judith accepted Marcus' comfort, reveled in the feel of his lean body pressed to hers. A warm, enjoyable flush suffused her. She sighed in contentment, knowing he would protect her. For now, she was safe.

Marcus slipped his hand along her neck to cradle her face against his chest. Her eyes closed, Judith nestled against him. "Thank you, kind sir," she whispered.

"Fair lady." His lips brushed her forehead. "If my circumstances were different, I'd deliver his head on a platter, not resort to trickery," he said, his voice hollow.

His words snapped Judith back to reality. Marcus Sinclair was naught but an actor, and she was allowing him to cradle her like a child—or a lover. Gathering her strength, she pushed out of his arms. "Thank you for your concern. But as you can see, I'm perfectly fine. Truly."

He gently rubbed the mud from her cheek. His touch sent a tremor of longing through Judith. "You're a terrible liar."

Judith gazed into his magnetic gray eyes. The man's presence—his smallest touch—sent a confused barrage of emotion through her. How much of the tawdry event had he seen? Had he merely heard enough to know he had to distract Mowbray? Or had he actually been witness to her shame? Suddenly, Judith wanted nothing more than to be alone.

She shuddered, wrapping her arms around herself and turning her back to him. "Please. I can't—I don't want to talk about it."

"Has Mowbray finally shown his true colors to you, in all their glory?"

His biting words prodded her anger, her misery. Judith's eyes filled with moisture. "He's horrid, despicable! This is my wedding feast! My family is visiting! And he's in here—in here with some—some—ill-bred doxy!" She faced him, blinking hard at the tears collecting in her eyes. "And then—and then, when I caught them, he wanted to do the same to me!"

"Judith." Marcus reached for her, her own pain mirrored in his handsome features. Judith fought the incredible urge to lose herself in his embrace. Instead, she retreated several steps. She couldn't allow him to comfort her. It was more than improper. The temptation he offered . . . it was so *wrong*.

With a frown, Marcus let her maintain her distance from him, but he obviously wasn't ready to end their argument. "Did you expect more from the man?" he asked sharply. "I can promise it won't be any better after you're married."

"I don't need you to tell me that."

"I know you don't. God knows, after what just happened to you, how could you even *think* of going through with the wedding? He's a cruel, vicious man. Everyone who works here knows it."

She hesitated. "Aye, I know. The gardener said something to me about it, just before . . ."

"What did the gardener say?"

Judith shivered as she recalled the macabre tale. "He—he said that Mowbray had beaten to death his last two wives and buried their bodies in the garden to hide his . . . crimes." She stopped, a new thought striking her. Marcus appearing when he did . . . the gardener's timely conversation with her . . . the way the gardener wouldn't face her. "You were the gardener, weren't you? You dressed up in some sort of costume, and—"

Marcus' eyebrows rose. "Me? Nay, I never played that particular part."

His innocent denial threw Judith. "But I thought . . . since he told me such a grisly story . . ." She sighed. "Nay, it matters not. There is nothing for it, after all." She looked away, the shame and terror of the past few moments coursing through her anew. The thought of being in the viscount's power chilled her through. She would never enjoy his licentious games. She could hardly stomach his touch! Yet she would be doomed to a hell of submissive obedience, a toy for his base pleasures. "It was awful!" she said, her voice catching. "I—I cannot stand to think of it, of being wed, of having my body used—"

"It doesn't have to be like that," Marcus said, his gaze probing hers. "That was the lust of a twisted mind, Judith. The viscount is incapable of anything else."

She laughed, a small, humorless sound. "What else is there?"

"Honor," Marcus replied. "Perhaps even love. You know that, Judith." The actor's gaze turned tender. He closed the distance between them to less than a foot. This time, Judith didn't pull away as his hands slipped up her back, sending marvelous, illicit thrills through her bruised body. "Sweet lady, I could never rest easy if I left you here. I beg you. Let me save you. You *can* have love." His jaw tightened a fraction. "Richard's love."

He looked at her so intently, she felt as if he saw something deep inside her that she herself couldn't see. She found it difficult to tear her gaze from his.

"Not me," she said softly. She looked at him a moment more—wanting to remember forever the way he gazed at her—before she forced herself to turn and leave him.

Chapter 3

"Did the gardener convince her, sir?" Alan asked as soon as Marcus returned to their room above the stables.

All the hired entertainers were staying in the long loft, so Marcus and Alan had strung up a blanket for privacy. It wasn't necessary right now, however, because the other entertainers were plying their trade at revels throughout the grounds, which meant the two men could speak freely.

Marcus tossed the gardener's toolbox aside and collapsed on an overturned barrel half. He clenched his fists on his thighs, rage he had barely held in check in Judith's presence now surging to the surface. "If I thought I could get away with it, I'd murder that sick bastard."

"Marcus," Alan said in a shocked whisper. "You don't mean that, sir. He's a nobleman!"

Marcus gritted his teeth. "By God, I do."

"Sir, this isn't like you."

The strain in Alan's voice finally registered. Marcus focused on his apprentice, saw that his fury had frightened the boy. He jammed his fingers into his long hair and sucked in a calming breath, using an old actor's trick of concentrating on the mundane to force himself to relax—in this case changing into his costume for the evening's performance. He rose and methodically began removing his black doublet. Alan jumped to help unfasten the sleeves and slip them off.

Marcus met Alan's gaze and forced a smile to his face. "She's damned stubborn, is what she is. Nothing terrifies her enough to make her leave, not even an obscene pawing from that wretched pile of horse droppings." He yanked his arm out of the second sleeve so roughly it tore. "Perhaps I'll have to try something else."

Alan inspected the damage with a sigh. "I can repair the pulled stitches."

Marcus shot him an apologetic smile. Properly maintaining costumes was paramount to an acting company operating on a strict budget.

Alan shrugged, as if to say it was all in a day's work. "So what will you try next?"

"I know not . . ." Marcus turned away from Alan and began to pace. "Mayhap she needs advice from a higher source than gardeners and maids, though you'd think she'd listen to the viscount's own servants. Of course, it's not that she doesn't believe the viscount is wicked—she had more than enough proof of such today. It's her damned sense of honor and duty. She can't imagine disappointing her father." Alan held up the ornate doublet Marcus would perform in that evening, and he slipped into it.

"Sir." Alan hesitated as he fastened the doublet's front. "Is it truly worth all this? Can't Lord Richard find another noble maiden to wed?"

Marcus considered his question as he yanked on the hem of the gold-flecked doublet. The irony struck him like a cruel blow. He could wear a nobleman's castoffs, even play the parts of kings, but he would always be common to the core.

Nobility. Gentle as Judith or cruel as Mowbray, God had seen fit to place them together in the same social class.

Marcus had never felt the pain of such differences before now. As a hired player, he earned eight shillings a week, less than the cost of one of Lady Judith's baubles. Someday, he might save the fifty pounds necessary to buy a share of the acting company. As a shareholder, he would earn a profit from each performance. That was as high as a country-bred lad such as he could possibly aspire. Will Shakespeare himself, the son of a glover, had earned the status of a property owner and gentleman only after years of dedicated work that pleased the queen.

"Richard thinks the lady is worth such trouble," Marcus said slowly. "I can't deny it." Holding Judith, comforting her after Mowbray's heinous assault—nothing in his experience equaled the frustration, the exquisite pleasure, the tremendous protectiveness that had filled him. Her gratitude as she had gazed up at him, brown eyes sparkling with unshed tears, had damn near torn his heart out.

But she was Richard's love. That was who he was doing this for.

Marcus never forgot that Richard had saved his life when he first came to London as an unsophisticated country lad six years ago. He had been seeking work in the exciting world of the theater then coming into its prime.

But his first day in the city, cutthroats had set upon him. Richard's quick sword had sent them running. Learning that he and Marcus hailed from the same country shire northwest of London sealed their friendship.

Since then, the two of them had been inseparable—carousing at the Blue Lion alehouse in Southwark, wooing wenches and barmaids, gambling behind Lord Grey's Inn, where Richard sometimes studied law to please his father. Indeed, it was easy for Marcus to forget the vast difference in their stations.

So when Richard sought his best friend's help to steal Judith away, Marcus didn't have to think twice. But he hadn't counted on involving his own heart.

Richard was going to be one lucky bastard married to Judith, Marcus thought as he collapsed on the barrel so Alan could remove his boots. And his lingering debt to his noble friend would be well paid.

Flames flickered cheerfully from the hearth in the corner of Judith's guest chamber, in contrast to the misery that hung in the air. Clutching a bedrobe around her, Judith sat on the edge of the four-poster bed and stared into the fire.

Her maid Audrey knelt at a washbasin, scrubbing gravy out of her gown. The noise of revelry rolled across the greensward from the banquet hall, reminding Judith of the horrible end to an even more horrible day.

During the banquet, the doxy who had so abused Judith had been assigned to serve her—a cruel joke on the viscount's part. Avis had sneered at Judith while waiting on her, finally going so far as to drop a platter of roast beef down Judith's front. Mowbray had laughed uproariously at the sight, and many of the nobles—people she had once thought well-bred and kind— had joined in.

At least it had given Judith an excuse to retire. Unfortunately, she would miss Marcus Sinclair's performance that night. And only one night remained.

"Richard," Judith murmured to herself. "Why did you send him to me?"

"Milady, don't waste your time fretting over Richard the Lying-hearted." Audrey laid the wet gown across a screen before the fire.

"I hurt Richard's feelings," Judith said softly, a tremendous pang of remorse stabbing at her. If she had only expressed more interest in the man, she might even now be wed to him, instead of being Mowbray's bride. "He must truly love me, to hire that actor to steal me away."

"Mayhap he does, milady," Audrey said. "But I truly doubt it. All those trinkets and poems—he looked to be playing at love. He has his eye on your dowry, methinks. That's what he wanted from you, an overindulged reprobate like him. You were a great catch that got away."

Audrey had taken a special dislike to Lord Richard, for reasons that weren't clear to Judith. Her maid had heaped him with insults when he appeared below Judith's window to serenade her and slammed the door in his face when he came to deliver gifts.

But Richard had behaved no differently than other lords who had tried to claim her hand, except he had been more ardent in his pursuit. In truth, he was the best-looking of her suitors, with his ginger hair and beard and his sturdy build. Some at Court considered him a no-account wastrel, though none could fault his knightsmanship and hunting skills—neither of which carried much weight with Judith.

"Besides," Audrey continued, "you couldn't possibly love that rogue, with all his fancy talk and false promises." She hesitated, gazing toward Judith. "Could you?"

"I don't know. Mayhap I don't know what love is. Now I'll never know."

Her back to Judith, Audrey smoothed the damp gown on the screen, adjusting it needlessly. "*I* can tell you about love," she said sourly. "It's not like in fairy tales. There's no such thing as handsome princes. Those are made-up stories parents tell their daughters so they'll be tractable about being yoked to a husband for the rest of their lives—and compliant in bed."

"Audrey, no." A sharp pang of regret coursed through Judith for Audrey's own lost dreams, whatever they might have been. Five years her senior, Audrey had always seemed so much older than her. But now that Judith had reached womanhood, she saw more clearly what an attractive young lady her maid was. Though petite, she was surprisingly well endowed, a fact Audrey tried to hide with a preference for oversized gowns. Her black hair was braided and rolled up in back of her head in an efficient hairstyle.

Audrey was merely two-and-twenty to Judith's seventeen. Yet she had never shown the slightest interest in leaving the employ of the Ashton household to raise her own family. Nor had she ever been interested in men.

Over the seven years Audrey had served as her maid, Judith had gathered through off-hand comments Audrey tossed out that she had endured a rough childhood. With it had gone any belief in the power of romantic love. Instead, she had dedicated herself to protecting the motherless Judith from a world she perceived as cruel and harsh.

Audrey came over to Judith and gave her shoulder a comforting squeeze. "I'm sorry, milady. I would rather you could keep your dreams."

"It's too late for dreams, Audrey." Judith couldn't cry. She had used up her tears after learning who her future husband was to be. Restless, she slipped off the bed.

Without conscious intent, Judith found herself at the balcony door. She pulled back the curtain and looked over moonlit greensward toward the hall beyond, its golden windows glowing with life. Yet the carousing had stilled, as if the guests had been struck with a spell of silence. Even nature seemed to be waiting, expectant and full. Then she heard it—a hauntingly lovely song in a man's rich alto, rising toward her on the evening breeze.

"Marcus." Judith would recognize his voice anywhere. No other singer possessed his facility with music, his ability to turn simple words into magic. He alone touched her heart with promise of love's fulfillment, a love she would never have the chance to experience.

His song held Judith spellbound until the last note. Gradually, applause swelled, long and thunderous. Then the sounds of revelry resumed.

Judith sighed, irritated at herself for her hopeless pining, hopeless dreams of an impossible future. She let the curtain drop back into place and turned again to Audrey. "Aye, I will put Richard out of my mind," she said with determination. "And what he tried to do for me by sending his friend. I must. Or I shall not be able to face it."

"Then, let's give the bright side a go," Audrey encouraged.

"The bright side." Judith shuddered. Audrey didn't know, for Judith hadn't been able to share any details of her experiences with the viscount. They were far too shameful.

"At least you won't be going into your marriage with a broken heart over Richard Lying-hearted," Audrey said. "There's a big worry off your shoulders. Who knows, you might even come to care for your husband."

Judith met Audrey's large brown eyes and knew her maid didn't believe her words any more than she did.

Only one more day of freedom. The thought resonated over and over in Judith's mind as she sat in the front pew of the small chapel, between her father and Viscount Mowbray. She tried to lose her worries in prayer, but couldn't shake her fears, especially with the viscount's hand inching up her thigh. Judith shuddered in disgust. Even within the House of God, he could not contain his base appetites.

Once the service ended, the guests filtered out, anxious to take advantage of the Lord's Day to enjoy lawn bowling, dances, feasting, and hunting. Judith stayed seated until the last parishioner had left.

"Judith, aren't you going to attend to the lord?" her father asked as he watched Mowbray exiting the chapel.

"I am attending to the Lord," she said wryly. Howard Ashton's brow creased. "Truly, Father, I just need a few moments alone."

Howard nodded. "As you wish, Judith, but don't be long from the viscount's side. You have been scarce as a flower in December. I know you are a trifle nervous about your wedding, but please, for my sake, show yourself more often or people will begin to talk."

Judith nodded, and her father left her there alone. She sighed, dropped to her knees and closed her eyes. She knew there was no chance she would be granted her fondest wish, to love the man who would be her husband and be loved in return. It seemed such a little thing for the Lord Almighty to grant her, but as impossible as putting a camel through the eye of a needle.

"I sense your sad heart, my child."

Judith's head shot up at the sound of the kindly voice. A pastor garbed in a black clerical robe stood before her, a hooded cowl pulled over his head. "Excuse me?" Judith peered at him, but the sunlight diffused by the arched stained-glass windows provided scant illumination in the dim church.

"You are distressed. I am here if you wish to unburden yourself. I need to help Reverend Bolton put away the vestments, but while I do that, I will listen if you wish to talk."

"I—I'm fine, thank you," Judith said hesitantly, sitting back on the pew. She was disconcerted to have her private meditations interrupted, even by a man of God.

"I know, my child, that you are pledged to marry the viscount." Judith's eyebrows rose, and he smiled gently.

"You weren't at the service," Judith said, eyeing the pastor suspiciously. Like the gardener and the Scottish "messenger," his appearance was exceptionally well timed.

"Nay. I just returned from a visit to the parish outside my lord's estate."

"Then, pray, lower your hood."

"Certainly, milady." The pastor flipped the hood back, revealing hair the color of summer wheat and a large, hooked nose.

"Oh. I apologize, Father. I thought mayhap—" She tried to search the pastor's face, but the man had dropped to his knees in prayer, his head bowed. "Never mind. It matters not."

The pastor completed his prayer. He rose after a moment and turned again to her, staying within the shadow of a pillar that fronted the nave.

"But it does," he said. "If you are distressed, you need to lay your burdens on the Lord. You have come to the right place. Do you have burdens, my child?"

Judith looked down at her lap and twisted her fingers together. "Aye. I'm desperately afraid."

"What do you fear?"

"The viscount. Being wed to him for life. He—he behaves so atrociously toward me. Toward everyone."

"I see." The pastor clasped his hands behind his back and paced before her, keeping nevertheless to the shadows. "Let me ask you this. When you are wed tomorrow, and say your vows to love and honor your husband, will you feel them in your heart?"

"I don't know, I—oh, yes, I do know. The answer is no, I won't feel them in my heart. Does that make me terribly sinful?" Judith was almost afraid to look at the pastor's face for fear of the censure she would see there.

"Not at all," the man said mildly. "You will be asked to confess on the morrow to God and man that you love this man, but you say you do not. It would seem to me that to make such a pledge while being insincere is a travesty of your faith. I would advise you to seek means to break such a betrothal."

Judith looked up at him in shock. "Do you mean it?" She had been expecting a lecture to "honor your father" and do her duty as his daughter, whatever that entailed.

"Yes, my child, I mean it. So does He." The pastor gestured to the heavens.

Her heart soared with fresh hope. "I've dreamed of doing that, I've dreamed of marrying a young man who might love me, but to defy my father—I don't know if I can. I know he isn't happy about this match either, but for some reason he wishes me to wed the viscount."

"He gave no explanation?" the pastor asked coolly.

Judith hesitated. She wished to God she understood why. "Nay. I asked him, of course, but he became furious with me."

"Is it because of all the men who sought your hand, Lord Mowbray was obviously the most suitable?"

"Absolutely not!"

Pacing before her, the pastor spread his hands. "You would prefer marriage to a younger man. One who displays a strong sense of honor, exhibits character." He paused before her. "Are these not values your father has worked to instill in you since you were a babe?"

"Aye! That is true," Judith replied, struck anew by the hypocrisy of being forced to wed a man who stood for all her father had taught her to hate.

"It would seem to me, then, that you are the victim of two men—neither of whom are dealing honestly with the sacred state of matrimony, or the weighty responsibility of seeing to your future. Mayhap, if you're strong enough, you might show your father the error of his ways by refusing to allow this travesty of a wedding to take place."

"I never thought of it that way," Judith said. Perhaps she could refuse, at that. She could withstand her father's anger long enough to get some answers from him, for her own sake. "You have given me much food for thought. Thank you." Judith rose to leave. The pastor turned toward the altar to straighten the altar cloth. Then another thought occurred to her, and she sat down. "Excuse me. Pastor?"

"Aye, milady?" He turned back to her, but he stayed well apart from her, in the shadows of the nave.

Judith swallowed hard. What she was about to discuss she

had never spoken of to anyone. Yet she felt she could share with this man of God, for she was desperate to unburden herself. "Something else is bothering me."

"Continue, child. I'm listening."

"I would never tell another soul, except perhaps my mother, but she died years ago. You've helped me much so far. It's about . . ."

"Aye?"

"It's about—"

"Go on."

"It's about . . . my body," Judith finished lamely, deeply embarrassed.

For a long moment, the pastor did not respond. "I see. Pray, continue."

"Is it natural for a woman to . . . feel certain things . . . in her body when around a man who isn't her husband?" Judith finished quickly, desperate to get the words out once she started them.

"Ah. You refer to . . . attraction . . . the physical attraction . . . between a man and a woman?"

"Aye." Judith sighed rather than spoke the word.

The pastor did not speak for the longest time. *I've offended him*, Judith thought, watching as he clasped his hands together. She focused on his hands—long, tapered fingers. Elegant hands.

He finally spoke. "It is important to wait until marriage to consummate such feelings, as I'm sure you're well aware."

"Oh, of course. Aye. I didn't mean I would—"

"But as long as the . . . attraction . . . you feel is for your future husband, there is no harm done. Is it mayhap the viscount you feel—"

"Nay," Judith interrupted.

"I see." Again, a lengthy hesitation. Judith wished she had never brought up the subject. "Another man, then, whom you have come to care for."

Judith nodded.

The pastor pulled in a deep breath. "One who has expressed his love for you, has courted you, mayhap, before you became betrothed to Lord Mowbray?"

He knows about Richard! Understanding came so suddenly it nearly knocked the breath out of Judith. She stared at the pastor—shock and dismay mingling with a guilty thrill at once again being alone with *him*. She jumped to her feet and advanced on the blond, beak-nosed pastor. "Forgive me, Father, but I ask you to step out here into the light for a moment. I need to see your eyes before I continue this discussion."

"Why, child, it's not necessary to—"

"Please, indulge me a moment."

"I believe Reverend Bolton is summoning me." The pastor turned away, but Judith caught his sleeve in both her hands. She yanked it for all she was worth, spinning the pretend man of the cloth into the bright light beyond the nave. She grabbed his face in her hands and stared into a pair of gray eyes that were becoming quite familiar to her.

"It *is* you! And I fell for it! I knew you were lying when you claimed not to be the gardener. I *knew* it! You must delight in making a fool of me." She yanked at his nose, and the beak fell away in her hand. It was slightly hardened bread dough. Next came his hair, a wig made of horse's hair.

"Making a fool of you is not my intention, Judith," Marcus insisted.

"I'm not Judith to you, sir. I'm a lady, and you will address me as such!" She pulled herself up to her full willowy height and did her best to look down her nose at the tall man before her. "I have a title, and I have not given you leave, do you hear me, you—you rogue!"

He grinned. "Excuse me, milady, I won't forget again. However, I prefer you to call me Marcus." He dropped his pastoral mein and became his arrogant self, closing the distance between them to a matter of inches. "I enjoy the sound of my name upon your lips. You spoke it often when I visited you in your chamber."

Judith's mouth fell open at the man's sheer audacity. "I don't want to call you anything, but gone!" She pressed her back against the cold wooden wall as he came closer. There was nowhere to retreat. Deep down, she knew seeing him leave was the last thing she wanted.

"I can't leave now," he said. "Time is of the essence. We have to arrange your escape this very night."

"I told you, I'm going nowhere with you. I'm promised in marriage to the viscount, as you are well aware. I can't just *leave*."

Marcus sighed and placed his hands on his hips, his stance cocky. "*Lady* Judith. You know as well as I do everything I said here today is the truth. You believed it when you thought it came from a man of God. Does knowing it comes from me make it any less truthful?"

"Aye! Nay!" Judith's haughty demeanor dissolved. She could not deny his arguments. It terrified her how desperately she wanted to believe him. "Oh, I don't know what to think!"

Marcus placed his palm on her chest. The heat of his hand seemed to touch her heart. "In here. In here you know what the truth is, Judith. You know you shouldn't be forced to marry Mowbray because of your father's lack of judgment. You *know* it! Richard is offering you an alternative. You have to make a decision, and you have to make it by tonight."

"But—" She bit her lip and turned her tortured eyes up to his. Her voice dropped to a whisper. "I can't, Marcus. I'm afraid!"

In response, Marcus swept her into his arms. Judith pressed her eyes closed as she laid her cheek on his shoulder. She absorbed the feel of him, so protective, so comforting.

So *right*.

"I'll be there with you, Judith," he said tenderly into her ear. His voice grew hollow. "So will Richard. Come away with me tonight. Let me take you to him, where a real future awaits you. Please, I beg you. I can't stand to think of you wed to that decrepit monster."

He was stroking her hair, sending tingles along her scalp and down her back. Flickers of desire ignited within her, wondrous, wicked sensations. She lifted her face to his, suddenly wanting, *needing*, more. . . .

Marcus held her only a moment more, before placing her firmly at arm's length. "Tonight, Judith. After my performance, I'll come for you."

Judith didn't reply. Her gaze clung to his. She knew he could clearly read her desperation, her desires. She wasn't worldly enough to hide her feelings.

After a breathless time, Marcus tore his gaze from hers and left the chapel.

The final night of the festivities arrived. With the wedding set for the morrow, just a few hours of freedom remained to Judith. At least tonight she would be able to look on the mysterious actor who had cared, who understood her pain, who had given her hope.

She could gaze at him unhindered once more before losing him—and her freedom—forever.

Marcus entered the banquet hall with only his lute, Alan accompanying him on a small cittern. He began his songs before the nobles were finished eating. But Judith noticed that many hands and voices stilled before he finished his first ballad, the women in particular gazing toward him with warmth. His music touched their hearts, his deep, melodic voice charming them, seducing them. Soon, even the men fell quiet to listen.

Judith was amazed how this man was able to command the attention of the unruly, self-satisfied nobility.

He again strolled up and down the tables while he sang as he had the first night. But when he completed the circle, he paused in the center, his foot on a stool to support his instrument. His gaze fell on Judith, and she felt his soul reach deep within her. The romance of his songs entranced her, the potent combination of his voice and the subtle heat of his gaze making her feel airy and light one moment, full of poignancy the next.

He commanded not just the audience, she realized. He commanded her. He urged her to feel what he was telling her in the words and music, experience the pain, the longing, the unattainable desire. She knew he was singing for her and her alone, despite the presence of several hundred other people in the banquet hall.

Fortunately for him, the other guests assumed he was singling her out because she was the guest of honor. As for the viscount beside her, he seemed not to notice, more concerned with whether his plum pudding had set. Judith ignored his complaints to his servant. She was no longer aware of anything but Marcus and his music.

> Come away, come, sweet love,
> The golden morning breaks;
> All the earth, all the air,
> Of love and pleasure speaks.
> Teach thine arms then to embrace,
> And sweet rosy lips to kiss,
> And mix our souls in mutual bliss.
> Thither, sweet love, let us hie
> Flying, dying in desire,
> Winged with sweet hopes and heavenly fire.

Marcus' fingers stilled on the strings as the last note vibrated in the air and died out. A spell had descended on the hall.

A sharp clap broke the spell, followed by another, then a flood of applause as the nobles showed their approval for his performance.

Judith alone sat unmoving. She still heard the song in her heart. It spoke to her as mere words could never do. Its power flowed through her like heady wine, intoxicating her with desire and longing. And a new conviction.

She would do it. She would follow her heart.

"Aye, Marcus. I shall come away with you."

"Eh? What's that, sweet?" Viscount Mowbray leaned closer to hear her over the thunderous applause.

Appalled she had uttered her heartfelt thoughts aloud, Judith swallowed hard. "I . . . it's nothing." She prayed her intention wasn't reflected in her eyes.

"Such a delicate flush to your face, sweet." Mowbray stroked a bony gray finger along Judith's cheek. She forced herself not to flinch. "Such a sparkle in your eye. Your excitement grows as our wedding approaches, hmm?"

Judith pasted a smile on her face as she looked at him, fighting down revulsion as flecks of food dropped from his goatee to his skinny legs.

"I thought so." Mowbray nodded in satisfaction.

Out of the corner of her eye, Judith saw Marcus take his final bows and leave the room.

"Excuse me, milord," she said. "I'm afraid the roast pork disagrees with me. I beg your leave to retire."

"Aye. Rest up, tender one. On the morrow, I will give you a meat that truly satisfies, eh?"

To Judith's shock, he grasped her hand and pulled it below the table, flattening it on his crotch. Judith registered only the silk of his padded trunk hose, but she knew he intended her to feel much more.

Inwardly recoiling, Judith managed to politely extricate her hand.

A few minutes later, she was racing across the greensward separating the banquet hall from the private chambers, toward a new future.

"That was fantastic!" Alan told Marcus as he walked with him back to the stables. "You nearly had me weeping like a woman!"

"Good practice for your roles," Marcus quipped.

"But, sir, the way you sang," Alan continued. "I've never heard anything so wondrously fine in my life! What's the cause of it, I wonder?"

Marcus shrugged and kept walking.

"Come on, now, Marcus. I know you better than that. Something's up. I can feel it right down to my toes, and my toes are never wrong. My mother used them to foretell the weather. And right now, I can tell something's going on with you."

"Naught that won't be solved tonight if I was able to convince the lady to come away with me."

Alan's smile broadened. "Come away with you, you say? Those are the words of that new song you wrote! Why, that's it! You've fallen in love with her, haven't you? You—"

Suddenly Alan's feet were a foot off the ground, Marcus' hands tight on his collar. "I am merely doing my best to convince her to accompany us. Whatever that takes," he said tightly.

Alan nodded vigorously. "I see," he squeaked out. "Like making her *think* you're in love with her."

Marcus lowered his apprentice until Alan's feet rested firmly on the ground once more. "If that's what it takes." He turned and strode toward the stables alone.

Chapter 4

Judith paced her floor once again, pausing every now and then to listen for the rustle of the bushes below her balcony. She counted the seconds, the minutes, the hours, but still he didn't come. Audrey appeared, and Judith let her disrobe her, not wanting to share her plans and worry her needlessly if the actor didn't appear. He said he would come. He *had* to come after the way he had sung to her this evening.

Audrey dressed her in a nightgown of simple cotton, with ruffs at the neck and cuffs. She was about to braid Judith's hair, but Judith declined, preferring to let her hair fall free down her back.

Audrey retired to her own bed, but Judith didn't even try to sleep. She had to keep waiting for him. She left the single candle burning on her night table to light his way.

Despite how anxiously she waited, Judith started when she heard the sound on her balcony. She sat up in bed, wondering if she had imagined it, or if he was really here now. He was, making a shadow in the doorway, the curtains beside him billowing out in the evening breeze. Judith slipped her feet over the edge of the bed and ran to him. She stopped just short of touching him.

He carried a cloth bundle under his arm. He tossed it aside and looked down into her face, a touch of humor on his expressive lips. "May I take it that since you left the balcony door open, I'm welcome here this time?"

Judith nodded, suddenly finding herself speechless.

"May I also assume that you intend to escape from here with me?"

Judith turned and stepped back to the bed. She sat on the edge. "Before I leave here with you, you must answer me a question."

"Aye?"

"This eve, when you performed your music, who were you thinking of?" Her gaze met his.

He stepped forward slowly, almost as if he were afraid to get too close to her. "Tell me why you ask this question."

"Answer it, and I'll leave here with you."

He gazed down at her speculatively. "It seems we're at something of an impasse."

"It seems to me you are afraid to say who you were thinking of. This means either that you are embarrassed to say who"— Marcus' eyebrow lifted as if to say he was never embarrassed— "or afraid." His other eyebrow joined the first one.

"Of what would I be afraid, Judith?"

"The truth."

"The only truth I know is that you must leave here tonight, or it will be too late for you."

"Then, answer my question."

Marcus glanced away toward the balcony doors. He wasn't accustomed to being so transparent, and it startled him. A master at disguise and impersonation, he was most adept at disguising his own feelings. He felt the soft warmth of her touch as her hands clasped one of his. His eyes fastened on her elegant fingers holding his rough commoner's hand, a hand that had grown up knowing hardship, and hard work. His eyes traveled up her fair arm concealed in her elegantly embroidered bedgown, the gown of a noblewoman. His eyes slipped up farther to meet hers. He found himself drowning in her gaze. He let her pull him closer, until he was sitting beside her on her bed. He could smell her skin, he was so close. She smelled of springtime flowers, of innocence and purity.

"I think of many things when I perform," he said quietly.

"You have yet to answer me. I asked what you were thinking when you sang your songs tonight."

His gaze moved over her face slowly, drinking in her features softly lit by the intimacy of her bedroom candlelight. "I was thinking of the impossibility of love."

"Of love you feel?"

He lifted his fingers to trace her cheek, running them caressingly over her skin. "What I feel matters not, and well you know it. I have answered your question, now answer mine. Why do you ask this question?" His tone held more agony than he intended to convey.

"Because of what *I* was thinking when you sang your songs."

"It's easy to confuse a performance with the truth," Marcus said quietly, trying to sound forceful and ignore the look of longing she was giving him.

"I know the truth." She moved her face closer to his, her soft lips parting slightly, inviting the touch of his.

Marcus was so tempted to follow through with the embrace, it took all his strength to resist. He forced himself away and stood up, deciding the best approach was to pretend the entire conversation never happened. "We must depart now. Are you ready?" He retrieved the bundle he had dropped and unwrapped it as he crossed to the hearth, where the coals glowed umber. Only once he had placed this distance between them did he face her again. "I've brought you a commoner's gown, and cloaks for both you and your maid. I had to guess at your size. I hope the dress fits." He tossed the dress toward her, and it landed hanging over the edge of the bed. "Hurry and dress. We don't have time to spare. And your maid, I take it she's accompanying you? You should wake her." He gestured toward the servant's door that connected Audrey's small closet with Judith's room.

Judith slipped off the bed, retrieving the dress. She walked quietly across the room until she was face-to-face with Marcus once more. "As long as you understand that I'm leaving here only because of you," she said softly, before turning toward the wardrobe to change clothes.

Marcus stared after her in shock, not sure how to take her words. Perhaps she meant only that she believed he would succeed in keeping her safe. Or perhaps she simply meant he had been very persuasive. But there was the possibility that she was telling him she expected to have a future with him. He was afraid to ask her to clarify her remark.

"Milady, are you certain you want to do this?" asked Audrey anxiously as she tightened Judith's corset. Judith had never defied her father in the seven years Audrey had served the Ashton family. She was deeply concerned over what may be driving her to do so now—namely a misguided infatuation with that actor.

Judith was not a woman to flirt with men lightly, so her reaction to Marcus Sinclair distressed her maid even more. Like all men, the actor was undoubtedly after one thing, and Audrey would be damned if she would let him attempt to steal it from Judith.

"Aye, of course I'm sure," Judith replied.

Audrey looked at her mistress askance, noted her flushed cheeks. Judith clearly anticipated the night's adventure. "But it's such a risk, and I didn't think you even liked Richard Langsforth!"

Judith held up her arms, and Audrey tugged the gown over her head. Judith pulled her hair free. "You're the one who dislikes him, Audrey."

Audrey cocked her eyebrow. "And how do *you* feel about him?"

"Who?" Judith was staring toward the closed balcony door, beyond which the actor waited discretely.

"Lord Richard, milady," Audrey said with a trace of exasperation.

"Oh." Judith bit her lip. She shrugged. "He's not Lord Mowbray, at least," she said with a grin.

Audrey frowned. Judith's flippant response made her dis-

tinctly uneasy. This entire escapade did not bode well for any
of them, she was certain of it.

Audrey followed Judith onto the balcony, and Marcus sepa-
rated himself from the shadows. His gaze fastened on Judith.
"Well, did it fit?"

In answer, Judith opened the front of her cloak, revealing
herself to him. Marcus smiled appreciatively. She was
enchanting dressed as a country maid. The simple burgundy
and cream gown showed off her slender figure, its snugly laced
bodice outlining the shape of her breasts. The rounded neckline
was low enough to reveal the milky whiteness of her neck and
chest. Puffed sleeves covered only her upper arms, leaving her
slender forearms bare and kissed by the moonlight. He had
thought a change of clothes might help hide her impossibly
wonderful attributes. But though she wore a common wench's
clothing, she was still obviously a woman of uncommon beauty.

"Well, do I look passable?" Judith asked.

For a moment, Marcus simply gazed upon her, wondering
what he had managed to get himself into. He grinned and said
lightly, "You are more enchanting than the very angels of
heaven."

A loud snort behind him drew his attention to her maid.
"Are we simply going to stand here all night?" Audrey asked,
giving him a chilling glare.

Marcus helped them climb down the balcony. It wasn't too
difficult for the women, he thought with satisfaction. Both of
them were young and healthy, and ready for the adventure.

The grounds were deserted and dark. The last straggling
revelers had collapsed in a drunken stupor either in the halls
or in their rooms. He led the women over the grounds, taking
full advantage of the shadows cast by the manor house. He
approached the wall of the estate and a clump of trees there,
then gave a low whistle. Instantly a rope appeared over the
eight-foot wall. Marcus tested its strength, then helped each
woman to climb over the top. Again, he was pleased neither
of the women had much trouble.

On the other side, Alan waited, holding the reins of their

two horses, which he had led out of the estate earlier in the day before the gate closed for the night.

Marcus lifted a woman onto each horse; then he and Alan led the beasts along the wall. They paused as close as they could to the forest that lay beyond the fields surrounding the estate. Marcus directed Alan to mount behind Audrey, as he himself mounted behind Judith. It made sense, he had decided, since his primary responsibility was seeing to the welfare of his friend's future bride.

But he couldn't deny he wanted to be near her as long as possible. He did his best not to think too much about the wonderful sensation of having her pressed against him as they shared the mount, the feel of her waist under his arm as he steadied her against him. Judith didn't seem to be bothered in the least by the unseemly contact. Rather, she fairly snuggled against him.

"When I give the signal, kick your mount for all it's worth and get into the safety of the forest as fast as possible, before the night watchmen have a chance to see," Marcus told Alan. He waited until the closest watchman who traversed the perimeter of the estate wall had passed on his way back to the front.

"Now!" Both mounts took off, speeding toward the safety of the forest.

They galloped without much noise until the horses crashed through the forest barrier. But by then they were safe in the concealing darkness. Marcus led them onto a forest track, through the dense underbrush, heading toward the road by a route he had mapped out the first day they arrived at the estate.

Before long, they broke through the barrier of the forest once again and entered the road. Moonlight filtered behind sporadic clouds, which were carried along by a light, caressing breeze.

To Judith, dressed without her heavy formal garments, the wind felt wonderfully free. She had never done anything remotely this adventurous in her sheltered life. She stifled a stab of guilt over disobeying her father and determined to enjoy her taste of freedom for as long as it lasted.

Marcus kicked his mount, and they started down the road,

toward the lands of the Earl of Langsforth, and away from the viscount's holdings.

Judith fell asleep in Marcus' arms sometime during their ride. In the middle of the night, she stirred awake, aware that a man's strong arms were holding her, the scratchy wool against her face carrying a warm male scent. Marcus was carrying her somewhere. "Where are we?" she mumbled, her eyes bleary.

"My family home."

Accepting his reply, Judith snuggled against his broad chest, completely trusting him to take her wherever he wished.

The piercing cry of a hungry babe woke Judith with a start. Her eyes opened, and for an instant, she didn't understand where she was. It was still dark, a leaden, predawn light coming through a small window. Oak beams crossed the ceiling above her head. Firelight flickered beyond the open door.

Judith glanced about in the dim light and realized the room she was in was much cozier than the vast chambers she was used to. She was in an intimate cottage. While small, it was clean, the air scented with fresh herbs strewn in the rushes.

She could tell by the furnishings that Marcus had put her to bed in a small chamber that undoubtedly belonged to the married couple of the house, for both men's and women's clothing hung on hooks on the wall. On a simple wooden bureau, a woman's brush lay alongside a man's grooming tools.

She lifted her head and looked toward the sound of voices that were coming from the main room. A tingling wove through her as she contemplated Marcus carrying her here and gently tucking her in. There he was now, lounging on a bench by the fire, engaged in a soft, intimate conversation with a striking young woman. The woman was nursing the babe that had awakened Judith.

Still muddled from sleep, Judith indulged in studying every detail of Marcus' face, absorbing his fire-touched features. Just looking at him gave her a sense that everything would end satisfactorily. He would take wonderful care of her. Sitting there with the lady and her babe, he appeared solid, a man a woman could rely on. She hadn't imagined her charismatic actor could fit so well into such a domestic setting. . . .

The homey scene suddenly struck a horrendous chord in her. *My family home,* Marcus had said. His family! Marcus was married—and father of a babe. She hadn't even imagined such a thing was possible—but then, why not? And what could it possibly matter to her, the future bride of Richard Langsforth, son of the Earl of Langsforth?

"He has a lusty cry." Marcus smiled indulgently at the babe, who suckled vigorously.

"Aye, a strong voice like his father's," his wife said fondly. Her eyes turned to Marcus, full of concern. "Are you certain you ought to be taking part in such a scheme? It's dangerous to cross powerful men."

Marcus shrugged. "Sometimes they need crossing, need to realize they aren't masters of the world. Besides, I'm not the one behind this. She's Richard's bride. He's taking full responsibility."

"But you did the actual deed. I don't like it, Marcus. Not one bit. You even had to leave your acting job!"

"Oh, come, don't worry so. Shakespeare will take me back. Besides, I'm still able to provide for you. Which reminds me—" Marcus pulled out a purse that jangled with coins and handed it to her.

The woman counted out the coins in her hand. Seeing the amount there, her eyes grew misty. She leaned forward on her stool, closing the distance between them, hugging Marcus tightly despite the babe at her breast.

Judith's throat tightened in dismay, and she turned away, curling into the woolen blankets to await the dawn, and the harsh light of reality. Everything she had believed was transpiring between her and Marcus Sinclair was as insubstantial as a dream.

A stab of jealousy pierced her, followed immediately by guilt. How could she resent Marcus' family life? He was obviously content. What was wrong with her? She resolved to stop imagining things that were impossible and begin dealing with the reality she understood too well.

* * *

Judith paced restlessly from one side of the cottage to the other. Though she had awakened to a beautiful spring day, Marcus had advised her to remain here, in the cottage. Then he had left to escort Alice and his baby to a May Day festival on the town green. Audrey and Alan had also gone to the festival.

The door slammed, and Judith spun toward it. Marcus stood there uncertainly, holding a garland made of pink roses and white baby's breath with wine-colored ribbons dangling from the back.

The delicate, feminine frippery looked out of place in his callused hand. Even he seemed to realize it. "Here." He thrust it at her, and Judith took it.

"Thank you." Was she expected to wear it while she sat here alone in the cottage?

For the first time in her experience, Marcus looked ill at ease. "Since you can't attend the festival," he said brusquely, as if that explained why he had given her such a token. "It's a tradition for maidens to wear flowers on May Day."

"Thank you, Marcus," she said softly, fingering the silken petals.

He glanced about the room, avoiding her gaze. "I know this cottage is poor compared to what you're used to, milady. But it shouldn't be long before Richard arrives. This is the last possible day for me to have gotten you away from Mowbray, so this is the day we agreed upon."

Marcus seemed to have erected a wall between them, again calling her "milady." It irritated Judith, even more because she knew it shouldn't. Restless, she strode to the door and looked down the street toward the field where the townsfolk congregated. Lighthearted music drifted toward her. "I didn't even realize it was May Day," Judith said on a sigh.

"Aye," Marcus said behind her. "The most important day of the year for a village like Lankenshire." Silence hung in the still air of the cottage. Every nerve in her body seemed aware of the dark man standing close to her.

A hand settled on her shoulder. "You wish to be part of it."

Judith hesitated, then nodded.

Marcus slowly turned her to face him. He lifted the garland and slid it over her head, the ribbons trailing down her hair. He squeezed her shoulders. "I've never been a particularly careful man," he said, his lips quirked up. "If we stay well away from the crowds, you can at least watch without risking much. Though Alice will have my hide if she learns of it. Come." Marcus grasped her hand and led her through the door.

Judith wasn't at all sure she should let a married man hold her hand, but the heat of his palm warmed her entire body in the most delicious way. As she walked beside him along the quiet dirt street, Judith realized how thoroughly alone they were. A sense of exhilaration, of freedom, filled her, washing away the worry and terror of the past weeks. Everything seemed lovely and new—the spring breeze, the fresh grass of the field they crossed, even her own body, tingling with awareness of the man beside her.

Marcus led her a roundabout way toward the east side of the green, then up a hillock dotted with large shrubs and trees, which gave them an excellent view. Judith sat beside him on the grass and watched the hundred or so people below, dancing and feasting. She caught sight of Audrey in a circuitous country dance and waved to her, happy to see her hardworking maid enjoying herself.

"The idea is not to attract attention, milady," Marcus said wryly, stretching out his long legs beside hers.

Judith shrugged. Danger seemed very far away as she watched the riotous celebration, which centered around a maypole bedecked with flowers and ribbons. Musicians on lutes, drums, flutes and fiddles filled the air with country songs.

Judith often danced at Court, but the informality of the country dancing touched something deep and uninhibited inside her. "They're so free," she said with longing. She felt Marcus' gaze on her and glanced over at him. The intensity of his expression stole her breath away.

"Today, yes, they are free," Marcus said, his gaze exploring her face. "Most days, they carry the burden of merely surviving. They would consider you the free one."

Judith opened her mouth to defend her statement, to remind

him how little say she had in her life, but he continued, "I know that's not true, Judith," he said softly. "Not after what happened at Mowbray's."

His understanding filled her with pleasure, and she realized with surprise that his opinion meant a great deal to her. "Thank you for rescuing me," she said. "Even if you did it for Richard."

He seemed to draw back at mention of Richard. He draped his arms on his knees and looked toward the festival. "You'll be with Richard again soon, and safely under the care of his family," he said coolly. "The Langsforths are quite powerful. There should be no difficulty for you or your family once they let Mowbray know who has possession of you."

In truth, Judith could hardly recall Richard's face. "I do not want to think about being possessed by anyone. Not today." She gave him a gamine smile. "Pretend I am nothing but a country lass."

His gaze swept over her body. Leaning close, he slid his fingers along a lock of her hair, where one of the wine-colored ribbons hung. "You are stunning, in any guise."

The husky rumble of his words resonated through her body, and she could scarce breathe. Why did he make her feel this way, as though nothing else mattered but being here with him? And she hardly knew him. She tore her gaze away and forced a light tone to her words. "So, tell me about you. What are your dreams, Marcus Sinclair?"

He laughed softly. "To make a decent living." He confided to her that his real dream wasn't to live hand-to-mouth, earning eight shillings a week as a hired actor. His goal was to become a shareholder in a theater like the Globe, to be one of the handful of men whose fortunes rose and fell with the theater's success, who earned not a salary, but took home part of the profit from each performance, who planned the theater's artistic endeavors, purchased the plays to be performed and determined how to cast and stage them.

Only as a sharer would he ever feel secure and one day be able to buy property. "But a share costs fifty pounds, and with one family crisis or another, I haven't managed to save more than ten pounds at a time," he said. "I know that sounds like appallingly little to a lady such as you." He smiled, and Judith felt her sense dissolving. The distance between them seemed to have grown smaller, yet the air vibrated with a powerful tension like nothing she had felt before.

His family . . . "Your wife," Judith said, clutching at reason, struggling to keep her senses in check. "You should be at the festival with her, not up here with me! Won't she miss you?"

A slow, teasing grin spread over his face, followed by a deep, sensuous laugh that rippled through her.

Judith stared at him in confusion. "What did I say that's so funny?"

"She's my brother's wife, dear Judith."

Relief poured through Judith, unwarranted, blissful relief. Then the endearment he had used sank in. The wall was again down, sending a thrill of delight through her. She felt as if a friend had returned to her, and she would no longer be alone. Still, she fought to hide her pleasure with a light remark. "So, that adorable babe isn't yours, then?"

Marcus cocked an eyebrow. "Of course not. He's my nephew."

Judith cast him a mischievous smile. "But I saw you giving Alice coin," she said. "That usually indicates a personal . . . obligation."

Marcus rolled his eyes at her teasing insinuation. "Aye, an obligation to my relatives. My brother's land isn't producing well, but he won't acknowledge he needs assistance. So, Alice and I, we don't tell him."

"That's terribly devious," she said, exploring his starkly handsome face with her eyes. "But very generous." Precious few of the men in her acquaintance would have set aside their own desires to help others.

Marcus grinned wryly. "I know."

"And where is this elusive brother? *If* he exists."

Marcus gave an exasperated sigh, but he was smiling underneath. "He's gone to market in Farthingham. He's a Puritan, so he leaves town on May Day. He will not partake of it, for he considers it wild, pagan revelry."

Judith laughed at the way he drew out the last words, as if the devil himself spoke them. "You make it sound deliciously wicked.'' She lay back on the ground, her skirts spreading around her, her hair blanketing the soft earth. She pillowed her head on one arm and sighed in deep longing for something she couldn't even name. She gazed up at the interlacing branches of the elm trees above her, until Marcus' face came into view. Then her eyes focused only on him.

He spoke tantalizingly low. ''Some say that the spirit of May Day is unstoppable, enticing one to lose all reason.'' He slid lower, until he was lying full-length beside her, and supported his head on his hand.

Judith looked into his lazy, sensuous eyes only inches from her own, hardly daring to breathe. His long, dark hair teased her cheek, he was so close. ''It seems remarkably powerful.'' So powerful, nothing else seemed to matter.

An alarmingly intimate grin spread across his expressive lips, and Judith knew then exactly what she wanted to happen, what had to happen, or she would forever regret it.

And she knew he understood. He slipped his arm about her, his palm cradling the curve of her narrow waist. She made no move to stop him. The weight of his arm made her aware of the rise and fall of her chest. Marcus' gaze drifted to her tightly laced bodice; then he lifted his eyes once more to hers. ''You have already succeeded in stealing my reason,'' he said solemnly.

Judith's smile faded as her eyes met Marcus' intent gray ones. He touched her cheek with two of his fingers, tracing the line of her cheekbone, the curve of her jaw, the small dimple in her chin. He ran his thumb gently over the full contour of her lower lip. ''You make me forget all else,'' he murmured.

Judith began to drown in his eyes, two kaleidoscopes of light and dark. ''As do you.'' She followed his example, her fingers tracing the sharper contours of his face, his long, aristocratic nose, his high cheekbones, his strong jawline, touching him as if to imprint his face on her memory forever. She ran her fingers over his lips. Marcus parted his lips, and her fingers slipped inside the edge of his mouth, touching the warm moistness there. He playfully bit the tips of her fingers. She smiled shyly.

''You taste marvelous,'' he said.

"I like the feel of your lips under my fingers," she replied softly.

"I long to taste your lips," he said, his unsteady voice revealing that he, too, felt the undeniable magic between them.

Feeling bolder than she ever had, Judith did not hesitate. "Then, taste them."

Marcus leaned over her, his mouth above hers. She prepared herself for her first kiss and was stunned when instead she felt the moist silkiness of his tongue. He outlined the curve of her upper lip with the tip of his tongue, tickling softly in the corners, sweeping down to explore her full lower lip.

His tender exploration sent a series of tingles through Judith, and she gasped softly in pleasure. In response, he touched his lips to hers.

His kiss was the soft brush of a butterfly wing, as tender and innocent as the first day of spring. Judith closed her eyes, the better to revel in the feel of this long-awaited intimacy. His lips were softer, more arousing than she ever imagined lips could be.

Marcus deepened the kiss, settling his mouth full upon hers. Gradually the kiss became more intense as their mutual passion grew stronger. Her lips parted under his. His tongue traced the inside of her lips, entered the soft recesses of her mouth, stroked her tongue with his own. She started in surprise, accepted the feeling, pleasured in it, moaned under the provocative onslaught.

Marcus pulled back, and his gaze met hers in unspoken communication. Judith reached up and cupped the back of his head, entwining her fingers in his thick hair. She tugged downward slightly, and he again brought his lips to hers.

This time, Marcus held nothing back. He kissed her as he had dreamed of kissing her, this untouchable maiden who looked at him as if she knew his very soul. Her uninhibited response to his kisses stunned and thrilled him. He pressed her sweet length against his, burying his mouth on hers as if to consume her.

Nor did she shy away from his brutally honest passion. She pressed her breasts tight against his chest, entwining her long legs with his own. He grew acutely aware of her hips lodged against his throbbing groin. He knew this embrace was wrong, knew it without a doubt. But she had so entranced him, he could not stop himself.

From far off came the sound of horns, trumpets announcing the arrival of a noble's entourage in the village. The sound remained distant and unreal through Marcus' passionate haze, until he realized the trumpets heralded Richard's arrival.

Reluctantly, he broke the kiss and glanced down the hill past the celebration to the main village road. Riding toward the green were ten horsemen in full livery, two trumpeters in the lead. He recognized the Langsforth crest on a standard being carried aloft by a bearer. Though Richard was more at home in rustic taverns, he had pulled out all the stops to collect his titled bride.

A surge of guilt swept through Marcus, but it did little to cool his fierce desire for the woman in his arms. "He's coming," he said tightly. He glanced down at Judith, drank in her face, her lips full and soft from his kisses. "Richard's almost here."

Judith looked toward Richard's entourage; then her gaze met his once more. "It will take them a few minutes yet to arrive," she said brazenly, her eyes dark with passion. "Those are my minutes, and I want them."

"Then, you shall have them," Marcus growled. His lips met hers again in a kiss more intense and frantic than he would have believed possible. Oh, God, how he wanted her. He wanted to absorb her into his being so that she would always be part of him. But he could never have from Judith more than he was taking at this moment. This was it. This was his life with her. In a few minutes, it would end, and she would be someone else's—not that she was ever his. His heart hammered in his chest painfully from the agony of having to pull away from her. But he did it just the same.

"Oh, Judith," he groaned. "It's over now." He sat up, turning his back to her, not trusting himself to look at her. He hung his arms on his knees and inhaled sharply in an effort to still his racing heart and control his arousal. A soft hand caressed his shoulder, but he didn't turn around. His gaze was riveted to Richard's men, who had entered the green, becoming the focus of the excited May Day celebrants.

He saw Richard scan the crowd. Marcus rose unsteadily to

his feet and pulled Judith up beside him. He swiveled her to face him. "This meant nothing, milady. May Day is a time for passions to leap the bounds of propriety. It happens every year. Do you understand me?"

Judith knew he was trying to recast what they shared into something casual, without meaning. She didn't believe him for a moment. "Marcus, I—"

"Let's go," he said, his voice husky. "Your future husband awaits."

Without waiting for an answer, he strode ahead of her down the hill to greet Richard, who was dismounting, his blue cape swinging about his shoulders.

Judith studied Richard. She had only seen him a handful of times at Court, never for longer than a few moments. He had sent numerous love notes and trinkets, however. A fortnight ago, he had come to her home to serenade her. But he hadn't made much progress in his suit, for Audrey had audaciously emptied the slop bucket on his head.

Richard was as well-favored as she recalled, with a square, youthful face and thick ginger hair. He sported a well-tended gentleman's beard and a satin midnight blue doublet shot through with gold thread, gold trunk hose, and expensive knee-high leather boots. He was extremely well turned out for a country ride, probably to make an impression on her.

His laughing blue eyes flashed with pleasure as Judith approached. She stopped before him, realizing he was a half head shorter than Marcus, though broader in the shoulder. *I will always compare him to Marcus*, Judith thought. She blinked back a sudden surge of guilty tears. Richard was completely unsuspecting of where her heart truly lay.

Richard stripped off his heavy gauntlets and passed them to his squire, who stood at attention behind him. "My beloved Judith, light of my life," he pronounced. He dropped to his knee before her, clasping her fingers in his. "Your ordeal must have been difficult. Are you well, my love?"

"Quite well," Judith said, trying to sound bright, trying to feel something for this man she hardly knew. "Your friend took excellent care of me."

Richard rose and faced Marcus. He pulled his friend into an

unabashed embrace and pounded him on the back. "You did it, friend. You did it. Thank you for delivering her to me." He grinned. "I'll owe you for the rest of my days—and nights!"

"I still have not repaid the favor I owe you," Marcus said. "If you hadn't risked your neck to rescue an unarmed country boy from London cutthroats those years back—"

Richard shrugged. "Not worth speaking of. Merely sword practice. But this"—Richard's eyes glowed as they settled on Judith—"it's more than I ever imagined. I'm truly the luckiest man alive, with the fairest flower for my bride." He addressed Judith. "Once you're safely behind our walls, we'll plan a fine ceremony, Lady Judith. What say you to a June wedding?"

Judith didn't reply, but, then, Richard didn't seem to expect an answer. He gave a command to his men to remount, ordering one of them to share his mount with Judith. The man-at-arms obediently pulled Judith up before him.

Richard paused before mounting his horse and scanned the gathering. "Judith, that saucy maid of yours, where is she?"

Judith hadn't been the only one looking Richard over. From where she stood among the guards, Audrey fought down a tingle of pleasure that the nobleman remembered her. She reminded herself how much she disliked him for trying to turn the innocent Judith's head with romantic songs and gifts. It was all a farce. He deserved no respect or courtesy, certainly not from her. She swept up to him boldly and planted her hands on her hips. "I'm here, my Lord Peacock. If you're going to force milady to go with you, I plan to come along."

"Damn right you're coming." Richard's eyes narrowed with menace. "I haven't forgotten how rudely you treated my wooing of her ladyship. I suppose I shall be generous and assume your emptying of the slops where I was standing to be an accident of timing."

Audrey lifted her chin defiantly. "From our balcony, your swelled head made an excellent target, your *lordship*."

Judith gasped. "Audrey!"

Audrey ignored her. Her gaze was riveted to Richard's face. The nobleman stepped closer, glaring down at her. But Audrey held her ground.

"You ruined my favorite doublet!" he said through tight lips.

Audrey felt a quick stab of satisfaction at his reaction. "It was the least I could do to save my lady's hearing from your incessant caterwauling. One shouldn't impose when one is so lacking in talent."

"Granted, I'm not gifted with Marcus' abilities, but my singing wasn't *that* horrid."

"I beg to differ. You were like to raise the dead from their graves!"

Richard's lips turned up in a stiff smile. His eyes sparked with speculation as he gazed at her. "You don't have the slightest fear of an earl's son, do you? Don't you realize how foolish this is for a woman of your station?"

"I'm perfectly aware of our respective stations, *lord*."

He nodded once, satisfied, and turned toward his steed.

Audrey added just above a whisper, "Otherwise I would have dumped the chamberpot instead of the slops."

Richard spun back, nailing her with a wicked smile. "I'll enjoy putting a sharp-tongued wench like you in your place."

Audrey stood stiff-backed as he swung his powerful leg over his steed's back. She knew she was treading on thin ice. Even Judith wouldn't be able to save her once the two were wed. Mayhap she should stay out of the man's way for a while, until he forgot about her.

Richard's next words shocked her. "Garrison, throw her up here." He gestured to a guard.

The guard complied, and Audrey sailed through the air to land in front of Richard. She gasped as the air was knocked from her. She worked to right herself, distraught that she would be forced to share a mount with this scoundrel of a lord when she could have ridden with one of his guards, as was her lady.

Richard's brawny arm tightened around her waist. He spoke low, his breath hot in her ear. "You're part of my household now, wench, and I'll not have any more of your tongue. You'll regret your tart words before long, I'll warrant." Audrey yanked away from him, but he merely chuckled and dragged her back against him, locking her there with a strong grip.

Just to spite him, Audrey muttered, "I'll die first, you ill-mannered boor.'' Futilely, she shoved at the gauntleted hand that imprisoned her.

Richard just laughed harder, tightening his hold. He called down a farewell to Marcus. ''You will attend the nuptials?''

''If I can get away,'' Marcus said, forcing a casual smile to his lips. ''I've been too long gone from my work as it is. Thank God this little escapade is over with. It's been more than taxing. It took every bit of my acting ability to convince Judith to escape, and to keep her entertained. You have no idea what I've had to put up with.'' He looked toward Judith in irritation, his hands on his hips. She did not appear hurt, as if she understood he spoke thus for Richard's benefit.

''Are you implying my beloved Judith was less than tractable?'' Richard asked with a touch of humor. ''She simply needs a man's strong hand, as all untried maidens do.'' His gaze fell on the shapely Audrey in front of him on the horse, who was trying vainly to keep distance between their bodies. ''I'll see to it.''

''Better you than me,'' Marcus replied with a laugh.

Richard raised his gloved hand in salute. ''Farewell, friend. I'll thank you all my days, or at least on my wedding night.'' He winked, then spurred his horse, and it bolted forward, leading the pack in a fast trot.

Marcus watched them ride away, his gut in knots, his heart shattering into a thousand pieces. His gaze stayed riveted to Judith, her blond hair flying behind the shoulder of the man who held her.

She turned her head once and looked back toward him. He was thankful that she was too far away to see that his expression was no longer masked, but torn with the agony of seeing her ride away the bride of another man.

He turned and walked back up the rise to the trees below which he had tasted Judith's lips for the first and last time. He collapsed on the grass, leaning in exhaustion against a tree trunk, feeling as if he would never celebrate again.

ACT 2

"Doubt thou the stars are fire;
Doubt that the sun doth move;
Doubt truth to be a liar;
But never doubt I love."
     —*Hamlet,* Act 2, Scene 2

Chapter 5

Judith felt distinctly uncomfortable being held in the arms of the stranger whose horse she shared. She felt lost, heading toward a future she wasn't at all sure she wanted, again trapped by her noble birth. She concentrated on the garland she had slipped over her wrist, watching as the wind stole the petals one by one, finally stripping it down to its frame of stems.

"Marcus," she said softly, only aware when she heard the word that she had spoken aloud.

"Say what, milady? Do you require something?" asked the man who rode with her.

"Nay, good sir. 'Tis nothing," she replied with a voice much firmer than she felt. Her heart ached unbearably. Her eyes began to fill with tears. She blinked to keep them from falling. She knew there was no other choice but for her to marry Richard, after what the nobleman had done to save her from a worse fate. She would become Richard's wife, as Marcus had said from the first.

The one bright spot was that Richard truly loved her. For that she was grateful. In time, she prayed she would be able to set aside her feelings for Marcus and come to love Richard in return.

Richard didn't speak much to Judith on the short ride back to his family manor house. Judith noticed that he seemed more interested in carrying on a verbal battle with Audrey, who was still positioned on his horse, much to her maid's obvious vexation. Judith had suggested allowing the two women to share a mount, but Richard just laughed.

Judith saw that Audrey was attempting to slide farther up the horse's neck to put space between herself and Richard. Judith knew well her maid's discomfort over men and wished Richard wouldn't bother her so. But Richard obviously thought teasing Audrey was most enjoyable. With a firm grip around her waist, he kept pulling the wench's rounded figure against himself. When Judith's mount came alongside her maid's, Audrey shot her an expression so filled with disgust, Judith fought not to laugh.

"Lucifer is a trained war-horse, sweet, but if you don't quit wiggling your shapely arse around, both he and I are liable to get excited," Richard commented to Audrey. "Of course, the consequences will be different, since *I'm* not going to throw you off."

"Being off this horse sounds like an excellent place to be," she retorted.

"You prefer landing on your fanny in the road?"

"Anywhere is better than with you."

"Nay, that will never do. It's 'Anywhere is better than with you, *milord.*' "

Judith was glad that so far Richard found Audrey's tart retorts amusing. Most lords would not take kindly to a servant speaking thus.

"Anywhere is better than with you, *milord*," Audrey replied, her voice dripping with sarcasm.

Richard chuckled. Audrey rolled her eyes for Judith's benefit.

Judith gave her a sympathetic look, but what could she do? She was even less comfortable squeezed in front of the bulky soldier, who spent most of the ride hawking and spitting in a stream onto the dusty road.

Richard called to Judith as they entered the long road to Langsforth Hall. "We'll have to find you a proper gown. I'm certain the countess will have something suitable."

Judith nodded. She would do whatever Richard wished. He had arranged for her rescue, and now he possessed her. "What about my father? Is he safe? He was still at the viscount's estate when we left. I worry about him."

"Lord Ashton has returned to London to await word of your whereabouts, which we'll send as soon as we arrive at Langsforth Hall. You needn't fear on that score, dearest Judith. I'll take care of everything."

With the gates of Langsforth Hall in sight, he spurred his horse ahead once more, with Audrey hanging on for dear life. The Langsforth family was ancient, and a castle had been its stronghold for generations. With the end of feudalism, the family had built a modern manor of more than a hundred rooms. Meanwhile, the neighboring castle was falling into disrepair.

Arriving at only a slightly slower pace, the man-at-arms helped Judith dismount. Richard and Audrey had already dismounted. Richard strode up, leaving Audrey standing by his horse, forgotten. He took Judith's arm and escorted her up the broad steps of the manor house.

They passed a group of nobles who called out greetings from their dice and card games in the elegantly paneled and carpeted salon. Another, narrower flight of steps brought them to the women's quarters.

"Don't look so worried, Judith," Richard said, pausing outside a richly carved door on the second level. "The difficult part of this enterprise is over. I'll dispatch a messenger to the viscount, and one to your father. I'll also include sufficient coin for each to pay them for their trouble. I'm sure they will be satisfied."

Judith didn't tell him that Langsforth money might not manage to ease her father's embarrassment, or the viscount's anger.

"You can change here, in the countess' chamber," Richard said. "Her ladies will outfit you properly. We'll send a message to my tailor in the morning to get you whatever gowns you need, and size you for a wedding dress."

Richard opened the wooden door and led Judith inside the large salon used by the women. Several women sat along cushioned benches set in the walls, embroidering and practicing their music on stringed citterns and on the virginals, a popular keyboard instrument. A thick, expensive carpet covered the floor. Intricate plaster moldings painted in bright colors and woven tapestries decorated the oak-paneled walls.

The eldest of the women rose gracefully to her feet and approached Richard. "So, this is the lady you've been nattering about," she said. The woman was slender, almost too thin, with a narrow, pinched face and pointed chin. While she was elegantly dressed, her skirt was so wide it almost dwarfed the woman within.

"Aye, Countess. This is my bride, Lady Judith Ashton, daughter of Baron Howard Ashton of Dunsforth House," Richard said. "My mother, Lady Grace."

Judith curtsied. When she looked up, she found Lady Grace Langsforth's lips pursed in displeasure, the woman's narrow gaze flicking up and down her body.

Lady Grace faced Richard squarely. "How dare you take it upon yourself to select a bride! As if you know anything about what makes a suitable mate for a son of the House of Langsforth. I warn you, Richard, your defiance of me will be your ruin. I have a mind to send her packing back to her father, and you to our relatives in the north country!"

Trepidation rippled through Judith. Apparently, Richard didn't have his family's full blessing for this dangerous enterprise in stealing her for his own.

"You can't possibly have a complaint against Lady Judith," Richard said, his voice a mixture of disbelief and anger. "She is well-bred, beautiful, of good family—"

"What dowry does she bring with her?"

"A substantial one, I'm sure. Her father's wealthy."

"That isn't for you to decide."

Richard gritted his teeth, and a pulse in his temple throbbed. "You wanted me to marry, so I shall," Richard said. "I had hoped you'd finally be pleased I was following your wishes."

Grace's eyes narrowed as she inspected Judith. "Her hips are too narrow." She faced Richard, her voice full of challenge. "Will she breed you sons? Does she have any brothers?"

"Well, nay, but—"

"Aha!" His mother crowed, as if she had won the argument. Richard was clearly fed up. He turned his back on both of them and stalked to the door. His mother's voice followed him. "Don't you walk out on me! Where do you think you're going?"

"I'm doing something *peaceful*, Countess," Richard shot back over his shoulder. "I'm going *hunting*."

The door slammed, the sound reverberating in the air.

Judith looked at the countess, who was still pursing her mouth fiercely. She seemed unconcerned that Judith, or her women, had witnessed the scene with her son. Nor did she seem concerned that Judith hadn't as yet spoken. Judith could have been a deaf-mute for all the woman seemed to care.

"If he thinks I'm treating him to a large wedding, he's more fool than I ever suspected," Grace muttered to herself. "That boy does not deserve such."

Judith fought down her anger toward Richard for so unceremoniously dumping her with this unpleasant woman. Lady Grace *was*, after all, a countess, surpassing her own rank by several notches. And she was her future mother-in-law. She would have to grow accustomed to her, she realized. Though apparently, Richard hadn't found a way to get along with her. It was no wonder he spent most of his time in London.

As Grace orchestrated Judith's transformation back into a lady, the countess spoke constantly, voicing her thoughts just to hear them spoken as much to communicate.

"Such lovely golden hair," Grace commented, picking up a handful. "So many women would kill for this hair. I'm afraid there's not a blond woman or child in our district that hasn't been asked to sell her locks for wigs. Human hair is so much more malleable than horse hair."

Grace accepted a gown handed to her by one of her own maids. "Perhaps the green silk." She held the gown up to Judith and inspected her closely, paying special attention to her eyes. "Nay, she has no green in her eyes. This color does her no favors. She needs a color that will bring out the shine in her skin, what shine there is. Perhaps this." The next gown was wine-colored embroidered with gold thread. "Aye, this will suffice." She passed the gown to one of her ladies-in-waiting. "Be quick about it, Martha. We can't let the dressing of this chit take up the entire afternoon."

Martha set about her task of dressing Judith. "But I brought my own maid, milady," Judith protested. "I haven't seen Audrey since we rode in."

Grace's hands stilled over the headdress she was studying. "Girl, you are a Langsforth now. All Langsforth servants come from Langsforth lands. Your Audrey, whoever she is, cannot possibly attend the wife of one of my sons. I hand-pick our personal servants. She will have to go to the kitchens or back to your father's house."

Judith gasped. Audrey in the kitchens? It was unthinkable, an insult. "But she's mine; she's served me since I was but ten years old—" *Been my friend,* she was tempted to add, but knew that would gain her no favor.

Grace stepped before her and placed her cool hand on Judith's arm. "You must make concessions to be part of our great family. Don't think I haven't thoroughly checked you out. Despite Richard's strong-headedness, I would not allow him to marry a poorly situated girl. That boy's head is full of romantic nonsense. He's hardly a proper Langsforth at all. One would think the nursemaid dropped him on his head when he was a babe." She turned away, effectively ending the one-sided conversation.

When the ladies-in-waiting were through dressing Judith, she was left feeling overdressed, gaudy even. The gown itself was luxurious and would be tasteful if worn by itself with perhaps a simple necklace. But she wore a ruffled collar at least a quarter-yard deep, embroidered so heavily she could hardly see the cambric it was made from. It was held in place by a combination of starch and a wire supportasse.

The bodice of the gown was thick with gold embroidery, the skirt supported at her hips by a heavy farthingale wider than Judith was used to wearing. It felt altogether cumbersome. On her head rested a crescent-shaped headdress at least six inches high, thick with pearls. Several gold necklaces were draped around her neck, hanging to her waist.

The rest of the afternoon, the countess kept her eagle eyes pinned to Judith. *As if she thinks I mean to steal the silver,* Judith thought in irritation.

Judith finally broke away when the nobles were heading to

the great hall for supper. She found Audrey in the kitchens, furious about her new situation, as well she should be. But she planned to stay at least until the wedding, she told Judith.

"Nay, this isn't right, you in the kitchens," Judith told her. "I'll speak to Richard about it. Once we're wed, no one will stop you from serving me."

"*No.*" Audrey nearly dropped the tray of bread-dough rolls she was carrying. She set the tray down. "If you plan to go through with this wedding, milady, I would prefer to return to London and seek a post elsewhere. Once you are wed, that is. Milady." She curtsied with uncharacteristic formality, her gaze skimming away.

Judith stared at her. She had imagined Audrey would always be her maid, regardless of who she married. "You dislike Richard that much?"

Audrey turned her back to Judith, as if pretending she hadn't heard the question.

Judith sighed. She left the kitchens and walked to the great hall, where the countess directed her to an empty seat next to Richard's. But Richard was not there. Their seats were at a lower table adjacent to the high table, with Richard's second youngest brother, Errol, and his wife Lettice.

She fought down her irritation that her future husband had chosen to spend his afternoon with his men and dogs instead of with her, when he had wanted so badly to win her. Apparently, the challenge was through, as far as he was concerned.

Worse, none of his family members welcomed her with open arms. Conversation buzzed all around her, but no one spoke to her. She wanted to talk to the other wives, hoped to find a friend among them, but none of them seemed the least interested in making her feel at home. She gathered from the whispered comments about her that Richard had done the unthinkable—selected his own bride rather than let the countess do it for him. For this reason alone, she was looked on with jealousy and suspicion.

Supper was half-over when Richard finally swept into the hall, wearing a dark brown, sweat-and-dirt-stained doublet and muddy boots. The conversation around Judith fell off as he approached and slipped into the chair beside her. He smiled at her, but his eyes were somber, distant.

"Richard!" The countess' high-pitched voice grated on Judith's nerves and attracted the attention of everyone in the large room. "How dare you come to table in such a state! You are an abomination to our fine house!"

Richard looked toward his parents at the high table, lines of weariness creasing his eyes. "Very well, Countess." He stood. Taking his plate in his hand, he strode to the end of the table used by the respected household retainers who were allowed to eat with the family and sat on the end of the bench. He studiously ignored his mother as she continued haranguing him.

"You left your bride this afternoon to go hunting, of all things! How could you desert her like that?"

Judith was surprised to hear the countess coming to her defense—until the countess continued speaking. "I have enough hard work to do without the difficult challenge of making this girl of yours into an acceptable bride for the House of Langsforth. Have you no concern for your mother's feelings? Ambrose, tell him!" The countess turned on her disinterested husband.

The earl shifted in his high-backed chair. "You heard your mother, son."

Richard bit into a leg of mutton and tore off a chunk. As he chewed, he glared at the high table from under his eyebrows. He swallowed. "I apologize, Mother," Richard said, his voice surprisingly even. "For all the errors I have committed today, for those I committed a fortnight ago, for those in years past, and in the years to come, because no doubt they will be legion. To spare you further agony, I'll take my leave now." He slammed down the leg of mutton and stalked toward the door.

Judith considered for only a moment before she rose to follow.

She found Richard pacing in the geometrically perfect knot garden. The sun was setting, and the dusk grew deeper by the minute. The perfume of spring roses hung heavy in the air.

Judith hoped he would talk to her about his difficulties with his family. But he didn't seem so inclined. He turned and smiled brightly at her as she slowly approached, as if she hadn't just witnessed a fierce family argument. "Beautiful eve, isn't it?"

"Aye, Richard." She tried to think how best to broach the subject of his family difficulties. There was no easy way, not if he didn't open the discussion himself. "Richard—"

He cut her off. "You ought to like living here, a refined gentlewoman such as yourself. What do you think of Langsforth Hall?"

"It's lovely," Judith replied. She sighed.

"Isn't it, though? I wish I could say it will be ours someday, but with three older brothers, that's not likely. We can still live here, of course. Though I prefer the excitement of London— the Court celebrations, the shops, the theater . . ."

London, where Marcus lives and works. In a flash, Judith recalled the seductive heat of his embrace, and she suddenly felt warm all over. She saw Richard's searching gaze on her face. In defense, she strove to cover her emotions with a bright smile.

Richard smiled in response. "Come." He took her hand and led her to a stone bench. "I know things are a little strange and new, but you're the type of woman I was destined to marry, Lady Judith. You'll soon fit right in."

"As well as you?"

Richard cocked an eyebrow at her ironic tone. "I shall, once we're wed. Then things will change. They must." His jaw muscle flexed. "They've been demanding it for God knows how long," he muttered as if to himself.

"Perhaps I can help?" Judith asked, inviting his confidence. She laid her hand on his where it rested on the bench.

Richard put on a cheerful smile. "Of course you can. That's why I wooed and won you. You are the perfect wife for me, everything a Langsforth bride *should* be. That whole incident with the viscount—it had me worried, I'll confess. But it all worked out in the end."

Judith cocked her head. Perhaps it was time for a little honesty. "Richard, why did you want to marry me?"

He smiled and clasped her hand. "You know why."

Judith was afraid she did, and it had precious little to do with love. But then Richard's eyes grew warmer as he gazed at her, confusing her further. "I've waited a long time to get you alone in a garden like this. I would have managed it sooner if your maid hadn't kept us apart."

"Audrey?"

"Is that her name? Audrey." He repeated it to himself, softly. His gaze drifted over the hedges and rose bushes. "It's romantic here, don't you think?"

"Aye, 'tis lovely." He certainly seemed inclined to romance now, Judith thought, hope growing within her. Perhaps they had merely gotten off to a rocky start, and he truly did care for her.

Still Richard paused, as if waiting for something else to happen. The silence stretched out, heavy and uncomfortable. "So," he finally stated.

Suddenly, his lips were on hers, without preamble, without warning. Judith started back in shock. Richard pulled back as well, a mystified look on his face. Then understanding dawned, and he sighed in relief. "I had forgotten for a moment that you've never been kissed before. You're a sweet, innocent maiden. But I'll show you everything you need to know about love making."

Judith breathed evenly to regain her composure and to hide a flush of guilt. She *had* let a man kiss her, a commoner—and this man's friend. "You took me by surprise, 'tis all," she replied. She smiled up at him as charmingly as she could manage. "Truly."

"Shall we try that again, mayhap?" Richard asked lightly.

Some of her apprehension eased. Richard truly was likable, with his boyish good looks and easygoing manner. She just needed to get used to him. "Aye, that would be nice."

Richard pressed his lips to hers more gently this time, with his mouth closed. Judith felt a slow, warm tingling at his attentions, and she clung to it like a drowning woman. In response, Richard tightened his arms around her and deepened the kiss, his fingers in her hair. Judith dutifully arched into the embrace, trying to show she welcomed his attentions.

But she felt no enthusiasm. She knew she should be responding better, as she had for the first man she had kissed.

But with Richard, she felt none of the wild, senseless urge to continue, to explore, to revel in desire as she had with Marcus.

To her relief, Richard broke the embrace first. He pulled back, his gaze roving over her face. "Well, that's a start, anyway. I promise you'll learn to like kissing, and all that follows after we're married. Trust me, I know how to treat a woman." He boldly placed his hand over her breast, cupping it solidly. His voice grew husky. "You've got a pleasing shape, sweet lady. I can show you things you never imagined." He kissed her neck. "You know, we're almost as good as married now. It wouldn't be unseemly for me to take my betrothed to bed. Perhaps then, you and I shall—"

"Richard, please give me time," Judith said, pushing his hand from her breast gently, not wanting to anger him. "It's all so new. I don't know you that well, and it feels rather strange."

"What feels strange? This?" Richard smiled suggestively and placed his hand on her breast again.

Judith sighed with a touch of exasperation and removed the questing hand once more. "No, everything. Our sudden betrothal, the escape from Lord Mowbray's estate, meeting your family—everything."

Richard nodded, his tawny brows lowered thoughtfully. "Judith, could it be that we . . ." He glanced away, his voice faltering. Judith tensed, but then Richard shook his head and broke into his familiar good-natured smile. "Never mind. I know how closely you have safeguarded your virtue. I can be patient. Lord knows I've been patient up 'til now. I can tell you, I spent most of my monthly allowance on those trinkets I purchased to woo you. I paid quite a bit to win you. Not to mention the cost of the poems—"

"Cost of the poems?" Judith asked in surprise. "What do you mean?"

Richard laughed self-consciously. "You know it's common practice to buy poems and letters to send to the woman you're wooing. It saved time, after all. I'm not a literary man, you know. Oh, I'm educated. I'm studying law. I can read Latin and all that. But I can't quite make the words flow like some men can, you know, men like Marcus."

"Marcus? He wrote the poems you sent me," Judith said in amazement, unable to hide her surprise and pleasure.

"I confess. And the letters, too, so you wouldn't wonder at the change in handwriting. But, of course, I told him in general what to say."

Judith hoped her pleasure wasn't too obvious. But Richard's smile had begun to fade, his eyes on her speculative. "Well, that's enough of that," he said. "Since I'm not going to be able to seduce you tonight, let's go back inside." He rose and held out his hand to her. Judith took it, grateful the seduction was over.

"At least I finally got you alone," Richard said cheerfully as they neared the house. "I never could with your maid about. Audrey," he added softly. "But I suppose I ought to be prepared, in case she comes at me with the chamberpot next time."

Judith laughed for the first time since saying good-bye to Marcus.

Judith spent the following week being properly clothed and schooled in Langsforth ways by the countess. She didn't see much of Richard. He spent his days hunting with his father and brothers, or practicing for tournaments in the tilting yard.

He did, however, take her for walks in the garden in the evenings. Things were fine when they chatted about mutual acquaintances or the latest news from Court. But he wouldn't discuss anything of a personal nature with her, such as his family difficulties, as if believing she was too gentle and refined to be disturbed by ill thoughts. Instead of talking, their walks usually ended on a bench, with him attempting to seduce her with kisses.

Judith began to dread their encounters. She could tell Richard was frustrated by her lack of enthusiasm for his love making. But she wasn't very good at acting.

Audrey fisted her hand and mashed it into the pile of bread dough with all her strength. For a moment, she had imagined it was Lord Richard Langsforth's mocking countenance. She squeezed in the sides and rolled it into a ball, then once again slammed her fist right where his aristocratic nose would be.

A lady's maid, Audrey knew next to nothing about cooking, but she was discovering it was hot, sweaty work in the Langsforth Hall kitchen. Her lady's intended—curse his black heart—had long wanted to humiliate her, and now he had done so.

Throughout their verbal sparring, Audrey had never imagined he would actually hurt her. She had been hurt and humiliated plenty in her dealings with males of his class. Illogical as it was, she hadn't believed Lord Richard capable of it. Like some innocent little twit, she had been taken in by his ready smile and warm familiarity.

It was all because of that horseback ride. He had spent the entire ride teasing her and baiting her and laughing in her ear, as if she actually delighted him. And she had spent the entire ride trying to ignore the clean, masculine smell of him, the strength of the thighs pressed against her own. One would think she had never been with a man before, the way he affected her. Why, of all the suitors who wooed Judith, did the lady's future husband turn out to be Richard the Lying-hearted?

She longed to return to London. But even if she hadn't promised to stay until the wedding, she had no one to travel with. Rather, people were coming the other way, already arriving for the nuptials. Which made the demands on the kitchen—and Audrey—escalate even more.

"Audrey, your presence is requested upstairs," said a young parlor maid, entering the kitchen. The formality of even the servants surprised Audrey. But the Dragon Lady, or so Audrey had nicknamed Richard's mother, would have it no other way and punished the servants accordingly to keep them in line. The nickname caught on like wildfire. Audrey wondered what the woman would think should she learn what the servants were now calling her behind her back.

She gave the dough over to another maid and followed the parlor maid. Judith must have finally gotten a few moments alone and wanted to see her own maid, not one of the stiff dolls the Dragon Lady had assigned to her.

At the top of the stairs, the parlor maid opened a door for

Audrey. She slipped quietly inside, and the maid closed the door behind her.

"There you are."

The deep male voice startled Audrey, and she forgot to answer.

Chapter 6

Lord Richard Langsforth rose from a chair at a table with a half-played game of chess spread upon it.

When Audrey realized she was simply standing there, she quickly curtsied and bowed her head. What on earth could Lord Richard want from her? She couldn't fathom it. Unless—she shuddered—unless he wanted to pay her back for all her barbs now that she was in his power. She lifted her chin and shot him a defiant look. She wouldn't allow him to get the best of her, even if she were punished.

Her gaze fell to the chess board, and she gestured to it. "Playing with yourself, milord?"

Richard arched his eyebrows at her bawdy remark. He walked slowly toward her, his eyes sparkling. "Care to . . . give me a *hand* at it?"

"So, you be that desperate for help?" she shot back.

Richard smiled suggestively. "Let's say I'm finding it increasingly . . . *hard.*"

Audrey eyed the black king piece he was unconsciously rolling in his fingers. "Perhaps you ought to stop fiddling with it and play a proper game."

Richard looked down at the chess piece in his palm and burst out laughing. He chucked her under her chin. "I'm glad to see living here at Langsforth Hall hasn't blunted your wit, Audrey. God knows it does little to improve mine."

Audrey spoke stiffly, her dark eyes snapping. "I'm a lady's maid, sir. I do not appreciate being sent to the kitchens like some untrained wench off London streets."

His tawny eyebrows shot up. "You're working in the kitchens? I had no idea. I had wondered where Judith's little protector had got to." His eyes assessed her, and he brushed a moist strand of hair from her face with tender fingers. "No wonder you look so flushed. And here I thought you were in a sweet sweat over me."

She scowled at his insolent grin and knocked his hand away. "You don't do this to punish me?"

"My God, what kind of monster must you think me? Nay, it's not me. It must be the countess' doing. Damn!" He sighed. "But don't fret. I'll take care of it somehow. She'll only want blood from me, after all, nothing I haven't given her before."

Audrey tried to squelch her pleasure that Richard wasn't behind her humiliation. It mattered not.

Richard raked a hand through his hair and began to pace. "Needless to say, I'm hardly her favorite son. She thinks I'm some kind of changeling or something, because I disagree with her views on just about everything. But who wouldn't? She's so damned strict and cold. I can't please her, no matter what I do. So now she's taking it out on you and Judith. I'm sure she has plans to manipulate my new bride into her way of thinking. Divide and conquer, that's her motto."

Fascinated with this confidential outpouring, Audrey didn't think before she replied. "I didn't realize Judith and I were engaged in a war with the Dragon Lady."

Richard stopped pacing, his blue eyes wide as he faced her. Audrey could have bitten her tongue. Insulting the lord's mother to his face was not a wise move for a servant.

"You call her that? Dragon Lady?" Richard stared at her a moment, then threw back his head and roared with laughter. "It's perfect. I'd love to see the look on her face if she knew!" He continued to laugh, then finally forced himself to catch his breath. "You're the cleverest little chit. That's why I sent for you. As her maid, you know Judith best of anyone. I want you to explain her to me."

"What do you mean?"

Richard sobered. He tossed the king piece on the board. It skittered and knocked over several pawns. "My sweet, beloved Judith cares naught for my attentions. She tries to conceal it; but I've experience with women, and I can see the signs. Now, I know she has a reputation at Court for being virtuous. But we're going to be wed! I had hoped for some sign she anticipates married pleasure." His tone lost a good deal of its arrogance. "God knows I can think of no other reason to wed anymore." He faced her squarely. "Am I so disagreeable?"

Audrey took in his aspect, her gaze playing over his brawny build. She well remembered the strength of his arms and the feel of being held against his broad chest. His thick ginger hair and trim beard were perfectly barbered. His royal blue clothing was impeccable, with knee-high leather boots and a satin-lined cape. But her gaze settled on his face, the fine laugh lines around his crisp azure eyes, the ready smile. He looked like a prince in a fairy tale. "I suppose I've seen uglier, milord."

"Milord, is it? I recall you addressing me as Knucklehead."

"Only because you deserved it."

"So I am witless, is that it?"

"Well, you are awfully naive about love."

"Am I?"

"All that nonsense you told Judith in those letters to her, about love overcoming all obstacles. How could anyone with half a brain believe any of it?"

"You don't believe in love?" Richard looked at her as if she had grown horns. "I didn't think that was possible. How sad."

Audrey grew uncomfortable under his stare. She hadn't meant to allow this man into her thoughts. In defense, her tone turned scornful. "I don't believe in fairy tales, wood sprites or St. Nicholas, either, but I suppose you do."

Richard grinned. "Of course!"

Audrey averted her eyes from his infectious grin. She retreated to a professional mein. "How exactly do you make love to Lady Judith now?"

"The usual way. Here, I shall demonstrate." He settled himself on the bench at the foot of his large, four-poster bed. He grasped Audrey's wrist and pulled her to sit beside him. She stared at him suspiciously. Perhaps she shouldn't have posed such a question. Yet her indifference to his lovemaking would serve to frustrate him even more. It would be worth putting up with him for a moment to knock his lordly arrogance down a few pegs.

Richard slipped his arm around her waist and pulled her close. "I've tried kissing Judith, of course." He cupped Audrey's cheek in his callused hand. "I've kissed her tenderly, like this—" His soft beard tickled her pleasantly as he touched his lips to hers. His mouth played gently over hers, sending a glorious tingling through her body. Audrey's thoughts grew misty, and she felt herself going lax in his arms. She was stunned by her reaction to him. She had the urge to kiss him back.

He outlined her lips with his tongue, prodding at the corners, entreating them to open. Audrey clamped her mouth tight to resist him. She stiffened her spine and clasped her hands in her lap. She was determined to show he had no effect on her, or he may press for further favors. She detested bedding men, particularly noblemen who only wanted to use her body for their own pleasure. There was simply no accounting for the effect of this man's kiss.

Richard lifted his eyes to meet hers, one eyebrow arched speculatively. Audrey spoke with as much cockiness as she could muster. "So, she didn't care for that either?"

"She seemed not to," he said slowly. "But sometimes women aren't honest about their feelings. So I tried kissing her with greater passion, like this—" Richard pulled her hard against him and buried his mouth on hers.

A shocking blast of sensation shook Audrey's entire being. This time, she found the urge to return his kiss irresistible. Her mouth opened willingly under the onslaught, her tongue meeting his thrust for thrust. Her hands slipped up his satin-clad shoulders, then higher, her fingers digging into his soft, thick hair.

Richard growled deep in his throat. Audrey felt his palm

cupping her full breast, stroking the apex. A burst of pleasure radiated outward from where he touched her. Audrey was melting from the heat of it, swept away on a tide of feeling. She lost all sense of where she was and whom she was with. With unaccustomed hunger, she arched into his embrace as he stroked her lush curves, his hands molding to her flesh.

Richard yanked her chest hard up against his as if he couldn't get close enough to her. He dropped his mouth to trace a path of sensation along her neck. "My God, woman, you're pure fire!" He groaned hotly in her ear. "If only Judith were more like you!"

The mention of Judith brought Audrey up short. Richard was her mistress's betrothed, and she was letting the man get fresh with her! "You must stop," she said, but her voice was entirely too breathless to be effective.

Richard only chuckled, his hand teasing her nape. "But you don't want me to, and a gentleman always fulfills a lady's desires."

"I'm not *easy*," Audrey replied more forcefully, pushing against his chest. "*Besides*, Judith *does* enjoy kissing, for I've seen her."

Richard drew back startled, as Audrey hoped he would. "You have! With whom?"

"On May Day, she was kissing someone."

Richard's eyes widened in shock. "May Day, the day I picked her up from Marcus?"

Audrey didn't reply, realizing she had already said too much.

"Marcus! He was kissing her, wasn't he? That scoundrel!" He pounded his thigh with a clenched fist.

Startled by his vehemence, Audrey raced to explain. "It meant nothing! Everyone was kissing everybody. Truly. It was a celebration, rather like being under the mistletoe at Christmas."

Richard still looked dubious, but she had managed to take the edge off his anger.

"Believe me, it meant naught."

Richard sighed, and his muscles relaxed. "Mayhap you speak true. After all, Marcus said she was a trial when he gave her over to me, hardly what a lover would say." His eyes glinted freshly, darting up and down her voluptuous figure. "So, everyone was kissing everybody, you say?"

"Aye. Judith was merely the same as everyone else that day. It would have looked odd if she hadn't taken part. It was part of her disguise."

"So who were you kissing?" he asked abruptly.

"Me, milord?"

"Aye. You."

"I—I don't recall . . ."

Richard gave her a devastatingly attractive grin. "You've forgotten his name already? Must not have been very exciting. Not like—" He pulled Audrey into his arms again and gave her a thorough kiss that sent her senses reeling. "This," he murmured when he broke it off. He lowered his mouth to hers again. With her last shred of self-control, Audrey yanked herself from his embrace and stood.

She nervously smoothed her skirts and clasped her hands before her to still their obvious trembling. "I told you, milord, I am not a cheap hussy you can make do your bidding without even a by-your-leave," she said icily. But she kept her eyes averted. "In future, I will expect you to deport yourself as a gentleman should, and remember our stations." She turned on her heel and left him, trying desperately to demonstrate a prim, professional air. Before the door closed behind her, she thought she heard Lord Richard laughing.

Audrey returned to London suddenly, joining a group of merchants passing through. She gave Judith only a terse goodbye, without any explanation. Judith didn't really need one, for she knew how unhappy Audrey had been since arriving here. She didn't blame her maid for leaving, and hoped Audrey would be able to continue in some post in her father's house. It was certainly better than working in the Langsforth kitchens. But Judith felt more alone than ever in her life.

Things would have been better, perhaps, if Richard had treated her like his future wife, or even his friend. Instead, he seemed unwilling to spend time with her. He stopped trying to seduce her. She caught him giving her the oddest looks when he thought she wasn't looking.

Now and then, he would make a comment about the London theater; in particular, his "good and loyal friend" Marcus Sinclair.

"Good and loyal friend." Always in those words.

Judith feared she would reveal her feelings and always steered the conversation elsewhere. But Richard continued to bring up his name. She suspected he knew her heart lay with his friend Marcus, but how could he possibly know what he meant to her? Besides, Marcus would remain forever in her past. She had best remember it.

So she told herself, but she could not stop thinking of the compelling actor, and the kiss they had shared on May Day.

Finally, a reply came from Judith's father in London. He wrote both to Ambrose, the Earl of Langsforth, and to Judith. In the earl's letter, he agreed to the betrothal and accepted the payment for damages. He pointed out, however, that it would hardly suffice to repair his friendship in the eyes of Viscount Mowbray. He promised Judith's dowry would arrive on the day of her wedding, which the Langsforths had set for the first of June.

He also sent his regrets about not being able to attend the wedding.

In his letter to Judith, he was much more to the point. Judith retreated to the solar to read it in privacy. She broke the seal and unfolded it, her gaze scanning the scratchy letters of her father's hand.

You disappoint me greatly, daughter. I fear I will never live down the shame and humiliation you have brought on me. Viscount Mowbray was noble enough to believe that I had nothing whatsoever to do with the plot to steal you from your own betrothal feast.

I would, however, like to get my hands on the man who took you away. Rumor has it he is an actor who performs here in London. If I find him, I will bring him to account for his actions against our family.

I will not be attending your wedding. I do this in

punishment of your unseemly behavior, as a stern warning not to go against the wishes of your father or your family ever again.

I would prepare myself, if I were you, for the Langsforths' disappointment when they receive your dowry. It will be substantially reduced once I have removed what I deem fair for damages caused by the way that family stole you. The paltry sum the earl sent me was nowhere near sufficient.

I do not, however, plan to inform him of this until you are wed into his family, and if you are wise, neither will you, for it will only decrease your value further. And I sincerely doubt I could find another man to marry you after a second such debacle.

Your father

Judith refolded the letter and began to slip it inside her sleeve. To her shock, the countess' narrow fingers extracted it. The woman had followed her! Without a word, the countess stalked off down the hall with the letter.

Judith didn't see the confrontation in the salon downstairs once Richard's family read the letter. But she heard their voices raised in a pitched battle with their "wayward son," who had risked a healthy dowry with his scheme to wed Judith. Naturally, they also blamed Judith for turning his head to mush.

From her window, she saw Richard storm out of the estate and toward the stables. A few minutes later, he was riding hell-bent for the forest beyond.

It occurred to her then that Richard was using her. He had known all along what it would mean to select his own wife. He had known stealing her from Mowbray would cause difficulties. He had known his father and mother would be dissatisfied with any woman he chose. But he chose her anyway.

Not because he loved her.

Because he could never please the earl and countess. So he simply made it easier for them to find fault.

Judith sighed. She was sick to death of being used by people. She wanted it to end. She wanted to be free, once and for all.

Yet it was impossible.

The letter Marcus had been dreading arrived a fortnight after his return to London. The messenger delivered it to him at the Globe Theater one morning during rehearsals for the afternoon performance of *Henry the Fifth*.

The richly embossed parchment with its seal at the bottom served as yet one more reminder to Marcus of the world to which he didn't belong.

He tore open the seal and read the letter, the words blurring under his eyes, melting like snow thrown into the fire. Judith and Richard were to be married on June first, a mere two weeks away.

Marcus was tempted to destroy the elegant invitation, but instead he refolded it carefully and tucked it into his tunic. He had to think clearly before he made a decision about whether or not to attend the wedding. His initial reaction was to make his polite excuses. But if he didn't attend, Richard might become suspicious as to why he was avoiding the wedding. He couldn't allow any suspicions to fall on Judith.

Judith—that was the real reason he wanted to go, and dreaded going. He knew it would be the most difficult thing he had ever done to watch her given in marriage to his friend. But he also wanted to assure himself that she was happy in her new life. If he saw that she was, perhaps he would be able to forget her more easily, knowing he had helped her life take its proper course.

"Marcus!" Richard called, approaching his friend.

Marcus dismounted from his borrowed horse on the front lawn of Langsforth Hall. He had entered the estate with another party of guests who had also traveled from London for the wedding.

"I'm so glad you could come." Richard clasped his shoulders.

"After all I went through to see this transpire, you don't truly think I'd miss it, do you?" Marcus smiled warmly. He noticed, however, that Richard looked strained, despite his broad smile.

"Come. I'll show you where you're to sleep."

Marcus walked with him toward the west wing, but they didn't enter the main door there.

"How is London?" asked Richard. "I miss it, I tell you. This marriage business sorely taxes my freedom. Of course, once I'm wed, I can leave Judith here and roam about as I did before. We can resume where we left off, drinking and wenching. I greatly look forward to it."

Marcus felt a knot of fury in his stomach at his friend's casual dismissal of the joy to be found married to Judith. "But, Richard, you told me you were in love with the girl," he said, striving to sound nonchalant. "Surely the fresh bloom of love hasn't faded so fast?"

"Love? Ah, yes. I do love her, after a fashion. Or at least I lust after her—somewhat. Of course, it's not altogether easy to love a cold fish. Her maid, on the other hand—"

"Cold?" Marcus asked in surprise. He caught himself and hid his amazement, worried Richard might detect that his surprise was from personal experience.

"Aye, cold. Just as she was rumored to be," Richard said pointedly, looking at Marcus speculatively. "Virtuous, untouchable Lady Judith. Now I know why they call her that."

Marcus realized then they were heading away from the hall toward the stables situated a good distance behind. "Is your hall full with the wedding guests?"

"Full? No, not really. We have so much room at Langsforth, half the county would have to be here before we filled it. Seeing as I'm only a fourth son, that's not likely to happen for this wedding." They had reached the stable door, and Richard swung it open.

"Then, why are you putting me up here?" Marcus asked,

trying to keep calm, trying not to believe something bad was afoot.

Richard had the grace to look embarrassed. "I'm sorry, Marcus. But it's the countess. She can't stand to see anyone attempt to rise above his station. I thought I could manage to have you as a guest, but she had a veritable fit when she found out I'd invited you. She forced me to agree that you would be here as a performer, rather than a regular guest."

"Oh, is that a fact?"

"Don't take it the wrong way, Marcus. You have to admit you'd feel a little awkward sitting at the tables instead of playing before them." He attempted a laugh. "You always did make fun of us nobles as gaudy peacocks, and vow you couldn't stand to trade places with us."

"I wasn't expecting to trade places with anyone. I was expecting to be treated as a guest, Richard, and sit down to a hearty supper."

"You'll be served supper in the kitchens, after the performance. You will perform, won't you? I'm sure Judith would be happy to hear you play. Why not give us a taste of your talent this afternoon, at our prenuptial banquet?"

Marcus' eyes narrowed as they settled on Richard. "I would be delighted to perform at your wedding, dear friend. I wish you had made your purpose clear to me. I did not come properly prepared. I have my lute, of course, but I haven't rehearsed."

"Aye, I realize that, Marcus, and I'm truly sorry." He laughed again, a strained sound. Marcus thought Richard had never looked so unlike himself, so tense and worried. "In any case, I put a couple of blankets in the loft for you to use." He elbowed Marcus familiarly and chuckled. "Certainly it's not any worse than some of the stews we've passed out in. I have to go tend to the other guests. If you need anything, just ask."

Richard hurried off, leaving Marcus to stare after him in amazement. Richard was not himself. Perhaps it was being back in the bosom of his cold, argumentative family; perhaps it was his impending wedding. Regardless, Marcus' role had just changed, and he was now expected to perform at the celebration of the wedding between his best friend and the lovely Judith. The thought fair made him sick.

Marcus appeared in the hall on cue, after the midday meal had been served, his lute slung over his back.

Judith stared in shock as Marcus entered. He was as handsome as she remembered, more so than any other man in the hall, with a regal bearing that belied his simple garb of black hose, breeches and doublet. At first, she thought he was only late to supper; perhaps he had just arrived and needed yet to find a place at the table.

He headed not for a seat, but for the center of the room. He faced the high table, pulled up a stool to rest his foot on, and began to strum his lute while the crowd quieted down. Meanwhile, he glanced over the nobles, particularly Richard's family.

Judith's heart stopped when Marcus' gaze fell on her. He gave her a cursory glance, no longer than the glances he gave any other member of his audience as he performed a popular love ballad. Disappointment welled in her chest, despite her resolve to forget him as well.

After Marcus looked away, Judith whispered to Richard, "Surely he's not here to perform for us?"

"He is an actor," Richard replied defensively.

"He's your friend!"

"Marcus is used to it. He's never known any better."

Judith's throat constricted with shame at what was transpiring. Tomorrow she would marry Richard, a man that treated his friends as hired help. "It's appalling, after what he did for you, for us!"

Richard's expression looked chiseled from stone. Judith could tell he especially disliked the fact she was the one to point out the error of his ways. Anger radiated from him, almost matched by Judith's own. Judith fell silent, barely able to hide her fury.

Marcus ended his song with a flourish and instantly had the attention of the nobles. He bowed low to the high table, and to each of the side tables in turn, and introduced himself.

"Good evening, ladies and gentlemen. I am Marcus Sinclair of Lord Chamberlain's acting troupe of London. Tonight, for your pleasure, I ask you for your attention only, a paltry thing for those who are so gifted with riches of the spirit and heart." He smiled right at Richard. "Indeed, one is considered blessed to have such friends, for one then learns clearly in what esteem one is held, and need never again wonder at the quality of the reception he will receive."

Richard clutched at his pewter cup, his knuckles showing white against the silver, his jaw clenched so tight a cheek muscle spasmed. Judith noticed that no other members of his family seemed distressed by Marcus' well-aimed words.

"Thank you, kind sir," replied Grace. "We are happy to receive you in our home. Pray, begin your show."

Marcus set his lute by the table and returned to the center of the hall. "The scene I shall perform for your pleasure tonight is about betrayal," he said, his hands held wide. "It's the story of a man who trusts his friend, but discovers the truth, to his own tragic end."

Richard watched in growing fury as Marcus began acting out scenes from *Julius Caesar*. The actor dwelt especially long on Caesar's speech after being fatally wounded by his friend— and assassin—Brutus.

Richard's gaze slid sideways, and he noted his bride's expression. Judith was clearly entranced by the performance, despite its cutting message. His fury intensified to an even greater pitch as he observed her watching Marcus, her eyes aglow, her cheeks flushed with delicate color. She had never looked at him that way, and he was her future husband! "Milady, I think you are forgetting your place," he said quietly, tightly.

Judith barely acknowledged him, she was so intent on Marcus' performance.

Richard's gaze switched back to Marcus, his suspicions more than confirmed. A sick feeling clawed at his gut. It was painfully obvious now—Judith's reluctance over the wedding, her disinterest in their future together, her lack of relish for his lovemaking, her seeming pleasure at his revelation that Marcus had authored the love poems. Not to mention that kiss on May Day. She wanted Marcus! All the wenches Marcus had at his disposal and he had flirted with Judith! Richard felt a sudden helplessness. He knew he wouldn't be able to fight Judith's feelings for Marcus, and he wasn't sure he wanted to try.

But Marcus had been his best friend, and he had trusted him. That galled worse than all else.

"Those actors, such baseborn fools, such lowlives," Richard muttered. He said it just loud enough for everyone in the hall to hear. "It's a wonder they can make a living at all, dishing up such drivel."

His words interrupted Marcus' performance. The actor stopped and stared at Richard, his hands on his hips.

"I thought you loved the theater," the countess exclaimed to her son. "You spend enough time there."

"That was before I realized what a thorough waste of time it is," he replied, his eyes fastened on Marcus' cold, gray ones.

"Nevertheless, son, I *was* enjoying the performance. Pray, continue."

Marcus began again, as if nothing had interrupted him. Judith yanked on Richard's arm, and he swung his gaze to her. She looked furious, and more full of passion than she ever had. "How could you say such things?" she whispered in fury.

"How could I not? After all, actors are little better than lawless vagrants," Richard said loudly, again interrupting Marcus' performance.

Judith jumped to her feet. "I refuse to stay here a moment longer with a man who treats his loyal friends so basely!"

The guests stirred in shock at the bride's outburst, but Richard was beyond caring what they thought. His best friend and his future wife—how could he have been so blind! Indignation swelled within him as he rose to face Judith. "I know all about you and Marcus! I have every right to chastise you! I refuse to spend my wedding night with my bride dreaming of another man!"

Judith almost looked ashamed, but she rallied quickly. "Marcus risked himself to rescue me from Lord Mowbray, and this is how you repay the favor? You are little better than a knave, and I will have nothing more to do with you."

"Richard!" The earl's voice shook the rafters. "What kind of Langsforth are you? Control your woman!"

All eyes in the hall were riveted to them. Richard knew he had to take control of the situation or be a laughingstock. He pulled at Judith's arm, trying to force her to retake her seat. "You will sit down and mind your place, or I shall beat you so hard you won't be able to sit!"

A collective gasp shook the onlookers as Marcus vaulted over the head table and grabbed the front of Richard's doublet. "You lay a hand on her over my dead body," Marcus said tightly, his lips thin over clenched teeth.

Richard needed no more proof of his best friend's duplicity. The betrayal pierced Richard's heart like a finely honed blade. "As you wish," he gritted out. He shoved Marcus back hard and swung his fist up.

Suddenly, Judith appeared between them. Richard barely missed striking her. Marcus grasped Judith's arm and pushed her out of the way, then dropped into a fighter's crouch.

"Enough!" The earl's heavy hand landed on Richard's shoulder and spun him around. "You've ruined this feast, Richard, and shamed us all before our guests. I've never seen the like!"

Richard's gaze darted from his father's furious countenance back to Marcus, who wore a calm innocence that only a professional actor could conjure.

Marcus swung his lute over his shoulder. "Milady, milord," he said to each of Richard's parents in turn, with a deep bow. "I fear I've overstayed my welcome. I'll take my leave of you now." He turned and strode toward the door.

"Excuse me," Judith said tightly. She shouldered past Richard and followed after Marcus.

Richard heard the guests whisper and saw their mocking gazes as they watched his bride walking out on him. He burned with humiliation. He wouldn't let Marcus win this easily. He hadn't treated Judith the wisest, but he would be damned if he would let her run off.

"Judith, stop it! Come back here!" She ignored him and

disappeared through the door. His brothers' derisive laughter trailing him, Richard stalked from the hall, his pride in shreds.

"Marcus."

Marcus turned from saddling his horse in the stable and found Judith behind him. His eyes met hers through the shadows, and he read the gratefulness there, saw, perhaps, something even deeper. He was suddenly filled with overwhelming euphoria at being with her once again.

"Would you be willing to escort me to my home in London?"

"I believe it's on my way," Marcus said calmly, trying hard to squelch his joy at this turn of events. It would mean spending the rest of the day and much of tomorrow in her company. "What about your maid, Audrey?"

"She already left. She couldn't stand it here."

"And you?"

"You know you needn't ask me that."

"No. I needn't ask," Marcus said as his eyes searched her face. In the space of a few short minutes, her countenance had transformed from the tense, pale woman at the banquet to a woman even more lovely and spirited than he remembered. He sighed with more than a trace of regret for his friend Richard over how poorly things had turned out.

"Ah, there they are, the two lovers planning their next tryst!"

Richard's raw voice cut into their privacy, startling them both. They turned to find him standing in the door of the stable, his face wearing a mirthless smirk.

Chapter 7

"Richard. Are you still determined to have it out with me?" Marcus asked tightly.

Judith stood frozen beside him, knowing how the pair of them must look to Richard, wishing she wasn't causing both men such pain.

Richard's voice shook, filled with accusation. "You set out to seduce my bride, the woman I love. You've been wooing her behind my back! I *trusted* you to take care of her for *me*, not for you! You're not even suitable for her!"

"And you consider yourself suitable?" Marcus shot back. "Judith needs a man who will put her interests first. You only think of yourself. You haven't even bothered to notice how unhappy she is."

Judith was stunned that Marcus could read her so well. He had only seen her in the hall during his performance. She hadn't thought he had even looked at her. She was torn between the two men, furious at Richard for dishonoring Marcus, yet upset at the distress she had caused a man who professed to love her.

"Richard, it was never as easy as you wanted it to be," Marcus continued with strained calm. "You can't make a woman love you. You never bothered to consider Judith's feelings.'' Marcus breathed deeply, obviously trying to rein in his own anger.

"So you think you're the expert? You, because you can bed any woman you desire? He can, you know.'' Richard turned to Judith, his eyes sparking. "I've seen him in his finest form. He can have his way with any wench he desires, noble or common.''

"You exaggerate, Richard,'' Marcus said.

At his words, Judith shivered. She forced her spine stiff, but she knew Richard had seen her shocked reaction.

"They see him on stage,'' Richard continued. "Sinclair spots them during his performances. When they're ripe for the picking, practically swooning over him, he directs a few of the more—romantic—lines to them. The next thing you know, they're sending him messages to meet them after the performance. You know what follows after that—an arranged tryst somewhere and Marcus has made another conquest.''

Judith's heart thudded heavily against her ribs. She recalled how quickly she had succumbed to Marcus' magic when he performed at Lord Mowbray's, how ready she was to believe he was performing only for her. She also remembered how easily she had given him the favor of her kisses.

"Richard, you know naught of what you speak,'' Marcus said.

"Hah! Of course I do! We've laughed about your conquests over many an ale, haven't we, Sinclair? Or have you already forgotten the good times we had, when I thought you were my friend?''

Richard circled closer to Judith, his expression stark. Judith knew he was making none of this up, and she could barely hide from the two men how upset she was. Only her training as a gentlewoman kept her from showing how deeply Richard's words stung.

"It would shock you to hear who he's bedded, Judith. You'd be surprised at the names I could share with you. There's that countess, the one with the prominent beauty mark on her upper lip.'' Judith knew exactly whom he was referring to. The woman was rumored to have many lovers. "She came to every performance of Sinclair's for three months—until her husband found out. Then, of course, that lady-in-waiting to the queen, the one with raven hair—she was practically making a scene until Sinclair noticed her." He spun back to Marcus with a biting laugh. "I bet if you set your mind to it, you could even bed the queen!"

Judith could not suppress her shiver at his words, and Richard pressed his advantage. "Oh, you didn't realize that about your beloved Marcus Sinclair, did you? Marcus is a rake. You probably fancied he cared only for you, that you were special to him. That's what they all think."

"No, I didn't feel that way," Judith said, her words sounding hollow to her own ears. "I know how he feels about me. I was merely a nuisance to him. He told you as much, if you'll recall." She forced a calm expression to her face and looked boldly at Marcus. He was gazing at her in dismay.

"Just don't forget Marcus is an actor, Judith. You can never trust anything he says."

"Richard—" Marcus said in a warning tone. "My love life isn't at issue here, for I have no designs on Judith. None whatsoever." Despite everything Richard had said, Marcus' warm gaze wrapped around her heart, making Richard's warnings meaningless. "It's true she's beautiful, the most incredibly beautiful woman I've ever seen. She's brave and good, clever and kind. A true lady in every way." Marcus tore his gaze from Judith and turned again to Richard, his voice low, but firm. "I would never dream of hurting her."

"You certainly never could," Judith said defiantly. She was determined not to show how much pleasure his sweet words gave her. "Marcus' reputation does not matter one way or the other, for I certainly wouldn't permit him to press his advantage with me."

"Truly?" Richard said in disbelief. "Then, why were you kissing him?"

The question hung in the still, dusty air several heartbeats too long. Judith wavered on her feet, finally forced her spine straight and looked toward Marcus. He appeared as chagrined as she felt.

"Don't look so shocked, Judith," Richard said sarcastically. "Your maid Audrey was glad to tell me the truth. She told me you were kissing Sinclair when I came to meet you and bring you here. Kissing him, there in front of the village, like a common country wench!'' He slammed his hand on a post. ''All along you've played me for a fool, Judith. You've wanted *him*.''

''Of course not! I confess we kissed, but—''

Marcus cut in. ''That was my fault, Richard, but it was a silly mistake. Leave her alone. You're badgering her, and I won't stand for it.''

''Badgering my own betrothed for kissing another man? I think not. And that's only part of it! I didn't understand at the time, Judith, but you certainly weren't upset when you learned Marcus had authored those love poems I sent you. You probably fancied he was actually writing them to you. But he had never even seen you when he wrote them. I paid him well for them. You meant nothing to him, I assure you.''

''I didn't think I did,'' Judith said coolly, determined to maintain her composure. ''Quit condemning me, Richard, before you know the facts. Marcus doesn't love me. I would never fool myself into thinking he does.''

''I forced myself on her, Richard. She was behaving a perfect lady until I—''

Judith interrupted. ''Don't lie on his account, Marcus. I'll not have it.'' She turned to Richard. ''I wanted him to kiss me. It was just a passing fancy that meant absolutely nothing. I understand that completely.'' Judith ignored the potency of Marcus' gaze and lifted her chin. ''In truth, Marcus probably thought it fair payment for the risk he took. But that's the sum of it.''

Despite her dismissive words, Judith found she couldn't look away from the face that dwelled always in her thoughts, couldn't turn away from his magnetism, the pure sensuality that she had tried so hard to forget. Her gaze drifted to his expressive mouth, and memory of the passionate embrace they had shared came flooding back, rocking her.

''I believe neither of you!'' Richard's incredulous voice echoed loudly in the stable. ''Mayhap you can't see it, but I can. I see it plainly now. You want each other, so desperately you can hardly withstand it.'' He threw out his hands. ''I say you're both mad! What do you think you'll get from this, Judith?''

Still gazing at Marcus, unable not to, Judith replied, "I expect nothing because I want nothing to do with him, nothing! I wouldn't think of loving him!''

"I think you are protesting too much, milady.'' Richard spun on Marcus. "You're a fool if you think she'll ever be yours, Marcus! She's much too valuable a piece of property for a commoner like you. Besides, you could never afford her!''

Marcus' eyes turned the color of storm clouds, his jaw muscles tense. "I have no designs on Judith. She means nothing to me, except she continues to throw my life into turmoil.''

"And I do not feel anything for Marcus,'' Judith repeated, still caught in his gaze. "Except, of course, I am grateful to him for saving me from another disastrous marriage.''

Richard grasped her shoulder and forced her to look at him. "From Mowbray or from me?''

As she looked into his distraught face, Judith's voice failed her.

"Do you love me, Judith?''

"Nay,'' she said quietly.

His voice became soft, desperate. "Do you want to marry me?''

Judith's breath caught. She couldn't stand hurting him, but she knew lying would serve no one. "Nay, Richard. I do not.'' She sighed heavily.

Richard looked defeated, and Judith's heart went out to him. He hadn't asked for things to turn out so poorly. "Richard—'' she began, in a sudden desire to comfort him.

Richard cut her off with a gesture. "There's nothing more to say, is there? Go on, Sinclair, take her out of here. She can take one of my horses. I don't particularly care. I would wish you luck, wherever this leads, but it will do neither of you any good.'' He turned on his heel and slammed the stable door behind him.

In the aftermath, the silence weighed heavily in the air, broken only by their breathing. Now alone with Marcus, Judith avoided his gaze. She wondered what he was thinking, then immediately told herself it mattered not in the least. He had certainly made it clear once again that she was nothing to him, despite Richard's claim to the contrary.

She lifted her gaze to meet his. "Hadn't we better leave now? I have no desire to linger."

"Aye," Marcus said curtly, turning away. He began saddling his horse as Judith tended to her own.

They were silent until they had walked their saddled horses outside into the bright afternoon sun. Judith approached him. "Thank you for rescuing me, again," she said quietly, her cool voice at odds with the warmth in her heart.

"I seem to be making a habit of it," Marcus said wryly. "Come now. We have to get on the road to reach an inn by dusk."

He slid his hands around her waist and lifted her to her saddle. Too soon, he released her and vaulted onto his own horse. They kicked their mounts into a canter and left Langsforth Hall far behind.

Marcus and Judith joined a party of travelers on the road to London, for there was safety in numbers. Judith was glad that Marcus kept close by her side, and not just because he was posing as her groom. She was determined to speak of the strong current of feeling that flowed between them.

Even now, she could see he was having difficulty keeping his eyes from her. She was sumptuously garbed for an afternoon's entertainment at her prenuptial feast. Her green gown was made of silk and velvet, and she wore a headdress decorated with seed pearls. Marcus had bade her remove her gold chains and strands of pearls, to discourage thieves.

Her corset thrust her small breasts high enough to offer a pleasing display of cleavage. Judith's exposed skin tingled when Marcus' gaze swept over her. His gray eyes lifted to hers in such a powerful contact, it seemed to vibrate the air between them. After a timeless moment, he tore his gaze away.

"Marcus," she said softly. "I've been meaning to apologize to you for causing a rift with your friend, Richard. I know I've been more than enough trouble for you."

"Don't think on it, milady. Look at that man." Marcus

gestured to a tall fellow dressed as a fool, in parti-colored clothing. "He's a jongleur by trade, but dabbles as a tailor. I met him a few years back when I toured with the players through the countryside. Does a marvelous trick tossing flaming torches about."

"Perhaps you can introduce us later," Judith said. Anxious not to be sidetracked, she continued, "As I was saying, I suppose it's all my fault. Richard could tell something was wrong. What I said, in the stable . . . I wasn't being completely honest."

"And that man." He pointed. "He's a merchant of good, sturdy fabric, wool and cotton mostly. Takes it through the countryside in that small cart he pushes. He has two wives, one in London and another in Shrewsbury." Marcus laughed lightly. "I'd like to be a fly on the wall if they ever meet."

Judith grew frustrated. She was about to try once more when another traveler rode up beside Marcus and asked him for news.

News often took weeks or even months to travel the countryside. Marcus shared the latest on the Essex rebellion with their fellow travelers, describing all the events surrounding the poorly planned, short-lived rebellion. He told who had been arrested, which ringleaders had lost their heads or been hanged, and who had been merely fined according to how much they could afford to pay. The Earl of Essex, of course, had gone to the block despite once being a favorite of the queen's.

Judith noticed that even though he wasn't performing, Marcus Sinclair had the natural ability to become the center of attention, even of this small group of disparate travelers. She watched the others listening avidly to him and began to realize Marcus had a charisma that affected all sorts of people, men as well as women.

Was that all it was? His personal charisma at work on her as it worked on so many others?

No. With a forbidden burst of pleasure, she understood the cause behind his distance. He was trying to keep the fire that lay between them from raging out of control.

When dusk fell, Marcus stopped at a large inn a half-day's ride from London. After securing Lady Judith a room, Marcus led her to the supper table. He found himself barely able to eat, despite having missed the midday meal he had been expecting at Richard's.

Richard. . . . Regret weighed heavily in his heart over the loss of his friend. But an entirely different emotion swelled in his chest when he gazed at the lady across from him. He watched the firelight play over Judith's delicate features, turning her hair molten, and a profound hunger swelled deep in his gut.

He noticed she also had barely eaten. Nor did they speak, as if talking would force them farther along a path that once taken, would change their lives forever. With this thought on his mind, Judith's lambent gaze lifted to his. As their eyes connected, he knew she could plainly see the raw emotion on his face. In defense, he shot to his feet and held out his hand. "We should get you to bed, milady. The hour grows late."

Judith rose slowly and gathered her skirts in one hand, then slipped her other hand in his. Marcus led her up the rough wooden stairs and stopped in front of a door wider than the others lining the hallway. "Here's your room." Belatedly, he realized he still held her hand and forced himself to release it.

"Where are you sleeping?" she asked softly.

"I'm bedding down with the other single men in the hall." He unlocked the door and opened it. Judith entered and looked around. Marcus stepped inside, but lingered near the door. "It's the best room they have," he continued. "It has a bed with a down mattress and a fireplace, though I imagine they're poor accommodations compared to what you're used to." The fireplace was already lit, giving the room an intimate, comfortable feel. The four-poster bed was piled with comforters.

"I don't find the lodgings poor at all. They're perfect," she murmured. Her eyes met his, softly highlighted by the glow of the firelight. "And you spent your last shilling on this luxury for me, didn't you?"

Marcus smiled gently. "You're a noblewoman."

She stepped close to him. "I'm a woman, with a woman's heart."

Despite his staunchest efforts, her words caused his mask to slip. His gaze connected deeply with hers, intense in the recognition of their mutual desire.

"I confess I gave Richard cause to think as he did about us," she said, her words shockingly honest. "I never told him anything, but I'm not the actor you are, Marcus. He could see it in my eyes."

Marcus absorbed her marvelous, frightening words. "Did you forget what I said to you after we kissed?" he asked carefully, almost afraid of her answer.

"No. But I never believed it meant nothing."

Marcus' heart pounded harder against his rib cage. "I see. Why might that be?"

"You know as well as I, Marcus."

"What about what we said to each other in the Langsforth stable? We were both very adamant."

Judith smiled. "You just answered your own question."

He absorbed the love in her eyes, her expression, the softness of her smile as she gazed at him. His hand seemed to lift of its own accord to touch her hair where it fell along her face. He stroked it gently, unable not to imagine how it would feel sliding against his naked skin.

Judith touched him in return, her fingers tracing the contours of his face, as if wanting to imprint him on her fingers for eternity.

Merely touching Judith wasn't enough for Marcus. He wanted to consume her, to fold her into himself until there was nothing separating them, nothing holding them apart. His heart constricted with unfulfilled need, with the certainty he must never succumb to his desires. His voice dropped almost to a whisper, his words deeply melancholy. "What have we gotten ourselves into?"

"I know not, except the hunger I feel for you."

Her words were sweet invitation. Marcus drew on all his strength to resist. She was untouchable, despite their circumstances. He had to remember that, or the consequences could be horrendous for them both. He dropped his hand and stepped back. "I know you are a noblewoman, Judith. You were today, and you will be tomorrow when I return you to your father." He moved farther away, into the shadowed hallway. "Good night, sweet lady." At the head of the stairs, he gave her one last lingering look, before descending the steps to the hall.

* * *

Judith couldn't stand to see him leave her, when their time together was so brief. She also was well aware of the difficulties that lay between them. It wasn't fair to him for her to desire his love when there was no future in it. But it was already too late for her heart and, she knew now, for his heart as well.

But they were running out of time. By midday tomorrow, her brief freedom would end. She would return to her father's care and submit to his plans to marry her off. The thought of being forced to wed a man—any man but Marcus—was a hundred times more disheartening than it had been before Marcus rescued her from her wedding to Mowbray. Casting darkness over her future was her love for Marcus. In a few short hours, she would lose him forever, this marvelous man who had come from nowhere to steal her heart.

She had never given much thought to carnal love before meeting Marcus, being reared to think of it only as a wife's duty to her husband. The thought of bedding a man before marriage had always seemed lewd, shameful, something women who lacked breeding might do.

But she knew how deeply her passion burned for Marcus Sinclair. The mere thought of lying in bed with him, her body alongside his, her thighs opening to him. . . . Why, she could not conceive of suffering another man to touch her in that way. And she could not conceive of denying that perfect consummation to herself and Marcus.

Nature had decreed it: They belonged together as she would never belong to another man. Now that she understood this, there was only one thing left to do.

Marcus lay wide awake while the men around him snored contentedly. After tonight he would deliver Judith to her father, and they would part. He would have to content himself with memories of the incredibly lovely creature he had been privileged to escort through the English countryside.

But his thoughts went far beyond memories of what they had actually done together, into a golden future he would never have with her. At times, the course of his imaginings was downright base. He chastised himself for the carnal nature of his fantasies, but would fall back into dreaming of her almost immediately. Any thought of making real such fantasies was entirely out of the question. But his mind persisted on the same path, for he had precious little mental discipline where Lady Judith Ashton was concerned.

A child's voice cut through the darkness. The only man still awake, Marcus rose onto his elbows and found himself looking up at a small boy.

"I have a message for Master Sinclair," said the lad, peering into the gloom barely alleviated by the glowing remnants of the fire in the hearth.

"I am he."

"The lady you came with sent me," he piped. "She's took real sick. She's spewing her supper into a bucket right now."

"Damn!" Marcus cursed. Judith sick? It didn't bear thinking about. He didn't hesitate to follow the lad, grabbing his linen shirt and slipping it on as he walked. He had been wearing only his breeches, and it wouldn't do to come to her room half-naked.

The boy led Marcus to Judith's door. His concern for Judith driving him, Marcus entered quickly, and the boy closed the door securely behind him.

Marcus' gaze was immediately drawn to the vision standing before the fire. "Milady," he murmured. A full bear skin served as a hearth rug. Judith stood beside it wearing only her silken chemise. Her bare shoulders were caressed by her curtain of golden hair, glistening in the firelight. Her only adornment was a gold pendant shaped like a star that dropped into the valley between her breasts, the mounds clearly outlined, her nipples pressing against the almost-transparent fabric. "You certainly don't look like you're losing your supper."

"Excuse me?" Judith clearly wasn't expecting that kind of statement from him at this moment.

Marcus grinned. "That's what your little messenger said."

Judith smiled at him sweetly. "As long as it brought you to me."

Chapter 8

Marcus' pulse quickened at Judith's seductive tone, as thick and sweet as honey. A corresponding ache began to grow in his groin. She was ethereal, a vision, a goddess. He backed toward the door.

Judith read his intention. She instantly moved into action, reaching the door before he did and sliding the bolt into place. She leaned back against the hard wood, breathing heavily, her breasts rising and falling invitingly. For Marcus to open the door, he would have to move her aside—and to move her, he would have to touch her.

Marcus made as if to do just that, but his hands stilled inches from clasping her narrow waist. He looked down into her face, his eyes burning, demanding she release him, demanding she keep him from leaving. "You are a vixen, woman," he said, his voice hot with tension, his gaze devouring her face, devouring the look of love and desire that lay naked there. "Are you trying to torture me?"

"No, my love. To satisfy your desire—and mine." She took his hand in hers and, lifting it, brought it to her lips where she gently kissed his palm.

Marcus smiled tensely. "Judith, you don't know what you're doing."

"But I do." She lifted a hand to his beard-roughened cheek and gently traced the outline of his lower lip with her thumb.

Marcus couldn't resist. He allowed her thumb into his mouth and gently bit down on it. In response, her eyes grew smoky with desire. He whispered tightly, "You will be the death of me. I'm only human!"

Judith ignored his plea. She slowly lifted his hand, turned it palm outward, then settled it on her breast.

Through the silk, Marcus felt the tautness of her nipple under his palm. Her breast perfectly filled his hand. Her audacity, her invitation, was beyond his control. His free arm encircled her, and he clasped her bottom hard, dragging her against him. His lips burned fire down the white column of her neck. "Darling, I cannot continue like this," he said hotly into her ear.

Her response was a heartfelt pledge of devotion. "I love you, Marcus, I adore you. I will never love another man as long as I live. Love me tonight, Marcus. I need you tonight." Her voice trembled with passion. "I need to feel your love around me, and inside me."

His heart filled with love for her as his body burned with desire, both forces obliterating once and for all his carefully constructed defenses. He tightened his hold on her as if determined never to let her go. His words were fierce, commanding. "I will love you, as you were meant to be loved." His large hands ran up and down her back, massaged her bottom, caressed her hips.

His touch, his heated words, played havoc with Judith's senses. She returned his caresses, slipping her hands under his shirt to slide along the flat plane of his stomach. Marcus slipped off his shirt and dropped it. He pulled her again into his arms, allowing her the freedom to explore his body in turn.

Judith ran her hands up his muscle-ridged chest, through the soft scattering of hair there. The crisp feel of it thrilled her as it slipped through her fingers, enticed her to greater boldness. She encircled his small male nipples with her fingertips, felt them tighten under her touch.

She felt his gaze on her, watching as she enjoyed his body.

She cocked her head and looked into his eyes, seeing in their gray depths his delight at her boldness. With unspoken communication, they acknowledged what they were about to do, the forbidden, irrevocable step they were taking. The shared secret bound them even tighter together.

Marcus cradled her face in his hands and entrapped her gaze with his own. "Aye," he murmured, his mouth just above hers. "You will be mine tonight, Lady Judith Ashton. Mine alone. I will possess you, love you until you are weak with my loving. I will strip away all your ladylike decorum until the passionate woman inside lies naked and wanton before me. Then, and only then, when you crave me as I crave you, will you understand what you've done to me."

He held her gaze for an eternity. Judith was afraid he would look away, afraid he would leave her and pretend he hadn't said these wondrous, frightening things. "Marcus. I want that, too," she quickly confessed, surprising even herself.

"Then, it shall be." Marcus lowered his mouth slowly and claimed hers in a searing kiss that sealed their fate.

His hot lips on hers were questing, seeking satisfaction, fulfillment of a promise too long denied. His lips roved over her face, her neck, her shoulders. His hands around her waist inched up her chemise, revealing more and more of her alabaster body in the bright firelight.

The gown was ruched around Judith's waist before she became aware of it. She glanced down to see her own nudity, her femininity exposed to his gaze. Being thus revealed to him gave her a decidedly sensuous feeling. She lifted her eyes to meet his, accepting this, and everything to come. She slowly raised her arms so that he could slip her chemise off the rest of her body. It fell from Marcus' fingers, forgotten now that Judith was once again exposed to the heat of his gaze.

Marcus' eyes played over her wondrous figure, more perfect, more sensual than he had imagined. He explored her with his gaze, from the golden hair that fell caressingly over one pink-tipped breast to the rib cage that narrowed to her flat stomach and tiny waist, to her gently flaring hips and satin-soft thighs, a crop of golden hair nestled between them.

For a moment, he no longer touched her, except with those

molten eyes. She prayed she wouldn't disappoint such a seasoned lover. Marcus slowly knelt before her, his hands running along the front of her thighs, then slipping inside to caress her most sensitive skin. Judith shuddered with pleasure. He cupped her bottom in his hands and brought her mound toward his lips. Judith stared in amazement at his worshipful posture. Then his lips made contact with the most intimate part of her woman's body in a liquid kiss.

Judith gasped at the sensation of his tongue slipping sensuously through her mysterious crevices, tantalizing the heart of her womanhood. She clutched his thick hair in her hands and felt her knees grow weak, her body shaking with need. "Marcus," she moaned.

His strong hands urged her thighs wider, and she complied, her legs shoulder width apart as he loved her on his knees. The slow, sensuous torture built a fire within her, bit by delicious bit, until she was arching with such need she could no longer contain herself. "Please," she cried, her senses spinning out of control. "Marcus, please."

With his considerable natural grace, Marcus rose slowly to his feet, his hands never leaving her body as they trailed upward along her thighs, her stomach, to her breasts. "You have utterly possessed me, Judith," Marcus said heatedly. "Do you know the power you have over me?" He played his roughened thumbs against each of her soft, pink nipples.

"And you me," sighed Judith, arching into his touch. "Oh, my lord, your hands are magnificent." Marcus pulled a sweet nipple into his mouth. Judith cried out at the tingling sensation, cradling his head in her arms. "Your lips are magnificent, too," she said with a gasp.

Marcus laughed, deep in his throat, his teeth tugging at her nipple. Judith finally collapsed against him, weakened beyond bearing.

He slipped his arm under her knees and lifted her, cradling her against his chest. Instead of carrying her to the darkened side of the room where the four-poster bed awaited, he laid her on the bearskin rug before the fire, stretching out beside her. The fur felt soft and erotically sensuous against her naked skin, the heat of the fire warmly caressing.

He searched her eyes for some sign of fear, of hesitancy, of second thoughts. There were none.

"Judith, are you certain? I can still stop now, though it will be damned hard. But once your virgin's knot is untied, it remains so."

"I have so little to give you, Marcus," she said. "I want to give this to you."

In response, he dropped his mouth to consume hers in a passionate chain of kisses. His chest pressed intimately against her own bare flesh, sending a wave of heat through her body. Judith's arms tightened around him possessively, trying to draw him nearer, ever nearer.

"God's blood, Judith, I ache for you," Marcus moaned. His hands explored her body as if to memorize every curve, every pore. His questing fingers brushed softly over her womanhood. Her body already well prepared for him, Judith's thighs widened in response, spreading to accommodate his stroking fingers.

Marcus left her there, craving much more. Her eyes were misty with desire, her skin flushed. Of their own accord, her hips arched upward, seeking what Marcus now was withholding from her. "Oh, please, my love, please," she moaned.

Marcus was stripping out of his breeches as quickly as humanly possible, anxious to hold her once more, to find fulfillment for his own pulsing desire. He swept her into his arms again, the contact of their naked bodies gloriously complete.

Judith felt his hard, hot manhood against her thigh. Marcus took her hand in his. "I want you to know me, Judith." He gently laid her hand on his manhood. Judith found him surprisingly silken to the touch.

Marcus groaned as she caressed him. "I would rather die than hurt you, darling," he said softly. "But I must. Do you trust me?"

Judith nodded, suddenly anxious about being able to accommodate him. But she did trust him, and she wanted him—lord, how she wanted him. He dropped a tender, loving kiss on her lips, the kiss achingly sweet. Then he slipped his hips gently between her thighs, supporting himself on his arms. Judith spread her thighs wider to receive him.

The tip of his manhood slipped inside her sex, prodding at

her maidenhead. As gently as possible, he pressed deeper into her. He felt a resistance at first, then a giving way, an acceptance, and he slipped halfway inside her.

Sure enough, Judith cried out. "Marcus, Marcus, yes," she cried at the wonder of feeling him inside of her. There was some discomfort, but it did not overshadow the immense connection she now felt with him. Her eyes dropped to their joining in wonder, then rose to meet his in unspoken understanding. They were one.

Marcus' long fingers stroked the hair alongside her face. "Does it hurt, sweet?"

"It—it hurts a little, but it feels so good. And you?"

Marcus was in truth almost in pain from the effort to hold back. "You are golden, my sweet," was all he could say. He gave in to his body's demands and pushed himself farther into the tight glove of her body. Loving her gave him the most pleasurable sensation he had ever experienced inside a woman. He groaned with the sweet heat of her.

He gently showed Judith how best to wrap her legs around him and move her hips with his. He gazed into her eyes as he began the ancient rhythm, the dance of man and woman that betokened spring's rebirth, life's renewal, and passion's fulfillment.

Marcus soon changed the rhythm of their loving, moving swiftly against her, pounding harder than he intended, considering this was her first time. But he was lost with it, with her, consumed completely by his passion for her. "God, I love you," he groaned.

Judith also was lost to the glorious sensation of her lover inside her. She knew only one thing before her mind and body lost control. She was right to give herself to this man. She would never regret it as long as she lived.

His loving swept Judith up until the full heat of summer burned within her, gloriously warm, fervent, golden. She cried out Marcus' name as he continued to work his delicious magic on her. She began to feel a need unlike anything she had ever known, a need so great she knew she would die if it weren't met.

When the heat inside her became too intense, it suddenly

changed, bursting into a thousand stars, pleasure coursing
through her, her fingers, her toes, all of her transported beyond
knowing, beyond caring. She shook with it as she cried Marcus'
name until her throat was dry.

Marcus gripped her tightly in her ecstasy as he found his
own release, his eyes meeting hers, his expression one of agony,
yet ultimate ecstasy, the face of a man blessed and possessed
by his love.

He collapsed upon her, sated, holding her, stroking her hair
from her face, unable to imagine life without her, unable even
to try. "Sweet, darling Judith," he breathed after a moment,
his head on her chest. "I have never felt with any woman what
I feel with you. You are all there is." He removed his weight
from her and lay on his back, pulling her into his arms.

For a long while, the lovers lay still, filled with wonder at
their joining, savoring every moment, every sensation. Judith
breathed deeply of his masculine scent, touched his skin to feel
the texture, watched the way the firelight played over his body.
She wanted to remember it all, every moment, every nuance
of the evening, so that tomorrow, when she became Lady Judith
Ashton once again, she would not forget, no matter how many
years intervened.

"Oh, Judith, my sweet, I love you so much," he breathed
into her ear. "I've tried to deny it, I've tried to avoid it, but
God knows, I do love you. From the first moment I saw you—"

"Aye, Marcus, I know," Judith cried softly, her throat thick
with emotion, her eyes filling with tears. She couldn't hold
back, and a sob tore from her throat.

Marcus pulled away and took her face in his hands. "Sweet,
don't cry, don't cry," he crooned. He brushed away her tears
with his thumbs.

"It's just that I'm happy," she gasped, before Marcus' mouth
came down on hers once more. Marcus knew she felt as he
did, ecstatic in their shared love, yet miserable in its hope-
lessness. But they had tonight, a slender moment in a lifetime
of sorrows and unfulfilled dreams. This alone was theirs to
share.

* * *

"This is what love between a man and a woman was meant to be," Marcus said fervently as he lay spent beside her. He had carried her to the bed and loved her again, more thoroughly than before, worshiping every inch of her. "You will never have this with the husband your father finds for you, I'll warrant, for he can't possibly love you as I do."

"Nor will I love him as I love you, Marcus. You know that's true," she sighed. "Yet I am lucky."

Marcus' mouth twisted. Conscious of how quickly the hours were flying by, he felt far from lucky. "Are you?"

"Most women, particularly noblewomen, must marry their husbands before they even know if they love them. They lose their maidenhead to a stranger. But you, a man I truly love, has shown me the way of loving."

Intense rage built inside Marcus at this reminder that he had merely been the first, that once she was married, she would belong to a husband who may or may not cherish her, mind, body and soul. Yet it was the thought that another man would lie between her thighs that filled him with a primal rage the likes of which he had never experienced. But he hid his fury, knowing there was nothing either of them could do about it.

"You have shown me the way of it, too, Judith," he finally replied. "Of love. It humbles me."

Judith lifted herself to her elbows to look into his face. "But why? I have given to you, but you have also given to me."

Marcus didn't feel like explaining to her how easily her gift could have been abused, her reputation destroyed, if she had given herself to a man who wasn't completely in love with her as he was. He knew the risk she was taking to give herself to a low-born man such as he. But then, she was well aware of it, too.

"Don't think it, Marcus," said Judith, as if reading his thoughts. "We have the rest of the night ahead of us." She kissed his lips gently. Marcus' large hand cradled the back of her head, and he explored her lips thoroughly with his, reminded once again that there would be a long, lonely lifetime ahead of him for poignant thoughts, for hopeless wishes, for regrets. But there were yet many hours until dawn. For tonight, they had each other.

* * *

"Sweet Judith, I have a confession to make," Marcus told her several hours later, cradling her against his chest. The fire had died to embers, but the sky through the window near the bed was growing grayer as dawn approached. There was so much he had yet to say, he would never be able to say it all. Perhaps now, as their time together drew to an end, Judith would see her future differently.

She lifted her head from his chest and gazed up at him. "Aye?" she asked.

"I did sing those songs for you, as you guessed," he said, a smile playing at the corners of his mouth. "I even wrote one for you."

"The one that asked me to come away with you."

"Aye. That one."

Judith looked at him carefully. "Is that what you wish me to do? Do you wish me to run away with you, Marcus?"

He gazed at her a moment before answering. "Would you say yes?" he asked, equally softly. But he awaited her answer in tense silence.

Judith's eyes filled with tears, more than enough answer for Marcus. He gritted his teeth. "You could never wed a commoner," he said tersely, "could you." A statement, not a question.

"You misunderstand, my love. I cannot betray my father. I love him, Marcus. I cannot hurt him so disloyally." She dropped her gaze from his and inhaled a quavering breath. Her body shook with it. "I cannot marry you. It would break his heart. He needs me."

Marcus sighed deep in his chest, an agonizing sound that signaled the end of his last hope. *I need you, Judith!* he cried silently. Yet, he had expected her to feel this sense of responsibility, of loyalty. It was one of the things he loved about her. They were not youths like Romeo and Juliet, caring for nothing but their love.

He knew the baron's need for Judith was more for her ability to secure a title and provide an heir for the Ashton wealth than for her alone. But Marcus couldn't force her, refused to cajole her. That would be not only wrong, but lead to ruin. "If that's truly how you feel, I cannot ask it of you. Our guilt would cripple us, were we to elope. And your position—that is too much for anyone to have to sacrifice."

"It's not my position. That means nothing to me. Nothing. If you don't already know that, you should." She searched his face with her eyes. "It's an accident of birth."

"It is more than an accident. It is a curse." Marcus' chest filled with pain. He wrapped his hand in her golden hair, imprisoning her head, his lips twisted into a grimace mere inches from her own. He shook her once, almost painfully. "A curse." He gritted out the word once more before his lips claimed hers hotly.

He pulled her down onto the bed and made love to her in rough, passionate silence, demanding she give herself to him completely in the last few moments before dawn, demanding she give him at least this much. She opened herself to him yet again, letting him fill her, letting him command her body into heights of ecstasy he vowed no other man could ever make her feel, for as long as she lived.

Marcus groaned as he found his release, his body shaking, sated only physically, for his soul would never again be satisfied. He lay beside her on his back, touching Judith only where their hands were clasped, their heavy breathing the only sound in the dark, silent bedroom.

"If you become with child after tonight, what will you do?" Marcus asked quietly.

Judith didn't reply at first. "I do not know. I haven't thought. It depends how soon my father finds me a husband, I suppose. I find I almost wish your seed does take root, for then I will always have part of you with me."

"You would not purge yourself of it?"

"Never."

Marcus wondered how he felt about that. Her words thrilled him, but he wasn't keen on his own child being raised as another man's. Even more frightening was the possibility that Judith could be punished severely. But there was little Judith could do, unless she took some dangerous midwife's remedy. He didn't want that, either. "We must simply pray you will not beget a child from this night," he said firmly.

"Prayers," Judith said hollowly. "They do little good, Marcus, or we would not be in this situation now."

"I should have thought of this. I should have spilled my seed," he said quietly.

"No. I wanted all of you," Judith replied solemnly. She lifted herself to her elbows and looked down at him, her shadowed brown eyes reflecting his own dimming happiness. "Marcus, my love," she said, her voice husky with emotion. "I fear I have done you a great disservice. I should not have brought this about—"

"I don't regret it, Judith," Marcus said firmly, conviction filling his heart. "I will never regret the gift you've given me tonight, the chance to love you so completely."

Judith's eyes filled with tears. "After tonight, after I'm married, don't think on it again. Don't waste your life thinking of us."

Marcus' lips twisted wryly, and he laughed, a deep, humorless sound. "I have no choice, Judith. You have thoroughly possessed me."

"I want you to marry someday, to find another woman to love and have children with."

"No." He said nothing else, and Judith gently rested her forehead on his chest, her hair fanning about them both. Marcus' hands gripped the linen sheets hard, his knuckles turning white with his agony. He forced them to relax and brought them up to stroke her silken hair. "Don't worry about me, sweet. Care for yourself." Marcus felt dampness on his chest and realized she was silently crying. He lifted her chin with his fingers and caught and held her gaze. "Oh, Judith—" His voice broke. "You are making it so hard for me to end this."

"I'm sorry, I don't mean to make it harder." She quickly wiped at her eyes with her hands and sat up, not looking at him. "But you are right. We must end it now. It grows light, and you must take me home."

"Aye."

"What will you do, after?"

"Work."

"And . . . women?"

Marcus grimaced. As if there *were* any other women in the world for him. "I can always find compliant country maids willing to share my bed," he remarked flippantly, knowing it would hurt her, suddenly wanting to hurt her.

Judith's eyes lifted, searing into his. "That's a horrible thing to say."

"Certainly no more horrible than the idea of you marrying and being regularly bedded by another man," he said bitterly, his eyes challenging hers.

She turned her head away. "It's odd how possessive we are of what we do not possess. I was just telling you to forget me, yet the thought of you bedding another woman cuts me to the quick."

Regretting his words, Marcus sat beside her and brushed the hair off her face, smoothing it over her shoulder. "We do possess each other," he replied, laying his hand on her chest. "In here. Always. I will be your champion, and you will call on me whenever you need me. Even after you are married, for your husband may not always have your own best interests at heart. You will always have me."

She smiled tenderly at him. "I think of this as my wedding night, for you are the husband of my heart." She slipped her hands under her hair and unclasped the gold, star-shaped pendant that hung between her breasts. Throughout their night of loving, she had worn the bauble, and Marcus would forever carry with him the image of it against her naked skin. She kissed the filigreed gold, then fastened the chain around his neck. It still carried the warmth of her body. "This was my mother's. Until tonight, I have always had it with me. Think of me when you wear it."

"I will never remove it." Marcus cradled her cheek in his hand. "This has been my wedding night as well, for I will never love another woman."

He could see his words were melting her strength, and he needed her strength now to be able to leave her, to reenter the hall and prepare for their departure, to begin the difficult task of pretending to the world that nothing had happened between them. "Help me say good-bye to you, Judith, for I am growing ever weaker," he said softly. "I need you, as well."

Judith responded to his plea. She slid off the edge of the mattress and retrieved his breeches and shirt from the floor. She brought them to the bed and held them out to him. He took the clothes, slipping them on as quickly as possible. Judith retrieved her chemise and put it on, as well.

She took his hand and led him to the door of her room. She reached for the handle, but Marcus caught her wrist and stayed her. "When next we meet, it must be as a lady and her escort." She met his eyes as he slipped his arms around her. "Good-bye, my Judith," he said, his voice achingly soft. His gave her a final kiss, chaste, loving—a kiss of farewell. Then he slipped out the door.

ACT 3

"The game is up."
—*Cymbeline,*
Act 3, Scene 3

Chapter 9

Soon, the spire of St. Paul's Cathedral came into view, rising above everything else in the city. Marcus and Judith slowed their mounts as they passed through the ornate Bishopsgate arch and into her neighborhood.

Marcus gazed about the neighborhood with curiosity. He had never been in this section of London. The wide lane was lined with the houses of nobles and wealthy merchants, brick and stone mansions decorated with gothic arches, intricately carved woodwork, and stained-glass windows.

Judith led him to an elegant three-story manor set back behind a wide front lawn and a small, unattended gatehouse. A six-foot-high stone wall segregated the property from its equally elegant neighbors.

They rode silently up the curving carriage drive to the front door.

"You should leave me here, Marcus," Judith said, dismounting.

Marcus remained mounted. His eyebrows rose. "Indeed?"

"I'm just not sure my father should see you."

Marcus had been under the impression he would not only be asked in, but was needed to help explain why he was delivering the baron's daughter to him. Obviously, Judith was embarrassed to come riding home with a man of his class. Despite the passionate night they had shared, she was ashamed of him. "I endeavor to please you, fair maiden," he said coldly, nodding his head formally and preparing to ride forward.

"Marcus, don't," Judith said, her expression suddenly anxious. She stepped up to his mount and laid her hands on his knee. "He threatened you, in a letter he wrote me while I was at Richard's. He said he wanted to get his hands on you and make you account for your actions in taking me from Mowbray's."

A leaden weight lifted from Marcus' heart, and his tight expression relaxed into a smile. "Ah, so it's concern for me, then?"

Judith nodded. "You should have known it was."

"Very well. Then I'll be leaving." But he was finding it extremely difficult to tear himself away. Judith also showed no sign of pulling away from his side.

Before he could leave, Baron Howard Ashton stepped from the massive front door onto the stoop and called out a greeting. Marcus couldn't very well ride away now, so he dismounted to explain to her father who he was and what he was doing with Judith.

But he was pushed to the background. "Father!" Judith lifted her skirts and ran up the short flight of broad steps to the front door.

"My sweet girl!" Howard called, his arms outstretched. He gave her a tremendous bear hug, swallowing her in a massive embrace. It was obvious how much love the two shared.

Howard pulled back and inspected her. "Ah, I should have come to the wedding. Perhaps I was hasty. But you look well, daughter."

"Father, I'm fine. I was very well taken care of, I can assure you." She cast an affectionate—and perhaps too revealing—smile at Marcus.

Howard Ashton also noticed the intimate gaze his daughter gave her new husband. She had never appeared happier over a man. His gaze traveled over the aristocratic features of Richard Langsforth. He was dressed simply—Howard wasn't certain why they arrived without the train and baggage of the typical traveling noble. But frugality was something he himself valued. Yes, he liked that in a man.

Despite the simple clothes, the man's breeding could not be disguised. Richard Langsforth was tall, well-proportioned, obviously strong and graceful. He reminded Howard of one of his prize racehorses. But then, breeding always showed. "Perhaps I was thoughtless when I allowed Lord Mowbray to convince me to give your hand to him. Perhaps I needed to work out some other arrangement with him," he said, his eyes on Marcus. "This man appears a fine specimen indeed. I can definitely see the value of mixing our blood with his."

Judith could hardly believe his words. He actually admitted she would do well to marry Marcus? It was incredible. "Oh, Father, you don't know what it means to me to hear you say that!"

"Indeed, the Earl of Langsforth is well-connected at Court. I am honored to join our family to his."

Judith's heart caught. "Excuse me, father, what are you talking about? Richard's not here."

Howard wasn't listening. He held out his hands to Marcus, who stepped forward and bowed his head.

Judith's heart fell to her shoes. "This isn't Richard, Father," she said in a dull, spiritless voice. The dream had been so sweet while it lasted!

"Oh? Then, who is it?" Howard stared at Marcus assessingly. Judith had a hunch her father recognized him, but couldn't place him.

"I'm Marcus Sinclair, Lord Ashton," Marcus said.

"Sinclair, you say? I don't know that name."

"Perhaps because we've never been introduced before," Marcus said pointedly.

Judith sighed, irritated by her father's presumption. "He's not a member of the nobility."

Howard's expression darkened. "Who are you, man, and what are you doing with my daughter? Tell me straightaway."

"I am an actor by profession," Marcus said with perfect composure. "I provided your daughter with an escort home from the Langsforths when it became clear the wedding was off."

Howard stared at them both, his eyes wide with shock. "Actor? You mean for one of those seedy Southwark theaters?"

Desperate to dispel her father's prejudice against actors, Judith spoke quickly, her hands on his arm. "What does his trade matter? Marcus took excellent care of me."

Howard's face turned ruddy. He yanked on Judith's sleeve, making her follow him onto the lawn at the side of the house. Marcus discreetly looked away. "He's the one who stole you from Mowbray in the first place!" Howard whispered angrily. "I recognize him now, for he performed for your wedding banquet!" He gritted his teeth. "And he's done it again! Is this man making it his career to steal you from your future husbands?"

"Of course not!" Judith cried. "He just happened to be there when I needed someone to take me home."

"Why *are* you home?"

"It's simple. I did not want to marry Richard, nor did he want me."

"You are becoming extremely difficult, daughter," Howard said. "I have told everyone at Court about your latest wedding. Now what do I tell them? I'll be a laughingstock! And now you come home in the company of *him!*"

Judith glanced toward Marcus, who was pretending not to notice their argument. "He's a good man. And my *friend.*"

"A *friend?* You're calling that man your *friend?* Judith! That type is poison, do you hear me? He's a bastard of the first order! I did not raise my daughter to go gallivanting across the countryside with vagrants and scoundrels!"

Judith was appalled at his sudden change of opinion. Her eyes snapped. "A moment ago you said you would be honored for me to marry a man like him."

"I thought he was Richard Langsforth!"

"What does it matter what his name is, or that he lacks a title? I once heard it said, 'A rose by any other word would smell as sweet.' It's the truth."

"He's a stage actor!" Howard's face hardened. "Do you know what they're like? They're rogues! It's not a proper trade at all, pretending to be other people, even kings and queens! I'm afraid even to ask about your virtue, daughter, afraid of what I might learn. You spent a night alone on the highway with him! The idea fair makes me shudder.'' He set his hands firmly on her shoulders, his expression softening with concern. ''What has he done to you? You must tell me true. I'm your father and I have to know, no matter how horrible the truth may be.''

''I'll tell you the whole truth. Marcus is not a rogue,'' Judith insisted. ''He saved me from two disastrous matches, and you owe him for that. He paid our way home himself. He never asked for a cent from me, or anything else for that matter.'' Indeed, she had given him a special gift most freely, she thought, fighting a telling blush. ''You're so prejudiced you can't see anything clearly! And you can't even thank him properly! I'm ashamed to call you my father!''

Howard looked at his daughter in consternation. ''It's not your habit to argue thus with me.''

''Nay, Father. But surely, if he had mistreated me, I would not now be defending him.''

He sighed, seemed to give in. ''Perhaps I have indeed jumped to conclusions.'' To her relief, he turned from her and approached Marcus. ''Excuse me, young man,'' he began hesitantly. ''It seems I owe you some thanks for what you did for my daughter.'' He cleared his throat, but was unable to sound less than stilted in his praise. Marcus gazed at him in stony silence, offering no attempt to make Ashton's task easier.

Ashton hesitated. ''My daughter feels you treated her well. Apparently you did well for someone who's not reared to caring for ladies of a gentle breed.''

Judith wished fervently she could sink into the ground and disappear.

''Aye, I managed to muddle through despite my coarse manners and regrettable lack of breeding,'' Marcus said, a humorless smile pasted to his lips.

''Ah, that's good, that's good,'' muttered Howard, not hearing the sarcasm behind the words. He smiled and raised a finger. ''You deserve a reward, young man, for helping Judith. I'll send you fifty pounds. Tell me where to deliver it—''

Judith knew it was a lot of money to Marcus. But she also knew how he would respond, his posture stiff with pride. "I didn't help your daughter for money, milord, but because she needed me."

Howard stared at him as if he had been insulted. "You must be joking. I see, it's not enough. Then, I will pay you one hundred pounds."

Marcus shook his head. "No, thank you."

"But, your payment . . . ," Howard began.

"All I ask in payment is that you ensure that Judith approves of your choice of husbands before you seek to wed her again."

Judith's heart warmed that even now Marcus thought only of her happiness. She could see her father considering the audacious proposal. Certainly, if she had approved of her husband in the first place, none of this trouble would have happened.

"Very well," he finally said. "I give you my word."

"Give *her* your word."

Howard sighed in exasperation. "Judith, on the Lord's good name, I promise not to marry you to a man you don't approve of."

Judith grinned and threw her arms around her father. "Thank you."

When she pulled away, she saw Marcus had already mounted his horse. She broke away from her father and stopped beside him. She didn't say a word, and she didn't have to. No words could express the melancholy either of them felt at their parting. A deep current of emotion passed between them, almost frightening in its intensity, communicating a palpable longing in the gently stirring morning air.

Marcus lifted his hand as if to touch her face, but hesitated. Judith caught it and pressed his palm against her face, wanting desperately to hang on just a little longer.

But the moment had to end. Marcus withdrew his hand, then kicked his horse into a brisk trot. He rode down the drive and disappeared into Bishopsgate Street.

Howard's voice brought her crashing back to reality. "You look like a lovesick cow, daughter, and I'll not have it!" He jerked her arm, and she spun to find his angry countenance inches from her own. "I don't care how grateful you are to him; your behavior is entirely inappropriate. I can see your distance from me this past month has done nothing but harm your refinement. We must work on that immediately so that you will be ready for your next—and I dare say last—betrothal, whoever the poor sot may be."

He turned and reentered the house. It was a long time before Judith followed.

Chapter 10

Judith reluctantly allowed Audrey to prepare her for a ball at the home of Lord Hutcliff, one of a score of such affairs she had been made to attend in the past three months. She lifted her arms, and Audrey settled a fine, sea green velvet gown over her figure.

Judith thought about Hutcliff, remembered he was an older man, a widower. Her father knew him well and had encouraged her to accept the invitation. She had little enthusiasm for the coming ball, but she did her best to mask it.

While Audrey was dressing her hair, Howard passed by on the upper landing and called out. "Judith, I would like to see you wear the gold star necklace from your mother. I haven't seen you wear it in weeks."

"Oh, my," Judith murmured, her gaze returning to her reflection in the polished metal mirror over her dressing table. Her hand flew to her throat.

"Milady, pray tell what the matter is," Audrey asked as she brushed out Judith's hair and began to plait it and puff it into an elaborate coiffure. "It's sure to be in your jewelry box."

Judith began to feel sick. "I don't have it anymore, Audrey."

"Whyever not?" Audrey's gaze met hers in the mirror,

undoubtedly noticing a hint of the secret Judith fought to hide. She knelt beside Judith and took her hands. "What's this all about, milady? You haven't been yourself, not since you returned from Richard Lying-hearted's estate."

Judith smiled at her maid's insult. "You are so wicked, Audrey."

"Aye. So you can tell me what's on your mind. I won't judge you. There's precious little in this world that would surprise me," she said ruefully.

Judith sighed, her voice dropping almost to a whisper. "I gave the necklace to Marcus."

Audrey's eyes widened. "To that actor? Marcus Sinclair? Whatever for?"

Judith couldn't contain her blush, and she knew Audrey guessed the truth.

"Oh, I see. A lover's gift."

Judith nodded. "A pledge."

"You and he . . . ," Audrey prodded, clearly anxious over her lady's infatuation with the actor. "Surely you didn't let him—"

"Oh, yes," Judith breathed. Even now her skin flushed with remembered pleasure.

"I see," Audrey said in a tone that said she didn't see at all.

Judith gripped her maid's hands. "Audrey, I won't ask you to lie. But please—"

Audrey squeezed her hand in response. "You surely don't have to ask, milady. No one will ever learn a thing from me. But why did you do such a thing? The only good reason to endure that nonsense is to make babes, which you certainly don't want now."

"It was my only chance to experience true love," Judith said simply.

Audrey gritted her teeth. "I only hope your heart won't be broken, or I will have to break that actor's head!"

Judith touched her throat where the necklace used to hang. "I don't regret it, Audrey. But now it appears I'll be paying the price."

Audrey sighed and squeezed her shoulders. "Don't look

so downcast. Chances are the baron won't even remember suggesting you wear it." She pulled another gold chain from the jewelry box and fastened it around Judith's neck. "Wear this one instead."

When Judith came down to the great hall, Howard bade her stand still while he circled her, inspecting her from head to toe. "I want you to look fetching tonight, Judith, for Lord Hutcliff may be just the man to tame you. He's extremely well placed at Court."

He stopped in front of her and stared in her eyes. "I grow weary of this, daughter. Very weary." Judith could sense the anger behind her father's cool demeanor. "I wish I had never given you my word that you could approve of your future husband. I would have had you wed and off my hands long before now. But none of the men I find for you are ever good enough for you. They all lack something, according to you. Brains, wit, looks," he continued in disgruntlement. "They're too young, or too old. It's turning me gray before my time."

Howard turned from her, and Judith breathed a sigh of relief. He hadn't noticed the gold chain that took the place of the missing pendant.

Grasping Judith's arm, Howard led her toward his favorite viewing spot in the center of the room, where the full panoply of the House of Dunsforth history stretched end-to-end across facing walls. A dozen pairs of eyes gazed down at them from their exalted positions high up on the walls, portraits of long-dead lords and their ladies—most painted in the last century as Renaissance realism took hold, and based entirely on family lore. Displayed with these noble visages were period swords, maces and gauntlets, most of them authentic, though there was no way of knowing whether they had actually been wielded by a member of Dunsforth House. A suit of armor stood at each corner of the hall, the oldest from the Norman Conquest, whence Dunsforth House proudly claimed its roots.

"This, Judith. This is why you must wed the proper man," Howard said, his voice taking on a reflectiveness all too familiar to Judith. "Your husband must be a man of such character that he can raise our family name to even greater heights. The Ashtons have been through much over the centuries. Many of the families that shared prominence with us have faded away. I'll not have that happen to us, Judith.''

"No, Father,'' Judith said softly, her eyes on Howard's portrait, painted when he was a young man in his prime. He stood leonine and proud against the backdrop of their country estate, which even now was only a shade of the vast estate it had once been. Judith supposed someday her image would hang on the wall, too, and her children and grandchildren would gaze at her. The thought did not make her feel particularly proud.

"We were earls, once, almost dukes,'' Howard continued. "We had the ear of the king. Now I'm merely a baron, girl. And I can scarce show my face at Court after the fiasco of trying to get you properly wed.''

"There's nothing wrong with being a baron,'' Judith said, anxious to turn his thoughts from her failed betrothals.

Howard snorted. He glanced at her, and his gaze fell on the gold chain at her neck. "Where is your mother's pendant?''

Judith stared straight ahead. "Excuse me?''

"I asked you specifically to wear your mother's pendant, the gold star. Where is it?''

"Oh, *that* one. I wasn't sure which one you meant.''

"Well, go put it on.''

Judith made no move to obey. "I've grown weary of it,'' she said on a sigh.

"I said, go put it on!''

"But we'll be late for the ball if we tarry longer—''

"Put it on!''

Judith jumped at the anger in his voice. "I—I—''

Howard shoved his face into hers, his eyes narrowing angrily. "You *what?*''

"I no longer have it, Father,'' Judith said softly, preparing herself for the inevitable scene.

Her father surprised her by stepping back and saying nothing. But he looked her up and down, from the top of her blond head to the tips of her gold satin slippers. "I see. You no longer have it. Why might that be?''

"I lost it, or it was stolen,'' Judith answered quickly.

"So, which is it? Lost or stolen?"

"I can't recall, I—"

Her father's lips pulled into a thin line as the color began to rise in his face. "I think I have been blind," he said finally. "Your reluctance to approve of any of your suitors, your missing necklace, the way you stared at that actor when he delivered you to me." His eyes narrowed, hardened, and she shivered. "You gave it away, didn't you, dearest daughter?" His voice was menacing. "Rather like a lover's token, wasn't it?"

Judith stared in shock at his accurate guess, her pulse beginning a nerve-wracking tempo in her veins. "Father, I—"

"Don't think to lie to me!" her father screamed at her. "You're in love with that *actor,* aren't you? Pining for him! I knew you were infatuated with him, and I forgave you for that. After all, he did help you out. But it's been three months! Three months!"

"It can be three years, thirty years, and I will feel the same," Judith said finally. A weight lifted from her heart as she confessed her love for Marcus. She felt suddenly brave, filled with the power of her love. She met her father's eyes. "I will always love him, Father."

His normally sanguine expression turned ruddy, every muscle in his face flexing. Judith knew then it had been a mistake to admit it to her father. His fists tightened with such rage, she was afraid he would strike her, something he had never done before.

"You can't love him. He's a baseborn nobody! What has he done to you, daughter, to make you think you love him? If he's laid one hand on you, I swear I'll—" He stopped dead in front of her and grasped her shoulders, his fingers tightening on her painfully. "Why, you were on the road with him twice! Without a proper chaperon! He had every opportunity—" The muscles in his jaws worked furiously. "I ask you, daughter, once and for all. Do you still have your chastity?"

Judith stared, unseeing, at her father's portrait behind him and tried hard to maintain her composure. She couldn't lie, couldn't deny her love for Marcus, the gift she had given him, the love they had shared. It would cheapen it. Nor could she tell her father the truth, or she might endanger Marcus, and herself. So she simply refused to speak. Her father ranted and raved at her, commanding her to say something, anything, but she stood as mute and unbending as a statue.

Which for Howard was answer enough. "There's one way to settle this, daughter, and your uncooperativeness has driven me to it," he said, sounding more weary than angry. "Go upstairs and remove that gown. You're going nowhere tonight."

He spun and left the room. Judith's knees buckled under her, and she collapsed on the nearest chair.

In less than an hour, three women came to the house. Judith had replaced her ball gown with a simpler at-home dress. She heard the voices downstairs and slipped into the hall, desperate to know what was going on. She had no idea what her father was planning, no idea why there would be visitors at this late hour.

She descended the steps to see her father talking with a small old woman with a wrinkled face and work-worn hands, and two surprisingly large women, one obese, the other simply strong-limbed.

Her father's eyes met hers. "Go on upstairs, Judith. Wait in your bedroom."

"But, Father, who are these women?"

She waited for an introduction, but it never came. The old woman, apparently the leader, took over. "No matter. We can get her back upstairs. Gilda, Hanna, take her on up. I'll join you as soon as we settle on the fee."

Judith didn't like the looks on the faces of the two large women who came to the foot of the stairs toward her. At the same time, she heard her father say something about "expensive midwife's fees."

Suddenly she knew exactly what these three women were here to do. She felt the blood drain from her face as a numbing dizziness swept over her. She gripped the banister and forced herself to remain steady. If she could rush past them and out of the house, there was still a chance her secret would be safe.

She ran down the stairs and tried to shove past the women, but one of them caught her around the waist and lifted her as though she were a sack of flour. Judith cried out, kicking and clawing, but her efforts were useless.

The burly woman dragged her upstairs to her chamber and threw her on her bed. She snorted. "As if we don't know the answer to the lord's question after seeing you try to run!"

Judith sat up and scrambled toward the head of the bed. "If you lay one hand on me, I'll scream as loud as I can!"

The woman's face split into a gape-toothed smile, and she started to laugh. "Your father's paying us, missy. Just be happy he's not doing this himself!"

"Hold her down," came the command from the doorway. It was the midwife, her face looking even more wrinkled and gray up close. Judith tried to squirm away, but Gilda and Hanna each took an arm and a leg and pinned her to the bed. Spreading her legs wide, they worked her skirt up over her hips. Judith wriggled and yanked at their grip. "Let go of me, you monsters! What kind of women are you, anyway? I thought midwives were supposed to deliver babes!"

"This is another service we perform," the midwife replied coolly. It was obvious Judith was not the first maiden whose virtue she had been called upon to guarantee. Judith cringed as the woman's cold hands poked and prodded at her private parts.

"Wider. She's resisting me," the midwife said. Judith was indeed clenching every muscle in that area of her body against the indignity of the woman's assault, thrusting her hips back and forth wildly. The midwife had one of her assistants press her knee down on her pelvis so hard it hurt to move or resist.

Judith felt at least three of the midwife's fingers probing at her painfully. "Yes, indeed, as I thought. As open as the door to a brothel." The midwife stepped back. "Let her up. I'm finished with her."

The weight was removed, and Judith yanked her skirt down. She didn't rise from the bed, however. She curled into a ball on her side and buried her head under a pillow. She felt so ashamed at having been forced to undergo the examination, and she was terrified of her father's anger. Any moment he would be storming up here to scream at her, to punish her worse than he had ever punished her. She dreaded his coming with each shaky breath she took. It was only a matter of time. First he had to pay off the midwife and her assistants; then he would come.

Despite how frightened Judith was, she still did not feel remorse over giving herself to Marcus. She would never feel remorse. She would do it again if the decision were presented to her today. Were that it were so! If only she could be with him again! She missed him dreadfully, night and day, despite the constant whirl of social events her father dragged her to.

Their time together had been so fleeting. In those hours, she had been gloriously free, free to think for herself, free to live her life as she wanted, free to be with Marcus, to love him as she burned to.

She would never wish ill on her father. But for the life of her she couldn't stand the conflict much longer between love of her father and love of Marcus. She was doing her best to forget Marcus, to be a dutiful daughter, but it was so difficult when she had her memories. To think he was here in the city, not far away, merely a carriage-ride's distance. Yet he was a world away, and those worlds weren't destined to touch, much less blend.

Judith waited for her father to come, to condemn her, to punish her severely. He never entered her room. Her fear was joined by crushing guilt when, some time later, she heard his uneven sobs as he passed her door and left the house.

Marcus left the Blue Lion alehouse and began the short walk back to his loft apartment. He hadn't stayed very late at the alehouse, not as he had in the old days. He thought of his life now as Before Judith and After Judith.

Before Judith, he ate, drank and was merry much of the time, entertaining friends, sharing pranks and living the happy man's bachelor life. But his life had irrevocably changed now that he had loved and lost Judith. It wasn't merely that the ache in his heart wouldn't go away. He simply had little desire to enjoy the company of his friends as he used to.

When he was with them, he was someone else, someone they used to know, putting on an act of easy congeniality.

The act exhausted him, however, and he sought the solace of aloneness as often as he could, a thoroughly uncharacteristic thing for him.

But there was no one he could confide in without endangering Judith's reputation, for they all were aware he had helped her family out. The only friend he could have imagined telling his woeful story to was Richard, a friend he had lost because of his love for Judith.

Marcus sidestepped a rowdy gang of revelers on the narrow street, but one of them bumped him hard. Marcus kept walking, adjusting his lute over his shoulder. Tonight would be like any other. He would sit on his sleeping pallet, or his chair if he felt like composing poems by candlelight, and sing for his own pleasure, sing the pain of his heart and soul to the walls. He was aware that other tenants in his building could hear him sing, but no one complained, yet. He wouldn't have cared if they did. His music was his soul's only consolation.

Marcus passed the front of his building, moving into the shadow of the second story that overhung the first a good eight feet. The stairs to his apartment were around the corner, on the alley side. The dim light from the few lanterns burning in the windows of the houses up and down the street did nothing to illuminate the alleyway. Marcus knew his way blind, however, for this had been his home for five years.

He strode the last few feet to the foot of the staircase, but he never made it. Something hard hit him in the stomach. He doubled over, spinning away at the same time to fight back. "What in the—" he began, but his words were cut off by another sharp blow to his gut.

His head spun from lack of air, but his blood was pumping, readying him instantly to fight off the cutthroat. He slipped his knife out and lunged at his attacker. The shadow of the man leapt back, but not fast enough. Marcus felt the blade sink into something, and the man screamed. Suddenly Marcus' lute was torn from his shoulder, and his arms were pinned to his sides from behind.

"The bastard cut me!" cried the man in front of Marcus. Marcus could only see his outline silhouetted against the light in the street. "Hold 'im!"

"I got 'im, Kyle," said the rough voice. "Take your revenge on him now."

The first rogue laughed. "We'll do more'n that, won't we?" He picked up the lute and smashed it hard against a nearby post. The sound of the wood breaking was like a death knell.

"My lute! God curse you!" Marcus cried.

In response, the rogue grabbed him by the hair and yanked his head back painfully. "So, ye're the actor who's been sticking his prick where it don't belong. Think ye're somethin', don't ye, swiving a maiden lady?" He punctuated his question with another blow to Marcus' stomach. Marcus gasped at the impact, and at the man's words. These weren't villains simply after his purse. They had been sent because of Judith.

Bracing himself against the man holding him, Marcus swung up his feet and kicked the man before him square in the chest. The man fell, but the second rogue never let up his painful grip on Marcus' arms.

"You bloody bastard!" the cutthroat said once he was on his feet again. He lifted his fist and slugged Marcus hard in the face. While his companion held Marcus' head by his hair, the first man delivered blow after blow into his face. Marcus knew he would be lucky to survive this evening. But then, if they had simply been sent to kill him, he would probably already be dead.

Marcus cried out as loud as his tortured lungs would let him, praying that someone might hear and come to his aid. He was well-aware of the unevenness of the fight, and of the vicious fighting ability of his attackers.

"Shut up, or we'll do more'n break yer legs and arms. We'll geld ye, too. Got it?" The first man, obviously the leader of the two, pulled Marcus' bloody face up and glared into it. The starlight glinted from his narrow eyes.

Geld him. . . . Prickles of sheer terror swept through Marcus.

"Cut open his doublet and see if it's there." Marcus' mind couldn't function well enough for him to know what they were talking about, until one ham-handed fist closed around the gold pendant Judith had given him and ripped it from his neck.

"I got it. Now we'll get the old man's money."

"Now bring him over here," said the leader. His burly

assistant dragged Marcus to a cluster of barrels. "Lay his arm over that one." The rogue did as bid. He delivered a crippling blow to Marcus' knees, causing Marcus to collapse on his side in agony.

The assistant brutally yanked Marcus to his maimed knees. The impact of his knees striking the ground caused such intense pain to shoot through his body, Marcus thought he would faint. The cutthroat stretched his left arm over the top of the closed barrel. Marcus swore and struggled, but each time he moved he received debilitating kicks to his midsection, until every breath was a torment and his strength began to fade.

Marcus saw through blood-streaked eyes some large object lifted in the leader's hands. It came crashing down on his forearm where it was stretched over the edge of the barrel. The sudden, violent break of his bones shot red-hot fire through Marcus' mind and body. He reacted like a wounded animal, screaming at the top of his lungs as his arm hung at an odd angle over the barrel.

The second cutthroat retrieved the rock the first had used to break Marcus' arm and lifted it above Marcus' head.

"Don't. We want him conscious for all of this, remember?"

The second man dropped the rock. Instead, he withdrew his knife and held it up where Marcus could see it. He lowered the point and scratched a line along Marcus' jaw from below his ear almost to his chin. "That cut will be lower if you make one more sound," he said, his fetid breath washing over Marcus.

"The other arm now," commanded the leader. His assistant positioned Marcus over the barrel so his right forearm hung over the edge. Again the first man lifted the rock. Marcus braced for the pain of the blow.

It never came.

A shrill cry rang out as the leader fell forward, rocking both the barrel Marcus was stretched across and the man holding him. Marcus was released, and he fell to the ground, painfully jarring his broken left arm. He could only dimly see what was happening—a third man had intruded on the scene and attacked the leader with his sword. The cutthroat lay moaning on the ground.

His rescuer, whoever he might be, was engaged in a sword

fight with the second man. In a matter of moments, the second man hightailed it out of the alley, running for his life from the swordsmanship of the newcomer. The leader made it to his feet and stumbled toward the opening of the alley, clutching his midsection.

Marcus closed his swollen eyes, trying to steady his vision through the blasts of pain from his arm, his stomach, his face, his knees, every part of him. He heard a familiar voice near him and opened his eyes. His rescuer was kneeling beside him.

"Marcus? Is that you under all that blood? My God, you look horrible!"

Marcus stared in amazement. "Richard?" he asked, his voice raspy, his lips so swollen it was difficult to speak.

"Aye. The very one. It seems we did this once before, eh?"

Marcus could barely focus on his words, remembered vaguely the night they had met.

"Only you didn't get near the thrashing then you got tonight," Richard said. "Can you walk?"

"I'll—try," Marcus replied as Richard slipped his arms under his and pulled him to sit. Marcus cradled his left arm in front of him. Even the smallest movement jarred him with fresh waves of agony.

Richard got behind him and tried to pull him to stand, but Marcus' knees wouldn't support him. "They did something to my knees," Marcus finally realized as he crashed back to the earth. The pain in his legs was excruciating, along with everywhere else.

"Christ's blood. I'll have to get help. Don't go anywhere."

"Don't make me laugh. It hurts," Marcus replied.

Richard began to move off. Marcus couldn't stand to see him go. He felt as weak as a woman—weaker—both in his body and his spirit. He didn't want to be alone, and had to bite his tongue to keep from calling Richard back.

Marcus lay there, one throbbing mass of pain, wondering what had triggered this cold-blooded attack, who had revealed his affair with Judith—who had caused his world to end so brutally, for he wasn't certain he would be able to survive the beating.

Richard returned with two other men from Marcus' tenement.

They brought a blanket with them and laid Marcus out on it. "Watch his arm," Richard said. Using the blanket, they dragged him to the foot of the stairs and began to pull him up the tortuously narrow flight. Marcus winced with each step that jarred under him. Surely hell had no greater agony than this. And the worst of it was how helpless he felt. Like a newborn kitten. It was utterly galling. Even now, he could feel tears of pain pressing against his eyelids—tears, as if he were a child.

The three brought Marcus into his apartment and lifted him to the bed. The landlord's wife followed and lit the lantern on Marcus' small table, illuminating Marcus in all his bloody glory.

The two men who had assisted gasped at the sight. Richard stared at his one-time friend. One eye was swollen shut, turning purple and red from the most horrific black eye Richard had ever seen. Marcus' other eye was only partially closed, and blood dripped from his swollen nose. His lips were also split and swollen, and there was a sizeable gash on his jaw. The only feature Richard recognized was one gray eye peering up at him. Even his hair had taken on a new appearance, matted and black with blood.

His doublet and shirt were torn down the front, exposing half of a badly scraped and bruised chest. But perhaps the sight that made them feel the most pain just looking at him was his left forearm, which hung at a decidedly unnatural angle.

"They did you up good, Marcus," said Richard, fighting the bile that rose in his throat. "There's no question their only aim was to beat the hell out of you. They weren't after your purse, that's a fact." Indeed, Marcus' purse was still fastened tight to his belt.

The only female there took charge. "Don't stand there gawking," she said curtly. "Paul, go get lots of fresh, warm water. And, Harrison, get your girl Irene up here. She knows some of the healing arts, don't she?"

"I'll go find a surgeon for that arm," Richard said.

"Good luck at this hour," the woman replied. "And that arm. I've seen less terrible breaks end in losing the arm. We might need the barber to cut it off."

Marcus knew then he would be sick. Lose his arm? His *arm?*

He made a living with his hands, playing music and acting! How many roles were there for one-armed men? Perhaps Shakespeare could write one for him—maybe one. "Not the arm, anything but the arm," he began to mutter. "God, no, not the arm."

At the door, Richard turned back to Marcus. "Don't worry so much. I'll find the best surgeon there is and make him set it, even if I have to hold him at sword point."

Marcus felt only a little more optimistic. How well could a surgeon peform with a sword blade at his neck?

In the next hour, Marcus had been washed and the cut on his jaw bandaged. Irene came and forced a few spoonfuls of laudanum down his throat for his pain. She helped remove his shirt and spread herb poultices on his wounds, their sickly sweet smell overpowering despite his broken nose. But he wasn't fit enough to complain. He needed their help, whatever form it took, for he had no one else.

Richard returned in another hour, alone. "The surgeon will be here in about an hour. He was a bit upset I woke him, so I threatened to run him through with a sword if he didn't show. He is the acknowledged best, however. He treats many of the nobles. I brought this to help you sleep until he arrives." He handed Marcus a tankard of ale.

Marcus took it, but was unable to drink it without being helped to sit. The effort to sit, even aided, caused him excruciating pain. "It's not worth it. Let me down," he told Richard and Irene. They did as he bid. Richard set the ale on the table.

"Someone has to stay with him, and I can't," said Irene. "I have a young 'un to look after."

"I'll stay," Richard said, stroking his gold beard. "God knows, I've stayed here before, usually after too much revelry."

Irene and the landlord's wife both left, and Richard pulled up a chair to sit by his patient's bed. Of all the places in the world, of all the situations he had imagined himself in, playing nursemaid to Marcus Sinclair had to be at the bottom of the list.

"Thank you," Marcus said. He seemed to have trouble staying awake and had drifted in and out of consciousness through the past two hours. But when he was awake, he was lucid.

"My pleasure," Richard replied awkwardly. "So, what was this all about?" he prompted, his curiosity eating at him.

"You should know."

"I should?" Richard stared hard at Marcus. "You mean— Judith?"

Marcus' swollen lips seemed to curl into a sardonic smile. At least, Richard thought it was a sardonic smile.

"My God, man, what in the name of the devil have you been doing?" Richard asked, aghast.

"Nothing lately," Marcus replied wryly.

Richard stared at him. "Then, what exactly happened to get you thrashed?"

Marcus turned his head enough to give Richard a look that said, *Can't you figure it out?* Or, at least, that's what Richard thought the look said.

Richard leapt up. "Did you and she—Christ's blood! That was incredibly stupid, Marcus. She's a lady, for God's sake!"

Marcus would have laughed if he wasn't in so much pain. "Think I don't know that?"

"Why in heaven's name did you do it, then? Why didn't you find some tavern wench to satisfy your lust?"

Marcus didn't answer. There was no explaining to Richard his all-consuming need to consummate his love for Judith. Everything he was, every dream he had had, was wrapped up in his desire for her. "I'd do it again," he said finally.

Richard stared at him as if he had seen a ghost. "No woman is worth this," he laughed wryly and shook his head. "You're more hopeless over this love nonsense than I ever was, Marcus."

He reclaimed his seat beside Marcus. "So, did she tell her father? Or did a new husband find out on his wedding night? No, I don't believe she's married yet, so it must be her father. I suppose if I were her father—"

"Richard—" Marcus began, no longer interested in discussing it. He was unsettled by the thought that Judith had told her father what they had done. It didn't bear thinking about.

"You can't trust women, Marcus. I've always said as much. Love 'em, but command 'em. Don't lose your heart to one," Richard continued. "Take Judith, for instance. I'm quite over her. It seemed once you took her away, all I really felt was relieved. She and I just didn't suit. Rather funny, after how hard I'd fallen for her. I suppose one never knows.''

"One never does," Marcus agreed.

"Well, you'd better try to get some sleep." Richard rose and lifted the tankard of ale from the table. He gulped it down and replaced the mug, then doused the candle and sat in the corner on a blanket to keep vigil over the patient.

"I'd do it again," Marcus murmured to the darkened room.

Chapter 11

Judith stayed curled on her bed for the next few hours as the house fell silent and the servants retired. She was desperate to know where her father had disappeared to. She was certain she had overlooked something, that her father was planning something she had to be on the alert for. Perhaps he was arranging her marriage even now.

Her father's voice from downstairs startled her, and she sat up. She decided it would be best to act as if nothing had happened, to maintain her composure and her grace, her dignity unassailable. She had nothing to be ashamed of, nothing.

Her father stood up when she came into the hall. He waited until she sat down at the table, as was traditional courtesy before resuming his seat. But he remained standing. He circled around behind Judith. She tensed, apprehension flowing through her, sapping her strength.

"Hold out your hand, daughter," he commanded. Judith did as bid. A flicker of gold caught her eye as a chain poured from her father's fist into her waiting palm. Her pendant, the one she had given to Marcus, lay pooled on her hand.

Terror unlike anything she had ever known gripped her. Her

eyes opened wide, and she was unable to tear them from the pendant. "He's—he's dead?" she asked, hardly breathing.

"I am not a murderer, daughter. But he has been paid back for what he did to you."

"Wh-what do you mean, paid back?" Judith was almost too afraid to hear the answer to ask him to elaborate.

"I had him beaten to within an inch of his life. He'll think twice before swiving noblemen's daughters in the future, I'll warrant."

Judith lifted her eyes to her father's and stared in shock at his self-satisfied smile. Her father was proud of what he had done. Proud! As if he had done something noble, something worth bragging about, something he expected that Judith herself would thank him for.

"Why," Judith's hand clenched around the pendant, which had so recently been torn from her beloved's neck. "Why, you . . ." She rose unsteadily to her feet. Then her fury caused a fresh burst of strength to enter her system, and she stood straight and tall, regally challenging the man who ruled her life. "You bastard!"

Her father actually jumped, he was so startled by her outburst.

"You horrid, disgusting, barbaric bastard!" Judith cried. "How dare you harm Marcus! You ungrateful, cowardly man! I am ashamed to be your daughter! Ashamed, do you hear me?"

"But, daughter, he took advantage of you—"

"I *gave* myself to him! I asked *him* to love me, to take me, because I love him! And he loves me! And I knew I could never marry him, and I wanted one night to remember all my life, because I know I cannot spend my life with him. But you can't understand that, can you? You cannot understand how I could love anyone without 'lord' before his name. You thought Marcus was wonderful when you thought he was Richard. But take that blessed title away and he's a nothing to you, despite all he did for me. You are the most hypocritical man I've ever known!" Judith spun and ran from the hall.

Her father stared after her, shocked and dumbfounded that his mannerly daughter, his well-behaved girl, should lash out at him like that. More than that, he began to feel the merest twinges of shame at what he had done. He had been so furious when he discovered the scoundrel had taken her chastity, so out of his mind with anger, he hadn't thought it through. Howard collapsed on the bench and tried to think clearly.

He knew that Sinclair had not pursued his daughter since they parted. But it thoroughly galled him that his daughter had succumbed to the commoner's charms. Nevertheless, he knew other noblewomen who had done worse than indulge in a one-night tryst, far worse. At least his daughter had realized her responsibilities and not run off with the man.

Just then he heard the wheels of the carriage pulling out into the cobbled street. He rose from the bench and ran to the front door. He swung it open in time to see Clyde, his groom, driving off with his daughter. *At least she hadn't run off with the man*— or had she?

Howard smirked. Once she saw the mess of a man that was left, she would be back in the blink of an eye, for no woman would want what the cutthroats had left behind in that alley, according to what they had told him.

Judith ignored the curious stares of the night denizens of London as she took her fine carriage over London Bridge to the seedier side of town—Southwark, home of rogues and thieves, whores—and actors. They passed amid the throng of foot passengers, carts, and carriages that crossed back and forth between the two sides of the Thames. On the bridge itself were houses, shops, monuments, and the ever-present pikes upon which were displayed the rotting heads of traitors recently beheaded at the Tower.

Since it was well past sundown, the guards at the Southwark gate questioned her thoroughly as to her destination before letting her pass outside the city limits. They gave her dire warnings that she was on her own if set upon by thieves.

Once on Bankside Street, Judith was appalled at herself when she realized she had no idea where Marcus lived. She sent her groom Clyde into taverns, the only establishments still open this late at night, barring brothels. While Clyde usually said little, his size alone intimidated the semi-inebriated customers into revealing what they knew. At the Blue Lion, he found more than one patron willing to reveal where Marcus lived.

In a few more minutes they were outside his small tenement. Judith's heart pounded in her chest. She felt a twinge of apprehension over the condition she might find him in, but it was overpowered by her excitement at seeing him again and the certainty he would need her help.

Clyde followed her to the rickety steps, his massive bulk protectively hovering over her. He held high a lantern, enabling them to pick their way through the rubbish strewn in the alley. The amber beams glinted off the steel bands of nearby barrels, some overturned, and shined off a slick puddle of some unknown substance that definitely wasn't water.

The light caught a polished mahogany finish near the bottom step. Heedless of her long skirts trailing in the refuse that lay thick on the ground, Judith stooped to retrieve the piece of wood. She saw the rest of the instrument scattered on the ground nearby. "They destroyed his lute," she said quietly, feeling new rage at the crime that had been perpetrated on Marcus. Her jaw tightened. "His music means so much to him."

She ran up the narrow steps and knocked on the warped door, leaving Clyde to guard the carriage. The door swung open to a tiny room smaller than her dress closet. Immediately her gaze fell on the bed where Marcus lay.

"Oh, Marcus," she murmured, her throat catching. She hurried to kneel by his bedside, her skirts settling around her like a blanket of new-fallen snow against the rough wooden floor. "My darling," she whispered, not wanting to wake him.

But his good eye slowly opened at the sound of her voice. "Judith?"

"Yes, it's me," she replied. She gently touched his face, not wanting to cause him pain, yet wanting so badly to touch him. "Look what they've done to you. The bastards! I hate him, I hate him for this."

"Who?"

"Father. He found out. I'm so sorry, Marcus. I kept expecting him to punish *me!* I never expected this! I should have warned you."

"How?" Marcus asked.

Judith knew what he was asking. She lowered her head in shame. "He—he had an idea when I wouldn't wear my necklace, the one I gave you. And I have not been very cooperative when he presents suitors to me. But when he asked me straight, I refused to answer; so he sent for a midwife, and she proved it was true."

"Bastard," Marcus grumbled through his split lips. "Did the woman hurt you?"

Judith gazed upon him. "What a thing to ask. Look at you. I'm fine. Oh—" She bit her lower lip, noticing again how badly his right eye was swollen shut. She leaned over and kissed his forehead, the only place on his face that seemed undamaged. She pressed her lips to his ear. "My darling, I love you so much. I'm so sorry my stupidity caused this. I should have known better."

"Judith, I'm not sorry," Marcus told her. "I'd do it again."

"You wouldn't."

"In a heartbeat," he murmured, his good eye meeting her liquid brown ones.

Judith felt her heart catch painfully as she gazed at his ravaged face. Tears stung her eyelids, and she blinked them back. She didn't want Marcus to see her cry. He needed her to be strong.

Marcus laid his good hand on her cheek. "You shouldn't be in this neighborhood, my sweet. You might be accosted. One of us in this condition is enough."

Judith took his hand from her cheek and kissed his palm. "That's hardly a consideration when you need me so. As long as you need me, I'll be here with you."

Marcus stared at her, his good eye dark with melancholy. "Don't risk yourself for me, Judith. I promised to be your champion, and I can't even tie the laces on my shirt!"

"Oh, my love." Judith touched his hand resting on the bed. Marcus cried out. She started, taking in the horror of his left arm, canted oddly, white bone pushing through torn flesh and congealed blood. Feeling ill, she rose to her feet almost in a panic. "You need a physician. I'll find the best one in the city and bring him to you."

"I've already sent for him, Lady Judith."

Judith spun. There by the door was Richard Langsforth.

Judith hadn't even noticed him. But, of course, someone had to have opened the door when she knocked. But *Richard?* He was the last person she expected to see in Marcus' home. "Richard! What are you . . ."

Richard bowed low before her. He was dressed as any noble-man would be, in fashionable trunk hose and plum-colored doublet with matching netherhosen and a starched cambric ruff. He was completely out of place in this room, as out of place as she with her farthingale-supported skirt of rich, cream-colored taffeta and her daffodil yellow velvet bodice with the wide, pearl-studded sleeves.

"History repeated itself—he rescued me again," Marcus replied.

Judith was still staring in shock. "Oh. Then I must thank you."

Richard smiled. "Marcus and I have patched things up. Of course, we haven't quite managed to patch him up yet."

Judith still watched him suspiciously. She wasn't sure the man should be anywhere near her Marcus. "Then, where is the physician?" she asked coolly.

"I sent for the best *surgeon* and bonesetter around to tend to Marcus' arm. He'll set the bone for him. A physician would just bleed him, and Marcus looks like he's lost enough blood to me."

Judith looked back at Marcus. Homemade bandages had been placed on the worst cuts, and bruises were starting to color his damaged flesh. He looked so awful, it twisted her heart in agony.

Another knock at the door announced the long-awaited surgeon, whom Richard had roused out of bed. The short, balding man was obviously surprised by the address and the contrast of the overdressed occupants.

"I was expecting a better address, particularly for a visit in the middle of the night," grumbled the surgeon. "I expect to be well paid." His attention fell to the patient, and he ushered Judith out of the way.

"His arm is broken, and he was complaining about his knees when I found him," explained Richard.

"Before I do anything, I need to have assurance that my bill will be paid.'' The surgeon glanced disparagingly around the simple, low-ceilinged room. ''Which one of you—''

''I will,'' said Judith.

''I will,'' said Richard at the same time.

''As long as one of you will pay.''

''*I* will,'' said Marcus in irritation. The others ignored him.

The surgeon glanced over Marcus as if he were an interesting specimen, taking in the misshapen arm lying on the outside of the blanket, the bone poking through in a grisly display of white bone and torn flesh. ''Nice compound fracture of his arm. I should be doing this in my office. I haven't the proper table here, nor the proper tools. I only brought a few. He's a big man, and if he causes trouble, I don't have my assistants to help. We could transport him—''

''No, he's in enough pain. Do it here,'' Richard said.

''I can't do it alone. I'll need help,'' the surgeon warned again, looking at Richard.

''Of course,'' Richard replied a little uncertainly.

''We're here,'' Judith assured him.

''You said his knees were hurt. If they're as bad as the arm, there may not be much left.'' The surgeon opened his bag and dug inside. He pulled out one wicked-looking tool after another and laid them on the floor—knives, saws, pliers, cautery irons. Judith prayed the surgeon wasn't planning to use all of the sharp-edged implements. ''This is the little helper I need,'' the surgeon muttered to himself. He held up a nasty pair of shears, the light from the lantern glinting off their sharp edges. He turned toward Marcus, whose eyes widened in apprehension. The surgeon bent beside the bed and began to cut off his breeches. Marcus exhaled and relaxed back on the bed.

With Richard's help, the surgeon stripped off Marcus' breeches. He bent to inspect his knees, which were misshapen and swollen. ''Dislocated, not broken. But a nice job of it. Professional, no doubt.'' He turned back to Richard. ''If you're involved in something against the law, I want no part of it. I make my living serving the nobility, not back-street ruffians.''

''He is *not* a ruffian,'' cried Judith, her irritation at the surgeon rapidly growing into anger. ''Simply do the best you can. If you don't, I will be furious.''

"And who are you?" the surgeon asked coldly.

"Lady Judith Ashton, daughter of Baron Howard Ashton," Judith replied in her most imperious manner.

The surgeon sighed and instructed Richard to help him lift Marcus to the floor, providing a level surface on which to work. Once there, he put pressure on his left knee. Marcus cried out until an audible pop was heard. The surgeon repeated the procedure with the other knee. He directed his instructions to Richard, the only other man present and the one he had decided was the responsible party. "He'll be sore for weeks. I'll bind his knees to support them. Change the bindings every few weeks, when they start to smell. After that, he should do fairly well."

"I'll be able to walk?" Marcus asked a bit apprehensively.

The surgeon didn't look at his patient. "Of course, of course." He turned back to Richard. "But don't let him try it for at least two months."

The surgeon inspected Marcus' ribs and announced that a few were cracked. He bandaged them and said there was nothing more he could do about it. "Don't let him sit up for a while," he said tersely. "Now to that arm, the most interesting part of this atrocious evening." The surgeon bent to inspect it. "A bad break. Through both bones. Torn skin, as well. I'll have to remove the arm."

Marcus' good eye opened wide, and his other one cracked open in spite of the swelling. "No!" he cried.

"Absolutely not," Judith commanded. Her voice sounded strong, but she flushed with fear—an image of an armless Marcus in rags, begging on a street corner, flashed through her mind. "Not only will you set his arm, you will do it perfectly, for if you don't, you'll suffer the wrath of my family."

Richard's eyes sparkled at her spunk. He pushed away from the wall he was leaning against and stood firm. "And mine. You might have heard of my father, the Earl of Langsforth?"

The surgeon seemed to pale. "I'll do my best, but there are no guarantees."

"I said *perfectly*," Judith replied imperiously. "He is the finest lute player in all of London, in all of England, for that matter. He needs both his hands working perfectly."

Marcus chuckled at her boast, but it came out sounding like a dry wheeze.

"All that time I wasted on sword practice and horse riding to impress the ladies, and all along I should have been taking lute lessons!" Richard exclaimed.

Marcus laughed again, but the laugh was cut short when the surgeon began poking at his arm to determine the position of the bones.

"All right, but perfect causes a lot more pain," he replied with disgruntlement. "And it's likely to turn putrid and need to be removed anyway."

"*Set it*," Judith said firmly.

The surgeon sighed. "You." He glanced up at Richard. "I'll need your help to straighten the bones."

Richard came over, his expression almost comical, he looked so squeamish.

"And you. Get some wine to kill infection." Judith jumped up to comply, and Richard pointed out a half-empty wine bottle he had been drinking from on the table. She retrieved it.

The surgeon pulled out several lengths of wood and measured them against Marcus' arm. He selected two of them. Then he pulled out a jar of a crushed boneset herb. He instructed Judith to dip linen rags in the herb mixture. She placed them by the surgeon in a neat pile.

"All right, when I give the word, pull on his hand as hard as you can and don't stop until I say so."

Richard nodded, grasping Marcus' hand tightly.

Judith positioned herself to take his head in her lap. She gently stroked his hair during the procedure. The surgeon passed her a strip of leather to put between the patient's teeth for him to bite down on.

When the surgeon commanded Richard to pull, Marcus screamed between clenched teeth, the cords of his neck standing out sharply. Judith kept her gaze locked on his, willing him to draw on her strength, on the love in her eyes, on the soothing words she spoke.

Richard kept up the pressure on the arm until the surgeon had evened the bones to his satisfaction and bound the arm tightly with the splints and the linen strips.

Marcus was drenched in sweat by the time the procedure ended. Tears trickled down his cheeks, and Judith brushed them away. "It's over, darling, over." She kissed his forehead and removed the leather bit from his mouth.

"Stay with me," he murmured, his gaze drinking her in one last time before he mercifully passed out.

"I will," Judith replied, stroking his hair, though she knew he didn't hear her or feel her.

The surgeon set about splinting and binding Marcus' knees. When that was done he sewed the gash on his jaw and reset his nose as best he could. Satisfied, he glanced over the rest of him and determined there was nothing more he could do. Richard helped him return the patient to the bed, then paid the surgeon, and the man left.

Richard came to stand over Marcus' bed, but his eyes were on Judith. "They were about to break his other arm when I came upon them," he said softly. "I gather from what Marcus said that they were going to break his legs next."

Judith shivered. Richard gently took her arm and led her out of the apartment and down the steps into the early morning sunlight. Judith hadn't realized morning had come, and she blinked against the brightness.

"I want to apologize to you, Lady Judith," Richard said suddenly.

Judith looked at him in surprise. This was the last thing she expected, considering how she had practically left him at the altar. "What for?"

"For not understanding." Richard looked away toward the river and the uneven skyline of London beyond the Thames. "I confess despite my protestations of love for you, I didn't understand until now what love truly means. Until I saw you and Marcus in there." His blue eyes met hers. "I always thought love was one more addition to life, like the decision to purchase property, or new clothes, or go to law school. I didn't realize it took everything over. When I courted you, I wanted you because of your beauty, and your title. Of course, you probably figured that out already."

Judith smiled at his confession.

"I didn't really know you. But Marcus saw who you were.

So when you ran off with him from my home—well, it hurt to think my bride preferred a commoner over me. But it was my pride that was suffering, not my heart. I don't blame either of you, not anymore. I know it was my own fault for not treating you right—and for throwing the two of you together."

"It was no one's fault, Richard," Judith said. "I'm not even sure that's the right word for it. It just—happened. I couldn't help it; Marcus couldn't. We tried to deny it, but we failed."

"Didn't I see this in a play before?" Richard asked with a laugh.

Judith shook her head. "I wouldn't know. I've never seen one."

"Never seen one? And your lover—is that what I should call him?"

Judith blushed and looked away.

"Marcus—that's what he *does*, act in plays. You've got to see him in a play."

"I would love to see him act in a play, but my father—"

"A pox on your father!"

Judith arched her eyebrows. "This, from a man who wanted nothing more than to win his family's favor?"

Richard smiled ruefully. "Aye, and where did it get me?" His voice lowered, intensified. "You've got to live for yourself, Judith. That's the key. I know that now, thanks to what happened between us."

Judith gazed thoughtfully at him. "My maid Audrey insisted you weren't a bad sort, merely confused. It appears she was right."

"She said that? Well." Richard crossed his arms and looked away. He pressed his fist to his mouth as if in thought, but Judith could see the smile he was trying to hide.

"Of course, I couldn't quite determine what made her soften her harsh opinion of you." Judith thought she detected a slight blush on his neck.

Richard turned back, neatly changing the subject. "You can both come see Marcus at the Globe when he's better."

"When he's better—that will be months." Judith faced Richard fully. "Oh, Richard, what will he do until then? He's an invalid! I would offer him money, but I know I would only be insulting him.''

"I like to insult him." Richard grinned mischievously. "I'll do it, unless we can think of something else.''

"To be honest, I can't stand to see him in that dingy little room. He needs to be where people can take care of him.''

"True," Richard replied, looking up at the little room under the eaves. "I can't take him in. I'm still living in the dormitory at Gray's Inn." He considered for a moment, then voiced a new thought with growing enthusiasm. "Actually, I know someone who is sure to help. He cares a lot about Marcus, and I know he'd understand the injustice of all this. His name is Will Shakespeare. He'll think of something, I'm sure of it.''

Chapter 12

In short order, the playwright William Shakespeare had helped Richard arrange for Marcus to be a guest in Hunsdon House, an elegant manor home in the Blackfriars district of London. Its owner was no less a personage than George Carey, the Lord Hunsdon, patron of Shakespeare's acting company and Queen Elizabeth's own High Chamberlain of England.

As patron, the young man considered well his investment, an investment begun by his father, a previous chamberlain. He was loath to lose his position as patron of the finest acting troupe in all of England because one of its most popular actors was incapacitated.

A man of the world, Lord Hunsdon certainly understood how Marcus could have gotten himself in such a scrape, at least the way Richard explained it. No lusty man of his acquaintance would have done any differently than Marcus had, given the opportunity to taste the sweetness of the chaste Lady Judith Ashton, the most untouchable maiden of Her Majesty's Court.

Richard made it clear Marcus was the cruel victim of circumstance. He didn't bother to explain Marcus' infatuation with the lady in question, for he was certain Lord Hunsdon would have laughed at his friend.

Richard knew Hunsdon considered himself too sophisticated for such profound soul-possessing love as Marcus and Judith seemed to share. Richard himself found it difficult to imagine feeling that strongly about a mere woman. So, to Hunsdon he painted his friend as the rake he had always known him to be, his reputation enhanced rather than damaged by his disastrously adventurous liaison with the forbidden Judith.

With great humor, Lord Hunsdon immediately dispatched a note to Judith's priggish father to let him know where his precious darling was, so the man wouldn't raise an unwarranted outcry at her disappearance from his home. Nothing could be more entertaining, Hunsdon told Richard, than for that straight-laced social climber Lord Ashton to learn his virtuous daughter was nursing a commoner with the utmost dedication.

Lord Hunsdon smiled as the messenger boy departed, no doubt anticipating the coming confrontation.

"Lady Judith, how fares our patient?" asked Lord Hunsdon. He rested an arm on the heavy carved banister, which led from his ornate grand hall to the second-floor gallery and the guest rooms. Marcus had been placed in one of them.

Judith paused on her descent, stopping a few steps above him. His red-and-gold clothing caught the flames from the dozen candelabras in the hall and seemed to cast a glow of success and power about him.

"You are doing such a remarkable job tending to him. Do you have all you need?" he asked.

"Yes, for now, your lordship. Thank you very much for your hospitality." She ran her hand over her brow, suddenly aware her hair had started falling from its elegant coiffure of the previous night. And, she supposed her wrinkled dress made her look frightfully undone. Somehow, being properly turned out seemed an incredibly trivial matter.

"Marcus is resting quietly, but his fever has risen," she said, knowing her voice reflected her deep worry. "We'll have to keep a close eye on it, the surgeon says. His blood's full of ill humors, and it could be very serious." She prayed she could help Marcus through the coming battle with the searing heat and the raging blood. She may not have much experience, but if there was a way on earth to save him, she would find it.

"Judith, I must say I do admire your dedication, particularly in the face of parental disapproval," Hunsdon said, sliding a lace-edged handkerchief through his manicured fingers.

"Disapproval?" Judith looked past him, through the door leading into the solar, and realized her father stood by the fireplace, waiting to confront her. Dread filled her chest. He must have come in pursuit of her, to drag her back home. She certainly had no intention of allowing that, not while Marcus was suffering upstairs on their account.

Judith felt Lord Hunsdon's sharp gaze and turned back to him. The lord had pressed his interest with her months ago at Court, and had accepted her rebuff with good humor. She hoped he would remain a gentleman while she was in his house.

As if reading her very thoughts, he lowered his voice and said, "You're showing more spirit than I knew you had when I tried to form an alliance with you at Court. I'm glad to see *some* man managed to attract your . . . loyalty."

Judith felt the blood drain from her face. What would the proud man think if he knew she had taken a common actor for a lover, over his lordship? The thought suddenly terrified her.

He brushed his handkerchief along the back of her hand where it rested on the banister. Judith jerked back, and Hunsdon chuckled. "Don't look so distraught. It would seem I'm the least of your concerns." He looked past her.

Howard Ashton had grown bored waiting for her and was barreling toward her. Yet Lord Hunsdon remained, a pleased smile on his lips as if he thought the situation most amusing.

Certainly, her father wouldn't dare attempt a scene in front of such a powerful personage.

"Father," Judith said coolly.

"Daughter," her father replied, equally cool.

Judith breathed a bit easier. "You must already know Her Majesty's High Chamberlain," she introduced her father to him. Howard mumbled acknowledgment.

"Certainly," Hunsdon said, grinning through a neatly trimmed beard. "Lord Ashton used to be a regular at Court. I haven't seen you but briefly lately. The last time you were truly involved with Court matters was ... let's see ... about February, I believe. You were there when we were all discussing that disastrous, ill-planned rebellion by Lord Essex.''

"Aye," Ashton said, shifting his feet. "Those were dangerous times."

"Only for the guilty," Hunsdon tossed off lightly. "Rumor has it the queen is still seeking conspirators who were involved with Essex."

"Nonsense," Howard Ashton replied with a wave of his hand. "The queen has already executed anyone who mattered, or so I understand." He slid a finger into his ruffled collar and tugged it.

"I don't know about that," Hunsdon replied significantly, eyeing Howard carefully. Howard wouldn't meet his gaze.

Judith had no idea what was going on in Lord Hunsdon's mind. She was too tense over what her father would do when he got her alone to give it much thought.

"I'll tell you, a common actor like Marcus Sinclair is certainly one lucky man to have a titled lady tending to him," Lord Hunsdon commented wryly. His tone turned probing, his eyes flicking from her father to Judith. "Things were so hectic when you and Richard Langsforth brought him here, Lady Judith. I'm not sure I quite caught the reason you are involved. Could you explain it to me again?"

Judith opened her mouth to reply, but her mind went blank. A hard knot formed in her stomach. Lord Hunsdon apparently gloried in her troubles, and a few more insinuations like that in the right ears at Court would brand her a wanton woman. She noticed that her father—ever conscious of his reputation, and hers—had lost his healthy ruddy color.

"She's helping Marcus as a favor to me," Richard Langsforth's voice came loud and firm, almost challenging in its tone as he entered from a side room. Judith sucked in a relieved breath.

"Why, Richard Langsforth," Lord Hunsdon said, his tawny eyebrow arched. "The second *gentleman* our lovely Lady Judith spurned at the altar."

Judith didn't miss the way he stressed "gentleman." But Richard smiled through it, obviously unconcerned. " 'Tis I.''

Lord Hunsdon tapped his lower lip. "Yet you remain friends. Most remarkable. Lord Richard, I trust you found my accommodations acceptable last night?"

"More than comfortable." Richard grinned. "You have a wonderful home here. I appreciate the offer of a bed."

"What else could I do, seeing as it was so late?"

"And I more than appreciate all you're doing for my friend Marcus."

"Providing one of my most popular actors with a place to recuperate is the least I could do. I'm only glad you brought along such a beautiful nurse." He grinned at Judith, who smiled stiffly and nodded her acknowledgment of the compliment. Hunsdon's smile became devilish once again as he turned to Howard Ashton. "And her father is here as well, fully supportive of his daughter's efforts, I'm sure."

"I appreciate you visiting my friend Marcus in his time of need," Richard said to Howard, feigning casual friendliness. "I know you must have been worried about him when you heard the dreadful news, as we all are. You *do* know the details, don't you, about the brutal beating he received by thugs right outside his own apartment?"

Ashton gave a curt nod, then cleared his throat. "That neighborhood's to blame, I'm sure," he said stiffly. "A hotbed of brothels, gaming establishments—all manner of vice and corruption."

"Aye, Southwark has its seedy side," Richard agreed. "Though it can be exciting. Why, there's nothing else in the world like the theaters. Wonderful places."

"Milady, I hate to interrupt—"

Judith turned from the group to find Audrey coming down the steps. She joined her halfway and bent her head to listen as Audrey lowered her voice.

"He's getting a fever something fierce, and he's calling your name," Audrey said.

Judith made her excuses and quickly returned upstairs, Audrey following behind.

Richard watched them go, his gaze on Audrey's shapely hips under her maid's skirt. He hadn't realized Judith's maid had arrived to help out. Why, that lent an entirely new level of interest to the goings-on in this house. He had not forgotten the responsiveness of Audrey's pert mouth under his own, the fire that ignited between them as she arched into his embrace. . . . *Later*, he promised himself. But not much later.

"Come home with me this instant, daughter."

Howard Ashton confronted Judith outside the second-floor guest room off the gallery. Marcus lay inside, unconscious, a fever raging. Judith had just stepped out to request more water from one of Hunsdon's servants.

She ignored her father until she dispatched her orders to the servant. Then she turned and met his gaze squarely. "I'm not going home with you, Father."

"No? Did you say no?" Howard's face began to redden.

"That's correct. I'm nursing Marcus. He's in terrible condition, and he needs my help."

A passing butler glanced toward them, and Howard lowered his voice. "You little fool!" he hissed, his face close to Judith's. "Obey me this instant, or I'll lock you in your room with nothing to eat but bread and water for a week! It isn't your place to care for that scoundrel!"

"Seeing as my own father's the cause of his distress, I feel it's my duty," Judith replied, her spine stiffening. "You should be aware that Lord Hunsdon and his friends suspect how he ended up in this appalling condition. But, for now, it's only speculation. I am quite able to supply the details."

Howard's eyes narrowed. "Are you threatening me?"

"Aye, I suppose I am," Judith replied, amazed at her own audacity.

Howard's face paled, and his jaw slackened in surprise. "You wouldn't dare. It will ruin your reputation!"

"My reputation is not so important to me. It means everything, however, to you, and could adversely affect whatever political match you hope to make with my marriage."

"Impertinent woman!"

But both of them knew Judith was right. For the moment, she had him.

Ashton's fist tightened at his side, and as suddenly spasmed open. "When I get you home, girl—"

"It's so sweet of you to come up to see how Marcus is faring, Father," Judith said in her best dutiful-daughter voice. "If you would like, you can look in on him now." She turned to the door of Marcus' room, her calm, ladylike demeanor a desperate attempt to conceal her inner anxiety. She half expected her father to whip her right there and drag her home. She had never behaved so disobediently.

Before she could open the door, Howard grabbed her arm and swung her to face him. "If you think I'll leave you alone in that man's presence, girl, you're a fool."

"Perhaps. You tell me." Tearing her arm from his grip, Judith entered the room, her father following on her heels like a guard dog.

Their eyes couldn't help but go straight to the large bed which dominated the room. At its center lay Marcus, his position unchanged from when she had last left him. Audrey sat beside him, her eyes wide at the sight of Lord Ashton. She quickly turned away and busied herself pressing a newly soaked cloth to Marcus' forehead in an effort to lower his fever.

"And your maid nursing him, too!" Howard said.

Judith stood quietly while her father took in the condition of the patient in the bed. She watched his face. His fury began to lessen, his color turning paler, reflecting his shock at the brutality of the beating. After a moment, the shock in his eyes turned to what Judith guessed might be revulsion at the sight of a man in such a condition as Marcus was. Her father had never had a strong stomach.

She was glad he was affected. She was determined to make sure he knew exactly what he had caused, exactly what Marcus had gone through and what he would have to endure in order to recover. She also determined to make it clear that his treatment of Marcus had not changed the reality of their love one iota.

Judith spoke in the cool, professional tone she had heard the surgeon use. "His arm is horribly, painfully broken, a compound fracture that punctured the skin. The surgeon says it's the most difficult break there is. He wanted to amputate, but I refused to allow it. Marcus makes his living with his hands, you know. He's a wonderful musician as well as an actor.''

Judith watched her father's expression as she detailed Marcus' injuries. She wanted him to feel contrite, prayed he would feel contrite. He deserved to feel such a heavy burden of guilt that it hurt for the bearing of it. This wish was so alien to her, so surprisingly strong, it scared her. Despite the fact her father still had possession of her and could do with her as he willed, he would never own her loyalty or her heart like he once did.

"The cutthroats who set upon Marcus dislocated his knees, causing him excruciating pain. The surgeon reset them, but it will be months before he can support himself on his legs, much less walk.'' Her eyes flicked to her father's face, noting the ashen pallor as he viewed the massive injuries of the man in the bed. She thought she saw a hint of shame underlying his expression. Taking hope, she continued.

"Those are the major injuries. There are minor ones, as well. His ribs—some of them are cracked. Probably, once he was down, they kicked him like he was a mongrel dog. The two men also took a stiletto and carved his jawbone. I'm not sure why—to frighten him, I suppose. One can only guess at the terror he must have felt as that knife blade neared his throat.'' She was unable to keep up the pretense of detachment, and her voice dropped almost to a whisper. "And his face—it's so badly abused, he can only see out of one eye. The surgeon says he may lose use of the other eye. It's too soon yet to tell.'' Judith's hands rose to her lips, but not in time to stifle the sob that rose in her throat.

"That's enough.'' Howard turned from the sight of the prostrate victim. His eyes fastened on Judith, and she felt victorious at the defensive expression he wore. She saw his anger; but she knew he no longer felt good about what he had done, and it pleased her. "Damn it, Judith,'' he cursed under his breath. But he kept his voice low, showing respect for the sick out of habit. "Was this his idea, to get you to care for him?''

"Of course not, Father. He hasn't even woken up since the surgeon had at him with his painful procedures. He roused once or twice in the carriage on the way here, but I don't think he understood where he was being taken.''

"Milady, I'm not sure I'm bringing the fever down. His skin turns these rags hot to the touch," Audrey interrupted.

Judith crossed to the bed and laid her palm on Marcus' cheek. It was as hot as a hearth before a fire. "That servant is certainly taking his sweet time fetching the water," she muttered in frustration. "Audrey, see what happened to him. We need lots of water, cool water. And get more towels. We'll have to bathe him all over." Audrey hurried out.

"Judith!" Howard said sharply, obviously shocked at the very idea. "Stay away from that man's side!"

"But, Father," she replied in an ironic tone. "He has nothing I haven't already seen."

"Judith! You've shamed me enough! You'll not speak of it, girl, not to me or to anyone. And you are *not* to touch that man."

Judith stood upright, her spine ramrod straight. She returned to her father's side, but she kept her chin high. "He needs proper nursing, and I intend to see that he gets it."

"Hunsdon should have sent him to a hospital," he said gruffly with a wave of his hand. "They're for people like him. He belongs there, not being pampered in a palace like this!"

Judith's fists clenched. "The hospitals are overcrowded, dirty and rat-infested! I would die before I allowed Marcus to be sent to one."

"I do not like you being anywhere near that man, girl, and I will not stand for it," Howard repeated uselessly.

"Surely you're not afraid he'll seduce me? My virtue, as you would put it, has already been compromised, father," she said bluntly. "And if you're worried about a recurrence, why, look at him! He can barely breathe, much less assault my virtue!"

She watched her father stare once more at the man in the bed. To her surprise, a smile twisted the corner of his mouth. "He is certainly a sight, isn't he? I imagine he needs around-the-clock care."

"Yes, he does." Judith hesitated, uncertain why he looked suddenly pleased. Perhaps he expected her to fail in her efforts to help Marcus. Perhaps he thought if she saw enough of him, she would become bored with caring for him. As if her love was worth so little!

As Howard Ashton moved toward the door, he smiled to himself. The answer was so simple. He had been fighting her willfulness far too hard. Things would take care of themselves in the end. Once Judith was around his puss-filled sores long enough, forced to clean them and change his filthy, bloodstained bandages, forced to handle his bedpans, she would lose all her so-called love for the blackguard.

The scoundrel was entering what would be a raging fever, probably a fatal one. He would most likely swear in his gutter language when he succumbed to delirium, offending every one of her gentlewoman's sensibilities. She would have to contend with his urine, his spittle and drool, his sweat and stink.

If he didn't die, he would probably be crippled for life, or blind in one eye. Judith wouldn't come near him then.

And if he died—well, so much the better. By the time the world saw the last of Marcus Sinclair, Judith would no doubt be relieved. Then she would be happy to agree to a permanent alliance with a man of good name.

Feeling better than he had in days, he turned back when he reached the door. "Since we seem to be striking a bargain, daughter, I'll agree to allow you to stay here under Lord Hunsdon's care only until that man begins to recover. Then you will never see him again. Meanwhile, we will find a proper husband for you as expeditiously as possible—before your wantonness makes you completely worthless to me."

Judith demurely lowered her eyes to hide the victory she felt over their skirmish. "Aye," she agreed softly, before turning back to her patient.

Audrey heard a step behind her. She turned and found Lord Richard leaning in the archway between the kitchen and the parlor. He smiled beguilingly. "Are you alone?"

"Foolish question," she replied pertly. "Do you see anyone else about?"

Audrey turned from him to the kitchen table, where she was folding the linen cloths she and Judith had been using to soothe

Marcus' feverish brow. She pointedly ignored Richard, but the man seemed intent on stalking her.

She had no doubt what he was after, but he wasn't about to get any favors from her. Lord Richard Langsforth was the last person she would bed with—the man was far too full of himself as it was. Lady Judith had been able to take him down a notch or two, but sure as grass that was stepped on, he had bounced right back up again—and this time, he wanted her.

A touch so gentle, so featherlight, it seemed she had imagined it brushed across the back of her exposed neck. Warmth radiated outward from his touch, sending tingles along the entire length of her spine. Audrey stiffened, fighting her body's betraying response.

Yet she allowed the touch to linger a moment too long—a moment she feared betrayed her pleasure. Quickly she spun away from him, heading toward the nearest sideboard. Forcing her back stiff, she set about ignoring him all the more.

"Audrey," came the soft rumble of his voice. "You are the most delectable dish in this kitchen."

She couldn't ignore *that* remark, try as she might. She turned to him, a saucy expression on her face. "And I'll bet you'd like a little taste, wouldn't you—Richard?" she asked, foregoing his title.

He grinned at the audacious intimacy. "Aye, you know darned well I would." He strode closer to her, his boyish grin transforming into a much more predatory one. Predatory, but too darned attractive to be borne.

Audrey used her most imperious voice. "Well, you won't be getting it from me, you rapscallion, so get on with you. I've work to do."

Richard ignored her. In a moment, he was before her, his sturdy frame imprisoning her against the counter behind her. His hand slipped behind her head and cradled it. "I've much better things for you to do." He brought his mouth low, almost to hers. Audrey held her breath, desperate to keep her senses. She would put the man in his place once and for all and be done with it. Unknown to him, her hand was reaching behind her, searching, until it made contact with exactly what it was seeking.

Richard's lips ran across hers in a touch so light, Audrey wasn't sure it was even a kiss. But it felt like a kiss—worse than a kiss, it felt like a taste of heaven itself. Her entire body cried out for her to give in to his attentions, to let him use her, have his sport with her. So many noblemen used their female servants thus. She was once used by such men, forced to do almost anything to keep her paying job when people were lined up three-deep, eager to take her place. Londoners were too many, and jobs too scarce.

But Richard was not her employer. He was a rake like any other, only after one thing. She was determined he would never get it from her. Her fingers tightened spasmodically on the handle of the knife behind her.

Richard's kiss deepened, and despite her resolve, her grip on the weapon loosened, her fingers becoming weak along with the rest of her. The soft point of his tongue probed open her lips and met her own, reminding her of the hot embraces they had shared at his family home, taunting her, daring her to forget. She could not. Nor could she give in to the desire that swept her body like wildfire.

As if her life truly depended on it, she shoved hard at his chest and, in the same instant, swung the dangerously sharp knife between their bodies. The sunlight pouring through the nearby window glinted on the knife blade.

Richard's eyes widened, and he leapt back as if he had been stabbed. "God's blood, woman, what do you think you're doing?"

"Keeping you in your place, you scoundrel."

"Hah!" Richard gritted his teeth. "My place is on top of your fine young body, and you know it as well as I do! Look at you!"

Audrey realized she was gasping, her chest rising and falling rapidly as she strove to catch the breath he had managed to steal with his kisses. She knew her face was flushed, her hair in disarray, her lips moist and swollen. But she would never admit what he did to her, what he made her feel. Never.

Richard didn't wait for her response. He took one step forward and wrenched the knife from her fingers. Audrey's eyes widened in fear. Richard threw the knife away expertly, and it landed solidly, its point digging deep into the wooden tabletop. Audrey couldn't tear her eyes away from the handle, which was still quivering as badly as she was. She knew if he pushed her, she would succumb. And there was nothing between them now, no defense she could call on.

Richard's hand on her chin swung her gaze to meet his. His large, warm fingers burned into her flesh. "No, I'm not going to force you, sweet. You are going to want me as much as I want you. And you will."

Remarkably, he winked. Then he grinned, that infectious, boyish grin that made Audrey want to slap him. Then he was gone.

Judith groaned and arched her back, grimacing at the pain in her lower spine. It had been seven days and still Marcus battled with the fever. She was exhausted, but doing her best. Audrey took over when Judith was too tired to see straight, allowing her to rest a few hours before again tending to Marcus. Hers were the only helping hands Judith trusted.

Judith had initially recruited a few of Lord Hunsdon's servants, with his permission, of course, to help nurse Marcus in shifts. But no one took care of him to her satisfaction. Not that she altogether knew what she was doing.

But when she saw one of the women sitting idly by while Marcus thrashed in delirium, calling for her—she knew then she belonged by his side. Why, at any moment the phantoms could overtake him again, and he could cry out for her, and what if she wasn't there to comfort him?

By the sixth day, however, the delirium had lessened considerably. Marcus' coloring, even on his bruises, had paled, and his skin took on a frightening gray, ashy tone. Judith was terrified this meant he would die. She sent for the surgeon, who had no advice to give her, merely patted her hand in sympathy. That's all she got from Marcus' acting friends and well-wishers, too, people from every strata of society, who came calling every day to see how their favorite actor was faring.

The only bright spot was that the swelling across his right eye had gone down. She was relieved to see that there was apparently no damage to it. Now he opened both eyes fully. But plagued by hallucinations, he saw nothing of what was actually before him.

Judith was terrified he would die, but she was determined to prevent it if it killed her. Impatient for her return home, her father came every day to check up on her—and to see if the patient had succumbed yet. Yesterday, satisfied that Marcus was failing rapidly, he had grinned briefly and promised to return for her tomorrow. When the door closed behind him, Judith had at last surrendered to tears.

She stopped crying when she realized her self-indulgence did nothing for Marcus. As quietly as possible so as not to disturb him, she sat in the chair by his bed. The chair had become quite familiar to her. So had her patient. She knew the extent of every bruise, every cut, knew how well most of them were healing.

She laid her hand on his forehead, exhilarated by its coolness. After his fever had reached the worst last night, it had broken. His color, too, was much healthier. She smiled tremulously and checked again with her other hand, pressing her fingers to his face and forehead in growing hope. Perhaps Marcus had gotten through the worst of it.

"You've fought so well, my darling. Just a little longer now," she said, more to herself than to him, for he hadn't heard anything she had said in almost a week. The scar under several days' growth of beard gave him a remarkably savage appearance. The swelling on his nose had gone down, but there was now a permanent bump on its bridge. She smoothed back his wild, unkempt hair tenderly. He was more handsome than ever to her, despite everything he had gone through.

Marcus stirred under her fingers. Judith sat back, her hands clenched in her lap, her breath caught in her throat. "Please, Marcus, come back to me."

From a great distance, Marcus heard her voice. He imagined he was in heaven—except for the throbbing pain in his arm and the equally vicious pain that radiated outward from his knees up and down his legs. He groaned and cracked open his eyes. The light was so bright, it assaulted his senses, and he shut his eyes against it. It had to be afternoon. But his window never let in so much light, for it was too narrow and high up under the eaves. Something else was different, too. The smell. Instead of straw and the earthy scent of his one-room apartment, the air was clean and sweet, like flowers in springtime.

"Are you awake? Marcus? Oh, thank God!"

There was that voice again, that enchanting voice. Marcus cracked open his eyes again. Sure enough, she was there. All he could see at first was a golden halo of hair shining in the light from the mullioned window beyond. "Judith?" he asked. His lips felt unwieldy, and his mouth was severely dry.

"Yes, it's me, it's me." Marcus felt cool fingers caressing his face. "You *know* me! I'm so glad! It's been days. I was so worried for you, we all were. You had such a terrible fever."

"Sweetheart, come closer. I want to touch you, to be sure I'm not still delirious."

Judith complied, sitting beside him on the bed as gently as she could. Marcus clasped her hand in his free hand, the other arm still bound in a splint. He gazed in wonder at her, and reality came home to him. His Judith. Images came to him of the past few days, cool hands, a soft voice cutting through the fiery heat and horrendous pain. His Judith had been here by his side. It hadn't been a figment of his fevered brain. She was truly here with him, nursing him back to health.

That must mean she had broken with her father, for how else could her presence by his side be explained? Her father would never have allowed her here otherwise.

Marcus' heart swelled with joy. She had given up everything to stay with him. He had one specific memory he had been certain was a delusion. He lifted his undamaged right arm and touched his throat under his shirt. The gold star pendant the thugs had ripped from his throat once again encircled his neck. This was the final proof, he thought, joy coursing through him as he gazed at Judith. "I love you," Marcus said softly, his voice scratchy, yet revealing an underlying strength. "You won't regret this. Ever."

In his pain-fogged mind, Marcus envisioned a life together with the woman he loved, accepting the vision without question, his passion obliterating his usual logic.

"Regret it?" Judith gazed at him quizzically. "You must be horribly thirsty. Here."

She helped him sit up and adjusted the pillows behind him, then handed him a glass of water. Marcus drank it down in one gulp. He gave back the glass and swiped at his mouth with his good arm. His eyes focused, and he took in the room. He wasn't in his own apartment anymore. The down mattress beneath him was too darned comfortable for that. He noticed now that the silken bed sheets were embroidered with an elaborate crest. At the foot of the bed was spread an intricately embroidered rug in blues and burgundy. A writing desk and chair completed the picture. "Where are we? What's going on?"

"This is Lord Hunsdon's home. Richard and I brought you here to take care of you, Marcus. I couldn't very well take you home."

"No, no, of course not," Marcus agreed. That would never do, now that she had left home to be with him.

So she had brought him here, to the Lord Chamberlain's home. It made sense the lord would want to protect his investment. The room was sumptuous. The top half of the walls had been whitewashed, the bottom paneled in oak. Both were joined by richly carved wainscotting. A chandelier hung from the high, molded ceiling, and the bed he lay in was a canopied four-poster of intricately carved mahogany.

Marcus turned to Judith again. He looked at her sweet, loving countenance. How had she managed it? Had she simply walked out on her father? Undoubtedly so, considering what the man had put her lover through. "God, Judith, I love you so much!"

Judith could hardly help but respond to such a pronouncement. She pulled him into her arms. Tears pricked at her eyes as she pressed his brutalized body to hers. "My darling, we must be careful," she murmured, pulling back. "I so want to hold you, but—"

"I know, I'm not yet ready for that," Marcus chuckled. "I just want to gaze at you." Marcus lifted her hand in his. Despite his cut lip, he kissed her palm, and she softly sighed. "Once I'm better, I'll show you how happy I am to see you," he said huskily.

"Marcus—" Judith slipped her hand from his. She glanced toward the door, as if nervous over something. "I can't stay much longer. I'm afraid tomorrow—"

"Don't be afraid of tomorrow, Judith. I vow on my life you'll never want for anything—anything that truly matters." Marcus thrust his fingers into her neatly coiffed hair, destroying its perfection, pulling her forward until his lips met hers. The sensation of kissing her again sent a welcome blaze of pleasure through his battered body, and despite his condition, desire heated his gut.

A loud bang in the gallery beyond the chamber door made Judith start. She jumped back from Marcus and nervously looked behind her. A chambermaid passed by, and she breathed in relief. Marcus stared at her, mystified by her edginess.

"I'm sorry, I thought it was my father."

"Your father!" Dismay swept through him.

"I promised him I would go back home once you were past the worst of it. That was our arrangement. He's been checking in on you every day."

Marcus' wonderful fantasy shattered, taking his heart with it. Judith had not run away with him. Of course she hadn't. She had too much to lose—her title, her wealth, her position at Court. What a fool he had been even to *think* it was possible! "And you would hate for him to see us in a lover's embrace," Marcus said tightly.

"I can't allow him to see. He would be hurt, Marcus. He trusts me. Or he has, until recently. He was furious with me over this, over us. And when I made him promise to let me nurse you, I had to shame him into it. I've never done anything like that before." She clutched his good hand in both of hers. "But I did it because I love you, because I wanted to make up for what he did to you, all on account of my own selfishness. I made you take me to bed, and this is what came of it."

Marcus hated to see her bear such a burden of guilt. "I don't blame you for this, darling, not in the least."

"But I blame myself."

"What happened between us—I knew what I was doing," he said assertively. But he wondered if he really had understood what it would do to his heart, his life. "As for your father's revenge on me, that was entirely his fault, and none of yours."

"But I drove him to it. I must never do anything so foolish again, never. I have to prove to my father that he can still place his faith in me."

"Your father means that much to you," Marcus said, his words hollow.

"I'm all he has," Judith said softly. "I want you to understand. I love you so much, Marcus. More than I can say. If things were different for me, if I had brothers and sisters—but I don't. Without me, there would be no House of Dunsforth to carry on. I wish you could see the look on my father's face when he gazes up at the family portraits in the great hall, all the faces of our ancestors. Every week he takes down one of the armaments on display and polishes it himself, even though we have plenty of servants to do such a task. It's—it's his way of ensuring immortality, of connecting us to a long line stretching back as far as William the Conqueror."

Marcus stared hard at her, wondering if she was speaking for her own feelings as much as her father's.

"I know I can't explain it very well," she said, as if reading his thoughts. "Our family lineage isn't a concern of mine. But I'm my father's only family. When my mother died, my father and I only had each other. I've always tried to be there for him, and I will continue to be, as long as he needs me."

I need you, Marcus thought fiercely. But he knew he would never try to convince Judith to give up her exalted position, forsake her blue blood, for a life with him. Such a decision would have to come from her, or she would never be happy. There was far too much for her to lose. He cursed her loyalty and sense of responsibility at the same time he fell more in love with her for it.

Judith took a shuddering breath. "I'm so sorry, Marcus. You would be so much better off if you'd never met me." Tears misting her eyes, unable to meet his pain-filled gaze any longer, Judith rose and hurried from the room.

* * *

Marcus saw nothing of Judith the rest of the day, which he acknowledged was probably best, but his heart ached over it. He received a visit from a friend, however. "Marcus! You are indeed looking a little more human."

Marcus laughed. "I feel like someone's kitchen leavings."

Richard pulled up the bedside chair and straddled it. "This is a strange situation all around, isn't it?" He shook his head in amazement. "I can't get over it. I think our good friend Shakespeare ought to write a play about it. First you fall in love with a woman, her father finds out and has you thrashed, the same woman manages to nurse you back to the living, and immediately disappears when you awake."

"Judith's gone?"

"Aye, and she took her cheeky maid with her," Richard said with disappointment. "Her father picked her up an hour ago."

Marcus turned from Richard and looked toward the window, gazing absently at the trees beyond. This was surely the severing of his link to Judith. The future couldn't possibly hold any other chance of an encounter, which he tried to convince himself was best.

"What *is* happening between you, anyway?" Richard asked, his voice dropping conspiratorially.

Marcus glanced at him, a wry twist to his mouth. He was determined to keep the tone light. "Not much, Richard. Do I look like a man ready to plan his next tryst?"

"I'm not talking about bed games, Marcus! I realize your reputation bespeaks your prowess as a lover, but even I am not so naive as to believe you could accomplish that in your condition!"

"Nor would I want to," Marcus groaned as he sought a more comfortable position.

Richard leaned close again. "What I meant is, are you and she working out a plan to thwart her father? He's a man who deserves to be thwarted, after all. Perhaps arranging to elope? I'd be happy to help in any way I can."

Marcus arched the eyebrow over his unbruised eye. "Oh, would you? And would that have something to do with her cheeky maid?"

Richard grinned sheepishly. "You've caught me out. A lady wouldn't elope without the help of her maid, would she?"

Marcus chuckled. "I suppose you're in love again. Why am I not surprised?"

"Never," Richard said decisively. "I'm never going through *that* again. It's all fun for me from here on out." He gave a heavy sigh. "Ah well, it would be fun, if the lady in question weren't such a tease."

"You mean you and Audrey haven't—"

Richard shook his head.

"Hmm. She doesn't strike me as a difficult conquest. God knows her body was made for pleasure."

Richard scowled. "Marcus! *You* haven't—"

"Of course not. I just meant—"

Richard's heartfelt sigh interrupted him. "She can't stand me."

Marcus raised his eyebrow. "Ah. That does pose a problem."

"In truth, she's driving me mad. I either want to throttle her, or throw her on the floor and show her exactly where she belongs—under me! After all, she's only a lady's maid. But to me she behaves as if she were the Queen of England herself." He propped his elbow on the chair back and rested his head on his hand thoughtfully. "But she's the bravest chit. Do you know she pulled a knife on me?"

"You're joking! She did that, to a nobleman? What were you doing to her?"

Richard grinned. "Only kissing her senseless. When she's not running from me, she's"—he flung his arms out—"she's pure fire in my arms! But she won't admit it." He shook his head in aggravation. "Sometimes I feel as if I'm bashing my head into a brick wall. But I know what's on the other side will be spectacular. So I'm chipping away at it bit by bit."

"Maybe you ought to build yourself a ladder." Marcus smiled. It felt good to have Richard here, another man he could talk to, his best friend restored to him. "I believe you're right in what you said. This entire situation is starting to sound like a play I acted in once. Four lovers were stranded in a magical forest and got thoroughly mixed up. By all accounts, Audrey the maid should be for me, and the noble Lady Judith yours."

"Aye, I suppose. But seeing as it's not that way, what say we defy convention and have a go at it? You and Judith can wed in secret, and I'll have plenty of opportunities to convince Audrey to allow me the pleasure of her company."

Marcus gave him a look of pure annoyance. "That isn't funny, Richard."

"But why not? I know her father may be angry when he finds out you're married, but with the power of both our swords—"

"Richard!" Marcus tried to shout; but his ribs screamed in protest, and the sound lacked impact. Marcus tried reason rather than force. "Are you forgetting why I'm lying here? Judith's father is a powerful man. He can hire men to kill me next time. But even that's not why I hesitate, as if it weren't reason enough. The decision must come from her, and that's too much to ask any woman. Do you think Judith would be happy married to a commoner like me? She's a *lady*, for God's sake! She's used to finery, clothing, quality food, servants, living in mansions like this one—things I'll never come close to being able to provide for her."

"But you're a successful actor," Richard said, yet his dubious tone betrayed his own doubts.

"Hah!" Marcus gritted his teeth, then forced his jaw muscles to loosen. It wasn't Richard's fault that Marcus Sinclair came from humble stock. "Very well, consider then that my career may someday be as successful as Will Shakespeare's. Perhaps someday I'll be a partner in the company, too. Shakespeare's worked hard all his life and only recently become a gentleman. And a gentleman is far below Judith's station. No, Richard. I don't even want to discuss it, much less imagine it. As soon as I'm well enough, I'm walking out of here, and if God grants my wish, I'll never see her again."

Richard stared at him. "Never see her—" He shook his head in bewilderment. "I don't understand you. I thought you loved her—"

"Goddamn it, Richard!" Marcus cried, grimacing at the agony as his chest burned in response. "It's because I love her! I can't stand it!"

Richard raised his hand, his brows furrowed. "All right, all right, Marcus. Calm down. This arguing can't be good for you.

Forget what I said. It was an altogether foolish thought. As foolish as me marrying Audrey—as if I'd consider it. What an idea! Can you imagine the look on the countess' face if I brought her home as my wife?''

Both of them paused to imagine Richard's domineering, class-conscious mother welcoming Audrey as a daughter-in-law. Their eyes met. Marcus' grin matched Richard's at the absurdity of it; then they both began to chuckle.

Chapter 13

The All Hallow's Eve at the Earl of Devonshire's manor ended early enough for the guests to reach home before midnight, when ghosts and ghouls would begin traveling abroad. Once home, Judith climbed slowly to her room, her legs aching from dancing, her feet as leaden as her dispirited heart. The entire house was dark, except for a single wall sconce on the stairs.

Lord Walter Kennington had been a marvelous escort—witty, intelligent, attentive. She hated him for it, while she also told herself she had best accept the man. She would never fall in love with her husband, whoever he may be, and Kennington was the best of the lot. Her father, too, would be supremely pleased. For some reason, he had taken a special interest in Kennington.

Judith had been back home for two weeks when her father told her he had found the perfect suitor for her. Her father droned on about the man's sterling future, the rumors that Queen Elizabeth was about to reward him for his diplomatic service with the East India Company—possibly make him a count or even an earl. But Judith barely heard him describe the man she was about to meet, for her heart was with Marcus, and Marcus alone.

The pain of not seeing him every day was almost unbearable. She worried about him, prayed he was receiving proper care. Prayed he was recovering completely and wouldn't be left lame, or with a useless arm. But she was not to know, at least not firsthand.

She was thankful that Richard regularly brought news of Marcus. Judith wasn't so blinded by her own loss that she didn't see that Richard also came because of Audrey. Her maid, however, managed never to be alone with the young lord, almost as if she feared him.

But it wasn't fear Audrey expressed when Richard was around. It was more like defiance, which continued to surprise Judith. Audrey had always been strong-willed, but she had also been deferential toward her employers and anyone of a higher class. For some reason, Richard alone she treated with disdain bordering on contempt. It was almost funny to watch the two together, except Judith was rarely in the mood for laughing.

When Judith reached her room, it was nearing midnight—the witching hour. Every year since she was seven years old, Judith had taken part in the maiden's ritual that only worked one day a year, on All Hallow's Eve.

She picked up a ripe apple from a bucket she had set on her dressing table earlier. Sitting on the padded stool, she also retrieved a paring knife. She began peeling the apple carefully, so the peel would come away in one piece.

The peel broke. "Darn!" She tossed the apple and peel into the slop bucket by the door and picked up another apple. This time she successfully unpeeled the apple in one strip. She sighed in satisfaction as she held up the long, unbroken peel. She closed her eyes and held the peel in both her hands, thinking as hard as she could of Marcus. Then, in one swift motion, she threw the peel over her left shoulder.

She heard it drop softly to the carpet. She took a breath and turned around to see what shape the peel had taken. It would reveal the initial of her future husband.

She gasped. It was definitely in the form of an *M*. "Audrey, come quickly," Judith cried, rousing her maid, who had long ago gone to sleep in her small room off Judith's. "Quickly!"

"What is it, milady?" Audrey's groggy voice preceded her as she padded sleepily into the room.

"Look." Judith pulled her by the elbow and pointed to the peel. "It's definitely an *M*."

After wiping the sleep from her eyes, Audrey gazed down at the curling bit of fruit peel. "It could be an *M*," she said thoughtfully. She walked around to the other side. "It could also be a *W*."

"A *W!*" Judith said in consternation. She tilted her head and stared hard at the peel. Walter Kennington, she thought with distress. Was this a sign she should stop fighting her fate?

"Even if it's an *M*, milady, that could be many men. You don't know if it's a first name or a last name. It could as easily be Mowbray as Marcus."

"Audrey, bite your tongue," Judith replied in mock chastisement.

Audrey sighed. "Milady, I know how you feel about Marcus. But it's foolish to hope for what isn't going to be. Life isn't like that. Princes never sweep damsels off their feet, and true love only wins out in fairy tales."

Judith sighed in disgruntlement. She retrieved the apple peel from the floor, then tossed it into the slop bucket. She knew she had no future with Marcus, but she didn't appreciate her own maid destroying her fantasies.

"Don't look so sad, milady," Audrey said, unfastening the back of Judith's gown. "Guess what! I had a visitor this evening, while you were out."

Judith spun to face her. "Marcus?"

"Marcus! He still can't walk. Besides, do you think he'd ever show his face around here with your father about?"

"I know, but—" She waved her hand dispiritedly. "Oh, don't look at me that way. I don't know what I was thinking." She turned back around.

"He may not be well enough to walk here, milady, but we're certainly able to walk there," Audrey said carefully, her fingers busy on Judith's corset laces.

Judith's eyes grew bright. "You mean visit him? My father

would never allow it. I've been a virtual prisoner since he dragged me from Lord Hunsdon's home, you know that.''

"I had heard he plans to leave town briefly.''

Judith gave her maid an assessing look. "Does this have something to do with your mysterious visitor?''

Audrey looked only slightly embarrassed. "Actually, it does. That annoying Lord Swellhead—''

"Richard Langsforth.''

"Aye, he came by with the suggestion. He thinks Marcus needs some cheering up, and a visit from you would work quite well in that area. He made me promise to relay his plan to you.''

Judith clutched her hands. "Well, don't just stand there. Tell me what it is.''

Marcus reveled in the feel of the sun bathing his face. He was relaxing on a stone bench in the garden beside Lord Hunsdon's house. Most of the roses and other shrubs were past flowering, but he wasn't here to enjoy the garden. This was the first time he had been outside since the attack almost a month ago.

It was Richard's idea. In fact, his friend had all but dragged Marcus outside. Now Richard was pacing back and forth in front of him. "If you're so bored and restless, why don't you go find something to do?'' Marcus asked in annoyance.

As for himself, he was content just to be upright for a while and absorb the weak autumn sun. He hadn't yet felt a return of that marvelous energy that used to propel him through each day like a wild horse intent on seeking whatever was over the next horizon.

Perhaps he was getting old before his time, he thought. He certainly felt old compared to Richard, who looked like a boy anticipating his schoolmaster's reaction upon discovering the frog planted in his desk.

"Richard, stop pacing in front of me. You're blocking the sunlight.''

"Sunlight! Is that all you think of these days? You are in need of a little adventure, aren't you?'' Richard crossed his arms and stared at Marcus. His friend was definitely skinnier, his complexion paler. He certainly was in need of sun, his muscles in need of exercise.

But it was more than that. Marcus was different somehow, less buoyant. He was more apt to question Richard's impulses, and less apt to laugh at them. Less apt to laugh at anything than he used to be. Richard was positive it was a phase that would pass once his friend was fully healed and back to his old self. His old lusty self, that was, and a woman was what he needed.

The gate to the street clanged, and Richard spun around. Marcus looked up to see two youths enter the garden hesitantly, looking lost. Both wore simple breeches and tunics, and floppy hats on their heads. One had a lute slung over his back. Marcus couldn't imagine what the boys were doing coming into a private garden—probably up to some mischief. The gate must not have been locked, which was a serious breach in Lord Hunsdon's household security.

"And what do we have here? Trespassers in Lord Hunsdon's private garden?" To Marcus' surprise, Richard sprang on the visitors. He grabbed one about the waist and swung him around. The boy fought viciously, pounding and kicking and shrieking loudly. "I'll teach you to break in where you don't belong. I'll thrash you first; then I'll throw you out on the street—naked," Richard threatened.

Marcus knew then he was only teasing the hapless youths. The boy in his arms continued to shriek, a girlish sound any self-respecting boy should be thoroughly ashamed of. The second boy shoved his lute farther up his shoulder and pounded on Richard's back, demanding he let go of his friend.

The boy in Richard's arms lost his hat, and to Marcus' amazement, a pile of waist-long black hair tumbled out. Then he realized he had seen this particular boy before, and he was really a she.

Richard stood there pretending to be stunned at the revelation. "Why, look at that! There's a woman hiding in those boyish rags. And what a woman!" He whistled low.

In response, Audrey jumped forward and slapped him hard across the face. Marcus winced at the sound. Richard swore. Audrey turned and ran away from him. Richard started chasing her, and in a moment, they were running down a path into another part of the garden.

Audrey wasn't running from Richard as hard as she could have. Still, Richard didn't catch her until they were toward the back of the garden, well away from Judith and Marcus.

"All right, you wench," he called. "No one, and I mean no one, strikes a Langsforth and gets away with it."

"You deserved to be slapped, and hard," Audrey tossed off over her shoulder. Her eyes widened as she saw that Richard had rapidly closed the distance between them and was right behind her. In an instant she was enfolded in his arms, pressed hard against the full length of his body. Audrey struggled for all she was worth. "Get your hands off me, you—" She brought her knee up and crashed it toward his groin. It wasn't a clean hit, but she managed to make her intention clear.

"You little hussy!" Richard dropped her so suddenly she landed on her bottom in the bare soil of the vegetable garden, sending a shock up her spine.

Breathing hard, she craned her neck to where he loomed over her, and watched his expression shift from pain to anger to something else, something even more dangerous. She had certainly pushed him too far this time. She scooted backward on her bottom until a trellis prevented her from going any farther.

Richard stared down at her, and she was unable to look away. "You're going to pay for that, but good."

"You deserve to be slapped, and you deserve even more to be injured in your privates," she retorted. "You're entirely too randy. I hope it hurt."

"Do you, now." Richard dropped to his knees before her. He grasped her by the upper arms and dragged her face to within inches of his own. "You are the most aggravating woman I have ever met." He shook her once, hard. Suddenly, he flipped her over his knees. Audrey found her nose inches from the black soil, her rump in the air. "I've never struck a woman before. But in your case, I'm making an exception."

Understanding his intent, Audrey began kicking hard. "Let

me up, you bastard! You have no right to lay a hand on me! Ow!"

Richard lightly swatted her rump. "That was for the slap. And this—"

"Ow!"

"—is for the knee to my groin."

"All right, Sir Pain-in-the-Backside, you've had your fun. Now let me up this instant!" Audrey demanded.

The spanking stopped, but he didn't release her. She heard him draw in a shaking breath, felt his hand drop once more to her bottom. This time he didn't swat her. The swats hadn't truly been painful, but this touch wasn't even the semblance of a swat. His hand cupped her bottom, molded to it, began massaging in soft, gentle circles, down, around, his fingers even drifting between her thighs. "What are you—"

"Just lie still," Richard said, his tight voice betraying his own reaction to their encounter.

Audrey knew she should get up immediately, but she was falling badly under his spell. She had helped Judith arrange this tryst with Marcus through Richard, and she knew why, though she vowed she would never let him get the better of her. Nevertheless, she wanted to see him, thought about him more than was good for her, about how his touch sent her senses reeling and dissolved her will. Worse, Richard knew how he affected her. But this time, Audrey gained an understanding of how she affected him, in more ways than one. Lying across his lap, she was thoroughly conscious of his rock-hard desire pressing into her belly.

His hand slipped higher; then his fingers made shocking progress down the inside of her waistband. The feel of his hand caressing her bare buttocks was provocative, tantalizing. His fingers dipped lower, lower still, between her thighs to tease her womanhood. His touch burned like pure fire. Audrey knew he felt betraying moistness there.

Desperate to keep her dignity, she tried to scramble away. Suddenly, she was looking at the sky, unable to move. She was lying on Richard's satin-lined cape. He must have spread it on the ground while she was distracted. Now he was lying beside her, his arms enfolding her, one leg pinning hers.

He slipped his hand up her rib cage outside the tunic and cupped her generous breast through the rough wool of the shirt, his thumb playing over her hardened nipple. "You have the body of a courtesan. You could never pass for a boy. You're too well endowed." He grinned rakishly, and his eyes met hers.

That grin was his undoing. Audrey suddenly came to her senses. She knocked his hand away and rolled from him. Richard dragged her back. "Not so fast, sweet."

"Unhand me, you blackguard!"

"Not until you admit it."

"Admit what?"

"That you dream of me."

Audrey's mouth dropped open. She was speechless. How had he known? She wriggled all the harder, but Richard just laughed and seemed to enjoy it.

"I don't hear you denying it."

"Of course I deny it. I dream of running a knife through your scoundrel's heart, when I think of you at all, which is never."

"You make me sound most horrible."

"You are horrible."

"Hideous," he said.

"A monster," she agreed.

He propped his head on his hand. With his other hand, he stroked wild strands of hair off her face. "Your sharp tongue seems to flay only me. Ever since we met you've been heaping insults on me. Why is that?"

Audrey's chest heaved in frustration. "Because you look like bloody Prince Charming! You came to woo Judith spouting enough nonsense about love to choke a horse." Her voice dropped. "I feared my lady would believe in you."

"Were you truly afraid for Judith—or for yourself?" He leaned closer, his hand so entangled in her hair, Audrey couldn't free herself if she tried. She began to feel lost in his gaze, both excited and comforted by being wrapped so completely in his embrace. He must have sensed her resistance lessening. His handsome face loomed closer, his grin vanishing. His hooded eyes burned with inner fire.

Audrey had seen that look on men's faces before, knew

exactly what he was anticipating doing to her. She couldn't stand the thought of enduring such humiliation at Richard's hands. Before he had a chance to press his advantage, Audrey did something she never imagined she would do to a lord, much less the son of an earl. She spat in his face.

Richard stared at her in shock. He shoved her aside and sat up, wiping the spittle from his cheek. He said nothing, but kept his back to Audrey. She pulled herself up and sat there, frozen, afraid any moment the blow would come, and this time it wouldn't be in fun. Perhaps she should run away? But he would surely catch her again, and running might aggravate him further.

"I was under the impression you wanted to see me, too. You did accompany your lady here today," he said coolly without looking at her.

"Richard, why do you persist?" Audrey asked in a sudden burst of honesty. "I—I want to know. There must be dozens of women . . ."

Richard turned around and stared hard at her. His eyes roved from the top of her decidedly disarrayed hair, down her poorly concealing boy's clothing now streaked with dirt, to the swell of her breasts under her tunic, her hardened nipples embarrassingly prominent under the cloth, then back to her face. "I honestly don't know why. But I want you more than I ever wanted any woman."

"You wanted Judith."

Richard smiled wryly. "It's not the same."

Because she's a lady, Audrey thought to herself.

He leaned closer, so that their bodies were almost touching. "I never burned for Judith," he said softly, his blue gaze holding fast to her own. "But I burn for you, Audrey."

The sound of her name on his lips sent a shiver of desire through Audrey. She had never imagined a man's voice alone could be so provocative. His eyes grew smoky with desire as he brought his lips closer to hers, his hand cradling the back of her head. She began to pull back, but he spoke her name again, so softly she couldn't bring herself to resist. Her heart filled with amazement over this lord, so many stations above her, yet wanting only her. She was stunned that he wasn't furious with her, that he still wanted her after she had slapped him in the face, tried to incapacitate his manhood and finally spat on him.

But his desire for her was unquenched. She knew he would try to kiss her again, and was entirely uncertain she could resist. But his warm lips landed on her neck instead. His tawny beard tickled the soft skin of her throat as he stroked his hands through her hair, setting her scalp tingling. "My God, I want you so much," he whispered in her ear. "But I didn't imagine taking you in a vegetable patch. Perhaps we can—"

"You're not taking me anywhere." Audrey shoved at him and pulled herself to her knees. She was not about to arrange a tryst with him! She simply had to keep her distance from him, despite her desire to be near him. She was like a drunk trying to stay away from wine. She craved him, but he would be her ruin.

Before she could stand, Richard gripped her wrist, forcing her to face him. "I'm telling you true, Audrey. I've never felt this way before. Sometimes I honestly think I'm going mad, I want you so badly."

Audrey could think of no reply. She had never felt this way before either, but she wasn't about to tell him that. After what seemed an eternity, she managed to tear her eyes from his and her arm from his grasp.

She rose and walked unsteadily away, trying desperately to still her breathing. How much time had passed? Should she return to where Judith and Marcus were, or did they deserve a little more time alone? Could she bear to be alone with Richard any longer? She was uncertain of the outcome if she stayed.

She could feel him coming nearer. From behind, Richard's hands settled on her shoulders. As if reading her mind, he responded. "Don't fret. I've said my piece. I won't bother you anymore—at least not today." He swept up her hair and planted a tender kiss on the back of her neck. His touch sent a delicious tingle through her. She closed her eyes tightly against the threatening feelings.

Richard stepped away from her. "You'd better brush yourself off. You look like you've been wrestling in the mud."

"I thought I had been," she replied ruefully. She shook out

her clothes and watched as the fine garden soil tumbled from her tunic and breeches. She knew the muddiest spot was her behind and tried her best to brush herself off there.

"Not good enough. Here." Richard grasped her by the shoulder and spun her so her back was to him. He dusted her off quickly and efficiently, as if completely uninterested in the woman underneath the clothes. He turned her to face him and knocked more dirt from her front.

"You should talk. Your cape's covered in dirt, and your fine satin doublet may never look the same again." Tentatively, she batted the dirt from it.

"No matter. It was worth it."

Audrey was appalled that a man could so easily dismiss the loss of such expensive clothing. Usually even the nobility treasured their clothing. Could he truly mean it was worth it for a few moments with her that had left both of them thoroughly unsatisfied?

Audrey realized his hands had moved to her hair. He plucked out a shriveled grape leaf and dropped it to the ground. She could hardly believe she was standing here quietly, allowing him to touch her like this. It was madness. Why, any moment, his touch may turn amorous. He could pull her once more into his arms, and—

"There you go, good as new." Richard began to turn from her. Audrey surprised herself completely. She caught his wrist before he left her, marveled at how thick, how muscular it was. Richard stared at her, his eyes glancing to where she clasped his arm, and back again to meet her enigmatic gaze. Both of them were breathing heavily, and the moment stretched into eternity.

An instant later, she was in his arms. He swung his lips down hard on hers, seeking, eager, drinking of her soft, pliant mouth until they were both breathless.

She wrapped her arms around his neck and clung to him as if her life depended on it. She had never been kissed so ardently before and knew something indefinable was happening, something that would change her life forever. Beyond that, she couldn't think at all, could only feel.

As suddenly as the embrace started, it ended. Breathing hard,

Richard firmly set her from him. Audrey backed away from him, her eyes drinking in his broad shoulders, his muscular, sturdy build, his intense expression. As if being pursued, she turned and ran toward the garden entrance.

Safely there, she laid her forehead on the cold metal of the gate, trying to catch her breath. Was she right to deny Lord Richard the pleasure he was seeking from her? Would she find any pleasure in it, too? Her body seemed to cry out for him, but she had never enjoyed the act of bedding. Men had used her, and she had been forced to let them. But perhaps with Richard it would feel differently. Perhaps because it involved her heart—

She shook her head, angry with herself. As far as Lord Richard was concerned, the heart had nothing to do with it, not where a mere servant was involved. She knew for certain after today that if she ever again allowed him liberties, she would fall so thoroughly in love with him, it would ruin her ability to work, to think. She would pine for him as Judith pined for Marcus, and no good would ever come of it. She mustn't allow that to happen. One dove with a broken wing in the Ashton household was more than enough.

As soon as Richard and Audrey had vanished, the other boy came to stand beside Marcus, gazing down at him with love in his eyes—or rather, her luminous brown eyes. "Marcus, you're looking wonderful," Judith said softly. She set the lute beside her on the bench and took his hand in hers.

"Judith, I wasn't expecting—"

"Of course not. I'm a surprise."

"You certainly are." Marcus gazed hard at her, wondering if she had somehow come to a decision about her future, one involving him. His heart thundered with pleasure at seeing her again.

"Richard arranged it," Judith explained. "He thought you needed cheering up."

"And he thought you were the answer." Marcus smiled wryly, masking his disappointment. Seeing Judith again was like opening a wound that refused to heal. Obviously, nothing had changed in their relationship. Again he had let his imagination get the better of him.

"Aren't you glad to see me?" Judith asked with a pert smile.

Marcus was unable to resist her charms. She was more enchanting than ever. "You are the essence of sunshine," he said softly. For a long moment, he was lost in her gaze. She moved closer, her thigh pressing against his, her full lips turned toward his. Marcus breathed deeply, determined to maintain his control despite his desire for her. "I have something to show you." He took up a carved wooden crutch he had laid under the bench and slipped it under his good arm. He rose and put his weight gingerly on his right leg. "See?"

"Oh, Marcus, that's wonderful!"

"I've been exercising my legs, bending the knees, trying to build up strength." He grinned down at her. "I'm going to return to the theater in a few days. Not as an actor, at first. But I'll be the bookkeeper for the company until I finish healing."

"What's that—a bookkeeper?"

Marcus settled once more beside her. "The bookkeeper is the man who makes sure the actors enter on cue, makes sure the play flows smoothly, that everyone has the props they need when they need them. He has the only complete copy of the script. The actors merely have their sides."

"Sides?"

"Their roles, the characters they're going to play. They don't need to memorize the other players' lines, so we don't bother to make them copies."

"Oh."

Marcus could see she had no understanding of the theater, his other passion, and it disturbed him how little they were able to share.

"Sides. Well, I think you'll be a wonderful bookkeeper. Oh! I almost forgot. I have a surprise for you, as well." She presented him with the lute.

Marcus took it, admiring the skillfully wrought mahogany. It was a work of art. "It's exquisite."

Judith glowed at his reaction. "I bought the best one in London to replace the one you lost."

"Thank you, sweet. But it must have cost a fortune."

Judith shrugged as if the cost were nothing, which for her, it undoubtedly was. Marcus' chest tightened at this fresh reminder of their vastly incompatible stations. He ran his hand along the smooth, polished wood, marveled at its exceptionally fine workmanship. Though his left arm was in a sling and splints, he managed to balance the instrument precariously on his knee. He began plucking notes with his free hand, testing the instrument's tone, hearing them sparkle cleanly in the crisp fall air. In all his life, Marcus had never touched such an exquisite instrument, much less owned one. "I can't accept this, Judith. It's too fine." Marcus tried to hand back the lute, but Judith refused to take it.

"Of course you can. You must accept it, Marcus. For me."

Marcus saw the pain of guilt shadowing her eyes over her father's brutal act against him. He would gladly accept this gift if doing so would abolish that shadow, would restore the radiant joy and pleasure he so loved in her.

"Besides," she said, "it would be a crime if the finest lute player in all of London did not have an instrument worthy of his talents." A teasing smile curved her lips, and Marcus chuckled. He didn't doubt that she believed what she said. Her faith in him, in his abilities, filled him with awe.

Judith's eyes were bright as they played over Marcus' face. Her heart surged with love for him. He was pale, but his eyes were full of vitality as he gazed at her. His nose now had a slight bump in the middle, and the scar on his jaw was a thin pink line. But she no longer ached in sympathy for his pain. Her physical desire for him completely obliterated any vestigial nursing instinct she may have harbored. If she were as objective as possible, she would have to say Marcus was more handsome than before, his ordeal having added a ruggedness to his features that only enhanced his masculine attraction.

Marcus knew if she kept looking at him that way, she would soon be in his arms. They were alone, and—

"Where did Richard and your maid go?" he suddenly asked.

Judith glanced around worriedly. "Goodness, I'm not sure. He won't hurt her, will he?"

"You know perfectly well Richard likes his women willing,"

Marcus said dryly, remembering how quick his friend was to relieve himself of Judith once she made known her heart.

"Well, I doubt he'll get far with Audrey, then," Judith commented, sounding relieved. "She dislikes men, particularly Richard. Though it's odd. She does not truly seek to avoid him."

"Richard said she couldn't stand him."

"Sometimes it's easier to tell yourself that, when a liaison poses problems." Her gaze fastened to his. "I know I wish I could find something unlikable about you, for then I wouldn't be dreaming of you every moment of the day and find you haunting my every dream at night."

"Is that all it would take, finding me unlikable?"

Judith smiled. "Well, not really. It's a silly idea. I can no more stop loving you than I can stop winter from coming." She hugged her arms about her.

Marcus took the hint and pulled her hard to him with his good right arm. She snuggled against him as if she belonged there. He pressed gentle kisses atop her head, stroking the soft tendrils of her golden mane. She turned her face to his, expectant, flushed with desire. Marcus knew he had to stop this dangerous dance with her, but of their own accord, his lips connected with hers, his hand cradling her head. With his other arm still in splints, it was up to Judith to draw him closer, and she didn't hesitate.

The sweetness of her kiss washed over Marcus like the taste of cool water to a thirsty man. He wanted so much more of her, wanted to drown in her delights. But she was as beyond his reach now as she had ever been, and he must never forget it.

When he finally broke the kiss, both of them were breathing heavily. "You torture me, woman," he said against her lips. "You know that, don't you?" But he didn't release his firm hold on her.

"It's torture for me as well," said Judith, her eyes burning with suppressed passion, "a slow, sweet death."

Marcus took a deep, steadying breath. "Judith, you're a noblewoman, remember? Sole hope for the House of Dunsforth."

"Aye, I remember." Her eyes grew misty. "But what I remember best is every precious moment I spent in your arms."

"Oh, Christ, woman!" Marcus yanked her against him and kissed her again, over and over, hungrily, feeling he would never get enough of her. His free hand roved over her body, caressing her hips, her waist, her breasts under the boy's tunic she wore. Suddenly, the fire of life, of passion, burned through his body once again.

"I didn't realize you were so healthy," Judith gasped.

Marcus lifted his lips from the soft curve of her throat. His eyes met hers in a piercing stare, inches from hers. "I'm only a man, Judith," he growled. "You must do your part to fight this."

Judith caught his face in her hands. "But I don't want to fight it, Marcus. I want you." She kissed him again, her tongue bringing forth unspeakable pleasure from his lips.

He groaned. "Sweetheart, we have to stop." Mustering inhuman self-control, Marcus managed to separate himself from her, his body shaking from the effort.

Judith also looked shaken. No doubt she hadn't planned on their tryst becoming so physical so fast. "Why does it have to be so hard for us?"

Marcus couldn't look at her. She was unable to commit to a life with him, and he did not blame her in the least. How could he when she had so much to lose? There was only one solution left to them. "We have to end this, Judith. I'm too healthy now, and the temptation is far too great. We must never see each other again."

"No!" Judith cried, flashing a determined gaze at him. "I can't imagine never seeing you again. I just can't. I tried, but it's no good, Marcus. I know it's dangerous; I know I shouldn't. My father would be devastated if he knew about even this meeting. He's anxious for me to accept Lord Kennington's suit."

Marcus felt a surge of anger toward her, and it surprised him. She wanted it both ways. She wanted to please her damned father, be an obedient, virtuous daughter, yet have a clandestine lover, too. But where would that leave him? Lying in an alley with his throat cut? Or simply more heartbroken than he already was? Neither prospect had much appeal. "No, Judith," he said, his voice sounding harsh to his ears. "It's not fair to either of us, and it's not fair to your future husband, whether it's this Kennington fellow or another man."

"I couldn't care less about him!" Judith replied hotly. "I owe nothing to him. Even if I wed him, all he would have are my name and my money. Never my love. Never. That's yours."

"Judith, you have to give him a chance. I don't want you to go into marriage pining for something that can never be."

"What about you? Are you going to simply forget me?"

Marcus stared hard at her before he answered. "No," he said quietly, that one word communicating a world of pain and heartache.

"And you ask me to love you less."

"I want you to be happy."

"That's asking the impossible." Her voice dropped to a husky whisper. "From the day we met, it became impossible for me to be happy without you."

"Oh, God, Judith, it hurts me to hear you talk this way," Marcus said, his voice cracking. All of his anger dissolved as he heard the pain in her voice. How could he think to blame her when he felt the same?

"It hurts me not to be able to love you as my heart commands me to." Judith's eyes filled with tears. "Sometimes I feel I'm going to die with it."

"Oh, darling, don't say that, I beg you." Marcus pulled her hard into his arms, cradled her, stroking her shoulders, her back, seeking to provide comfort where none was possible. As he clung to Judith, more valuable to him than life itself, understanding filled Marcus' soul with a painful dread. As sweet as their love was, it could only hurt Judith. Marcus vowed to find a way to set her free.

"Well, you two look cozy!" Richard's voice startled both of them.

Marcus let go of her and sought to control the emotions Judith had set loose. "Richard always did have incredible timing," he said under his breath.

Despite the painful emotions of the last few minutes, they

shared a faint smile. Marcus cupped her cheek. "Go on now," he said softly.

They both knew there was nothing more to say. Judith rose reluctantly and walked toward the garden gate, where Audrey was already waiting. The gate squeaked noisily as Audrey swung it open, and clanged as loud as a cell door when it closed behind them.

"All right, you can thank me now," Richard said jovially.

"Thank you so very much, Richard." Richard was obviously so pleased with himself, he completely missed the heavy irony in Marcus' voice.

ACT 4

"I must be cruel, only to be kind."
—*Hamlet*, Act 3, Scene 4

Chapter 14

Marcus fiercely doubted his sense in attending Lord Hunsdon's Twelfth Night revelry the moment Judith entered the parlor. On this, the final day of the Christmas celebration, greenery decked the halls and draped the mantel where a Yule log burned, and dozens of candelabra bathed the room in a golden glow. All in all, it was a particularly festive setting for the ornately garbed aristocracy.

The brightest jewel among them was Judith, dressed in a sky blue silken gown shimmering with gold embroidery and underlaid with the richest royal blue velvet. The gown's neckline scooped wonderfully low, revealing her soft feminine curves. Her golden hair was piled in an intricate configuration on her head, gold and blue ribbons threaded through it. In the French fashion, one lush love lock brushed her bare shoulder. She was easily the most breathtaking woman in the room.

Marcus stared at her. His throat thickened, and his eyes became moist. He cursed himself for a sentimental fool, but he knew he couldn't help dwelling on how much he loved her, how proud he was of her elegance, her grace as she turned her head in answer to a comment from the man beside her—

Marcus' gaze sharpened, and he stared hard at Lord Kennington. He was handing Judith a chalice of wine, taken from the generous hand of a nearby servant. Her long, elegant fingers took the chalice, holding it in her fingertips as she had been trained since birth to do, as if it weighed nothing. She wore no rings on her fingers and no necklace about her neck. As if she had decided to wear no necklace, since giving hers to him, Marcus thought triumphantly.

He shook his head hard and cursed himself. If he were successful tonight as he planned, he would learn that she would soon be wearing a wedding band, one bestowed by the man at her side.

With Richard's influence, Lord Hunsdon had graciously provided Marcus with this opportunity to learn for himself if Judith had found a suitable match. And, for Judith to discover the "truth" about her beloved Marcus Sinclair, stage actor and incorrigible rake.

Of course, Lord Hunsdon knew nothing of Marcus' full plans, or of how involved his heart was. Marcus had merely expressed a desire to ensure Lady Judith's future would not be adversely affected since he had threatened her reputation. As far as Marcus could tell, Lord Hunsdon bought the lie, and even enthusiastically lent him proper gentleman's clothing.

Again his gaze turned to Kennington, appraising him as dispassionately as his fierce passion allowed. As an actor, Marcus could read people fairly well, and he saw that the man with the striking mane of blond hair and cultivated beard was definitely a likely match for Judith. With a sinking heart, he could easily see what the man had to offer her.

To begin with, he wasn't bad-looking. He had a friendly, but not overly gregarious, disposition. His subdued clothing told Marcus the man didn't put on airs. In fact, standing beside Judith, he appeared her mate, neither of them wearing the excessively gaudy attire that was the height of fashion and the choice of many of the arriving guests.

Richard had said Walter Kennington was a diplomat. Perhaps, if Kennington had been away from Court, he was immune to its petty intrigues. He was mature, which would be good for Judith, most likely with a level head on his shoulders, a man who would indulge a young wife, but only insofar as it was good for her. Marcus clung to the idea that Kennington might serve as a second father to her, guiding her and protecting her. Certainly not her lover, never that. The thought made the ale Marcus had just swallowed churn sickeningly in his stomach.

"Judith, that man is staring at us," Kennington remarked to Judith. "Do you know him, perhaps?"

Judith looked past Kennington to the gentleman leaning against the mantel. Her breath caught in her throat. She was certain her eyes were betraying her. But no, they told true. It was Marcus, her Marcus, dressed as a gentleman and attending the party as a guest.

Her shock over seeing him quickly transformed into delight, and amazement at his elegant appearance. Forgetting the wine in her hand, she drank in Marcus instead, from his properly barbered hair to his feet, encased in fine leather boots. He wore perfectly acceptable attire for a gathering of the upper strata of London society.

In fact, he was indistinguishable from the rest of the gentry surrounding her, appeared aristocratic, noble even. He belonged so well she wanted to cry with the sheer joy of it, shout to the world that Marcus was worthy, as worthy as any man there to be her love, even her husband.

He appeared wonderfully healthy, and more handsome than he had been before the beating. As he slowly crossed the room toward her, she saw he favored his left leg slightly.

Judith's heartbeat accelerated. She wasn't sure how well she would handle her clandestine lover meeting the man who wished to be her husband. To her relief, Kennington caught sight of a colleague and excused himself to go speak with him.

Marcus stopped before her, his face wearing a cool, polite smile.

"Marcus," she said softly on a breath.

"Milady." His voice carried a wry note Judith hadn't heard before.

"You look wonderful. You're well again. I'm so happy for you."

"Aye, I'm doing well enough," Marcus replied evenly.

"I see that." Her eyes roved over his gentleman's attire. If Marcus' circumstances had changed. . . .

"They're borrowed," Marcus replied curtly. "From Lord Hunsdon. I'm still a simple country boy underneath."

Marcus had perhaps come from the country, but simple he was not. Even now, his eyes and voice seemed to be sending her a confusing array of messages, desire mixed with disdain, blended with an odd remoteness—or was it sadness? "Well, you look marvelous, nonetheless," she said.

"Thank you. You also look incredible, as always." His gaze slid along her body, turning molten, making her blood heat.

Judith glanced about, to be sure no one would overhear them. She lowered her voice. "When I allowed my father to pressure me into coming tonight, my love, I didn't have the slightest idea I would be seeing you again—"

"I am an odd sight amid the sparkling nobility, aren't I? A stone among diamonds, wouldn't you say?"

"Marcus, don't speak that way when it isn't true. I didn't mean it that way. I'm just surprised to see you here. I thought perhaps you came because—because of me."

Marcus shook his head, a wry twist to his lips. "Judith, I'm here for the same reason you are. To enjoy myself." He looked over her shoulder. "Now, if you will excuse me, I mean to do exactly that."

Judith followed his gaze to where Lady Alice Chancery, a lush brunette, was making her way through the crowd toward them. Marcus left Judith's side and met Alice a few feet away.

He grinned down into her coy face, and a stab of brutal jealousy pierced Judith's heart. Lady Chancery was staring at Marcus as if she were starving and he was a tender, mouthwatering steak. Judith *knew* Alice Chancery changed lovers as often as the seasons despite being married. As usual, her sickly husband hadn't managed to make it tonight. The dark lady's renowned escapades always appalled Judith when she caught wind of them. But not nearly as much as the woman was disturbing Judith now.

"Why, Marcus Sinclair. It has been an age. I've missed your inspired . . . performances."

"On stage?" His tone turned blatantly suggestive. "Or in bed?"

In *bed?* The blood drained from Judith's face, and she nearly dropped her wine goblet. Marcus could never care for that noble hell-cat, he simply couldn't. Not *her* Marcus.

Lady Alice laughed coquettishly, her fingers drifting along his arm. "You know the answer to that. Perhaps you would favor me with a repeat performance? That is"—her eyes flicked to Judith—"if you're through dallying with inexperienced little girls."

Judith's eyes widened, fastening on Marcus' face. Instead of defending her, his seductive expression as he looked at Alice never wavered. This, from the man who claimed once to always be her champion? Judith stood immobile from shock as he pressed his hand to Alice's back and led her into the crowd.

"The typical blackguard, moving on to a new conquest," came a voice in her ear.

Judith swung around to face her father.

"You will keep your distance from that—that man," Howard said in disgust. "It's appalling that he's even here, among proper gentry." His gaze riveted to Judith's. "You had best step carefully tonight, daughter. I expect you to comport yourself as a true lady, and not forget your place."

His lack of trust stung Judith. "What is there to remember? Haven't I been fulfilling my daughterly duties adequately? Lord Kennington seems pleased enough in me."

"I am pleased you care to win Kennington's favor. For there are others about who would prefer to see the match never come off."

"Father?" Judith expected he was talking about Marcus. Howard gestured, and her eyes followed not to Marcus, but to Lord Mowbray, who had just entered the parlor. She shuddered. She had no wish to be in the same room with such a man.

"I am aware how his presence disturbs you, daughter," Howard said, his voice displaying tender warmth. "I will soon be joining him in the gaming room, and he will be out of your sight."

Judith smiled. "Thank you."

Before leaving her, he leaned close and whispered softly, "Stay close to Kennington."

Judith watched him leave, confusion swirling through her at his mysterious tone.

* * *

"I admit he's a right ugly one, my master is. But he wears the most elegant clothes of any lord, and he has the queen's ear," insisted a skinny butler.

A matronly servant sitting beside Audrey snorted. "Well, you can brag, but my lady's the most beautiful at Court, admired by every man who meets her. They all wish to win her favor."

Audrey knew the woman was the personal maid of Lady Alice Chancery, renowned for granting her favors far and wide. "And their wishes are granted," she mumbled into her hot spiced ale. She sat with other lords' and ladies' servants at the long oak table in the huge chamberlain kitchen, idly watching the household cook and his staff frenetically prepare an astonishing array of dishes for the esteemed guests' dinner—and anticipating the leftovers.

"What's that you say?" asked the plump maid. When Audrey didn't reply, the maid continued singing the praises of her employer, for when her lady was admired, it enlarged her own reputation.

Audrey stopped listening to the discussion of the servants around her. She wasn't about to get into an argument over whose lady was the most favored, though everyone knew it was Judith Ashton, not that debauched witch Alice Chancery.

"My, my, there's a sight," sighed the plump maid. "What a handsome young buck."

Audrey's eyes flicked up, and she froze. She suddenly felt both hot and cold, unable to move and desperate to flee. Richard was leaning in a decidedly rakish way against the kitchen doorjamb, an inviting smile playing about his lips. But his eyes—they were looking straight at her, as if he knew exactly what she was feeling when she looked back at him.

"I'd say there's a gentleman who'll be wanting a little Christmas cheer," snickered the maid. "And it looks like he's wanting it from you, girl."

Audrey couldn't tear her eyes from him. She had accompanied Judith tonight knowing she might see him, almost wanting to see him, yet terrified of what might follow. In the previous weeks, they had met only briefly, when he called at the Ashton household on some pretense or other. Always Richard implied that when the opportunity came, he would have her. His words meant little when, in her own home, she could leave the room or shut the door if he pressed for favors. But here, tonight. . . .

No, she couldn't let it happen. He stood there in all his finery, decked out in emerald satin and gold brocade for the festivities, a golden velvet cape falling almost to his knees. Even his stance—arrogant, self-assured—screamed out his wealth and high station. What a fool she had been to entertain the briefest daydream that such a splendid lord might actually want anything but an entertaining tumble from her!

Richard's smile faded slightly, and he gestured with his head, indicating she should join him outside the kitchen.

Lady Alice's maid nudged her hard in the side. "Well, don't just sit there, girl, go be friendly to him. It doesn't hurt to have friends in high places, if you know what I mean."

"I'd rather not."

"You'd rather not! My, aren't we getting too good for ourselves." The maid turned to Richard and spoke loudly enough for the entire room to hear. "She'd *rather not* join you, milord. Ain't that sweet for you!"

Richard stared at Audrey a moment longer, not saying anything. His lips twitched, and a grin slowly grew. He straightened up. Audrey suddenly understood that if she didn't immediately come to him, he would come get her. She collected her composure as best she could and rose from the table. As nonchalantly as possible, she came toward him, then slipped past him out the kitchen door.

Once outside, Richard grasped her upper arm firmly. He steered her underneath the stairway that led to the gallery above and, above that, to yet another gallery flanked by bedchambers. The passage here was unlit and secluded. Richard wasted no time pulling her hard against him and burying his lips on hers, reminding her thoroughly of the intense kiss they had shared in Lord Hunsdon's private garden.

To Audrey's dismay, she was still as easily swept away by him as ever. His hand weaved into her hair and secured the back of her head as he guided her lips in the kiss. Through a haze of desire, Audrey was faintly conscious that her breasts were plastered against his padded doublet, vaguely thankful that the padding would keep him from noticing how quickly and completely he aroused her.

Richard broke the kiss. "You came tonight," he breathed into her ear as he stroked her shoulders. "I knew you would. It's been so bloody long since we've been properly alone."

"I came to accompany my Lady Judith," Audrey protested, fighting the urge to arch into his kisses as his sinful lips played along the sensitive nape of her neck.

"Her father and Lord Kennington weren't escort enough for her?" he chuckled, bringing his head up to meet her eyes in challenge. "You probably could have had the night free, to spend with family or friends. But instead, you chose to come here."

"I have no family."

"Friends?"

"A few. They were spending the evening with their own families."

He ran his thumbs along her lips, rubbing them gently. "You are a terrible liar, Audrey. I know why you're here. For the same reason I am. It's going to happen tonight, and we both know it."

"All I know is you're making a pest of yourself, Richard." Audrey shoved hard at his chest and attempted to move past him. Richard's arm shot out and caught her around the waist. He pressed her back against his chest, imprisoning her with his arms.

"You know the truth of it. You can't play coy anymore, Audrey." His voice became silken, seductive. "I've been dreaming about you constantly since we kissed in the garden, right here at this same house. I take that as a sign. Have you been dreaming of me?"

"Not at all."

"Liar. Lord Hunsdon has made chambers available upstairs for any guests who desire a little privacy." With one hand he expertly opened the top buttons of her dress before she even realized what he was up to. He slipped his hand inside, along her generous cleavage. "God knows I desire it, and every sign shows me you do, too."

"You're reading the signs wrong," Audrey said, but her body's reaction to him belied her words as he slipped his fingers inside her corset and fondled one of her taut nipples.

"Am I? I think not. I think that by dawn tomorrow, you and I will have come to a new understanding."

Audrey's knees were weak, but she forced her voice to be strong. "You talk nonsense, milord."

"I talk truth." Richard pressed her hips hard against his arousal. His hand slid down her thigh and back up, sending a path of fire straight to her womanhood. Of its own accord, her body had collapsed against his, her head heavy on his shoulder. His voice was a hot, sensuous whisper in her ear. "The hungry beast will be fed, our desires appeased, the banked embers within our souls ignited into an inferno of all-consuming passion until we're out of our minds with ecstasy."

"Your attempts at poetry are improving, but you're no Will Shakespeare," she said, trying for a dry tone. But her words were alarmingly weak at the images he invoked.

Richard laughed and turned her around. His hands cradled her face. "God, you are brutally honest."

"Am I?" she breathed, unable to tear her gaze from his.

As soon as the words escaped her lips, Audrey wished for all the world she could recall them. He knew for certain now that her protests were as thin as gauze. He was the honest one, and she was indeed lying.

Richard sobered as he gazed into her eyes. He hugged her tight, pressing her close to his heart. "Ah, sweet Audrey, I swear I've been looking forward to this all my life. On my heart and soul, you won't regret it." He pulled back and buttoned up her dress. "After supper, I'll come for you. Don't go anywhere. I'll be sorely disappointed if you're not here." He kissed her on the forehead, then disappeared through the door to the parlor where the guests were in full celebration.

Audrey collapsed against the wall, willing her body to calm itself. She was stunned at her reaction. She could have fought him, for God's sake. She had allowed him to hold her, allowed him to kiss her, allowed all manner of unmentionable liberties. She was a complete idiot, and she should never have come tonight.

She considered walking home. It was a long, cold walk in the January weather, dangerous this time of night when people were engaging in drunken celebration all across London.

But then, perhaps Judith would need her later. She had noticed that Marcus Sinclair was, of all things, a guest at the same party. That might prove sticky for her lady. No, she shouldn't desert her now.

She decided to do nothing yet. There was still time to avoid Richard. Feeling thoroughly enervated, she slowly walked back to the kitchen.

"I thought this was a gathering of some quality. Lord Hunsdon has lost his sense to allow such riffraff among the gentry."

Marcus nearly spilled the drink a servant was handing him. After seeing Judith with Kennington, he had retired to the side of the room to gather his thoughts and down some much-needed ale from a table spread with all manner of holiday cheer.

He turned slowly in response to the unwelcome voice to find Howard Ashton assessing him insolently with his lackluster blue eyes.

"Lord Ashton," Marcus began, determined to maintain his temper and show this pompous prig just how civil the "baser sort" could be. "And who might we be plotting against this week?"

Howard looked up at him from under shaggy eyebrows. "Be lucky I didn't have you killed. I thought I had managed to teach you a lesson. You apparently are a very slow learner. I had expected that you would have crawled back into whatever gutter you crawled out of. Get out of here, Sinclair. You don't belong here among decent folk."

Intense frustration welled up within Marcus. Who was Howard Ashton to say where he could be? It wasn't to be borne. "Lord Ashton, I am going to speak plainly," Marcus said. "You may command a vast sum of money. You may have a title. But that doesn't give you the right to dictate other people's lives. I am a free man, and I go where I choose. It happens I'm a guest of Lord Hunsdon's tonight, and if that doesn't suit you, you may certainly take your leave."

Howard moved closer to Marcus, further emphasizing Marcus' height. But Howard's blue eyes bore hatefully into Marcus' own. "You have caused enough of a breach between me and my daughter as it is, Sinclair. She came here to enjoy herself, not to be reminded of her folly where you are concerned. I'll not have you around where only decent people belong."

Marcus's stony glare met his. "And how do you intend to keep me away?"

"Simple. If you do not leave, I will tell the authorities how you forced yourself upon my daughter and stole her virtue."

A wry grin tilted Marcus' mouth. "It will never hold up. Judith will never claim I raped her. She came to me. There is no law against that."

"So she said," Howard replied tightly, his face coloring. "But whose story do you think the authorities will believe, yours or mine?"

Every muscle in Marcus' face tightened. To think Howard Ashton would create some rape story to explain the exalted experience that he and Judith had shared—it was reprehensible. "Judith would have to come forward and testify for the charges to carry any weight," he said icily.

"And you would put her through that?"

Marcus paused, realizing Howard's tactic. "I see," he said with a curt nod, almost admiring his adversary's ability. "You are right, of course. I wouldn't want to put her through that. Nor, I think, would you." He stared hard at Howard, and the other man was the first to look away. "However, as it's a matter of risking such an experience for Judith versus me leaving, I will take myself off." He began to move slowly from the sideboard.

"I'm glad you see it my way," Howard replied with a sigh.

"When I'm good and ready." Over his shoulder, Marcus gave Howard a devilish grin, knowing he had called the man's bluff. Judith's father wouldn't dare create a scandal about his daughter. He didn't have the guts.

Howard Ashton glared at him as if he were the lowest worm alive. Marcus turned his back on the man and tried to put him out of his mind. He had more important tasks ahead of him tonight than worrying about Judith's father.

Chapter 15

As Marcus took a healthy swig of mulled wine, he studied the man standing beside him. Supper had come and gone, and Marcus needed to get on with his task. He had approached Lord Walter Kennington and introduced himself while Judith danced with another lord.

So far, he could find no failings in Kennington, no sign of questionable character, odd preferences, nothing that might warn of impending unhappiness for Judith as his wife.

While they talked, Marcus probed Kennington about his views on a variety of subjects. The man passed every test. Even the last one.

"The ladies are truly lovely, as graceful as angels," Marcus remarked as they watched the women and men move in a stately, courtly dance. "You know, I have a friend who has recently wed a lady such as one of those," he commented to Kennington.

"I fancy that state myself," Walter replied jovially, his eyes seeking out Judith.

"Ah, yes. So did my friend. But he believed his bride an untouched innocent. And once they were wed, he learned quite the opposite."

"She was a wanton?"

"No, not at all. But she enjoyed a lover in her past."

"Just one?"

"Aye, I believe so."

Kennington shrugged. "Then, what is the man so concerned about? Your friend ought to be a little more tolerant. I'll wager he himself has had his affairs before committing himself to this woman. And as long as she is committed to him, what damage has been done?"

"Why, none, I should think." Marcus smiled at Walter. The man was almost too perfect—assuming he truly held to these views and didn't state them merely to impress people with his open mind. Apparently Kennington wouldn't even condemn Judith for her past liaison with Marcus. If he ever learned of it, of course.

"You know, it's odd you should mention such a thing," Kennington said thoughtfully. "I know another lady in the same situation. She's not yet wed, but she has confessed to me her previous liaison with a man."

Marcus stared at him. Surely Judith hadn't confided in him. "Has she really?" he said casually. "And what did you think of this?"

"I fault her not in the least. Of course, the man who dared take her was a scoundrel of the worst sort. To deflower a noble maiden! Who would stoop to such vileness?"

Marcus swallowed his wine. It went down like bitter gall. Had Judith painted their affair in such a light—perhaps out of shame? "Is this how the woman in question described her past liaison?"

"Not exactly, but one becomes expert at reading between the lines with ladies." He smiled. "Then again, I'm not altogether sure I want to know any more details, as long as it's over."

"Aye, it's over."

Kennington looked sharply at Marcus, and Marcus realized belatedly what he had said. He smiled disarmingly and quickly added, "If she knows what's good for her, for surely she should be watchful of her reputation."

Kennington appeared relieved. He nodded. "Aye, often a

lady has little else to recommend her. Now, Lady Judith Ashton, however, has much to recommend her.'' He sighed. ''Ah, look at her! She's a perfect flower, the most exquisite creature in all of London. And as lovely inside as she is outside.''

''That she is.''

''Gently bred, mannerly, intelligent enough to be interesting, but not brazenly so. Aye, she will make a fine wife.''

As he listened to Kennington, Marcus allowed himself the luxury of drinking in Judith's beauty as she moved with grace through the courtly dance steps. Her partner was a man Marcus didn't recognize, but he was old enough to be her father.

The real concern was Kennington. Not taking his eyes from Judith, he continued his probing. ''So, do you plan to seek her hand?'' he asked conversationally. His heart began a relentless pounding against his rib cage as he waited for the man's answer.

''I already have. But my Judith has not yet said yes.''

His Judith? Marcus kept his lips turned up, but the man's possessive endearment pierced him like a stiletto. He had never felt such savage pain, even when he lay beaten almost to death in the alley beside his house.

''Just look at her,'' Kennington said. ''She puts the angels to shame.''

''Aye. Yet she hasn't turned you down?''

''Thank goodness, no. But she hesitates.''

Marcus forced himself to firm his resolve. From now on, he would be on the rim of Judith's life, looking in. ''You will simply have to work harder on her.''

Kennington chuckled. ''I certainly intend to.''

Unfortunately, as far as Marcus could determine, that settled it. Judith belonged with this man more than any other, more even than himself, for Marcus Sinclair, the actor, could not give her even a fraction of what this gentleman could. He would simply have to ensure that Judith agreed to wed Kennington.

Richard looked among the thirty or so servants in the kitchen engaged in their own Twelfth Night celebration. Audrey wasn't among them.

''Ah, the lord's back, and he's wanting some goodly entertainment. He's come to the right place," said a skinny cook's assistant with prominent pock marks marring her face. The woman pressed herself against him in a most familiar manner. Richard backed away from her fetid breath stinking of garlic combined with heavy ale.

He pushed past her toward the other end of the long, narrow kitchen, peering into the open pantry door. "Where's Audrey, Lady Judith Ashton's maid?" he demanded to the room at large.

"You be wanting that one? You're too late. She's already got herself a lord," Miss Garlic said. "He took her upstairs a few minutes ago." She pressed herself against Richard again. "Let's say you and me finish celebrating this night together."

Furious at her news, Richard grasped her shoulders tightly. "Who did she leave with?"

"Lord Mowbray," the maid answered, suddenly sobered by Richard's anger. "But she hasn't left. She's upstairs, I say. Maybe once he's through with her you can have a go."

But Richard didn't stay to listen. He was taking the stairs two at a time. How could she do it? How could Audrey go with that disgusting, debauched man when he had been pursuing her for months to no avail? Audrey was purposely taking his heart and smashing it into a thousand pieces, merely to be cruel. How could such wickedness exist in such an exquisite body, behind that sweet face? He wouldn't stand for it.

Feeling for all the world like a cuckolded husband, Richard strode along the upper gallery. At each closed door, he pounded until he heard complaining voices that were neither Audrey's nor Mowbray's. He didn't have to knock on the last door in the hall, for it stood partly open.

Oblivious to possibly invading some other couple's privacy, Richard kicked in the door. It swung wide to reveal a man and woman, still clothed for the most part, engaged together on the bed, the man atop a thrashing woman. Both looked toward the door when Richard strode in.

It took only a moment for Richard to recognize both Mowbray and Audrey, and one second longer for him to realize that Audrey was not a willing participant.

''Richard,'' Audrey cried, her voice weak from lack of air, pressed down as she was into the feather bed.

''Get out of here! This is private business,'' said Mowbray imperiously.

In three quick strides, Richard was upon Mowbray, grasping him and flinging him to the floor. Audrey's bodice had been slashed open, one breast exposed. She quickly sat up and strove to pull the torn gown over her nakedness. Her hair tumbled about her shoulders, and the fear on her face made Richard seethe. Audrey's eye caught movement behind him. ''Watch out!''

Richard spun just in time to avoid the flash of a wickedly sharp stiletto aimed at his back. He pulled out his own dagger and met Mowbray's next stroke in midair, their blades crossing with an alarming shriek of metal. Richard shoved the older man backward, and again Mowbray hit the floor hard, his breath expelling in a loud grunt.

''Get the hell out of here, Mowbray.''

Mowbray rose, his eyes squinting in fury. ''You are an impudent scalawag to steal my wench out from under me. I'll get you for this.'' Mowbray attacked again. When the deadly stiletto arced toward him, Richard swiveled out of the way. Catching the man's wrist in his hand, he twisted the limb for all he was worth. Mowbray let out a howl of frustration and pain, but he was forced to drop the weapon.

Richard shoved him up against the wall. ''How dare you lay your filthy hands on this lady!''

''Lady! Look at her, she's nothing but a wh—''

Richard's strong hands grasped his neck and squeezed hard. ''A lady, damn you!'' He whacked Mowbray's head against the wall. The man grunted, clawing at Richard's hands.

Richard shoved him bodily out the door and kicked the stiletto after him. ''I'll kill you if you come anywhere near her again, do you understand me?''

Mowbray once again regained his feet and slowly retrieved his stiletto from the floor.

Richard vaguely realized several people were watching the exchange, some in the gallery, some standing in the doorways to the rooms. He left Mowbray standing there, the old man glaring murderously at him, and entered the room, securing the door and sliding the bolt home.

He turned. Audrey was sitting on the edge of the bed, obviously badly shaken by her ordeal with Mowbray. She brushed awkwardly at her tousled hair with one hand while holding her dress together with the other.

She lifted her eyes, meeting Richard's, reading the intensity of his concern for her. All of her attempts to be strong crumbled at the sight of his commanding strength, strength she badly needed to lean on. "Richard," she gasped.

Richard was beside her in a heartbeat, sitting close to her and cradling her gently. He pressed her head into his shoulder and murmured soothing words, sweet assurances that could only come from someone who cared deeply. Audrey gave in to her relief at being rescued, and the tears came, copious tears, all over his fine emerald doublet. Richard didn't even seem to mind.

"He had a knife," she sobbed after a moment, needing to talk about it, to explain it to Richard. "At my throat. He threatened to cut me if I didn't let him—use me."

"My God, my poor baby." Richard stroked the hair from her face, smoothed the moisture from her cheeks. "I was too late to be the one to meet you in the kitchen like I had planned. I came after you had gone, and I thought—I actually thought—" He was too ashamed to admit what he had believed of her.

"That I went willingly," Audrey finished for him.

"Aye." In a burst of clarity, Richard understood. What recourse did a servant like Audrey have against powerful men like Mowbray—or himself? Precious little, that was what. Richard had never before truly considered what Audrey must be going through during his amorous pursuit of her. He had considered it playful flirtation, believed she was teasing him mercilessly. In fact, she knew him to be of the same powerful class as Mowbray, a man it would be dangerous to deny.

"Audrey." He pulled back and looked in her eyes to learn the truth from her. "What Mowbray was doing, attempting to get from you. When I've pursued you so relentlessly ... Do you consider me to be like him?"

"Nay," she answered immediately. Then she hesitated. Richard *had* pressured her, though it was of a much gentler nature, and if she were honest with herself, it had been welcome. But it had been pressure from a powerful lord nonetheless. She breathed deeply to bolster her courage. "Aye, in a way."

Richard sighed heavily and pulled her even closer, stroking her back. "I never realized. I've been so callous, so unconcerned with how you must feel. The strain I've been putting you under is inexcusable."

His hand inadvertently slipped upward and brushed the side of her exposed breast through the slashed fabric. Alarmed at what she would think of him, he yanked his hand away. "Here." He began unfastening his doublet.

"What are you doing?" Audrey asked, puzzled. Nevertheless, though he seemed to be undressing, she felt perfectly safe in his presence.

Richard shrugged off the doublet and placed it around her shoulders. Audrey relaxed completely as he again draped his arms around her. "There you go. You can't very well go downstairs in that torn dress."

She smiled and wiped away the last of her tears. "No, I don't suppose so. But I'm not quite ready to go downstairs."

"I'm sorry, Audrey, for ever trying to pressure you into making love with me. It was unconscionable."

Audrey shrugged. It was a fact of her life. "Men think they can easily take liberties with the likes of me, since I'm not a lady."

"You *are* a lady, where it counts."

Audrey reveled in his words. She snuggled up against him, smiling into his silk shirt, one arm around his broad back and one hand fisted against his chest, childlike. She gazed up at him through her long black eyelashes and admired his tawny beard, reveled in the tenderness of his gaze.

He was so solicitous of her, showing his concern for her—and not making any move to seduce her. It was a new experience for her, and it made everything clear. She loved this man, despite their class difference and the pain he would undoubtedly cause her. She loved him with every fiber of her being. But she still would not give herself to him, because she knew she could never stand to lose him.

As if reading her thoughts, Richard spoke, his voice thick with emotion, and more than a little amazement. "Audrey, I believe I've fallen in love with you."

Audrey pulled herself away from him, the better to see his eyes, read his expression. "What did you say?" She brushed once more at her disarrayed hair, suddenly self-conscious of her appearance.

Richard smiled tenderly, then joyfully. His assurance grew with each passing moment. The astonishing revelation locked into his heart, finding a permanent home there. His heart brimmed with it, overflowed, elated him in a way he had never felt before. When he spoke, his voice rang with the confidence of truth. "I said I love you, Audrey. Deeply and utterly."

Audrey looked away from his penetrating gaze. "You said you loved Judith once."

Richard laughed deprecatingly. "That was a mere schoolboy's crush to what I feel for you. And I'll prove it." Richard slid to one knee before her and took her hand in both of his. He tenderly kissed her palm, then wrapped her fingers tight, as if to keep the kiss there. Audrey felt like the most honored lady in the land, like the queen herself.

Richard lifted his cobalt eyes, and Audrey gasped at the intensity in them. Her heart began pounding, crying out with joy.

"I pledge myself to you, and you alone," Richard said. "I'll keep you and care for you, in sickness and in health—"

Audrey had to stop this incredible, unexpected declaration of love before it went any farther. She could see where this conversation was leading, and she would not allow herself to even consider such a proposal. She sat up straighter, speaking quickly. "I will not become your mistress, Richard Langsforth. I said so before, and I still feel I can never risk—"

"Then, you must marry me."

Audrey's protest died in her throat. Her eyes widened impossibly huge as she stared at him in shock. "What—what did you say?"

His lips turned up in a wry grin. "Are you suddenly daft? I said marry me."

"You're the daft one! You're out of your mind!"

Richard's boyish face suddenly looked hurt, and Audrey had the urge to hug him and comfort him. "You don't want to marry me?"

"I—I—"

"That's what I thought." He smiled in satisfaction.

"But your parents—the earl and the countess, their friends—all those lords and ladies!"

"I don't give a hang about my parents!"

"But they would be furious! They would be shocked! I'm a commoner, if you haven't noticed, and a servant at that. A woman of no family. With no dowry. There's a world of difference between our stations."

"Oh, my family will shake their heads and roll their eyes, scream a little perhaps. Maybe disown me." He grinned as if it were a great joke. He rose and sat beside her once more, pulling her close.

"Is that why you want me to marry you, to shock them?"

"Of course not! You're wonderful and I love you." He dropped a kiss on the tip of her nose.

"Oh. You do?"

"Of course! Even if they disown me, I'll support you. I'll finish law school. I'm actually quite good at law. I have a gift for persuading people."

He gave her a brash grin, and Audrey had to agree. He was starting to make her believe in this outlandish idea.

"Once I start practicing," he continued enthusiastically, "we can buy a small cottage somewhere. Nothing fancy, I'm afraid, at least not at first."

He was already making plans for their future, as if this magical dream would actually happen! "You really mean it, don't you?"

He gave her an indulgent smile. "Do you think I'd want to marry you and raise babies with you and watch you grow old with me if I didn't love you?"

"I thought it was because you wanted me in your bed."

Audrey's gaze strayed to the full length of the soft mattress upon which they sat.

Richard's eyes followed. But he wasn't ready to think about the physical side of loving Audrey just yet. He was too overwhelmed with his discovery that he loved her, and with the incredible, marvelous idea of making her his wife. "Well, of course. We'll make love all the time. That's what lovers do."

"Is that what we are, lovers?"

"Certainly, if we love and desire each other. Unless, of course, you don't love me—"

"But I do. Truly I do."

"Then, that settles it." He grinned once more and leaned forward to kiss her. Audrey slipped quickly from his grasp. She needed to put distance between herself and Richard, for she knew she could never live with herself if she allowed Richard to marry her and did not tell him the full truth about herself.

"Audrey?" Richard asked in surprise.

She didn't speak for a moment. Richard had a sickening feeling that when she did speak, he wouldn't like what he would hear. She would reject him. She would scorn his vows of love. He had been a fool to so openly confess his feelings before being sure of hers. He would die a miserable and lonely man.

Audrey's first words shocked him by their nature, but relieved his heart nonetheless. "I'm a bastard. My mother brought a lawsuit against my father to make him pay for my upbringing, but he refused to acknowledge me. He was a simple cooper, a poor man."

She didn't feel she was good enough for him. He would have to relieve her mind of that concern. "Audrey, that doesn't matter to me. I still—"

"Let me finish." She continued to speak with her back to him. The tension in her stance, the way she wrapped herself in her arms, was testament to her distress. Her voice softened to the tone of one making a confession. "I matured early, and my bosom—which you've probably noticed—draws men's attention. Men think it means I'm free with my favors.

"The first man to think that was my stepfather. He kept

coming into my bed at night, even though it was in the loft not far from where he shared a bed with my mother. He would— touch me, and threaten to beat me if I told. One evening, when my mother was down with a stomach malady, he forced me to tumble with him. I had just turned thirteen.

"I tried to tell my mother, but he told her I had tempted him, undressed before him and teased him like a wanton. Mother was furious with me, and she sent me away. I lived hand-to-mouth for a while in the village, stealing what I could from the markets and table scraps from the slops left outside the nicer manor houses.

"I eventually found myself on the estate of a powerful gentleman. His butler caught me at my thieving and began to beat me. But the gentleman"—she sucked in a deep breath—"he rode up on a beautiful white horse and made him stop. He looked me up and down and offered me a post as a chambermaid. I was so excited by my good fortune. I thought he was a prince."

Her shoulders quivered, and Richard's hands tightened into fists. "So there I was, working as a chambermaid in a fine gentleman's home, in the countryside not far from London. I thought I was in heaven, for a time. Until the gentleman returned from business in London several months later. He spotted me again, and made advances to me. I tried not to let him catch me alone. I was terrified of denying him what he wanted, for I knew it would cost me my post. One night when he was drunk, he forced me to tumble with him. He came for me a few times after that. I couldn't think of how to escape him, and I had nowhere else to go.

"One eve, the gentleman came home extremely drunk. He stumbled across me before he found any of the other maids, whom he also used as he wished. The other women heard him coming and hid themselves. That night, he beat me harshly until I complied with his wishes, which I would prefer not to discuss."

Fury welled up inside Richard, a feeling he was growing increasingly familiar with on Audrey's behalf. But he said nothing, knowing Audrey needed to speak more than she needed to be comforted.

Her voice shook as she returned to her tale. "I managed to

run away that night, after he had finished with me. I came to London, as so many young people do, looking to make a new start. But there was no job to be had for one like me. By the time I arrived in the city, I was bedraggled, not dressed properly to apply as a chambermaid. But that work was one of only two things I now had experience in."

The pause that followed lasted too long. Richard wanted desperately to go to her, to hold her, but he held back, sensing her tale was not yet complete.

"I—I was starving, my meager coins had long run out, and begging got me nowhere. Men assumed that I was willing to provide services for their coin." Her voice dropped so low, Richard had to strain to hear her. "And so I did. I did it enough times to buy myself a decent dress. Then I applied for posts and found the position at Lord Ashton's house, as lady's maid to his young daughter."

Now that she had spoken the worst of her tale, her voice grew stronger. "I haven't sought out men since those days. I've dedicated myself to Judith, and raising her to be a proper gentlewoman. She has relied on me as no one ever has, and given my life meaning I never expected. I long ago decided there was no place in my life for men—or a man."

Richard's hands settled on her shoulders very gently. Audrey froze instantly at the contact. As if handling a precious, break-able statue, he turned her around and pulled her into his arms. He spoke gently into her ear. "I suppose you told me all this because you think it might make a difference in my feelings for you, and my proposal for your hand. It doesn't. I would never condemn you for what you were forced to do."

"There's something else, Richard." Her eyes were luminous with unshed tears as she gazed up at him. "There's something you want from me that I can't give."

"You mean you're not through with excuses yet, my sweet?" Richard asked with a tender smile. He was certain nothing she said would change his mind. Perhaps she was barren. He didn't care. He could do without children if it meant having her.

"I know you want a willing bed partner."

Richard's expression lost some of its softness, frown lines appearing between his eyebrows. "You aren't willing?"

She sighed. "I dislike bedding. But you make me feel it won't be too distasteful," she added hopefully.

Richard's eyes absorbed her completely honest expression. She truly believed this of herself, he could see. He didn't believe it for an instant. Throughout their tumultuous flirtation, she had responded fervently to every one of his kisses, every caress. She was certainly of a deeply passionate nature. She just didn't know it yet.

"There's something you don't know about *me*, Audrey," he said gravely. He slipped his hands up the column of her neck and gently held her face. "I'm a very patient man." He dropped kisses on her brow, her nose, her eyelids, moving slowly, undemandingly, only wanting to express his love for her.

Audrey began to feel soothed as he gently kissed her face, her tense muscles easing. He had not been repulsed by her confession. Hadn't been disgusted or disturbed. Didn't seem to think it mattered in the least. Tears pricked her eyelids; she felt so overwhelmed with love for this man, a man so unlike the others she had known.

Closing her eyes, she leaned her head back farther, welcoming the warmth of his lips on her face. His mouth settled on hers, and his kiss was exquisitely gentle, undemanding, not even asking to be returned. But she did return it, and soon the kiss turned passionate, recalling the other times they had embraced. Passion then denied could burn fiercely now, tonight.

When Richard broke the kiss, they were both breathing hard. "Let me love you, Audrey," Richard murmured in her ear.

"Aye, if you wish," she replied, her spine involuntarily stiffening at the prospect.

Richard vowed to give her all the time in the world. He continued to kiss her, running his hands up and down her back, underneath his own doublet, which she still wore about her shoulders. She raised her arms to encircle his neck, and the doublet fell to the floor. Audrey had forgotten about her slashed dress, until Richard's hand slipped up her rib cage, his palm forming against her bare nipple, which rapidly hardened in his hand. Audrey drew back, and her gaze met his.

It was as if Richard could read her mind. "Yes, Audrey,

you have a magnificent body, the body of a goddess. But that isn't what first attracted me to you."

"Oh? You didn't notice?" she asked in disbelief.

"I didn't think on it." He grinned. But his hand still hadn't stopped caressing her ample breast, and Audrey's words came out slightly breathless.

"Then, what was it that attracted you?"

"Those horrendous tongue lashings you gave me."

"Be serious."

"I am. You're the bravest woman I know, and not afraid to be honest. Then there's your tremendous spirit, and your loyalty to your lady—a hundred things. You looked as if you needed to be shown how to smile. I want to see you smile."

His hand slipped below her breast to her stomach. Suddenly he was tickling her. Audrey was so startled she gasped. Then she started to giggle. The laughter grew uncontrollable as his tickling grew relentless.

"Richard, stop, I can't stand any more," Audrey cried. She fought to free herself from his grasp, but Richard scooped her up in his arms and carried her to the bed.

"If you can't stand any more, then you must lie down. I wouldn't want you to fall."

"You mistake my meaning," she gasped in protest as he tossed her on the feather mattress. His hands came at her again, finding the most sensitive spots on her stomach. She allowed him this sweet torture, reveled in his laughter that drifted about her, echoing her own. His playfulness relieved her tension, and Audrey forgot to worry about what might come.

Finally, Richard ceased his torment. Audrey hadn't realized he had slipped onto the bed beside her. She gasped for air, enjoying the pleasure of his sturdy, muscled body lying against hers.

"Now that I have you in my power, woman, I'm going to drown you in kisses," he said lightly. His lips on hers left her breathless, then trailed down her collarbone and chest to that incredibly full, alluring breast. Audrey gasped as his tongue teased her large, dusky nipple. No man had ever drowned her in kisses. They had been after one thing, and this wasn't it.

Before she realized it, Richard had loosened the rest of her torn bodice and was now lavishing the same attention on her other breast. Audrey caressed his muscular arms and broad back, moaning at the torrent of sensations that poured through her body. He was touching her as no man ever had, and she was overwhelmed with a sudden desire for his attentions to continue, everywhere, to be swept away on the tide of desire that surged within her.

Richard understood. He helped her slip out of her dress, chemise and what was left of her slashed corset. Soon she was clothed in nothing but her hose. She trembled as he gazed at her, afraid his animal passion would suddenly overwhelm him and he would be upon her fiercely, without warning, heedless of hurting her. Instead, Richard's fingers slipped under the garter on her left leg and slid it down past her delicately arched foot. He tossed it aside. Rolling down her stocking, he kissed the length of her creamy white leg as it became exposed to him.

His beard tickled her as his lips traced a path of fire along her skin. He stroked her hips, caressed her thighs, her calves. Everywhere he touched his lips followed, equally caressing. He cradled the sole of her foot and took each of her toes into his mouth, sucking gently. Audrey gasped at the surprisingly exquisite sensation. His attentions were so obviously intended to pleasure her, tears burned behind her eyes at his generosity and love.

And pleasure her it did. After giving luxurious attention to each toe, each foot, he shifted his attention, moving his hands and mouth higher, closer to her womanhood, where his fingers began caressing her with deliciously delicate strokes so light, so gentle, Audrey did not withdraw in fear from his intimate touch.

Unconsciously, she began to arch up on the bed, seeking more than Richard was yet giving her. She was after an elusive something, something out of reach, something she knew wouldn't come from the act itself, for it never had before.

He again stretched himself beside her, his lips engaging hers while his fingers worked their delicious magic. Audrey buried her fingers in his hair, pressed him closer. The sensations grew so great, she had to force herself not to tear at his hair. ''Richard,'' she panted, her head rolling back and forth on the down pillow as her hips strained against his questing fingers. ''Please.''

Richard didn't miss his cue. He moved to his knees and stripped off his shirt. He shoved down his breeches, freeing his manhood, then discarded this last article of clothing that lay between them, tossing it to the floor.

Audrey braced herself as she eyed the upright, demanding strength of him. This was the part she hated. She prayed he would be done with it quickly, and he wouldn't be too disappointed in her afterward.

Murmuring endearments to her all the while, Richard stretched himself above her, not touching her, supporting himself on his arms. He began moving back and forth in imitation of the rhythm of mating, brushing her engorged nipples with the tawny pelt of his chest, stroking his manhood across her sex, engaging her eyes with his in open acknowledgment of their shared delight.

But still he withheld himself from joining with her, until she bucked beneath him, until she spread her legs in invitation, until she cried out for him to relieve the exquisite torment. Only then did he accept what she was at last ready to give him, what he had so long been seeking from her.

His long, slow thrust within her took her completely by surprise. A river of pure fire, sensation beyond measure, flowed into her body, into her being. She gazed up in wonder at the man arching above her. In amazement, she reached up and clutched at his tightly bunched shoulders, stroked his tawny chest.

He smiled into her eyes, still deeply nestled within her, sharing with her their moment of union. Then just as gradually he withdrew from her. Audrey cried out in sheer pleasure.

As Richard repeated the motion, Audrey found herself wrapping her legs tightly around his slender waist. She urged him onward, no longer content with the slow, delicious torment he was causing. She wanted more, harder, faster, was driven out of her mind with need.

Richard fed her desire, gave it free rein, allowed her to make demands on him, and gave himself to her commands in return.

His thrusts were for her, to give her pleasure, his intent to hold back his own culmination until she had achieved hers. He had never given himself so unselfishly, and it gave him more pleasure than he had ever thought possible in bedding a woman.

Audrey arched hard against him, pushing his hips against hers with her legs, burying his manhood deep within her, deeper still. Richard watched in pleasure as she cried out at the pinnacle of release, holding him, scratching at him, out of control completely as she bucked against him. Seeing her so open to him, so fulfilled, was the purest aphrodisiac, and he quickly came inside her. Before she had finished with the highest plane of sensation and begun to spiral back to earth, he was there with her. He came with her to the soft, golden completion, more fulfilled in body and soul than he had ever been.

He pulled her against him, cradled her gently, held her close in perfect contentment as they both waited for their heartbeats to return to normal, their breaths to steady.

Audrey spoke first. "Richard."

"Aye?"

"I no longer dislike bedding."

Richard chuckled, and tightened his arms around her.

Audrey continued, "It's as if I've never been with a man before. I didn't know I could feel so—loved. I've never felt this way before."

"Neither have I."

Audrey lifted her head, her lovely eyes wide. "You've been with so many women—"

"None like you. I love you, Audrey, and I know now that I truly have never been in love before. I wanted other women, but I wanted them for what it meant for me. I want you for yourself."

A slow, sweet grin spread over her lush mouth.

"What's that for?" he asked in amused wonder, outlining her lovely full lips with his finger. He had made her smile, and his happiness was unbounded. But her next words sent him even higher.

"I'd be happy to marry you, Richard Langsforth."

Chapter 16

Marcus stood with a different woman a short while later in front of the cheerful fire in the hearth, which burned in discordant merriment to Judith's depressed mood.

Standing nearby, she sipped her wine without tasting it. She tried not to stare openly as the voluptuous redhead threw her arms around Marcus' neck and kissed him full on the lips. Marcus returned the kiss willingly, his large, sensuous hands fitting snugly about her corseted waist.

Judith's pain at the sight began to turn into anger. Marcus certainly did not have to do this in front of her! The woman was named Susan Dirby, and Judith knew she was married. But her husband was nowhere about.

Walter stepped beside Judith and gave her a tender kiss. "Perhaps next year, we'll be celebrating Twelfth Night together at my home," he said softly into her ear.

She smiled up at Walter as brightly as she could. But she couldn't keep her eyes from flicking toward Marcus. Marcus looked past her the minute her gaze fell on him, then made some remark into Susan's ear which caused her to gasp and blush.

Judith took another strong gulp of her mulled wine and

decided she hated the woman, all the women here, with a lividness she had never felt before. Every one of them seemed to be eyeing Marcus, with one thing on their minds.

But it only seemed to get worse. Somehow Marcus and Susan came to stand right beside her. Judith couldn't help hearing every word of their intimate discussion. It was as if Marcus intended her to hear it, intended to hurt her.

"You will come, then?" Susan asked anxiously. "He's gone most of the day."

"I give my best performances in the afternoons," Marcus replied drolly.

The woman almost swooned with pleasure. "Then, we must set a date."

"Shh. Not here," Marcus replied softly—but loud enough for Judith to hear. "I'll send a courier, a poem. The time and place will be part of the poem."

"What marvelous fun! I can hardly wait." Susan hung on Marcus' arm as if afraid he would run off. Marcus didn't appear to have any intention of leaving her side. Judith watched in dismay as the woman rubbed her large breasts against Marcus' arm, her exposed cleavage heaving with each breath she took, revealing how aroused she was.

"Nor can I. Now, if you'll excuse me, I think I see your husband coming this way." Marcus slipped his arm from her grasp, but not before trailing his fingers along her generous cleavage. Susan pressed her hands against her pale, freckled skin where Marcus had touched her, and sighed deeply.

As Marcus passed Judith, he glanced disinterestedly at her.

A violent wave of nausea struck Judith, and she thought she was going to be sick right there. Did this mean Marcus didn't love her anymore? Did he ever love her like he had said? She pressed her hand to her stomach and took a deep breath to steady herself.

"Judith, are you all right? You're looking pale," commented a concerned Walter.

"I'm quite fine. Look. A new dance is forming. Let's take part."

"You're going to wear me out, Judith. I'm not as young as you, you know."

Judith pulled him into the ring of dancers. As the musicians began the lively tune, she began to dance with more abandon than she had all evening. Many of the guests were just as heedless of proper courtly behavior, for it was growing late, and they had consumed vast quantities of wine and ale.

But Judith had a different reason for wanting to expend energy. She was furious with Marcus. Despite how she had longed to see him again, he was acting as if she meant nothing to him. He wasn't even trying to be near her. Why, if he had shown the slightest inclination, Judith would be joining him in darkened corners to talk, perhaps even sneaking off to rendezvous with him in one of the upstairs chambers she had heard the lord had reserved for that purpose.

But Marcus seemed perfectly able to enjoy himself without her. More than able. He was having the time of his life, what with the exquisite noblewomen hanging on his every word. Even the men appeared fascinated by him. His charisma seemed to fill the room, center the party around him. And she was no part of it.

Well, Judith determined, her gaze turning to Walter Kennington across from her. Walter at least was gazing at her, with a longing Judith understood quite well. She knew if she so much as crooked her little finger, Walter would follow her up the stairs. She had no intention of doing that, but she could certainly show Marcus that she was no more affected by his presence in the room than he was by hers.

The song ended, and an even livelier tune began. Those not dancing were engaged in spirited discussions, some arguments, even a brawl or two that Lord Hunsdon's servants made certain to break up before the participants did any damage to his fine home.

The tenor of the evening had decidedly changed. What had started out as a formal occasion had transformed into one of high festivity. Some couples vanished upstairs for a private celebration. Many of the older guests departed, and men uninterested in flirtation or dancing had disappeared into a room in another part of the house to gamble, including her father and Lord Mowbray. Judith was relieved that Lord Mowbray was no longer about, for his presence in the room had been one more thing to worry about.

Judith noticed that Susan was no longer hanging about Marcus, for her husband had returned to her side. Instead, her place had been taken by a petite blonde not much older than Judith. Marcus had joined her in a dance, and he was spinning the woman about right in front of her.

At the end of the dance, he swung the blonde up high in the air, and she screamed prettily before landing right in his arms. Judith refused to watch what came after. She turned her back on Marcus and threw her arms about Lord Kennington's neck, pressing her body full against his.

Taken by surprise, Lord Kennington took a moment to respond, but soon he was avidly kissing her, as she intended. *Let Marcus stew on this,* she thought with satisfaction. But she wondered if he would even notice.

Marcus was indeed watching her over the head of the silly woman who kept chattering at him. Judith had definitely seen what he was doing with the other women at the party, and she was repaying the favor in kind. Marcus knew he should be glad, but he had the urge to pull Kennington off of her and smash his face in.

Instead, he tore himself away from the blonde and retrieved a full mug of ale from a passing servant. He downed it in one gulp and wiped the froth from his mouth. His knees weren't hurting him too badly right now, since he had stayed off his feet most of the night. If he continued dancing, they might begin to throb in protest despite the ale he was consuming.

But he didn't care. He was suddenly intent on dancing, intent on dancing with one particular woman.

Judith was stunned to find herself in Marcus' arms. He had practically torn her from Kennington's embrace. He had acted so distant all evening, she had even doubted that he still loved her. But the tight set of his jaw told her he was hiding emotions she could only guess at.

"You seem to be enjoying yourself," he said as he swung beside her with a kick and returned once more to face her.

"As do you."

"I make it a point to enjoy myself. You, however, make it a point to be a good girl."

"I'm not that good, as well you know."

"I see it differently."

"Oh, do you?" Judith saw that she had finally affected him. He was coming back to her again. Perhaps this had all been a stupid attempt to get her to forget him. It had infuriated her, but it had not even begun to make her fall out of love with him.

"Aye," Marcus continued, his tone biting. "You are so *damned* good, you think everyone is as good as you."

"I do not! I've seen *certain* people tonight behaving less than good."

Marcus smirked. "Oh, so what's good enough for you isn't good enough for me?"

"Lord Kennington isn't married."

"Yet."

"I think you're drunk."

"Not drunk enough."

So he did care. Judith's heart took flight. "Marcus, I—"

He teeth gritted. "Don't even think about saying it. You're the good little girl, remember? It's a role you're very *good* at. I wouldn't recommend changing it now; you might fall flat on your face, and I doubt pratfalls are your style."

Marcus swung her around so hard, she stumbled and almost did fall. Marcus caught her, but before she could even think about being held close in his arms, he shoved her hard toward Kennington.

She stumbled once more, but kept her balance. She straightened herself, inwardly fuming at such treatment from Marcus, a man she had thought would always treat her like a lady.

Marcus watched her stumble toward Kennington, and suddenly became furious with himself. The ale was definitely making him lose control, lose hold of his intentions.

He was actually angry with Judith because she had it in her power to be with him, but couldn't give up her title, her birthright, couldn't disappoint her father.

He was furious with her for thinking he ought to be pining for her while she flirted with her future husband.

He was livid with her for a million small things, the way she allowed Kennington to touch her arms, her back, even kiss her. The way she smiled at the man, her face alight. The way she ignored his attempts to make her jealous. The way she was taking part in the dancing with sensual abandon. She was killing him by being herself, and he almost hated her for it.

Marcus looked up as a group of people around Judith started pointing toward her and laughing. Judith looked around in consternation. Soon half the guests were looking her way.

"Why, you're right under the mistletoe, Judith!" said Lord Hunsdon, smiling at her jovially. "You know what that means."

It wasn't all that funny, thought Judith, despite the enjoyment the guests got out of it. She almost moved away, but thought better of it. "That means I get a kiss," she said, smiling demurely. She glanced around at the group, seeing she had their attention.

"Who will she choose?" asked the little blonde.

"Me! Me!" cried a young nobleman Judith had given a few dances to. The man started running toward her until his wife stuck out her foot and tripped him. Everyone laughed.

"No, I have someone else in mind," Judith said with a smile. Everyone waited, watching the fun, certain she would select Lord Walter. Instead, she looked right at Marcus and smiled with the most seductive look she could muster. Marcus stared at her in shock. She relished his expression for a lingering moment, then slowly reached out her hand and offered it to Walter.

Walter didn't hesitate a moment. He pulled her into his arms and gave her a hearty kiss while the guests roared their approval.

The kiss seemed to last forever. When Walter finally released her, Judith was gasping for air. The man had crushed her lips, her dress, everything. He had even thrust his tongue deep in her throat in his enthusiasm, nearly strangling her.

But she smiled up at him as endearingly as possible, his arm tight around her waist. "You must give me your answer, Judith," he whispered in her ear. "Waiting will be hard enough even without a long betrothal. Unless, perhaps, tonight—" Mercifully, his suggestion was cut off by a call from one of the guests.

"Music!" the man cried. The musicians began playing once more, with lutes, pipes, tambourines and citterns, and the dancing resumed in earnest. In between, other couples rushed to try out the mistletoe.

Judith was in the middle of being swung around by Walter in a lively dance when she saw Marcus in a hot embrace under the mistletoe with Lady Alice. She tripped and fell over Walter's feet.

He caught her before she hit the floor. "Too much ale?" he asked her lightly.

Judith laughed, her face tilted close to his. "Not nearly enough," she said. She spun near the kegs at the side of the hall and retrieved a mug of ale from a nearby table—someone's mug, she had no idea whose, and the guest probably didn't remember leaving it there, anyway. She gulped it down quickly before rejoining Walter in the dance.

The dancing turned even more riotous as she was passed from partner to partner. Someone cried out instructions, and the guests formed two circles, the men on the outside, the women inside as they began a complex dance where the partners interchanged almost as fast the music moved. Judith gritted her teeth each time Marcus ended up being her partner, but did her best not to show any change in her reaction. He certainly didn't.

Then someone—Judith thought it was that young nobleman again—came up with the bright idea that the musicians should stop the music suddenly so whichever couple ended up under the mistletoe had to kiss their partner. He was looking right at her when he said it. His young wife elbowed him in the ribs.

But the guests loved the idea, most of them too drunk to care. Kissing was a longtime English custom, after all, and a kiss for luck under the mistletoe would only increase their good cheer in the new year.

After a few turns around, Judith, fortifying herself with even more ale, ended up under the mistletoe with the young gentle-man—she knew he had arranged with the musicians when to stop the music. She turned her face just in time so the young man kissed her cheek. The other guests roared.

After a few more drinks, Judith forgot how many times she ended up under the mistletoe, and who she had kissed. She didn't care when Walter got a brief kiss from Alice, though she thought she ought to care. But then, she didn't even care anymore when she ended up as Marcus' partner as the inter-twined rings of the dance passed each other. On the next pass, she noticed Lord Hunsdon beside the musicians, a devilish grin on his face. Then the music suddenly stopped.

Judith found herself face-to-face with Marcus, and waited for the music to start again so she could move off, until she realized people were hooting for them to hurry up and kiss. Her gaze flicked upward, and she saw to her dismay that they were directly under the cluster of mistletoe.

She met his aloof gray eyes and determined then and there not to let him bother her in the least. She would prove to him she could as easily do without his attentions as he so plainly was doing without hers.

Marcus moved his face closer, his lips over hers, then directed them to land on her cheek. Judith anticipated his move and turned her head so his lips landed full on hers, anxious to show him she could easily kiss him and have it mean nothing, as it so plainly meant nothing to him.

She instantly realized her mistake as the sensation of kissing him went straight to her head. The feel of his lips on hers burned her, consumed her, filling her drunk brain with an even sweeter intoxicant. She found herself folding up against him, her arms around his shoulders, and was dimly aware that he was pressing her as close.

Somehow the kiss deepened. Whether she did it or he, she had no idea and didn't care. His tongue was stroking hers, sending waves of pleasure through her body. Walter never had and never would kiss her like this, she knew with a certainty. Marcus had hurt her, embarrassed her, insulted her, and still she craved him. She was a fool, a besotted fool, and she wanted to consume him.

Neither one was aware that the noise in the hall had abated substantially as the guests watched with interest to see how long the kiss would last. ''If kissing under the mistletoe means they'll marry, then these two look like they're already on their honeymoon!'' called out one man. His companions hooted with laughter.

The guests started hooting rhythmically, louder and louder, as if counting off how long the embrace was going to last. The increasing noise penetrated Marcus' brain, fogged as it was with drink and arousal. He broke the kiss and stepped back from her, realizing he had made a critical mistake. In one moment he had wiped out all of his hard work this evening.

As the party resumed around them, Judith crossed to the curtained entrance of a darkened anteroom off the gallery, sending him a meaningful look over her shoulder. Marcus could read her expression as clearly as if she had spoken. Like a man possessed, he dutifully obeyed her summons.

The moment he slipped through the curtain, she was in his arms, their embrace resuming in a frenzy of passionate kisses. Marcus crushed her hard against him, devouring her mouth with his own.

''Marcus,'' she gasped when he released her mouth to trail fire along her face, her neck, across her tantalizing cleavage. ''I knew you never intended to be distant. I knew it. Those ladies mean nothing to you, do they?''

''Nothing, nothing.'' Marcus buried his lips in her hair, breathed once more of her intoxicating fragrance.

''Do you think I would believe you so fickle, Marcus? I know you were only using those women to get back at me for being with Lord Walter. I hurt you, and you were striking back. But I know even if you bed them, it will never match what we shared.''

Despite himself, Marcus found pleasure in her unshaken faith in him, though his plan had failed. He reflected ruefully on how he had believed that a few well-placed scenes designed to arouse her jealousy would completely turn her from him, and turn her toward Kennington. He had badly overestimated his ability to control his heart, badly overlooked her own sensual powers of persuasion.

Judith breathed deeply, her lips inches from his own, her arms locked around his neck. "Marcus, remember when you suggested that we run away together, and I refused?"

"A man doesn't forget such things, Judith," Marcus said thickly, sudden irrational hope blooming in his chest.

"I want to now," she said, searching his eyes with hers, revealing her love for him in every look, every word. "I want you to possess me again. Tonight, and forever. All of this, it's nothing but shadow and show. But we're real."

"Ah, darling Judith," Marcus murmured. "I know you too well to think you'd be happy married to me."

"I feel such a hunger for you, inside—" she cried.

"Shh." Marcus laid his fingers on her lips. "Don't say it, darling, or you might convince me."

"That's what I want to do, convince you." She stroked his cheek. "I can never marry another man, Marcus, I realize that now."

"Your father wishes it."

Judith's eyes darkened. "I know if I defy him, it will hurt him, Marcus. But what is that compared to what we have? How can he ask me to give you up in order to make him happy? It isn't fair, and I'll prove it to you."

Marcus was not convinced. When he spoke, his voice was heavy with sadness. "Darling, it will never work."

Judith refused to listen, didn't really hear him. "I'm going to leave here soon, return home, and I want you to come to me," she said audaciously. "Come to my home. Visit me in my bedchamber."

"Aye, milady," Marcus murmured hotly.

"Soon, then." Judith kissed her fingertips and trailed them along his lips. Marcus clasped her hand and buried his mouth in her palm. A moment later she had slipped from his grasp and was gone.

Marcus collapsed in the nearest chair and hung his head. His hands shook badly, and he tried to still them on his knees. He was again completely under her spell. He had miscalculated badly, thinking he could turn her against him so easily. He should never have allowed them to enter into this battle of wills, for it had only heightened the latent passion that always lay between them, set fire to the embers of their desire.

It didn't work, it didn't work, came the litany in his drink-fogged brain. *You failed.* If only he had stuck to his original plan, made her believe he was nothing but a rake who had fallen completely out of love with her, perhaps had never even been in love with her. He had thought to make her see he was over her, show her that any woman could take her place, any woman here tonight.

But their love was too strong, their passion too undeniable. Judith simply had too much faith in their love. That had been his mistake all along, attempting to be subtle. He needed to cut to the heart of her to succeed in turning her from him. Nothing less would do.

Why did he have to kill what lay between them? Why could he not accept her offer? They could be gone tonight, go to the nearest country parish, be wed before morning. It could be done, had been done many times before. Secret marriages were almost commonplace.

Of course, what came after often was no honeymoon, depending on who was involved. Sometimes even the queen herself was wroth, if the bride or groom was one of her favorites. In this case, that wasn't a concern. Just that damnable father of hers. But Marcus wasn't afraid of him. Not afraid. He could do it; they could. It would be a finished act before anyone was the wiser.

He breathed deeply to get his raging passion under control enough to think clearly. Once they were wed, where would they go? To his family home in Lankenshire, perhaps. That would do for a start. Then what? He couldn't work in the theater if he wasn't in London. If they stayed in London, they would be near Lord Ashton, and Lord Kennington, who might also be wrathful. Marcus was not a cowardly man, but he was realistic enough to know their power far outweighed his. If they desired to destroy him—destroy them—they could find a way.

Beyond that, however, above all that, lay Judith herself. What would become of her married to an out-of-work theater actor? Would she travel the countryside with him while he played town taverns for a few coins? She was not destined to be the wife of an itinerant musician. She would find it romantic at first, perhaps, but after a while, months, even years, she would come to hate her life, come, perhaps, to hate him for dragging her to such a low. Even assuming they remained in London, she had no concept what it would be like, living with him on his actor's salary.

And her father—she would never forgive Marcus if he caused such a breach between them. She was too devoted to the man. Even though she tried to convince herself she could make that sacrifice, Marcus knew better.

As his desire and his common sense waged war in his drink-fogged mind, Marcus realized how completely Judith had changed his view of the world. He had never thought about another person's fate as hard as he thought about Judith's, never thought of sacrificing any of his personal pleasure for another person's welfare. Judith had affected him, changed him with her love, made him care so much he would do anything to keep her from making the worst mistake of her life.

Anything.

Chapter 17

As soon as practical, Judith asked Walter Kennington to escort her home, pleading a headache. Kennington was not about to let her get away easily, however. Once in the carriage he lost no time in confronting her.

"Dearest Judith, I couldn't help but notice—along with everyone else in the room—the inordinately improper kiss you gave to that actor, Sinclair," he said tensely, his hands fisted on his thighs.

"It was nothing, Walter," said Judith, looking out the carriage window. His possessive tone irritated her. She had more important matters to think about than offending Walter Kennington's sensibilities, such as arranging to run off with Marcus. "Everyone was kissing everybody, you know that as well as I."

"Still, it was highly improper. One would almost think you'd been intimate with him."

Judith shot him a look of defiance. "You're not my betrothed yet, Walter, to judge my actions so."

"Speaking of our betrothal, I have danced on the end of your string long enough, Judith."

"Are you tired of waiting?" she said, wondering if he could hear the hope in her voice.

"Aye." The carriage rattled to a stop, and Kennington's groom opened the carriage door for her. Judith stepped out. "I will return first thing in the morning, Judith," Walter continued. "And I will expect your answer."

Kennington gave the signal, and the carriage departed into the night.

Marcus stepped down the front stairs of Hunsdon House and pulled his cloak about him. The air was cold, but not unreasonably so, considering it was almost midnight. He could see his breath, but knew the walk to Bishopsgate where Judith lived would warm his blood, if not his heart. He had waited a half hour before leaving the celebration, not wanting to draw too much attention to the timing of his disappearance so soon after Judith's.

A carriage pulled past him up the drive, and a man leapt out. "Sinclair! I have a matter to settle with you."

Marcus turned in annoyance. "Kennington." He waited while Walter Kennington came closer, irritated beyond measure at being detained at this crucial point in the evening. He had a chore to do, and he wanted to complete it before he again was swayed from his course.

Without warning, Kennington threw a sabre at Marcus, its deadly silver blade glinting in the golden light of the lanterns illuminating the drive. Marcus caught it automatically. Damn, he thought, dueling with Kennington was not what he needed.

Kennington was clearly livid. He moved into a fighting stance. "You have offended a lady, taken rude advantage of her innocence, and I am calling you out," he said with brazen confidence.

"I'm not interested," Marcus said, ready to toss the sabre back.

"That cowardly, are we?" Kennington taunted, his lips curled up in a humorless smile. "Too ill-bred to take up arms?"

Marcus set his jaw, furious that the idiot before him should be keeping him from doing him a favor, a favor the man would never even know about. He decided it was best to get it over with. He tossed his woolen cloak on the nearby lawn and moved into a defensive stance.

Kennington immediately attacked, furiously lashing out at Marcus, who parried quickly but began to lose ground. But Marcus had no interest in continuing this contest beyond what was necessary. As soon as practical, he took the offensive, pressing Kennington back with a series of rapid thrusts. "You are an idiot, Kennington. But I will forgive you since you are acting on Judith's behalf."

"Hah! What would a despicable rake like you know about protecting a sweet woman like Lady Ashton?" panted Kennington, slicing his sabre toward Marcus' chest.

Marcus leapt out of the blade's way. "More than you'll ever know," he replied through gritted teeth, again taking the offensive with a thrust that narrowly missed Kennington's thigh.

"I'm going to settle with you, sir, make you sorry"—Kennington sliced toward Marcus and was instantly repelled with a clanging parry—"sorry you ever laid a hand on her." Their blades locked a moment, each man pressing hard against the other, their faces inches away. "I will delight in bringing you low," Kennington said through gritted teeth. "Howard can have Mowbray, but you are mine!"

"Am I?" Marcus wondered at Kennington's remark, but didn't have time to contemplate it. He silently thanked Shakespeare for making his players train in arms so their battle scenes would play out realistically. He shoved Kennington back hard and moved into a blinding offensive, his sabre almost invisible as it sliced the night air. He was tired of Kennington's show of gallantry, sick to death of the man. He swung his blade up in a hard spiral and sent Kennington's sabre spinning into the night.

Empty-handed, Kennington stepped back in shock and embarrassment as his weapon landed with a clatter on the gravel drive five feet away.

Marcus immediately tossed his own weapon away. It clanged discordantly against the first. He turned his back on Kennington and retrieved his cape, then strode off.

* * *

The balcony door swung inward, and a cloaked figure slipped through. The light from the full moon behind him outshone the meager candlelight of the room, leaving him in shadow. A stray wind caught at his cloak, swirling it hard against his lean legs. For an instant, Judith thought he looked almost devilish, cloaked as he was in the black of the night.

But he had come. She rose quickly from the bed, her heart pounding in excitement. "Marcus, my darling."

Marcus lifted his hands. "Stop. Come no nearer." Judith paused a few feet from him. She opened her mouth to speak, but Marcus anticipated her questions. "Shh. Say nothing. Just do as I bid."

Judith nodded, her wide eyes full of trust. Marcus felt his confidence in his ability to carry out his plan begin to waver. This angered him, for he had barely begun. He avoided looking in her innocent doe eyes, which threatened to melt his resolve. He turned from her to light the tapers in the candelabra by her bedside. More light would surely add to her shame. His back still to her, he issued a terse command. "Remove your bedgown and kneel on the bed."

Judith was confused by his actions, by his manner, but her desire for him was so great, any concern she might have felt weighed nothing against her anticipation of being once again in his arms. She felt no trepidation or concern. She did as he bid, slipping her gown down off her shoulders, beginning to feel almost sinfully erotic at the pleasure of fulfilling such an intimate command. Whatever Marcus was planning, she trusted him completely and knew it would only result in exquisite pleasure for them both.

Her bedgown pooled silently at her feet, and she stepped from it. As she knelt on the silken sheets facing him, she watched Marcus remove his cloak and fling it aside. He casually set each foot on a nearby chest and methodically unlaced his boots, throwing each in turn after the cloak. His clothes soon followed, and he was standing before her fully aroused, wearing nothing but the gold pendant she had returned to him.

Only then did he approach the bedside. Judith expected him

to pull her into his arms, to join her in a warm embrace that would lead to love as they had experienced it in the inn that glorious night.

But Marcus issued another command. "Turn over and grasp the woodwork on your headboard." The request was so unexpected, Judith disobeyed his command to silence. "Marcus, this is rather odd. I don't understand—"

Marcus reached over and grasped her hands in his, then pulled them forward so her fingers rested on the intricate carved wood. "Grasp it." Judith adjusted her body more comfortably, which left her kneeling facing the headboard with her back to him.

"Do you have a surprise for me, is that it?"

"Shh!" Marcus commanded once more. Then he joined her on the bed. He knelt behind her and grasped the front of her thighs none too gently in his large, hard hands.

He drew her hips backward, and suddenly he was thrusting deep within her. Judith cried out in shock and arched away. Nevertheless, she was surprisingly ready for this intimacy despite his lack of foreplay, Marcus noticed as he sank deep within her moist recesses.

But he also noticed how tense she was as he used her. She was startled and, he hoped, disgusted. His silent, cold domination of her was surely more than a gentle lady such as she could bear without complaint.

Judith did seem repelled, or at least frightened, as he thrust back and forth rhythmically into her. But she uttered not a word of complaint.

She had not expected this from Marcus, who had always treated her with the utmost respect. Perhaps she should have, considering how Marcus had positioned her nude body. Why he had chosen to love her in this way she could not fathom, but she was willing to meet his needs in their time together in whatever way he demanded, particularly when the sensations he was sending through her were so exquisite, so intense, she could hardly stand it. She belonged with Marcus, and nothing they did to pleasure each other was wrong.

After a moment, to Marcus' consternation Judith began to join in with a rhythm of her own, her alabaster back arching as she offered him deeper and deeper access. Her knuckles grew white, and she appeared glad to have the carved woodwork of the headboard to cling to as he pounded ever harder into her.

She groaned, and picked up his rhythm, which Marcus increased as their mutual excitement escalated out of control. His hands clutched harder at her white thighs, and he moaned as if in agony. He had meant to maintain complete mastery of his emotions, but he could not help himself. She transported him out of his mind.

Neither said a word, there being no need as the pleasure swept them forward into oblivion. Judith's soft pants became louder, increased, until a cry issued from her throat, a sound so wanton, so utterly unladylike, that it startled Marcus, and he quickly spilled his seed inside her.

Marcus collapsed upon her, his desire spent, his sweat-slicked body pressing into her own moist curves. Marcus had never believed such unabashed carnal lust lay within Judith's heart. Her golden hair was tossed aside, revealing beads of perspiration along her soft nape.

Marcus had the overpowering urge to lay kisses along that tender skin, to enfold her in his arms, his heart was bursting so with his love for her. But she must think of him as an unaffected participant except in a purely sexual way, and even that with much less passion than he had ever before displayed.

Now that the edge of his desire had been spent, he was able to think once more of his purpose in being here tonight. He pulled himself from her and knelt on the bed. He was angry with himself for assuming this act alone would disgust her enough to anger her, to precipitate a confrontation of the sort he was determined should take place between them before the night was through.

Judith lay where she was, shocked and amazed at herself and her reaction to Marcus' purely physical loving. He had said nothing to her, touched her body as little as possible, yet she had succumbed to ecstasy as easily as she ever had with him.

He was no longer touching her, but she could hear his heavy

breathing behind her. Gradually he brought it under control.
When next he spoke, his tone was remote.

"Your scarves. Where do you keep them?"

"Scarves?" Judith spoke breathlessly, still affected by his
loving, by how he had come on her like a wild animal in heat,
and by how she had responded in kind. She turned her head
to where he now stood by the bedside in all his naked male
glory. She drank in his well-defined legs, his muscle-ridged
chest rising and falling with every breath. His face was drawn
and tense, wearing a mysterious expression unlike any she had
seen before. He was more enigmatic and distant than he had
ever been. Perversely, this aroused her.

"My scarves are in that chest." She pointed weakly, still
exhausted from passion. "Why?"

She watched as Marcus opened the chest and retrieved a
handful of her brightly colored scarves. He returned to the
bedside. "On your back," he commanded. Judith thought his
tone similar to what a father would use to a child about to be
punished. She grew bewildered again, but if whatever he
planned had been anything like their first encounter, she was
perfectly willing to comply.

Marcus had grasped both ends of a scarf and spun it until it
formed a soft rope. He leaned over and took her nearest arm
in his hands, then tied her wrist to the corner of the headboard.
Judith gasped as she realized his intent. "Marcus, is this something you always do with women? I'm not sure I think it's a
good idea."

"It's a good idea," he said, again sounding remote. But his
eyes burned with unholy fire as they played across her body.
Judith relaxed and let him continue, her confusion over his
intent squelched by her love and trust for him. She knew he
would never hurt her. An unfamiliar sense of eroticism began
to grow within her as he finished tying her ankles to each
bedpost and she realized she was completely at his mercy. But
the bonds were not uncomfortable. Marcus stood by the bedside,
and Judith blushed at the look in his eyes as he gazed upon
her. She felt shockingly wanton, and as she began to anticipate
his next move, a fresh flush of heat coursed through her.

Marcus saw her reaction and prayed it wouldn't last. She

may be titillated now, but when he delivered his final coup de grace, she would be appalled at what she had let him do to her, he was sure of it. No well-bred lady would be able to look back on such a night, on such acts, and not be appalled.

Marcus settled himself between her thighs and scooped up her hips in his hands. His mouth went straight to her femininity, and his tongue set to its delicious work. Judith moaned, her hips arching in pleasure. Marcus continued his assault until she was thrashing on the bed. He lifted his head, now using his hand to keep her at the same threshold of exquisite tension. "Do you want me, woman?" he asked as coolly as he could.

"Aye, you know I do," Judith cried, her eyes on him. "Take me, Marcus. Don't leave me hanging like this."

"Are you begging me?"

"Marcus, please . . ."

"Beg me, Judith. Beg me to end this torment."

"I beg you, Marcus. Take me now, please."

"Say it again."

"Marcus, I beg you, please, take me now. Finish this before I go out of my mind!"

Satisfied at last by her acquiescence, Marcus thrust himself full into her. Judith arched her hips against his as much as she was able, bound as she was.

Once more, Marcus was shocked by her willingness, her raw sensuality, her lack of shame over her desire for him. He kept his body from touching hers once again and could see Judith's thighs quivering as they strained against the bonds toward ecstasy, her arms stretching the scarves taut as if she wanted to pull him against her.

He would not give her that intimacy. He would only satisfy her lust, he vowed. But he was finding his determination wavering the more he laid eyes on the woman he loved as she rocked in the throes of passion. He allowed one hand to settle on her chest possessively, his other hand supporting his body by her side. He closed his eyes so as not to gaze into her face, for then he would lose all his resolve.

The fierce culmination of their passion was as great as before, greater, and as they spiraled down together, Marcus prayed she would soon realize what he had done to her and begin to feel ashamed and angry.

This time he did not collapse upon her, for the intimacy would have been too great. He lifted himself away and leaned against the footboard of the bed. He let his head drop back and waited for her to come to her senses enough to begin to feel humiliated. On no account would he look in her eyes.

"Marcus," Judith panted, still short of breath. "Will you free me now?"

"Aye." As dispassionately as possible, Marcus leaned over her and began to untie each of her bonds from around her ankles and wrists. Once she was free, she would react to what he had done with anger and mortification. Then he would go ahead with the rest of his plan.

Judith sat up in bed, stunned by what had happened, but not in the least ashamed. Marcus looked somewhat ashamed, she decided, but there had certainly been no harm done. Except that things had been uneven. In fact—

She slipped off the bed and stood near where Marcus rested, one hand buried in his thick hair. He avoided looking at her. Without a word, she took his nearest ankle in her hand and began to tie it to one of the scarves dangling off a bedpost at the foot of the bed.

"Judith, what are you doing?" Marcus asked in consternation.

"I'm repaying the favor, sweet."

Marcus was unable to tell if she was angry with him. Perhaps so. Perhaps this was her way of letting him know how angry. He thought if he played out what she intended, he might get her to reveal pent up anger and frustration at how he had humiliated her. It was worth trying, since nothing seemed to be going as he had expected.

"Lie down," Judith commanded. Marcus did as she bid, and soon he was bound as she had been, his large body taking up much more of the bed than she had, fairly dominating it.

Judith knelt between his thighs, as he had done with her. Marcus' eyes widened. Was she actually going to do the same thing to him that he had done to her? No, it couldn't be. Not a gentle lady like his beloved Judith. She would never stoop to such whore's tricks.

Unlike Marcus, Judith had no compunction against indulging in foreplay. She ran her hands along Marcus' muscle-ridged legs, from his bound ankles all the way up to his thighs, teasing him, tantalizing him with the direction she was headed. Marcus watched as impassively as he could, but was filled with amazement at the actions of this woman he thought he knew so well.

He was also startled by the sensuality of seeing her command him. He had never been in a woman's power like this, and the sensation was overwhelmingly erotic. He had already loved her twice, but he was becoming aroused yet again, his eyes on her firm young breasts as she moved, her rib cage tapering to her narrow waist, her luscious hips even now thrusting in the air as she leaned over him.

She was bringing her face near his, and Marcus was terrified he would lose his resolve if she came too close. He was so tempted to speak words of love, tender endearments, to gaze into her eyes and share his soul with her. He shut his eyes against her approach and issued another stern command. "Take me in your mouth." If that thought hadn't been on her mind, perhaps his command would disgust her, Marcus hoped.

"It's my turn to decide what, and when," she said coyly. Then she was kissing him, pressing her soft lips against his. Marcus could only respond, his tongue hot inside her mouth, stroking hers possessively, drinking in her taste, her sweetness. He tried to bring his arms around her, but the scarves prevented him. He groaned in frustration.

Judith's mouth deserted his, and her lips traced a path of fire down his chest. She licked each of his nipples in turn, encircling them with her tongue as he had done to her in the past, then teasing them with her teeth.

Marcus quivered under her tender assault, and she smiled in satisfaction. She lifted her eyes to catch his, and in an unguarded moment, Marcus let her see how much she affected him. He instantly turned his head away, praying he hadn't revealed his heart in his gaze.

Judith seemed not to notice his emotional distance. She continued loving him, taking her time pleasuring his body in the way he had not with her.

She did not consider now why he had made love to her in such a strangely dispassionate way, for she was content to have him in her power.

As she worked her way down his lean frame, she found herself once again confronted by the seat of his masculinity, rising taut and thick above a patch of black curls.

Marcus saw her hesitate. He had to hit her with force now, to make her continue her intent, to give her something to later regret. "Take me in your mouth, Judith," he said. He intended to sound commanding, but the words were strained with passion. Judith touched him, felt his silken skin hot under her fingers. She began to lower her mouth to him.

Marcus' voice stopped her. "Not my shaft. My stones."

Judith's gaze fell to this most sensitive part of a man's body. She had been curious as to whether he would mind her touch there. When she complied, Marcus groaned in response. After a while, without needing to be told, her tongue strayed upward, and she took his thick shaft in her mouth. Marcus gave her more commands, instructed her how to pleasure him.

Judith was a willing pupil, thrilled by his own excitement. He was so completely hers, so much a part of her, he would not be able to deny they belonged together. Once their loving was done, together they would make their plans to be true lovers for life.

Her thoughts briefly straying, Judith was startled when Marcus cried out, liquid warmth pouring into her mouth. She drank of him until his pleasure was complete.

"Oh, my God, my God," Marcus cried as he crashed back to earth. "I can't believe—my God, woman."

Judith met his eyes and smiled. "You taste better than dessert," she said with a teasing smile.

Marcus sighed and dropped his head back on the pillow. His Judith was more and more surprising. More and more appealing, more and more lovable. But surely though she was enjoying all they had done, after his revelation, she would be mortified at how low he brought her, how he made her succumb to the basest carnality and allowed him to vent his animal lusts upon her gentlewoman's body.

Marcus expected Judith to untie him, but she wasn't moving to do so. "Judith? We are finished. Free me now," he said, his words taking on a deeper level of meaning that Judith wasn't yet aware of.

"I'm not finished with you yet," Judith said tenderly. "We're not yet even."

"Judith?" What was she intending? Surely she didn't expect to get more from him, for he was thoroughly sated now.

He soon discovered her intention. She began by lying full against him, positioning herself so their bodies touched from their feet to their chests. Then she began making love to him as they hadn't since their encounter began. She laid tender kisses on his face, along forehead, mouth and chin. She paid special attention to the scar along his jaw, which he had received because of her. Her kisses were sweet, sensuous, loving, and completely irresistible.

"Marcus, my darling," she breathed softly in his ear. "I have so many nights imagined you here in my bed with me. I am so happy it has finally come to pass." Her mouth moved to his neck and dwelt there awhile, laying a line of tender kisses from his earlobe to his collarbone.

She didn't see Marcus grit his teeth as he attempted to fight his overpowering attraction to her. His heart hammered in his chest, his breath came short and fast, and his body began to betray him yet again, despite the fact her intimacies magnified the pain he would have to bear. His heart was shattering into a million shards of glass the more she loved him, and he could not let her see his inner agony.

Judith slipped higher, her breasts caressingly soft on his chest. She lifted herself higher still and slipped one taut ruby nipple between his lips. Marcus groaned, his lips pulling and tugging on her, his tongue loving her as he refused to allow his words to.

Judith arched her back, now resting full on him, her golden hair a curtain surrounding them. "Oh, yes," she breathed. "Yes." She offered him her other breast, and he took it greedily, his mouth hot and wet and incredibly sweet.

Marcus strained against his bonds now, his entire body trembling. He thrashed, infuriated that he could not touch her, enfold her body against his. Judith sensed his distress, saw his arousal, and slipped him inside her, this time taking him within her at her command, at her pace.

Marcus cried out, amazed that he should once again be ready for her. She was a witch to possess him so, a wondrous, enchanting witch. But he refused to remain under her power, for his need was too overpowering.

With a brutal cry that startled Judith, he ripped each of his wrists from the scarves, the sound of tearing cloth shattering their tender loving. Marcus sat up, roughly dislodging her so he could free each of his ankles.

Judith suddenly found herself pressed back into the mattress with Marcus upon her, dominating her, loving her so completely that tears filled her eyes. She had slipped past his strange wall of remoteness and retrieved him from whatever dark country he had been visiting. Marcus was back with her, the passionate lover she had known before, the man who would hold nothing back in his adoration of her.

Marcus indeed held nothing back. He was lost this time, and he knew it. His desire to express his passion for Judith went beyond all his reason and his firm resolve. Nothing this night had turned out like he expected, so he cast aside his plans to shame her physically in the heat of his burning need for her. He consoled himself that it no longer mattered. What would follow would work regardless of this pure physical passion, for it had to work.

He used his mouth, his hands, his caresses to express what he dared not let his voice reveal, for he had yet to play out the evening's drama.

That would come soon enough. For now she was his love, his life, and he would allow himself one last opportunity to express the feelings he had bottled up, feelings that yet threatened to overpower him.

Still inside her, Marcus rose with her in his arms and leaned against the headboard. He held her close as she sat astride him, his mouth playing over her neck, her face, as he gently rocked her up and down upon himself.

Judith reveled in it, arching her head first to one side, then the other, inviting him with every gesture to ravish her with his lips, his tongue, his hands. Marcus cupped her breasts softly, gently, then with increasing urgency as their passion mounted yet again, his fingers lifting, tugging, then gently pinching her nipples as she responded with greater and greater urgency.

Her endearments poured forth like fine wine to his senses, words of love he would always hold in his heart. In response, he only allowed himself now and then a softly murmured affirmation. He would give her no sweet endearments to thrust before him later, no proof of what he truly felt.

A spine-jangling scream tore through the air and jolted Richard and Audrey from the cozy nest they had occupied for the last two hours.

"What in the—" Richard bolted out of bed stark naked, his hand going straight for the rapier he usually wore at his side. He drew thin air.

The pounding feet passing their door indicated that the scream had come from another part of Lord Hunsdon's huge manor house.

Richard began slipping on his shirt and hose. He glanced at Audrey, who was clutching the sheet against her chest, her eyes huge. "I'll go see what all the ruckus is about." He slipped through the door before she could respond and followed a few guests to a small parlor on the floor below, just off the stairwell. Cards and dice littered the floor by the large gaming table. A few chairs were overturned.

A knot of people had gathered, staring at something on the floor. Richard shoved his way through. His eyes fell on the body of a gentleman who lay on his back, the blade of a stiletto protruding from his chest. Blood dripped down his chest onto the wooden floor, staining it a dark burgundy. Richard's eyes swung up to the man's face. It was Lord Mowbray.

"Christ's blood, what happened?" Richard asked, now realizing the murmured speculation running rampant around him. Names were proffered and rejected, the words "murder" and "authorities" bandied about. The night was not over yet, and it wasn't going to get better.

"That's him! That's the man I saw fighting with the lord," said a pale woman. The woman stuck out her skinny arm and pointed straight at Richard. Richard realized she had been one of the guests at an adjacent door when he and Mowbray had fought. "He and Lord Mowbray were in a terrific fight earlier this evening, in the gallery upstairs. They were threatening to kill each other."

"And what's your name?" The squat, ruddy-faced city constable turned to Richard, his tone almost bored. He had brought along two burly guards from the nearby prison, Richard saw. The responsiveness of the otherwise slow and disorganized law-keeping force of London amazed Richard. It must have to do with Lord Hunsdon's high standing as the queen's chamberlain that he was able to have them brought here so quickly on a holiday.

"Lord Richard Langsforth, son of the Earl of Langsforth," Richard supplied.

The constable seemed singularly unimpressed with his title. "This woman here says she saw you engaged in a sword fight with Mowbray earlier this evening. Can you explain what that was all about?"

"It had nothing to do with this!" Richard exclaimed. "I haven't been anywhere but upstairs since around ten o'clock."

"Upstairs? Doing what?"

The skinny woman shoved closer to the action. "He stole a wench from Mowbray. That's what the fight looked to be about."

Richard wanted to glare at her, but he had a sense it wouldn't help to appear furious just now.

"It doesn't take hours to swive a serving wench," Lord Hunsdon said. "We think Mowbray was murdered between midnight and one. Where were you at that hour, Richard?"

"He was with me."

All eyes turned to Audrey, who was standing outside the circle, her gown rumpled and her hair hanging to her waist. She had bypassed her corset the better to clutch together the tear in her bodice, and her figure appeared in all its unbound glory. Richard pulled her against him, trying to protect her from the salacious gazes of a dozen men.

"And who are you?" the constable asked.

"Audrey Higgenbotham, milord." Audrey curtsied as best she could pressed against Richard. Richard looked down at her in surprise. He had never even known her full name until now. "I'm Lady Judith Ashton's personal maid." Audrey looked toward Lord Ashton for his confirmation.

Howard scowled at her, but he nodded once, curtly. "She's my daughter's maid," he said.

"And where is your daughter?" asked the constable.

"She has gone home, milord," Howard said.

"And left her maid behind?"

Howard seemed extremely discomfited by the direction of the questions.

"I'm taking her home," Richard supplied.

"So, this girl's a servant," observed the constable. "Well, as Lord Hunsdon said, it doesn't take but fifteen minutes to swive a serving wench. What were you doing the rest of the time?"

Richard's fists balled up in fury, and he had the fierce desire to strike the constable.

"It doesn't matter," Audrey urgently whispered.

"No answer? Guards." The constable gestured to his guards to stand near Richard, preventing him from leaving the room. Audrey was crowded away from his side.

"If Richard did it, he didn't act alone."

Everyone's attention turned to Lord Howard Ashton, who appeared unduly pale. His remarks were directed at the constable alone. At his side stood Walter Kennington, listening closely to every word. "It was that actor that was skulking about earlier."

"Marcus Sinclair?" Lord Hunsdon looked at Howard in disbelief. "What makes you accuse Marcus?"

"I saw him running from here a few minutes before Lord Mowbray was discovered. He was heading off into the darkness, as if desperate to get away from here."

"That's hardly enough," Hunsdon said dubiously.

"I saw the actor dueling Lord Mowbray earlier," Walter Kennington said.

The constable sighed. *"Another* duel? And where was *this* one?"

"Outside on the lawn. I'm positive it was Sinclair."

Richard saw a look of understanding pass between Walter Kennington and Howard Ashton. Something foul was definitely afoot tonight.

"I saw that, too!" another guest, clearly half drunk, said.

"I overheard them arguing, right here in this room," Walter said. "It was a most vicious argument."

The constable cast about the gathering. "So where is this actor now? What does he have to say for himself?"

"You don't think a guilty man would linger about the scene of his crime, do you?" Howard asked.

"He disappeared immediately afterward, I'm sure of it," Walter said.

"Marcus would never murder anyone," Richard protested hotly. "He's being set up!" Richard stared hard at Howard. Howard's face lost the little color it still possessed. He quickly glanced away from Richard's penetrating gaze.

"That's a serious charge, son," said the constable. "Do you have any proof of that?"

"If anyone's conspiring, it's you and that actor," interrupted Kennington hotly. "You both want Judith, and now that you can't have her, you're taking your revenge on any other man who wants her. You sicken me!"

"That doesn't even begin to make sense!" Richard cried. "Lord Hunsdon, you aren't going to allow this, are you? Marcus is your man!"

"Not if he's guilty, he's not," Hunsdon said flatly. Richard was appalled. As easily as that, the man's allegiance vanished. "I can hardly continue to defend my players to the Puritans who would shut down the theaters if I allow a murderer in their midst."

Richard protested hotly at his lack of loyalty. "How can you even think Marcus would—"

"Halt! This has gone far enough," cried the constable. He turned to Richard. "You, I'm taking into custody. As for this actor, this Marcus Sinclair, we'll track him down, don't worry. Let's be done with this. I left a warm bed to come here, and I have work in the morning.''

The constable led the way from the parlor. The guards shoved hard on Richard's back, pressing him to follow. Richard quickly turned to Audrey. ''Warn Marcus,'' was all he had a chance to say before he was forced, stumbling, down the stairs.

Chapter 18

"I've been so blind, Marcus, to concern myself so with my father's wishes, my family line. What does any of that matter in light of what we share?" Judith snuggled deeper into his embrace. She lay beside him thoroughly content in their loving, one leg flung over his thighs, her hair fanning out on his chest. "You're here with me, and from now on we'll be together, build a wonderful life together. Tomorrow we'll go to the countryside and be married. I know of a parish priest who will be willing to marry us in secret. He won't care who I am, or who you are."

"And your father?" Marcus asked dryly.

"Once we're married, I'll return here and gather my things, explain it to him—or perhaps just leave a note. Then I'll join you, wherever you are."

Marcus pictured Judith showing up at his meager apartment with her trunks of finery and her lady's maid. She had no concept of what would lay before her if she married him, a man who was paid only eight shillings a week. A few short months after they were wed, she would be miserable.

Judith didn't miss the frown of consternation on Marcus' face. "Don't worry, I know my father won't harm you once we're wed. He wouldn't dare, for I would go straight to the authorities this time.''

"That's not my concern.''

"Then, if you're worried I don't have the strength to escape him, you're wrong. I do. Once we're married, I will owe my allegiance only to you, my love.''

"I believe this charade has gone far enough,'' Marcus said grimly. He freed himself from her embrace, swung his legs over the side of the bed and sat up.

"You don't believe I'll go through with it, do you, Marcus?'' Judith laid a hand on his tense shoulder. "I know you think it will be hard for me to give up my name, my wealth. But it won't.'' Her voice softened, caressed him. "Not when I have you.''

Marcus stretched his arms and back languorously, as if he had not a care in the world. Inside, he was girding himself for a tremendous battle against his own desires. *Farewell, Judith.* The words came without warning to his consciousness, but they spoke true, even though he kept his tongue still.

Keeping his back to her, he finally let his words take part in the charade, his trained actor's voice taking on a lightness he did not feel. He breathed deeply one more time, a trick he employed before going on stage, a symbolic transfer of his character's spirit into his own body, a temporary possession. Then he slowly turned and looked straight at her. "That's not it, Judith. I just don't love you.''

Judith stared at him in confusion, certain she hadn't heard him right. "Marcus?'' She barely whispered his name. Judith felt as if she were on the edge of a precipice, that if she could keep time from advancing, she would be safe from what the next moment would bring, though as yet she didn't know clearly what was coming, only that it was horrible, menacing, killing to her mind and soul.

To her shock, Marcus laughed at her confusion. "I admit I fancied myself in love with you once. It seemed so romantic, our situation. Two star-crossed lovers and all that. Like one of the plays at the Globe. I'm embarrassed now to think what a lovesick swain I was, playing every scene between us as if we had an audience.''

Judith felt herself grow pale as a wave of nausea twisted her stomach. "I—I don't understand." She was surprised she could get even these words out, her throat was so constricted.

Marcus rose and casually began to dress. Judith clutched the bed sheet around her, frightened suddenly of being with Marcus, frightened of his words and of the pain they were starting to inflict.

"After I delivered you home from our first tryst, I admit for a while I thought you and I were destined to be together. But the more time I spent away from you, the more I realized you are not as special as my fancy had me believe. There are numerous ladies who vie for my attention, as I believe you're well aware. I have found consolation in their arms more times than you could possibly believe, innocent that you are—or rather, were." He smiled in an offendingly rapacious way, his gaze flicking over her body.

Judith's pulse pounded, her heart twisting in anguish. All this time she had been so concerned for Marcus' feelings while she spent time with Walter Kennington, and he had been with other women, dozens of them. She recalled bitterly that he had certainly never said she was his only lover.

But he was her one true love! What was happening now was simply impossible; it had to be. Judith shook her head, moisture sheening her vision. "How can you speak to me thus! After all this, after—after what we just did—what we said to each other! I don't understand. Marcus, why—"

The answer came easily, smoothly. "How could I not, you were so easy."

"Easy!"

Marcus fastened his breeches. "You threw yourself at me, Judith. Think about it. Our liaisons were always your idea. I got tired of saying no. Particularly when all it took were a few sweet words. You completely forgot what an accomplished poet I am. Words of love roll trippingly off my tongue with almost no effort. Or haven't you noticed?"

Had he been a rake all along, and she too naive and overly romantic to see it? In truth, she had always been the pursuer in their relationship. From the first, she had made the effort to draw him close. She had flirted with him, arranged their first

night of lovemaking, cared for him when he was racked by
fever, even taken part in a garden rendezvous. And tonight—
whose idea was it? Again, hers.

"Your little ceremony of calling me your husband that first
night—it amused me to play along with it. I had gotten what
I wanted most—in your bed. And I certainly knew how to
achieve my ends, didn't I?" He chuckled derisively as he pulled
on his shirt. Judith shivered at the sound. "I didn't chase
you; I let you chase me. It worked perfectly." He sighed in
remembered pleasure as he tucked his shirt into his breeches.
"And it was more than worth it; don't sell yourself short on
that score, Judith. It felt good to have a woman who was a
guaranteed virgin. I never had one before you. Men of my sort
rarely do, unless they marry, and that, fair Judith, is a fate
worse than death."

Judith's face had grown hot with shame. But she didn't give
him the satisfaction of looking away from his piercing silver
eyes.

"All the women I've bedded are used to men. It was one
of the highlights of my life, being the one to breech your
maidenly defenses, or to be more blunt, the first man to thrust
my cock inside you."

Tears started from Judith's eyes at his crude description of
what they had shared. She swiftly brushed them away, determined not to let him see her weakness.

But Marcus showed no indication he even saw her heartbreak,
her distress, her tears. He casually sat on the chest to pull
on his stockings. "Our night together was so memorable, I
continued to wear this little gold trinket you gave me." He
smiled in fond remembrance as he fingered the gold star that
still hung at his throat. "I even showed it to my alehouse friends
and told them how I'd earned it. It got to be quite the joke at
the Blue Lion."

"Joke," Judith gasped as the room began to spin about
her. She grasped the carved bedpost for support, her hands
tightening spasmodically as she tried not to fall from the bed.
She thought she would be sick.

Marcus didn't show the least bit of concern for her reaction.
He unclasped the pendant and tossed it toward her as if it were

nothing but a cheap bauble. Numb with shock, Judith stared at the pool of gold that landed on the sheet beside her as he relentlessly killed the heart of her.

"Everything was fine until your father paid me back for my little escapade," he continued in a bitter tone, as he tensely yanked on the laces of his boot. "That thrashing I could have done without. But you *had* to tell him, unfortunately." He gave an irritated sigh. "Of course, there was one benefit. I got my friend Richard back. It was a shame to lose him over a woman, after all, especially when it was merely a bad case of lust."

Marcus rose and began to don his doublet. "Then I wake up to find you nursing me, and I have to go along with the game even longer. I have to continue to pretend that I love you. For if you knew the truth, you would complain to your father, and he would finish the job!"

As he spoke, he carefully straightened each ruffled shirt cuff in turn, as if he were dressing in the privacy of his own room and not obliterating the heart of her.

"Well, little Judith, now that I'm back on my feet, I'm tired of all the pretending. I don't love you, I never loved you, and I wish you would quit mooning after me, for it will only cause your father to finish what he started, and I happen to like the use of my arms and legs!"

Judith stared at him aghast, her heart shattering into a thousand pieces. He was so thoroughly cold, so calm about it, so devastatingly composed. "But tonight—at Lord Hunsdon's— when we talked—" Judith began, her voice almost a whisper. "What we meant to each other—how can that be nothing?"

"I merely said what you needed to hear to invite me here. There's nothing like a good tumble after a party. Particularly between the silken thighs of a noblewoman."

Now dressed, Marcus strode toward the bed and leaned casually against the same bedpost Judith was clutching so desperately, naked but for the bed sheet she had wrapped around her. Crossing his arms nonchalantly, he leaned in close to her, his face composed, his gray eyes coolly boring into hers. "It's quite simple, sweetheart. I lied. Once I realized I no longer believed myself in love with you, I decided to continue the farce awhile longer. I lied about loving you, Judith. It's the biggest lie I ever told. Because I wanted you again. I wanted to feel your soft noblewoman's body under mine, at my command. I wanted to make you perform for me, and perform willingly. And you did it very well, too," he said with a rapacious grin. "Hot and willing, begging for my cock, just as I imagined it. And to think I made a virtuous lady such as you stoop to this."

His offensive description of what they had done together brought a fresh burst of shame-filled tears to Judith's eyes. She desperately blinked them back. "No," she whispered tightly.

"Aye." Marcus straightened and retrieved his cloak from the floor. "Barmaids stink of ale, country girls of sour milk, and whores—they harbor all sorts of diseases, such as the French pox, that will rot a man's pecker right off. But a noblewoman—you smell the sweetest, your skin's the softest, and heaven knows, it's good to know legions of men haven't been there before me." He turned back to her with a sharp look. "Perhaps they've been there since?"

Judith pulled in a sharp breath and clutched the sheet more tightly to her chest. "You know they haven't!"

"Not even Kennington?"

"Nay!" The word was barely a whisper.

"No matter. I'm sure he'll appreciate your charms once you're married. I've trained you well enough. Until then, spread your thighs for whomever you wish. You may smell sweet, but now that you've performed like a seasoned whore for me, I find I grow bored. From now on, I will seek my satisfaction elsewhere."

"I see," she said thickly as hot tears clogged her throat. "I didn't understand how little some things mattered to you. I didn't realize you were lying. Now I do. Thank you for telling me."

Her aplomb amazed Marcus. He was battering her with every word he spoke, worse than the harshest physical blows, yet she maintained her composure. She was more a lady than any woman he had ever known. Poignantly, he realized he was intensely proud of her.

She was only a few feet away from him, the candlelight accenting her hair and the soft, sweet features of her face now tightened with pain. His heart ached with the need to hold her, to tell her he was even now lying, lying because he loved her so.

He swung his cloak over his shoulders. "Well then, I'll be off. Thank you for a memorable evening, Judith. But keep in mind that I'm not pining away for you, milady, and I hope you realize now there is certainly no reason to pine away for me. It's all nonsense, after all."

"Aye," Judith whispered in reply. Marcus swung open the balcony door and slammed it behind him, rattling the panes in the wood.

Only then did Judith allow a cry of anguish to issue from her throat.

Marcus was unsure how much time passed before he came back to himself. He was leaning against an oak tree on the street, its branches silhouetted against the diffused moonlight attempting to break through the cloud cover. He breathed deeply of the chill night air, his heart thumping like a leaden weight in his chest. He prayed any moment it would cease its beating and he would be put out of his misery. But it continued its relentless task of keeping his body alive, even though his spirit was dead.

Marcus steadied himself, fighting the nausea that writhed in his stomach. His body revolted against what he had done, his gut seething in agony. He lost the battle and retched violently into the street.

Finally, he could give no more. He swiped at his sweat-coated face. His head throbbed wickedly, pounding mercilessly so he could hardly think where he was. Again he sucked in the brisk night air to clear his head, relax his aching stomach. But he knew no relief would come from that quarter, nor from anywhere else.

He shoved away from the tree trunk and found he could barely stand on his feet, so enervated was he by the effort he had expended to turn Judith against him. Stumbling like a drunk, he began the long walk back to Southwark and his meager apartment. As he walked, his mind served as his torturer, replaying again and again what had transpired a few moments ago in Judith's chamber.

He had been thorough, convincing, of that he was sure. It gave him small satisfaction. But she had believed him. He had succeeded in turning her against him. She was in great pain now. But when she had more time to reflect, to realize how he had abused her, that pain would be nursed into a kernel of anger within her, anger that would transform into hate. He had laid the groundwork for her to hate him, and she would be free to live the rest of her life without carrying the burden of their forbidden love.

And he would continue to love her.

Marcus knew he had never done a better acting job in his life. Shakespeare would have been proud.

A moment later, the clouds broke. A brilliant shooting star coursed across the night sky, trailing through the heavens in a burst of fire. As quickly as it appeared, it was extinguished, never to be seen again. Marcus believed then that the stars had indeed influenced his fate, just as Judith had said all those months ago when he visited her chamber at Mowbray's.

Somewhere, the gods were laughing.

Audrey had never run so fast. She had a good idea where Marcus was, but she suspected Lord Ashton did, too. The murder had naturally cut short the celebration, and Lord Ashton would soon be on his way home. If she wasn't quick enough, he might arrive first in his carriage and find Marcus there with Judith. There might be another confrontation. Marcus might even end up in a duel with him. Nothing would be more damning.

As soon as Audrey reached Judith's door, she knocked. She heard a muffled sound inside, but no answer. She knocked again, harder. Beginning to get worried, she became less concerned about invading her mistress' privacy, and she cracked the door open. The room was dark, the candelabra extinguished.

A huddled form lay in the center of the massive bed. Audrey could see Marcus was nowhere about. She came in and lit the wall sconce by the door, illuminating the room. Judith was curled into a tight ball on the bed with the sheet twisted haphazardly about her.

"Milady?" Audrey hurried to her side, knowing something was desperately wrong. "Milady, are you ill?"

Judith didn't respond.

Audrey sat on the edge of the bed and pulled the sheet back enough to see that Judith was actually awake. Her hair was a mass of tangles about her head, her face streaked with the tracks of a thousand tears. "Milady, what happened?" Audrey cried. She pulled Judith into her arms and held her tightly.

Judith barely acknowledged her maid's presence, or her concern. "I can't," was all she said, her throat thick and raw with tears.

"You can't? You can't what?" Audrey asked anxiously.

"I can't." Judith's voice cracked, and her shoulders began to shake as fresh tears began to flow.

Audrey pulled Judith's head against her shoulder and stroked the hair from her face, murmuring meaningless endearments. "Judith, please tell me what it is. I have to talk to you, and I need you to be strong."

Judith took a shuddering breath, her entire body trembling in Audrey's arms. "I can't hate him like I should," she said finally, her voice flat, spiritless.

"Hate him? Hate who?" Audrey was still mystified. Then a thought began to push itself to her consciousness. Marcus. Who else? The bastard had broken Judith's heart. "What happened? What did Marcus do?"

Judith shook her head. "Nothing I shouldn't have seen coming," she said weakly.

"Did he hurt you?" Audrey asked, fury sparking to life inside her. Some men definitely didn't deserve to live.

"Aye."

That one word was enough for Audrey. "How dare he hurt you! That man is scum! To think Richard wanted me to *warn* him! Warn *him?* I'd rather see him rot!"

"Warn him?" Judith's head finally came up.

Audrey had no intention of lifting a finger to help that cad of an actor now. "Never mind, milady. It's nothing for you to be concerned about."

"Audrey, tell me. Warn him about what?" Judith pulled the sheet to her face and wiped away her tears.

Audrey hesitated. "It's Richard I'm worried about, milady. He's been arrested."

"Arrested? I don't understand." Judith shook her head, clearly dazed from pain.

Audrey explained the events surrounding the murder as well as she could, and that Marcus and Richard were now considered suspects. "And now Richard's in prison. They may even have taken him to the Tower. I don't know."

"You—you care for Richard?" Judith asked, a bewildered expression on her face.

Audrey's heart went out to her lady. "Aye, milady. Tonight we—" She felt a rush of warmth as she remembered all that had happened between them, the entire new world they had created together. She looked at Judith and was struck suddenly by how cruel it would be to thrust such a miracle in front of her mistress' shattered heart. She would remain silent about her engagement, for a while.

"You what?" Judith pressed.

"We . . . became friends," Audrey supplied. "But he's innocent of the charges against him. We have to think of something."

"Think . . . I can't think." She fell back on the bed, her body instinctively reverting into a tight ball, her arms wrapping tightly about her knees.

Audrey knew she had no right to ask Judith to share her own immense burden of worry. Judith had no more heart to give, for that scoundrel of a theater actor had stolen her generous heart and crushed it. She would let Judith alone tonight. In the morning, she would go to the constable and plead on behalf of Richard, plead for his release. Her resolve firm, she rose and left Judith, now breathing softly in a troubled sleep.

That night lasted an eternity for Judith. She slept only to dream of Marcus, as things were before, warm and golden. Her spirit was briefly satisfied for a time. Then a feeling of foreboding stole over her pretty memories, a feeling that nagged, telling her she had overlooked something important.

She didn't want to look closely at this thing, but knew she was deluding herself not acknowledging it. Then suddenly, relentlessly, the curtain slid back, and it lay before her in brilliant, razor-sharp, undeniable clarity, everything he had said to her—done to her—the night before. She would snap awake, shaking and ice cold, red-hot pain piercing her shamefully, feeling horrendously alone, the horrible images and vile words brutally fresh in her mind.

Over and over her mind would torture her, replaying their loving times together, reminding her how she had felt, times she had believed in with her whole heart that now meant nothing, absolutely nothing.

The torture didn't end there. Relentlessly, she relived every memory in its minutest detail, laying over it the new truth Marcus had revealed. In the process, her mind tainted each and every word, every gesture, every loving remark she had once treasured and transformed it into something loathsome.

Loathsome. Loathsome and vile. That was Marcus Sinclair. He was loathsome. Hateful and wicked. Evil. Horrible. The devil in disguise. Raper of innocents, stealer of virtue. He was everything nasty anyone had ever said about anyone all rolled into one. . . .

Judith began to cry again, sobs racking her body painfully. She was attempting to fool herself, but it wasn't working. She didn't feel any hate toward Marcus despite what he had done to her. She couldn't. Perhaps one day. But for now she still felt something quite different for him, and it frightened her terribly—frightened her because it meant she had no spirit, no will, no pride. She still cared for Marcus. My God, she was such a fool! But she still cared for the rogue.

She knew the officials were planning to arrest him. Audrey had made it sound as if her own father was involved. Her father. What was happening? She couldn't think clearly. She tried hard not to care. She didn't love Marcus Sinclair anymore. She didn't. He could suffer, and she would be glad, suffer for making her suffer. . . .

If found guilty of murder, a nobleman could expect a quick

beheading—assuming the blade was sharp and the executioner able to cut cleanly on the first stroke. Sometimes even that wasn't enough, and it took several attempts to sever the head from the body. But a commoner who murdered a noble would be taken to the gallows at Tyburn, a noose put round his throat before a jeering mob, then the cart pulled out from beneath his feet. He would dangle there, struggling futilely, until his life left him.

Judith's gorge rose as she imagined such a fate befalling Marcus. He must never suffer for a crime he didn't commit. Never. She knew he wasn't a murderer. He wasn't. Not only wasn't it in him—as if she even knew him anymore!—but he had been here, in this room, during the midnight hour when the murder took place. He was innocent. That was all there was to it. Innocent. If he was arrested, he had no alibi except for her.

But to publicly proclaim that he had spent the hours with her, to let everyone know that they had been engaging in the most intimate acts, right here in her private chamber ... the thought was appalling. Hot shame flushed through her as she recalled what he had done to her, what she had willingly let him do, participating in with such relish. The thought of even mentioning last night to another living soul was devastating.

She knew she would find the strength to do so, should she have to, to save Marcus from the gallows. Certainly she could never live with herself if she refrained from speaking up merely to protect her reputation and hide her shame. But if she acted quickly enough, if she reached Marcus and warned him, the need to confess the truth might be avoided altogether. . . .

As Judith came to this understanding, she realized day was already upon the world, bringing with it the heavy burden she knew she had to bear. Early dawn light splashed against her white sheets, turning them a leaden shade of gray. The day was going to be overcast, fitting her mood and the distasteful chore before her. She was going to find Marcus Sinclair and warn him that his liberty was in jeopardy. He would have time to leave London, perhaps travel to his home in Lankenshire.

But it was the telling that would be painful, facing him again, seeing that sneer on his face once more. He would think she still cared for him, to bother herself so. But it wasn't that. It wasn't. She would have to steel herself for this ordeal, not let him believe she came for other than simple decency's sake. *Please, Lord,* Judith cried silently. *Don't let him think I care!*

ACT 5

"Some are born great, some achieve greatness,
and some have greatness thrust upon them."
—*Twelfth Night*, Act 2, Scene 5

Chapter 19

A chill wind bit at Judith as she hurried toward the Thames, and she pulled her cloak tighter. She knew Marcus was a player at the Globe, and she knew about where the theater was. From the other side of the Thames, she would occasionally catch sight of its flag flying high to announce a play.

It was already past noon, and a black silk flag fluttered above the wooden *O* of the theater. Judith knew the flag had been hoisted to signal to London citizens that a tragedy would be performed later that day. She prayed Marcus was still free, and at the playhouse. Anxiety clutched at her as she made her way down the slope to where theatergoers boarded the wherry to take them across the river.

She knew she was more anxious than she should be. She shouldn't be so concerned about Marcus' fate. Not after last night. She told herself over and over it was her own reputation that concerned her, the fear she would have to reveal that Marcus had been with her. That was all it was.

But then, why did she feel so tense, so uneasy, as if every moment took on vast importance?

She gave the wherryman her farthings and sat beside a rotund banker and his colleague. She gathered from their conversation that they were also bound for the playhouses in Southwark.

"Which will it be today, the Rose or the Globe? Or perhaps you prefer bear baiting?" the banker asked his friend. Judith shuddered as she thought of the blood sport where a chained bear was pitted against wild dogs.

"The play at the Globe is rumored to be rather exceptional," the man replied. He produced a handbill a boy employed by the players had passed about town an hour before.

The banker took it. "So what's it about?"

"A Danish prince. He thinks his father's been murdered—perhaps he has—and he is torn over whether to avenge the murder. I've heard there's a lot of sword fighting, and lots of murders."

"Ah."

Judith shuddered. A play featuring murder? She wasn't at all interested in hearing about more murder.

"May I see that?" she asked. Perhaps she wouldn't even see Marcus' name on the list of players. If not, she had no need to go to the play. She would try his home instead.

Her heart dropped into her stomach the moment her gaze alighted on the page. Marcus Sinclair was listed at the top, next to another name, Hamlet. She saw then that was the name of the play.

"Is this Hamlet a large part?" she asked the banker.

"Well, the play's called *Hamlet*! What do you think?"

Judith shrugged. She was trying not to think about Marcus. The wherry slipped up the south bank with a slow shudder. The wherryman helped her alight onto a wooden causeway laid over the mud of the riverbank. From there, it was a short walk to the theater on Maiden Lane.

A crowd was already milling about the main entrance. Judith pushed past the hucksters plying their wares, oblivious to their calls of delicious roasted peanuts and fresh apples for sale, and gazed up at the thirty-foot-high walls.

Above the main door hung a wooden sign depicting Hercules bearing the world on his shoulders. The sign let the mostly illiterate populace know that this was the Globe Theater, but the slogan *"Totus mundus agit historionem"* (All the world's a stage) was also posted out front.

Unaccustomed as to how the theater worked, Judith found herself shoved along with the boisterous crowd through the narrow entrance and a short passage. At the other end, a man holding a box demanded she pay a penny, so she did. She didn't understand that a second penny would gain her entrance up a staircase leading to the stands on either side, and a third penny would buy access to the galleries even closer to the stage. So she ended up in the yard of the circular, open-air playhouse, among the milling throng shouldering for the best spots for a performance they would be standing throughout.

Judith gazed up in awe at the splendor surrounding her, feeling she had entered another world. Three tiers of galleries rose dizzyingly upward, the people inside overlooking everything below. Each of the thirty pillars supporting the galleries was brightly painted, almost fooling the eye into thinking the sturdy wood was crafted of finest marble gilt with gold, like columns in a royal palace. The deception angered Judith. It reminded her of the delusion she had been under in loving Marcus, who also was not as he appeared.

The stage itself was a rectangular platform about five feet high and forty feet across, carpeted in fresh rushes. A short roof covered half of it, supported by two pillars.

Probably since she was a lady, she found herself within a few layers of spectators to the stage itself. Two double doors flanked the stage, and Judith suspected that was where the actors were hiding. She immediately looked around for a way to get onto the stage, but was at a loss. There were no steps.

Frustrated, she clasped her hands. She wanted to get in, do the deed, and get out. Instead she was forced shoulder to shoulder with this mob of unruly spectators, most of them working-class citizens who were hooting to each other, elbowing her, jockeying for position, making rude remarks, spitting on her shoes, calling out to friends and trying to force their way past—if this was what the theater was like, thought Judith, no wonder her father didn't want her to attend!

Perhaps that wasn't altogether fair, she thought as her gaze played over the galleries. There were places to sit up there if she had been able to figure out how to get up there. She was struck by the wide cross section of citizenry that made up the play-going populace. There had to be several thousand people here, crammed shoulder to shoulder, even though the playhouse auditorium was no more than sixty-five feet across. Every social class was represented—from nobles such as herself to wealthy merchants, to tradesmen and their wives, to apprentices, to common laborers.

The sound of a horn cut through the clamor. Judith's eyes followed the sound to a small hut several stories above the stage. The trumpeter was just withdrawing, closing doors behind him. The sound was apparently a signal, for the people in the galleries began taking their seats, the crowd around Judith growing quiet.

Spectators rushed to buy bags of nuts, apples, and tankards of ale before the play began. Next to her, a burly man had several apples in his arms and was munching one. "If the play stinks, they'll get this core from me," he exclaimed to his neighbor with a grin. Judith's eyes widened. For only a penny a performance, she was surprised spectators could be so cruel.

The trumpeter appeared a second time, giving another warning signal. Time was running out, and she hadn't accomplished anything. She pushed forward toward the stage, but was rudely elbowed back. She realized then that even if she made it to the foot of the stage, it was as tall as she was. How was she planning to climb up there?

Perhaps there was another door in the back of the theater. Judith turned and began to push her way through to the entrance, thinking she would walk around and look for an outside door.

She was too late.

A third trumpet blast came. The play was about to begin.

Two men appeared on stage. Judith guessed them to be soldiers by their breast plates and spears. They were soon joined by two others and began discussing a strange occurrence they had witnessed while standing watch. Judith looked at each man closely, but none of the players was Marcus.

To Judith's surprise, a trapdoor opened in the stage floor, and the most odd and frightening man emerged. He was painted a ghastly white and wore scarred battle armor. "It's a ghost," murmured the people around her. Some of them looked almost afraid. Judith didn't blame them. Something about the makeup, or the costume, or the way the creature spoke, made her shiver. As the unearthly apparition confronted the sentries, Judith realized the actors were pretending it was a dark, bitter night outside a castle in Denmark. The audience had no trouble believing it despite the filtered afternoon light, and they stilled to listen to the play.

After a while, Judith began to believe it, too. She was jolted back into reality with the next scene, when Marcus appeared from the nearest of the two doors in the back of the stage with several other players. He was dressed all in black, and the king addressed him as Hamlet.

Excited whispering from behind her caused Judith to turn. Three women were gossiping about Marcus—of course. "He makes a marvelous prince," one lady sighed. The man beside Judith hissed at them to be quiet. Judith almost thanked him.

Since she was stuck there, jammed into the crowd with nowhere to go, Judith soon found herself lost in the story. She even began to think of the man on stage as the Prince of Denmark, a melancholy soul tortured by the plea for revenge made by his father's ghost.

The audience didn't throw any nutshells or apple cores at this performance. Knowing next to nothing about acting, even she understood how intently Marcus absorbed the character of Hamlet, draping himself in another personality. His gift astounded her. As Hamlet, he was vacillating, melancholy, plagued with doubt—so unlike the decisive man she knew. He had ceased being Marcus. For a few precious hours she could even set aside the quelling pain the actor had caused her. And she knew obliterating such pain, even for an afternoon, took extraordinary talent.

She winced at one point, when Hamlet turned on Ophelia for being overly obedient to her father. She could almost recognize herself and Marcus—the old Marcus—in that scene.

By the time the climactic ending came, Judith was so engrossed, she was unconsciously gripping the sleeve of the man next to her. The audience watched with baited breath as Hamlet engaged in swordplay with Laertes, sending sparks flying. The spectators emitted screams and groans in response, as if feeling what the characters were feeling. The women behind Judith shrieked when Hamlet was struck by the poisoned tip of Laertes' sword. Judith then realized she had screamed, too.

"It's just pig's blood," her neighbor told her sympathetically, thinking the fake gouges Hamlet and Laertes had received had upset her. "None of them are really hurt."

Judith barely heard him. She watched enthralled as Hamlet stabbed the king, then forced him to drink a cup of poisoned wine. Finally, Hamlet himself succumbed to the poison racing through his veins. Judith moaned through clenched hands.

Judith was still shaking as the four bodies were borne backstage to the incessant pounding of a bass drum. A canon shot signaled the end.

Applause thundered around the small theater. Judith returned to the cold afternoon in the wooden theater and realized her knees were shaking from having stood so long. Amid the thunderous applause, the players returned through the stage doors, bowing briefly before moving to the sides.

Judith's shoulders slumped. She was glad the tension was over. But she still reeled from the raw emotion she had seen displayed on the stage. The line of actors parted, and Marcus stood alone before the crowd and bowed, his triumphant smile obliterating once and for all the gloomy visage of Hamlet.

Judith realized with a shock that she had completely forgotten she was watching a play with Marcus in the lead role. He had transformed himself so utterly into someone else that she had forgotten the ache in her heart and believed along with the rest of the audience that he was the tortured prince of Denmark.

She began to understand what Richard meant when he said she simply had to see him act—he was so gifted at becoming someone else. Of course, that did nothing to absolve the callous, cruel way he had treated her, making her fall in love with him only to rudely shove her away, acting for all the world as if she had meant nothing to him. . . .

Acting for all the world—

Acting. A swell of emotion expanded Judith's chest—a new conviction, a thought so impossibly wonderful, she knew it could sweep all sense from her if she wasn't careful. *Acting.* Oh, Lord, what a fool she had been not to realize it sooner!

The man she loved was skilled in deception—how could she have forgotten that? When she first met him, it had been as an actor, displaying many different guises. She had seen him perform brief scenes. But until today's performance, she did not realize how fully Marcus could project the emotions of another man, submerge the yearnings of his own heart.

With a lover's certain knowledge, she accepted the possibility without question. Even before the idea fully formed in her mind, the truth blossomed in her heart. With each passing second, the conviction solidified, exhilarated her spirit, and lifted the chains from her heart.

The night before, Marcus had become someone else in order to disavow their love and set her free. He had been acting.

Marcus straightened up from his last bow and couldn't resist looking toward the crowd of groundlings to where Judith was standing. He had noticed her almost the instant he came on stage, but had purposely avoided looking toward her throughout the performance for fear it would disturb his concentration. He could hardly believe his eyes weren't lying. What on earth was she doing here? How could she bear to look at him?

His gaze leapt over the distance separating them and connected with hers, illuminating for a split second his concern, his regret, his inner pain. In that instant, Judith recognized the man she fell in love with. Marcus had never really left her.

The actors left the stage, Marcus with them. Judith turned to the burly man next to her who had eaten all the apples—and the cores. "Can you lift me onto the stage?"

"What?"

"I can't get up there without help, and I no longer have time. I have to get back there immediately."

"Well . . ." the man hesitated.

"I'll pay you."

"Okay." Judith was instantly on the stage, as if she weighed less than an apple core. She tossed down a shilling, and the man grinned as he caught it. She hurried through the left door and found herself in a dark area backstage.

The room was narrow, but riotous. She moved behind a prop

throne near the door, staying out of sight as she watched actors elbow each other for dressing-room space between stacked props. Costumes flew through the air; men pounded each other on the back, shook hands, hugged, kissed—proud of their successful performance.

Except one man, who lounged by himself against the wall. This man accepted the accolades of the others and quietly dispensed a few. But he obviously wasn't in the mood to celebrate. Judith knew why.

"Cheer up, Marcus. You were outstanding!" said Alan Tremaine, who was half in and half out of his Ophelia costume. "It's too bad about Richard Burbage taking ill, but you did really well!"

The "ghost" settled his hand on Marcus' shoulder. Judith recognized the man from a visit to Hunsdon's, when Marcus was recuperating. He had introduced himself as William Shakespeare. "Indeed, you did exceptionally well, Marcus. I had a hunch there was a tragic element in you I could draw on, despite that devil-may-care front you always show the world. Most remarkable. I believe you explored elements in Hamlet even I hadn't thought of."

"It's time to leave Denmark behind," said the actor who had played Claudius the king. "What say we head on over to the Blue Lion for a celebration?"

Marcus gave him a tense half smile as he began unbuttoning his costume. Shakespeare offered him another option. "Perhaps, Marcus, you would like to join me and a few of my friends at the Mermaid Tavern tonight? You seem more in the mood for scholarly discussion and debate than rabble-rousing." The playwright and director cocked an eyebrow at "Claudius," who shrugged with a smile.

"Thank you both, but I'm feeling drained," Marcus said quietly. "I'll just go home."

"Very well. Take care, and thanks again for donning the spirit of Hamlet with such distinction." Shakespeare slipped past the ebullient actors to his desk in a corner, where he began gathering up the playbook.

Marcus shrugged out of Hamlet's doublet and returned it to a rack.

Judith slipped around the prop throne to stand before him. "Marcus?"

Marcus spun toward her, his face frozen in shock. The other actors' heads whipped up at the sound of a woman's voice. One man quickly yanked his shirt back on.

"Lady Judith!" Alan cried.

Marcus stared at her. For once, he was at a loss for words.

"It's urgent I talk with you," she said. "In private."

"Milady, you shouldn't be back here," Alan said, his adolescent voice cracking. "Tiring houses are for men only."

Marcus glanced back at the other actors, then led Judith through another door to a room filled with props.

Judith spun to face him, her words urgent, anxious. "The authorities plan to arrest you for Lord Mowbray's murder. You must leave London immediately."

Marcus stared at her. "I heard Mowbray was murdered, but why would they think I—"

"I don't know! I only know they're seeking you. I don't know when they plan to arrest you, but it's going to happen today."

"I see."

Judith began to grow anxious for him, inexplicably anxious, as if something were happening that was out of her control, as if no matter what she did, how urgently she spoke, how hard Marcus tried to leave, he would not be able to escape the fate that loomed closer, minute by minute.

Marcus did not seem to share her sense of urgency. He remained standing before her, looking at her curiously.

"Marcus, I beg you to leave, now."

"You want to protect me?" he said in disbelief.

"Aye! I know you didn't commit the murder."

"Oh?"

"You were with me the entire time."

"Consider me warned. You may go." Marcus settled his foot on a nearby stool and stooped to lace his boot. Judith had the sense he relished the excuse to avoid looking at her.

"It didn't work," she said quietly to his back.

"I don't know what you're talking about," Marcus replied,

but Judith could hear the tenseness in his voice, saw the way his gaze avoided hers.

"I don't believe a word of what you told me last night. That wasn't you speaking." Tentatively, she lifted her hand and smoothed a stray tendril from his forehead, found it still damp from his exertions on stage, found him trembling slightly. "You're a wonderful actor, Marcus. Too wonderful. When I saw you act today, it became clear to me what you had done, and why."

Marcus slowly stood upright. For a moment, he stood frozen. He had given it his all, he had put his heart and soul into it, and still she saw through it. He didn't know whether to be bothered that he had failed to convince her despite his acting prowess, or relieved that his beloved Judith had seen through to the real man beneath.

But he couldn't give in to his gladness. Taking a deep breath to firm his resolve, he turned casually to face her, his eyes snapping with disdain. "You think I was lying?"

Judith jerked back at his derisive tone. Then she lifted her chin. "Aye, I do."

"You can't accept what I said, is that it?" he asked scornfully. "Too much the noblewoman to believe a common man like me would use you in that way?"

"Too much the woman to believe it meant so little." She threw her arms around him. Marcus shivered in response, betraying the longing and desire that surged through him. She laid her cheek against his, tears squeezing from under her eyelids, wetting his beard-roughened face. "You fool, do you think what we have is so easily discounted?"

"No!" Marcus grasped her wrists and brusquely shoved her back. He shook her arms for emphasis, his teeth gritted in frustration. "No."

Judith ignored his denial, her tear-sheened eyes filled with love, crumbling his carefully constructed pretenses.

"No," he whispered once more, but it had become the answer to her question, and no, he knew he could never again deny what he felt for her.

She leaned into him, offering her lips, her body if he desired it. Marcus resisted mightily, his hands pressing into her arms almost painfully. But he failed miserably. He dropped her arms and enclosed her in a hard, possessive embrace.

Almost brutally, he crushed her full-length against his lean body, holding her as if he would never let her go. In response, Judith buried her face in his neck, her slender body trembling in his arms. Marcus clenched his eyes and breathed deeply of her. To his surprise, tears stung his own eyes. "You are remarkable," he murmured into her hair.

"I love you, Marcus. Forever," Judith said softly, her words entangled with tears. Her arms tight around his neck, she pressed her lips feverishly along his face, his lips, his eyebrows.

Marcus took a deep breath to regain his senses. But when he spoke, his voice was thick with passion and longing. "My sweet, why didn't you believe me?" he cried softly. "There is no future for us."

"You fool for thinking you could fool me."

Marcus cupped her face in his palm. "Darling, I wanted you to be free of me, free to find happiness without me. Now it seems your heart will never be rid of me while I'm alive."

"Never," Judith affirmed breathlessly.

Her mouth touched his, and a blaze of desire burst through Marcus like a thousand candles ignited at once.

Judith responded eagerly. Far too soon, she pulled back. "Marcus, quickly. We have to leave now." She clasped his hands. "Come away with me."

Marcus wondered if she realized she had used the words from the song he had written her. He squeezed her hands in understanding, ready to commit to the path they were about to take together. "Aye, I'll come."

Judith smiled with joy. Marcus let go of her hands and laced his other boot. He swung on his cloak, then grasped her hand and led her through the back of the tiring house to the door leading outside.

Marcus didn't have the faintest notion where he was headed, but he knew one thing—he was taking Judith with him, and the consequences be damned.

He opened the door into the fading light of day and hurried down the steps, Judith right behind him.

"Marcus Sinclair?"

Marcus turned at the sound of his name. A plump gaoler stood there, two burly guards standing beside him like a pair of oversized bookends. "Aye," Marcus replied, dread coursing through him.

"You're under arrest for the vicious, brutal murder of Lord Mowbray, an esteemed peer of the realm. Guards, take him."

The guards surrounded Marcus, cutting Judith off. They pinned his arms behind his back and used a stout rope to tie his wrists together.

"Stop it!" Judith cried, her hands on the gaoler's sleeve. "He didn't murder Mowbray, no matter what anyone told you."

The gaoler shook her off rudely. He seemed singularly disinterested in what Judith had to say. "Get back to your father, lady."

Her father? Was he speaking generally, or did he know who she was? How could he know? The gaoler led the procession toward a nearby wagon, the guards shoving Marcus before them.

Judith made a move to cut off the gaoler's strides. But her own strides were cut off. Walter Kennington stared down at her. He yanked her aside. He and her father had apparently been standing nearby, watching the arrest. "My God, Judith!" Walter cried. "What are you doing here—with *him?*"

Judith gasped. "*Me?* Perhaps you should explain your own presence here!"

"We're here to assist in carrying out the queen's justice," Walter said.

"Identifying Sinclair to the authorities," her father added stiffly. "Judith, I'm ashamed to see you still associating with that man!"

Judith ignored him, yanking hard against Walter's imprisoning grip. "Let go of me, Walter. They're arresting an innocent man, and I have to stop them!"

Walter tightened his grip. "How would you know, Judith? You weren't even at Lord Hunsdon's when Mowbray was murdered!" Walter's gaze traveled over her face, revealing his anxiety.

Judith met his eyes fiercely, but she was thinking of Marcus, who was even now being shoved into the back of the gaoler's wagon. "Because, Walter, Marcus was with me when the murder took place. He couldn't possibly be guilty."

"With you! Judith, you can't expect me to believe that! You're lying to protect him," Walter said. "You heard he was being arrested, and you came to warn him. I realize you are fond of him—*were* fond of him—but my God, Judith, this has gone too far!"

Judith gritted her teeth, furious at these men, both of them trying to sway her, convince her she wasn't doing what was right, what was essential. "Let go of me! I have to make them listen to me."

"The gaoler won't listen," Walter said derisively. "He's only acting under orders."

"Whose orders?"

"The city constable's."

Indeed, it was too late to prevent the arrest, assuming she had been able, which she truly doubted. Walter was right about that. The gaoler had his instructions. He was not the judge. Even now the prison wagon was entering the road, with Marcus inside.

"Where are they taking him?" Judith cried. She would have to be able to find him if she was going to convince the judge he should be let free.

"Newgate, so he can receive the punishment that's his due," Walter said.

Judith shuddered. She had heard tales of Newgate Prison, tales of its brutal treatment of suspects, even before a trial. And she knew well the fate of anyone found guilty of murder.

Her eyes turned fiercely back to Walter's. "Then, I'll go there and find a way to get him out. I'll tell all his friends, and the constable, and the judge, and anyone else I can get to listen that he was with me."

Walter's mouth dropped open. "You'll ruin your reputation!"

"What does that matter when Marcus' life is on the line?"

"It will change nothing!" Walter said, becoming more and more agitated. "Do you know how many women say the same about their men in a poor attempt to keep them out of prison?" he said furiously. "Why should the judge believe you?"

"Why should he not?"

"I'll not have you publicly dragging the Ashton name through the mud of the city courts," Howard said, flushed in anger. "You have caused me far too much trouble, girl." In a move so sudden Judith didn't see it coming, her father slapped her hard across the face. She fell to the ground from the force of it. For a moment she was shocked into silence. Her father had never hit her before.

Her eyes shot up and met his, her gaze accusing, not remorseful. Howard was the one who appeared remorseful, perhaps even shamed. Walter helped her to her feet, too embarrassed to look at her.

Judith ignored him. She pressed her hand to her stinging cheek and turned her large, pleading eyes on her father. "Father, *you* know Marcus is innocent, don't you? You must!"

Howard wouldn't meet her intense gaze. When he spoke, he mumbled his words. "I know nothing of the sort. That type is capable of any depravity, particularly against his betters."

"Father!"

"And you are saying nothing, Judith. Nothing." He and Walter pulled her toward their waiting carriage. "And I'm going to make certain of it."

Nothing she said could sway her father. During the long, painful ride back home, her father and Walter had argued with her, tried to convince her alternately of the futility of her plan to speak up for Marcus, and of Marcus' guilt.

But neither had any real evidence he had committed the murder. All of it was innuendo, conjecture, except for the witness Walter and her own father were planning to speak against Marcus. And the trial was set for tomorrow, an inordinately quick proceeding. Judith wondered if her father had something to do with how swiftly justice was being meted out in this particular case. It was odd for a man who bore Lord Mowbray no love to be so desperate to see his supposed "murderer" punished. But Judith knew the real reason. Her father hated Marcus' power over her, knew she loved him still. Both men were appearing as witnesses against her own lover. It was appalling. Judith silently vowed she would appear, too, and tell the truth. Nothing could keep her away.

The dankness of the cell was relieved only by a thin amber light that came from a wall sconce down the hall. Marcus sat on the driest spot on the floor not already taken by another of the half dozen prisoners, his back freezing against the stone wall behind him. He wished fervently he had his cloak with him still. But the guards had stolen it. Meanwhile, he shivered in the dark.

The clang of the cell door startled him, making a din in the echoing corridors. Six pairs of eyes swung upward, some baleful, some glinting in fear as the gaoler entered. Most of them knew he was coming for one of their number, and at this time of night, the summons could only lead to agony.

The man's hulking shadow crossed over Marcus and settled there, making the hair rise on the back of Marcus' neck. He was the one being summoned now.

"Up," commanded the gaoler dispassionately as he kicked Marcus in the thigh.

Marcus rose unsteadily to his feet, finding his knees stiff with cold. They were still not as strong as they could be, and he felt it when he walked too much, or stayed in one position too long.

He followed the gaoler down the corridor, swerving along with him to avoid the drips that came down the walls and ceiling in places. It had begun raining outside, and Newgate was not watertight. Marcus thought of these things idly, trying at all costs not to give in to fear. It was difficult with the sound of fear thick in the musky air about him. Cries of pain, moans of unhappiness, screams of terror—

The screams suddenly came sharper as the gaoler opened the thick bound door at the end of the hall. Marcus shuddered. The gaoler shoved him forward, and he landed sharply on his knees on the floor of what only could be called a torture chamber.

"You want a confession from this one?" asked a thick, ugly

man with a bull neck. He pulled Marcus to his feet, his hand tight on his shirt.

The gaoler glanced about the room. "The rack's in use?"

"Aye."

Marcus felt his stomach lurch, and an empathetic pain swelled in his knees. His body would never be able to withstand the rack, with his knees still healing from dislocation. Not for more than a moment.

"Confession's not necessary," said the gaoler easily. "Too much evidence. Just give him the usual."

"Good enough." The enormous torturer shoved Marcus against the wall as if he were as weightless as a child. He yanked off the rope still binding Marcus' wrists and pulled his hands up into manacles attached to the walls. "That'll hold you." With one swift jerk, Marcus' linen shirt was ripped from his back, the sudden cold air sending goose bumps up his exposed flesh.

Marcus couldn't see a thing, could only smell the mildew stench of the stone wall under his cheek. But he knew enough about Newgate to understand what was coming before the whip struck his back for the first time.

He had never felt the sting of a lash in his life. He cried out as the blaze of agony tore into his flesh. He wasn't a hero; he had no desire to prove his ability to withstand pain, no need to appear brave here in the prison torture chamber. Marcus was not accustomed to such stinging, relentless pain, the fear of anticipating the next stroke causing almost as much torment as the searing of the lash when it sliced into his flesh. His mind fogged with red heat as the lash snapped into him again and again.

After a while, his voice joined those of the others in the room screaming, until he lost the ability to cry out and the sense to understand anything but the seething ocean of pain drowning him.

Chapter 20

Judith dashed to her room the moment the carriage slowed in the drive of her home, anxious to get away from both men, anxious to think, to allow her mind to start putting everything that had happened in such a short time into some sort of order. Everything was happening too fast, as if she were aboard a runaway wagon, the horses tearing across the countryside, bound for a dangerous precipice.

If only she and Marcus had never attended the same party at Lord Hunsdon's home—but then she would never have realized she had the strength to run away with him.

If only she had reached Marcus sooner, warned him of the arrest before the play—but if she hadn't seen him act, she would never have known he truly loved her.

If only her father and Walter hadn't been there to identify him to the gaoler—but someone else surely would have.

The last few hours were a string of connections impossible to separate, impossible for her to bear, taxing her heart, promising unattainable happiness and unbearable pain.

Weary from thinking, she started down the stairs, planning once and for all to explain to her father why she so badly needed to convince the authorities that Marcus was innocent.

She would tell him everything if need be. Tell him how Marcus had made love to her in an attempt to hurt her, to make her stop loving him. Perhaps if he understood the reason Marcus had visited her, he would understand not only that Marcus was innocent, but that he was good, as noble in heart as any member of the nobility.

She heard her father and Walter speaking intently in the parlor. She was surprised Walter was still about. She had thought he would have long since departed.

"Are you sure she won't ruin everything?" Walter asked.

Judith froze before entering the parlor. *Ruin what?*

"I looked in on Judith a moment ago," her father was saying. Judith realized he must have done so while she was resting, for she hadn't seen him. "She's a smart enough girl, though she has made her mistakes. I've trained her to think of her reputation above all. I'm sure she understands she can hardly rush into the Court of Law with such a tale without damaging our place at Court."

"I hope so," Walter sighed. "I can't tolerate the idea of marrying a bride with that kind of background hovering over her."

Judith gritted her teeth. She would never marry him.

"She understands, my Judith. She knows her personal feelings are nothing compared to our position."

"She seemed adamant to me," Walter said darkly.

Her father was silent a moment, and then the conversation resumed in a new direction. "It's worked out well, I'd say," Howard said, his voice betraying satisfaction. "Tomorrow is the trial, and once we've done our duty there, it will be over for good. And none too soon, I tell you. I've been fighting this for months. At every turn I've had to take steps to protect our family name, all because of my daughter's naiveté where that actor is concerned. The man has some power over her that's inconceivable to me. As if she's bewitched. Once he's out of the picture, she'll settle down and be the responsible girl I raised so well."

"That's what attracted me to your daughter, Howard. That and her dowry, of course." Both men chuckled. "That man Sinclair wasn't difficult to find for the arrest, appearing on stage as he did. It's good no one warned him or he may have left London.''

Howard snorted. "Then all the authorities would have is Richard Langsforth.''

"Not bloody likely *he'd* lose his head over this,'' Walter said.

"Never necessary, after all,'' Howard said. "He only needed to be arrested to keep him from using his family's power to save that actor.''

"But he'll be free soon? If his father becomes involved, things could get out of hand.''

"Just as soon as Sinclair hangs, which should be day after tomorrow.''

Judith was appalled. They were conspiring against Marcus, heedless of his guilt or innocence. Righteous fury consumed her, and she entered the room ready for battle.

Startled, both men looked up at the same time. Judith took no time grabbing center stage. "You sicken me, both of you!''

Howard quickly rose, his hands extended in a calming gesture. "Judith. Now there, I'm sure you misunderstood what you heard—''

"I misunderstood nothing! Father, you can't do this! It isn't right!''

"Judith, steady yourself,'' Howard said. "You don't know everything. Walter and I know facts you don't, know why justice is truly being served.''

"You know nothing about justice.'' She spun on Walter. "And you! I hate you, do you hear me? I can't stand you! I will never marry a man as vile, as low as you.'' Walter had also come to his feet. He moved closer to Judith, fury contorting his features at her insults. "I told you Marcus was with me at midnight, but you can't stand to think of it, can you? He was with me, in my own chamber, loving me. As I was loving him, worshiping him with my body and my soul.''

When the hard blow came across her cheek, Judith was almost glad, victorious she had hurt him. She wiped blood from her lower lip. Her eyes snapped as they bore into his. "You can beat me if you wish, but nothing you do can ever change how I feel, Walter Kennington. My heart belongs to Marcus

alone. If you think you're going to kill my love for him, you're
both wrong. It will never die. Never!''

"Damn you, daughter, damn you!" Howard said. "You will
stay locked up in your room until that man swings from a stout
rope! And furthermore, you will stay there, and starve, until
you agree to marry this fine man and go begging on your knees
for an apology from him, and from me! In a few hours, Sinclair
will be found guilty of murder, and he will cease to cause our
family this torment!''

The image of Marcus dangling from a hangman's noose
knocked the underpinnings from Judith's anger, severely weak-
ening it. She was shrieking like a fishwife at the two men who
had the power to change the course of events, men who held
Marcus' precious life in their hands. She was only making
matters worse. Feeling suddenly, intensely frantic for sympathy,
for understanding, she dropped to her knees in front of her
father and clasped his hands. "I beg you, Father. Don't do this,
you mustn't! Marcus is innocent! You can't let him die!'' Her
tears overflowed and streaked down her face. "Father, I will
never see him again, I promise. I will forget him completely.
I will apologize to Walter; I will marry him. But you can't
murder Marcus like this! Please, Father! I beg you. Please.''

Judith gazed up at him, all the pain of her soul revealed to
him in her tear-filled eyes. Her father looked shamed, and Judith
prayed her heartfelt appeal was having an effect on him. When
he spoke, his voice fairly shook with the stress of emotion.
"Do you love me, daughter?''

The question seemed so out of place. "Aye," Judith replied.
"You know I do.''

"Then, let go of me, Judith," her father said, his voice
weary. "Let go, and go immediately to your chamber and
remain there.''

Judith rose to her feet. She was shaken from her pleading,
shaken by the raw emotion coursing through her. Her begging
had failed with the only other man she truly loved, her father.
Once more fury began to well up in her, frustration coupled
with rage more powerful than she had ever felt. "You will not
make me stay in my chamber! You will not keep me from
doing everything I can to save Marcus! I will go to the queen

herself if I must, but I will not see him hang for a crime he didn't commit!" She ran through the parlor door and into the great hall, heading for the main door.

"Dunley! Stop her!"

Howard's bellow brought his butler into her path. Obeying his master, Dunley swiftly bolted the door before Judith reached it.

Unable to go forward, Judith turned and ran toward the kitchen door. Howard and Walter intercepted her. Walter crushed her against him, imprisoning her in his arms.

"Take my daughter and lock her in her chamber," Howard commanded Dunley.

"No!" Judith kicked and scratched at Walter. Dunley stood there a moment, stunned at his master's request. But receiving a stern look from Howard, he moved to assist.

Between the three of them, they dragged Judith, kicking and screaming, up the stairs and secured her in her bedchamber.

Dawn was beginning to break. Marcus was going to be tried for murder. Even now he lay in a horrible, dark cell in infamous Newgate prison. Judith was as much a prisoner, still locked in her chamber.

She was desperate to get free, but had not found a way to accomplish that. Her father had posted Clyde, the burly groom, outside her door to guard her. Her balcony door was also locked, of course. Her father had thought of everything. For the first time Judith truly understood just how important form and reputation mattered to him. He would even stoop to imprisoning his own daughter to keep her from sullying her reputation in public—despite the fact an innocent man would hang as a result. Fury and desperation driving her, Judith lifted a chair and smashed it against the balcony door window. The thick glass cracked, but the steel panes were set too closely together in the mullioned window to allow her to slip through anyway. It was hopeless.

"Milady?" came a whispered voice.

Judith dropped the chair and hurried to her maid's closet door. The room on the other side adjoined her own and opened on a landing and steps leading to the kitchen. This door, too, was locked. "Audrey! Where have you been?"

"Shh." Judith obeyed, and heard a key moving quietly in the lock.

When Audrey opened the door, Judith was so relieved she hugged her as if she wouldn't let her go. "Where have you been? You've been gone so long."

"I'll explain everything, but you must be quiet. The other servants might hear. If they do, my goose is cooked." Audrey closed the door quietly behind her. She turned back to Judith. "They all think your father has lost his mind, locking you up like this. You have their sympathies."

"But not their help," Judith said bitterly.

"Nay. Think on it, milady. They could lose their jobs if they defy Lord Ashton."

Judith sighed. "Aye, you speak truly. It isn't right to expect such a sacrifice. But Audrey, *you* are risking it."

"That's different," she said pertly. "You're my lady. I would have come sooner, but for my trip through town."

"Where have you been?"

"Trying to find Richard. I finally located him in the Clink on Maiden Lane. It's not one of the worst prisons, at least. I was told he won't be mistreated; but I can't get near him, and no one will listen to me."

"I know how you feel," Judith said. "Marcus is in Newgate."

"Newgate! How horrible. But—" She looked carefully at Judith. "That concerns you, milady?"

"Aye, more than I can say." Judith swung a cloak onto her shoulders. "I have to leave now, Audrey. I have to help him." She peered out the door. "Is it clear? Or is my father about?"

"Your father has already left for the Court of Law," Audrey said.

"He's left? Then, it may already be under way!"

"What may be under way?"

"Marcus is on trial today."

"That soon! That's unusually quick, isn't it?"

Judith grasped her arms. "Come, Audrey, we have to leave now or we might be too late."

* * *

The room at the Court of Law was crowded with spectators, all elbowing for the best position from which to watch the drama that played out before them. Judith no less fiercely elbowed her way to the front.

The judge was speaking, asking questions of a ragged prisoner standing before him, wearing nothing but a pair of knee-length breeches. His wrists were tied behind him, signaling the man was most likely violent. His bare feet were filthy. Crusted blood striped his back, marks from a whip, no doubt. Marcus wasn't on trial here after all, she thought for one wild moment. This was some horrible criminal, some depraved murderer—

Her eyes raised a notch to his strong profile, showing the shadow of a beard, and her heart twisted in agony. It was Marcus. Her gaze fell once more to his back, fury and compassion warring within her. "They whipped him!" she said in dismay to Audrey.

"They whip all the prisoners, for good measure," said a scrawny man nearby. His grin revealed two missing front teeth. "Sometimes they confess. This one didn't, but he's hanging for sure."

"What makes you say that?"

"All the witnesses who saw him. He ain't got a chance."

Judith had no idea who had testified, but as the judge continued to question Marcus, she quickly pieced it together.

"Did you have an accomplice, or did you act alone?" asked the judge, glaring down at Marcus from his bench as if Marcus were lower than an earthworm.

"How can an innocent man possibly answer such a question?" Marcus asked.

"I'm the interrogator here!" the judge cried. "I repeat: Did you have an accomplice, or did you act alone?"

"I didn't act," Marcus said with chilling calm.

"Hah! You are a liar. You are an actor by profession, are you not?"

"I have already said that I am."

"Then, you lie when you say you did not act, for you act all the time!" The judge smiled at his witty victory. "Now, what say you to the charge that you kidnapped Lord Mowbray's bride from his own bridal feast?''

"No, it is not true."

"Lord Ashton has testified that it *was* true."

"It was not a kidnapping, but a favor for a friend."

"A favor for a friend?" The judge smirked. "I suppose the lady in question enjoyed your foul treatment of her, as well. Is it not true that you were dueling on the lawn of Lord Hunsdon's home the night of the murder?"

Marcus kept his chin high. "Aye, that is true."

"And after you engaged in this duel with Lord Mowbray you reentered Lord Hunsdon's home and viciously murdered him—"

"That is *not* true."

"Lord Kennington has testified he saw you engaged in such a duel."

"I was dueling Walter Kennington himself."

"Kennington? How could you possibly duel the man who was watching you? Again you are caught in an outright lie."

"It is Kennington who lies."

"I will not have you slandering members of the peerage in my courtroom!" the judge cried.

"Milady—" Audrey nudged her and pointed. Howard and Walter were making their way toward her through the crowd.

Judith knew they would prevent her from giving the evidence that could save Marcus. She shoved her way toward the judge. "Your Honor! I haven't testified."

All eyes turned toward her, including Marcus'. Judith read surprise and concern in his eyes. Rather than appearing relieved at the fact she was here to deliver testimony that could save him, she saw his jaw harden as if in resolve. She didn't understand why until much later.

"We do not need your testimony, young lady, for we have enough," the judge said. "Marcus Sinclair, I find you—"

"No! He didn't do it!" Judith cried frantically. "I can prove he didn't do it, for he was with—"

"I confess!" The thunderous statement from the accused instantly silenced the courtroom and drew all eyes to the actor. Marcus had projected his trained actor's voice at its full volume, a voice able to reach the farthest gallery seats in the Globe Theater, even above the most raucous crowd. "I murdered Lord Mowbray! I am guilty."

The courtroom was stunned for one long moment before the crowd went wild. People hooted, people argued, and some jeered and hollered.

Judith alone was shocked into silence. She stared aghast as the guards surrounded Marcus. He had confessed! What had possessed him when she was so close to saving his life? "No, Marcus!" she screamed, knowing it was futile. "No, he's innocent!" Her voice was only one more amid the babble.

Her father and Walter had reached her side and were dragging her outside. Above the tumult of the crowd behind her, the judge quickly passed sentence. "Marcus Sinclair, I find you guilty of the vicious, depraved murder of a peer of the realm, Lord Mowbray. At dawn tomorrow, you will be taken to Tyburn and there hanged by the neck until dead for your crimes. Guards, take him away."

As her father and Walter shoved her inside their waiting carriage, Judith vaguely realized they were silent, as if also shocked by what had transpired.

Chapter 21

Not until she had been locked up again, this time in the dark pantry off the kitchen, did Judith realize neither her father nor Walter had spoken to her on the ride home. Neither man chastised her for escaping her locked room or for trying to help Marcus. They had said nothing. She was so fraught with anxiety, she hardly noticed at the time.

As each minute passed in the dark silence, she grew even more frantic. Marcus was going imminently to his doom, each tick of the clock bringing his death closer, and she was powerless to stop it. She pounded on the pantry door, begged anyone who heard her to release her. She scratched at the lock until her fingers were bleeding, slivers embedded under her nails.

"Let me out! Father, you must let me out!" she cried, pounding her fists on the door, rattling the handle. "Dunley! I know you're out there. You must free me. I have to do *something!*"

The servants had apparently been given strict orders to ignore her. No one responded to her pleas, though Judith could hear the kitchen servants preparing supper as usual, as if this were a usual evening. The hours were passing relentlessly; minute by minute the shadow of death drew closer. She could feel it as surely as if it were coming to smother her own life.

"Somebody listen," she cried. "Go tell Lord Hunsdon, tell Marcus' friends. Somebody must help him, somebody." Her voice fell to a hoarse whisper, and her head dropped against the heavy oak door in exhaustion. She slid slowly down the door until she was huddled on the floor, sobbing.

"Marcus, why? Why did you confess?" She asked herself this so many times, she grew weak with it. Her reputation was nothing compared to Marcus' life. How could he even think it compared? As she reviewed what she had seen, as her memory replayed the events leading up to his confession, a deep chill crept up her spine. He had done it because he knew he was as good as dead already, she was certain of it. Her sacrifice would have been for nothing, discounted as the raving hysterics of a lady who was no better than a harlot.

Judith indeed verged on hysteria. She felt overwhelmed by events, as if she were losing her grip on reality in the dark pantry, the only light a thin line under the door. Marcus could not compete with the combined forces of her father and Walter in setting up a case against him. His own friends were either as common, as unconnected as he was, or—in Richard's case— also in prison. Richard—was he going to be executed, too? Judith doubted it, for Marcus had confessed to the crime. Richard had only been put out of the way temporarily. It was much more difficult to manage the death of an earl's son, after all. And for her father and Walter Kennington's purposes, it was unnecessary.

The kitchen fell silent, and the light under the door disappeared, leaving Judith in total darkness. *The darkness of a grave,* she thought, her heart thudding heavily against her ribs. She wished it would stop beating, for she could stand the agony no longer. She could do nothing to stop the inevitable approach of her lover's death, the creep of despair's frigid fingers upon her heart. She shuddered hard, knowing she would never again experience such agony. It was impossible for anyone to feel more impotent, more heartbroken, than she felt now. The forced inaction would drive her mad. She prayed for release from her prison, but was afraid of her prayers, for she would not be released until Marcus was dead. She prayed she would never see the end of the long, dark night. She would go mad with it, mad.

Relentlessly, the hours passed, and the line under the door again began to be visible. Judith blinked her eyes and looked into the pitch darkness to readjust her gaze, then focused once more on the base of the door. The line of light was almost imperceptible, but definitely brighter than before. Dawn was approaching. Marcus would soon be dead.

Her terror surged once again, more powerful, more dreadful than before, reality crashing into her brain, her heart pumping wildly. For a split second, Judith knew she teetered on the brink of madness. She shrieked as if all the demons of hell were pursuing her. Shrieked as if she had to make the entire world hear her. She screamed until her voice was hoarse, until her lungs would burst with it.

"My God, my God, I can't bear it!" cried a voice on the other side of the door.

So she wasn't alone, Judith vaguely realized. She wasn't alone. Her screams became spoken words once more, pleas for release. "Let me out, let me out, I beg you, whoever you are!"

"Do you no longer know your own father's voice?" came Howard's weary words.

How long had he been there? Judith wondered. Had he sat up all night guarding her, sitting in vigil with her? "Father?" Judith cried, fresh tears welling up. Her hands scraped the surface of the door, rattled the handle once more. "Let me out, Father, please." There was no answer, but Judith could distinguish his heavier breathing. "My God, Father, you can't do this! He's going to hang, and I can save him, I swear it! Let me out, I beg you," she whispered in supplication. "I beg you, I beg you, I beg you."

"I cannot," Howard said weakly.

A cry of anguish tore from Judith's throat, taking with it her last shred of hope. The light under the door had turned a murky gray, but Judith knew it was dawn beyond her family kitchen. Marcus was dying, and it was too late to stop it. There was nothing she could do. Judith collapsed on the floor, no longer having the will to move, to speak, to breathe. She would prefer to die.

* * *

The moment the door was unlocked, Judith left the pantry. Full sunlight played on the rushes about her feet, touched her golden hair, turning the disarrayed mess into a halo about her dazed face.

Judith was unaware of how unearthly she appeared, her eyes unable to focus beyond her pain. Her steps were leaden, her eyes blind to the sympathetic gazes of the servants around her. She didn't see her father, who looked away as she walked past him. Out of habit, she found herself at the bottom of the staircase. Gathering her skirt in one hand as a lady is always taught to do, she gradually pulled herself up by the banister, intent only on making it to her bedchamber before she collapsed completely.

It was as if there had been a death in the family, Audrey thought with sorrow. The servants whispered among themselves, and all of them steered well clear of Lord Ashton. The master himself looked his name, his face gray as ashes. When the door knocker banged around midday, it startled everyone in the house.

Dunley the butler accepted the delivery from the courier.

"I'll take that." Lord Ashton snatched the letter from his hand and read the name scrawled on it. It was for Judith, and it had come by way of Newgate.

"But, master, it's for Lady Judith," Dunley protested.

Howard ignored him. Holding tight to the letter, he wandered back into the great hall toward the massive hearth. Once there, he made a move to throw the letter in. But curiosity piqued him, and he decided there was no harm in reading it first.

My beloved Judith:
   When you read this, I will be with our Maker, as they say. I hope that may be true. As Shakespeare terms it, it is an undiscovered country, and I am departing on a voyage from which no man can ever return. But I will

*be beyond the reach of earthly turmoils, which I imagine
brings with it a form of peace. I pray that this is so.*

*I don't write these words to upset you. I hope that you
will understand why I did what I did, and not think the
worst of me. I knew things about that night that you did
not. I know why the accusing finger turned to me, though
we both know I was not present at the time.*

Howard's hand spasmed uncontrollably, his fist tightening
on the letter. Marcus Sinclair *knew?* He knew and he didn't
reveal what he knew, faced the gallows instead? It was too
much. Too much. Howard shook, the guilty monster inside him
growing stronger the more time passed. It was going to overtake
him if he wasn't careful. Like leaden fingers around his throat,
the shame threatened to strangle him.

Almost reluctantly, his gaze turned to the printed words once
again. He found he had to blink hard to clear his eyes enough
to read them.

*Remember that I always loved you. From the moment
I saw you, my soul was entirely yours. Even tonight, in
the darkness of this cell as I write by the light of a single
guttering candle, my thoughts turn not to what is yet to
come when dawn breaks, but to you—my candle, my
light, my glorious morning.*

*I would do nothing differently if I were given the chance
to live my life over, despite what has come to pass. Though
our path together was fraught with obstacles, our love
made me truly alive. I never understood what I was
lacking until I found you.*

*Shakespeare once told me I had yet to experience life,
to truly feel the depth of emotion mankind is capable of
experiencing. I did not understand him, until I met you.
Through you, I discovered these emotions, and a profound
love the likes of which I had never comprehended existed.
You gave this to me. My life may not have been long,
but it was rich.*

*I pray for many things on my last night on earth.
Foremost is a prayer that you will put our love behind*

you and go on to live a full life, as is your right and your destiny. Darling, for my sake, do not let what was between us shadow you for the rest of your days. Grant me this last request.

Please, when you think of me, if you think of me, consider me a brief act in the long life that has yet to play out before you, and face your future purposefully and without remorse. Stay vital, and gift this world with all you have to offer—your wonderful goodness, kind heart, and true nobility are rare in the world, and mankind is richer for it. I know I was richly blessed to have loved you.

Eternally yours,
Marcus

Howard froze. An incredible weight of guilt crushed down upon him, making it almost impossible to breathe. His fingers, tightening around the letter, grew numb.

His daughter. His daughter—what had he done to her? What had he done? He had murdered the man she loved, murdered him as surely as if he had wielded the noose and the sword. He had murdered a man who loved Judith enough to give his life for her. He had done this to his own flesh and blood, to his beloved Judith, for whom he wished only the best.

His eyes fell on the display of his ancestor's portraits, lined so proudly on the wall of the great hall. Above and below were the family arms, which he so lovingly cared for himself, polishing them religiously. Weapons handled by his esteemed ancestors as far back as four centuries ago. Was this worth what he had done, this preoccupation with his noble name?

His heart thudded, and his eyes grew wide. One of the daggers was missing. He was certain it had been there just hours before. His vitals churned in fear. *Judith.*

He rushed from the room and pounded up the stairs. *Put our love behind you, and go on to live a full life, as is your right and your destiny.* Marcus Sinclair had known she might consider this option. He had known. He had written her words asking her not to take this irrevocable step. He was facing the gallows the next morning, and he had thought beyond, to what his death would mean for Judith, the woman he loved.

He hurled the door open, and it crashed against the wall. Judith started, but did not release her hold on the dagger, which was pointed straight at her heart as she knelt on the floor. "Judith, my God, daughter, no!" Howard cried. He was afraid to come closer, afraid she would shove it deep inside her in the moment he reached her.

Judith raised her face to his, and Howard felt her devastation like a wasteland. Her spirit was gone from her already.

"You mustn't do this, daughter. Don't revenge me in this way. I beg you. I know I deserve worse, but not this, please!"

Judith was still contemplating this irrevocable step when her father burst in, not yet decided whether to carry out the deed. She knew if she did, Marcus' sacrifice would be for nothing. But her father's words incensed her, denigrating as they did once again her love for Marcus. "Do you truly think it would be for you?" Judith asked coldly. Even now, her father thought only of himself, and it sickened her.

Howard thrust out a paper toward her. "Marcus told you not to. He wrote you shouldn't do it."

Judith's hands shook, and she began to lower the dagger. "He wrote me?" she said, her voice dropping to a whisper. She set the dagger down beside her on the floor.

In an instant, Howard had grabbed it up and placed it out of her reach on top of a bureau. In exchange, he handed her the now much-crumpled letter.

Judith read the words, recognizing Marcus in every word, every phrase. His last words to her. A fresh sob caught in her throat.

"Marcus," she sighed, pressing the letter to her chest. She wouldn't take her life; she would listen to her lover even though he had departed from this world. She would listen to no one else ever again. She would move beyond her shock, come to terms with Marcus' death. She was growing stronger. Marcus was helping her, even now, as he had helped her in life, to understand fully her own strength.

Throughout the long night locked in the pantry, as Judith had lain in a cocoon of darkness, something had changed within her. She had undergone a transformation. Her previous conceptions had fallen away, her love no longer blinding her, and she had become fully aware of the world in a way she had never been before.

She no longer was blind to the hate in people, even within those she loved. She understood their weaknesses more readily. Kennington, for instance. How could she ever have considered marrying him? She would never marry that blackguard. He thought he was naturally superior to Marcus when he was the least moral of any of them, for he had deliberately lied. He had dueled with Marcus, yet testified that he had seen Marcus dueling with Mowbray. Judith would never marry him. And she knew now she had the strength to keep it from happening.

And her father. She knew her father for what he was, a weak man overly concerned with public opinion, frightened of what those in power might think of him. More than frightened. He was terrified. He had been terrified for a long time, but she had been so blinded by a daughter's love for a man she considered a strong father, she hadn't seen it.

She read Marcus' letter over again and concentrated on words she had barely understood before. *I knew things about that night that you did not. I know why the accusing finger turned to me, though we both know I was not present at the time.*

Judith turned and looked hard at her father, thinking of all that had happened. Her eyes widened as she studied him. It was writ plainly on his face, on his features—even now he was burning with guilt and shame.

She rose to her feet and stood tall before her father. Her voice was unnaturally calm. "*You* killed Mowbray."

The weight of the statement was heavier than an accusation, because they both knew it was true.

"You killed him, and you made it look as if Marcus did it."

Her father could no longer meet her gaze. He was shaking, visibly shaking from her words.

"And Marcus knew you did it, and he kept your guilty secret." As Judith said the last, heavy scorn colored her words.

Howard Ashton lost his control. The mask tumbled from his face. "Aye, daughter, I did it, all that you say." His shoulders shook, and he buried his face in his hands, as if too mortified by shame to have her gaze upon him. His moan tugged at Judith's heart, but she was past playing the role of the loving daughter.

She watched impassively as her father crumpled before her, collapsed on the edge of the bed. She watched him brush tears from his eyes, and waited. "I didn't mean to kill him, you must believe me. I'm not a murderer, for God's sake."

"Not a murderer because your blood's too blue, is that it?" Judith said, her voice thick with sarcasm.

Howard pulled away from her voice as if struck. "No, no. It was an accident. Mowbray was threatening me. He threatened to reveal what I had done, money I had given Lord Essex for his rebellion against the queen. That's why you were to marry him; it was payment for his silence."

Judith was amazed. She had never known any of this.

"You assisted Essex? But why?"

"He told me he would make me an earl," her father said bitterly.

"An earl?" Judith shook her head in amazement. "All of this—this tragedy, this farce—all this is because you wanted to be one more step up on the ladder of nobility? Oh, it's too rich to stomach!"

"Not just the title. He was to give me lands, and estates. They would have been yours, too, one day."

"I want them not! I want none of it, not even what you already have! You're already as rich as Midas, Father!"

She could see his shame rising once more to the surface and ceased berating him. She knew he hadn't yet told the entire sorry tale. "What happened when Mowbray lost me?" she asked quietly, yet forcefully.

"He began to blackmail me. He threatened me again with revealing my part in the plot. But he didn't really want revenge. He wanted money. So I paid him. And that Richard Langsforth. He complicated matters badly. I was glad when you broke with him, for there was once again a chance to make a sensible political match. That chance was Lord Kennington."

"Whose side was *he* on?"

"Ours. Or rather, his. He wants you badly, Judith, despite all that's happened. He is an ideal match, truly. He is very well situated at Court. And he will keep our name clean there, that's his promise.''

'.'Now that Mowbray's dead, there's not so much fear of that anyway, I'll warrant,'' Judith said ironically.

"Perhaps. This was before. Your affair with Sinclair threatened to ruin all of this. My reputation was on the line. There had already been talk linking me to Essex. If you had run off with Sinclair, it would have left me open to even more ridicule. My daughter, eloping with a stage actor!'' He shook his head at the thought.

"That night at Lord Hunsdon's, Mowbray again threatened me,'' he continued. ''We were playing dice with other men, but the hour grew late and the others left. He had me alone. He told me he was going to the queen with what he knew because he had heard about the negotiations for your hand to Kennington. He is not a man who likes to lose. Perhaps, if you had been less reluctant, if I had been able to marry you to Kennington sooner—''

"Don't lay any of this at my feet,'' Judith said coldly. ''You did not confide one word of this to me. You cannot expect me to feel sympathy for how you wanted to use me to clear your own name, which you yourself managed to sully.''

"Daughter,'' Howard said pleadingly. Judith heard the weakness in his voice, and it disgusted her.

"You haven't yet revealed the end,'' she said.

Howard waited a long time, as if unable to put it into words. ''Mowbray threatened me, and I knew I was running out of choices. He called me out, insulted me. I was afraid someone else would hear. I urged him to take our argument outside, but he was not concerned. He pulled his stiletto from his scabbard and began to threaten me with it. I was positive he was going to kill me. I jumped away and kicked at his hand. The blade went flying, and we both fell toward it, landing almost on top of each other. I found the blade first, and as I was raising it from the floor, it accidentally slipped into Mowbray's chest. I didn't intend to kill him; it was an accident.''

Judith was aware of her father's choice of words. He didn't stab Mowbray; the blade ''slipped into Mowbray's chest.'' She didn't know if the act had been as accidental as her father said, but it didn't matter. Marcus was dead.

"And somehow Marcus knew it was you," Judith said, wonder mixing with the scorn in her voice. "Marcus went silently to his own death, knowing you were the murderer, knowing even that you were the one sending him to the gallows. By giving his own life, he was protecting you. He did it out of love for me because he knows how much I love you." Her voice sharpened. She became the parent, trying to lead the man before her to a moral viewpoint. "Do you fully understand the significance of what he did?"

"I'm beginning to," Howard said miserably.

"How did Marcus know you were the guilty one?"

"I'm not sure. He's a wily one, that man."

"He *was* a wily one," she reminded him coldly. "But not as wily as some, it seems."

"He was the logical choice, daughter," he said, lifting his hands. "You must understand that. I needed you wed to Kennington, with no hint of scandal. I needed that more than anything. But you wouldn't give up Sinclair. Kennington told me how you and he were, together, at the party. He told me you spent time alone with him there. He had reason to fear what it meant, as we both learned later. He mentioned how you both left early."

"And Marcus was a commoner, without your connections, your money, your power," Judith said coldly. "That made him the perfect one to frame."

"Aye." He turned his pale blue eyes up to her, imploring her to understand. "But it was my *life,* Judith. I could have been sent to the block!"

A cleaner death than Marcus suffered, I'll warrant, Judith thought. She couldn't bring herself to say the words aloud. She still loved her father, despite everything. Just not enough to sacrifice herself for him any longer.

"Now that you know everything, you can forgive me, daughter, can't you?" Howard asked softly, as if certain his gentle Judith would soon be comforting him.

Judith stood as still as a statue looking down at him, her contempt warring with her love, with her sorrow and pain over

Marcus, with her lack of respect for the man she used to worship as a young girl. "Aye, I will forgive you," she said slowly. Her father's face began to brighten. "I will forgive you on the day you return Marcus to me." She turned and walked out of the room, as regal as a queen pronouncing an irrevocable sentence.

Behind her, Howard cried her name once, then dissolved into tears.

Chapter 22

The house was as silent as a tomb. Only the crackling fire in the hearth of the great hall gave evidence that people still lived and worked at the great Ashton manor house on Bishopsgate Street.

Lord Ashton had retired into his parlor hours ago and not emerged. Judith was resting quietly upstairs. Audrey had taken the opportunity to have time alone. She watched the fire crackling in the hearth, its orange tongues licking at the wood hungrily, determined to consume it. *At least something is alive in this house,* thought Audrey distractedly.

"Audrey, a gentleman is here to see you," said Dunley softly.

She looked up. Richard stood there in the great hall. In a moment she was in his arms, reveling in his warmth, his solidness, how protected it made her feel.

"I'm free, Audrey. It's all over."

She pressed her face into his broad chest. "I'm so glad. I was awfully worried."

"I knew you would be. I came as quick as I could after they let me out."

"I looked everywhere in London for you," she said, her

eyes hungrily playing over his face. "When I finally found you at the Clink, the gaoler refused to allow me to see you. Said you were not allowed visitors." The gaoler had also hinted he would make an exception if she allow him to tumble her, but she knew she needn't tell Richard that.

"That's true, I had no visitors," Richard said wryly. "And here I thought I was terribly unpopular."

"Don't joke about it," Audrey chastised. "Haven't you heard?"

Richard looked at her hard, his eyes revealing intense pain in their blue depths. "Aye, I heard. My best friend is dead."

"I'm sorry, Richard."

"It was the talk of the prison." He turned from her slightly, every muscle in his body tense with fury. "I could kill whoever did this to him, for I'm sure it was a setup. But I don't have any evidence of it. And it won't bring him back. I'm only glad he died peacefully, instead of at Tyburn."

"Peacefully? I haven't heard this. What do you mean?"

"When the gaoler came into Marcus' cell to escort him to the wagon that would take him to the gallows, he discovered Marcus was already dead. Someone had apparently poisoned his wine. Or—and I rather like to imagine this is so—perhaps God took him early to save him from a painful and torturous death."

"Hah!" Audrey said disparagingly. She didn't think of God as being personally involved in people's affairs. Her childhood had been too hard to maintain that notion for long. "If God could do that, he should have released him altogether."

Richard sighed deeply. "Perhaps you're right." He collapsed on the bench beside the fire. "If only I'd been able to do something! I'll tell you, Audrey, if I had been free, none of this would have happened. I would have called on all my friends, my father and his friends, and we would have put a stop to it, given Marcus a fair trial, gotten him freed. I swear it." He clenched his fists in frustration.

Audrey sat beside him and pulled him against her. "I'm sorry, Richard. But I'm glad you told me about the poison. It will relieve Judith's heart, somewhat, I believe. To think he died quietly in his cell and not in a public display for the crowd's entertainment.''

"Aye, that's one drama I don't think even Marcus would want to act in.'' He clutched Audrey to him and rocked with her. "God, I miss him, Audrey. I don't know how I'll be able to stand it. Except for seeing you, being with you.'' He cupped her head against his shoulder, then kissed her hair tenderly. "I think I'll be able to get through this, now that I have you.''

"Richard," Audrey said hesitantly, anxious about breaking his heart further.

"I have to leave London immediately, Audrey. I can't bear to be here any longer now that Marcus is gone. How soon can you be ready?''

"Richard," Audrey hesitated. "I can't go with you.''

Richard pulled back. "What? You have to come. We can be married on the road, or at my family estate, wherever. But I don't intend to leave you behind.'' He gave her the smile that always melted her heart.

Audrey fought the feeling. "Lady Judith needs me, Richard. I can't leave.''

Richard's face darkened. He released her, but kept hold of her hand as she spoke.

"Think on it. She's suffering more than any of us. She relies on me. I have to stay with her, help her get through this time. You know how much she loved him.''

Richard's eyes betrayed his hurt.

Audrey tried to explain. "She needs me, Richard.''

"I see. And you don't think I need you?''

"Not as she does. You're strong, Richard.''

Richard dropped her hand as if tired of holding it. "Then, there's nothing more to be said, is there?''

"Nay, I don't suppose there is.'' Audrey pulled both her hands into her lap, closing in on herself for protection. Richard was angry with her, and he would break with her as surely as night followed day. It had all been too good to last; she had known it at the time, but had been swept away into the fantasy.

Richard rose, his stomach muscles knotted with hot anger. He strode toward the door, his cloak swirling against the rushes.

He was determined not to look back. He would walk out of here and forget her, that was all there was to it.

At the door he paused, shame washing over him. The woman he loved was behind him, unhappy, devastated as surely as he was. And all he was thinking about was his own pain. He turned, and the sight of her cheeks moist with tears cut straight to his heart.

In a moment she was in his arms. His voice was tender in her ear. "I'm sorry, darling. I love you. I'll always love you. When you are ready, I'll be waiting, whether it's next month, next year, ten years from now. I'll be waiting for you."

"You may not want to wait." Audrey looked in his eyes, exploring their brilliant blue depths, seeing his commitment to her clearly reflected there.

"I'll wait," he said firmly, brooking no argument. He brushed her tears away with his thumbs. Then his lips descended on hers in a slow, deep kiss—a kiss of good-bye.

A moment later, he was gone.

The thundering wouldn't cease. It pounded relentlessly in his brain, over his body, up and down his spine. Black shards of discordant images floated past, but no attempt to grasp hold of them and clarify them was possible. A ringing began beyond the dark well of despair, a painfully sharp noise. If only it would quit.

Consciousness seeped back slowly, like a drug through his system, in bits and pieces. A disembodied voice floated high above in the stratosphere, but the words were unintelligible. The sensation of temperature came next—cold, so very cold. With it came pain, throbbing pain radiating from his back outward, and from his extremities, his legs and arms setting up a loud cacophony of tingles.

He became aware of his tongue, which felt like a lump of cotton in his mouth, a dead weight. He moved it slightly and tasted anew the odd flavor that had permeated his last cup of wine on earth.

With that realization, the terror flooded back. *His last.* He had fallen asleep, and this was morning. He wasn't alone; he was aware of voices about him. This was dawn, and he was going to his death—

A loud moan drowned out the babble that seemed to surround him. It was a moment before he recognized the sound of his own voice, before he felt the delicate vibration of his vocal chords.

"He's coming round," said a voice. Marcus understood the words. Consciousness was returning relentlessly now. But this particular voice was out of place here in this hellish cell.

"That's it, warm him up as well as you can." Hands on his body, blankets, the rough scratch of wool on his face, his skin. "He's getting better color now. He just might make it. Just might. Keep working."

Dull discomfort now, in his limbs. His knees and arm were throbbing from their previous injuries, from the cold. He was lying on something that gave under him, he realized finally. A mattress, a rough one. Not the cold stone floor of his cell in Newgate.

His eyelids felt glued together. But he could see golden-red light through them. He realized he had control of them again, yet he was reluctant to open them and be jarred back to reality. He preferred the soft cocoon of whatever place he had been dwelling. It had given him no dreams, no memories, only an appealing nothingness.

"You're awake, Marcus! I can see it." A man's hand touched his face, gave it several small slaps. "That's it, wake up. You're back among the living now."

Reluctantly, Marcus cracked his eyes open. The shadow of a man hovered above him. His voice and silhouette were familiar, but did not belong in this place. "Will?" Marcus asked, attempting to speak. The sound came out like a groan.

"We did it!" The man disappeared from above him, and Marcus heard his voice join two others, who were disordinately pleased about the fact he was awake—even though it meant his execution was merely moments away.

Marcus opened his eyes fully and tried to focus on the scene. Will Shakespeare was pounding his apprentice, Alan, on the back gleefully. Richard Burbage was still rubbing at his legs with a wool blanket. "Can you move your toes?" Burbage asked with concern.

Marcus attempted it, and it seemed to work. But nothing about this scene made sense. What was he doing in this small yet comfortably appointed chamber? Whose was it? And what was Richard Burbage doing playing the physician? The last thing he remembered before this inordinately deep, dreamless sleep was drinking a cup of wine delivered to his cell. He had refused his last meal, having no stomach for it, but the wine—that was a different matter. He needed all the help he could get to steel his nerves for the ordeal to come in a few short hours. Before drinking the wine, he had written a letter to Judith. Hadn't he? Or had the entire play of events been a dreadful dream?

He pulled himself up on his elbows and knew instantly it had been no dream. The lash wounds on his back, now scabbing over, cracked in protest. "What in the hell?" Marcus asked. Swinging his legs over the side of the bed, he rubbed at his temples, which were pounding like a team of runaway horses. He squinted at the light of one lone candle, which was as bright as looking directly into the sun. The rest of the room was dark. It must be evening still. Dawn had not yet come.

"Don't worry, Marcus, the effects of the poppy juice will wear off soon," Will said, his voice ebullient. "I thought for a moment I'd given you too much. But I was worried I may not give you enough, so I had to risk it. One sign of a pulse, or of life of any kind, and you'd be a dead man now."

"Dead. The execution. It must be in a few hours."

"It was hours ago this morning!" Will said happily. "Or would have been. But you were dead already, so there was no reason to go through with it."

At Marcus' mystified expression, Burbage explained. "Will bribed a guard to smuggle in some wine tainted with poppy juice for you. It was a special gift for your last night. Will heard that given enough, it can give the appearance of death—for a while, anyway, enough to fool the guards at Newgate."

"Like in *Romeo and Juliet*," Marcus said, amazed it had worked. He had always thought that was the least believable part of that particular play.

Will grinned. "Of course!"

"When they found you dead, the guards wanted to run you through to make sure, but Will stopped them," Alan said.

Marcus shuddered. "Thank you for telling me, Al."

"The one I bribed stood with me on that argument," Will continued. "He's a regular playgoer, and he knew who you were. He was in on it. When the guards brought out your dead body, I laid claim to it, and I gave them a stirring speech about the importance of not desecrating the dead. Then I brought the corpse home, with the help of these two."

"Why, thank you, Will," Marcus said in awe. The situation was almost humorous. "I'm sorry I missed your performance."

"And did you ever look the part!" Will continued. "As pale as death, not a breath of life to be found. I was certain it was hopeless, but at least I had managed to save you from a more hideous death on the gallows."

"Aye, you did that," Marcus said, smiling wryly. His mind had cleared considerably, the symptoms of the powerful drug receding, and he was able to think. Was it truly over? Did the authorities accept that he was dead? "So, that makes me a walking dead man, is that it?"

"Aye, it does." Will ran his hand over his balding pate. "That's the sticky part I haven't figured out yet how to handle, for the authorities must continue to think you dead. At least you're alive. That's what counts."

But what next? Marcus asked himself. He couldn't very well perform at the Globe. Someone would recognize him. Unless he was wearing a good costume, of course. But his name appeared on the playbills. "My name, I'll have to change it."

"Good point. That would be wise."

"And you'll have to give me parts where I can wear costumes, or makeup."

Will nodded. "Another good point. You have returned to the land of the living, with all your senses intact." He patted his shoulder. "Perhaps there's a play I can write to make use of your talents without anyone knowing who you really are. It's a challenge, but I'll think on it. Eventually, people may forget Marcus Sinclair, or at least what you look like, and you'll be able to go on stage in your own form again."

Marcus clasped his friend's hand in a firm grip. "I owe you, Will. I owe you for saving my life."

"It was the least I could do. I saw what happened when you were arrested. The way the nobility abuses its power appalls me." He sat beside Marcus and threw his arm around his shoulders. Marcus winced at the contact, but he didn't complain. "I don't have the power or the unlimited funds our esteemed members of the nobility do," Will continued. "But we common gentlemen have our own means to wield power in this world. Even the son of a glove maker such as I am, with the help of a lowly guard at Newgate, can thwart the most powerful in the land."

"Now can we go tell her?" Alan asked excitedly. "She'll have to know soon."

Marcus looked at Alan sharply. His mind had already been tussling with that issue, but he hadn't particularly wanted to discuss it. "No."

"Your lady, I mean," Alan continued with all the optimism of a fourteen-year-old youth. "Once she knows, you and she can marry in secret, and—"

"And her father will find out, and I'll be a real dead man next time," Marcus said bluntly.

Will sighed. "Marcus is right, Alan. It can't be done. Not safely. Unless she were willing to run away with you—"

"She offered, but it still won't work," Marcus said, his voice covering the depth of his pain. "We would be found out eventually. Think of the trouble it would cause for you, Will— for all of you. You would be implicated in the plot to free me." He looked at the three of them, seeing their concern, their sympathy. He would never risk friends such as these. "No. I won't be able to tell her," Marcus said slowly. "Neither must any of you. In a short time she'll be married to a man of her own rank, and it won't matter anymore."

The three stared at him in silence, their eyes reflecting his own pain. It was a conundrum, a dilemma with no exit. None of them must ever let Judith Ashton know that Marcus was alive. Too much was at risk.

Another thought occurred to Marcus, one inviting still more pain. "Richard Langsforth. Where is he?"

"He was released from prison this afternoon, I heard," Richard Burbage said. "He doesn't yet know about you."

"And he shouldn't," Marcus said firmly.

"Not even Richard?" Will asked.

"If he knows, Judith will know. He has a fondness for Lady Judith's maid and would be sure to tell her. And Audrey would surely tell Judith."

The three stayed silent, contemplating all Marcus was giving up—the woman he loved, his best friend, possibly his career. It was too much to ask any man, but there was no choice.

Marcus himself relieved the depressed mood that had descended on the group. "Now, is there anything about to drink? I'd die for a good strong ale."

The other three exchanged glances over his choice of words, then burst out laughing.

"So he must not have suffered much," Audrey told Judith that evening. "That's one small thing to be grateful for."

"Aye, that's true," Judith said as Audrey brushed out her golden mane. Judith's eyes were dry, her composure that of a well-bred lady. Underneath, however, she had grown a new spine of iron. "Do you think someone poisoned him?" she asked quietly.

"I wouldn't know, milady. Richard seemed to think it was an act of God, that the Lord took him peacefully to keep him from being executed for a crime he didn't commit."

The familiar way Audrey said Richard's name wasn't lost on Judith. She watched her maid closely as she tended to her duties in the same efficient, caring manner she had done for years. "If it were poison, it may have been a painful death, nevertheless," Judith reflected.

She couldn't help but think on it, either way. She was grateful Audrey was willing to discuss it, for not to talk about Marcus' death, not to share her thoughts, would have been so much harder. She was grateful to Audrey for innately understanding this—grateful to her for so many kindnesses over the years, for nurturing her through so many difficult periods.

"Mayhap it was painful. We will never know," Audrey said sagely.

Judith's eyes met hers in the polished glass. "It was kind of Richard to come with the news. I'm glad he was freed."

"Even though Marcus paid the price."

"Even so. Will Richard be coming again soon? I should like to talk to him. He loved Marcus, as well."

The brush froze in midair. Judith watched closely as Audrey again resumed brushing her hair as if she had never interrupted her movements. "I think not," she said slowly. "He mentioned returning to his family estate, to recover from his sorrow."

"That's a shame. What think you, Audrey?"

"About what, milady?"

"About Richard leaving London."

"If it's what he must do, then he must do it."

"A pretty statement, Audrey. But will you miss him? You told me you had become friends."

"Aye, milady. Friends miss each other, of course."

Judith listened to Audrey talking softly to her, listened closely, and heard something new in her maid's voice, something that may have been there before, but Judith had been too entangled in her own agonies to notice. "You love him, don't you?"

Audrey met Judith's eyes in the mirror briefly, then quickly looked away. "Milady asks too many questions."

Judith spun around on the stool and took the brush from her hand, setting it aside. She clasped Audrey's hands. "Audrey. You don't have to hide it, not from me."

"I can't say I understand what you mean," Audrey said, not looking her in the eyes. She withdrew her hands from Judith's and turned away.

"Audrey," Judith said softly. "I was so caught up in my own pain, I never saw it. You must forgive me for being so selfish, so blind. You've fallen in love with him, and you were as distraught over Richard as I was over Marcus, when we didn't know what would happen to either man. But you shared none of your pain, while I poured out all the agony in my soul onto you. It hasn't been fair, not fair at all."

Audrey smiled weakly. "You're my lady. I'm your maid. That's my job."

"Don't be silly. Now, tell me everything, Audrey. I order you to. When did you know you loved him? Does he love you? Tell me true, Audrey, is he merely toying with you? If he is, he's going to hear from me straightaway."

"Nay, milady. Don't fret." Audrey retrieved the brush and resumed stroking Judith's hair. Her voice deceptively casual, she added, "The scoundrel asked me to marry him."

"Marry him?" Judith turned around and faced her maid, temporarily speechless. A nobleman taking a common woman as his mistress was a frequent occurrence. But it was extremely rare for him to give her his name, and ask her to be the mother of his legitimate children. That it was Richard who was defying convention, when the approval of his domineering family had meant so much to him. . . . Judith shook her head in awe. "Why, that's wonderful, Audrey! Why didn't you tell me sooner?" She rose and hugged Audrey tightly, then looked in her distraught eyes. "He must be madly, passionately in love with you! When is the wedding?"

"Milady, I cannot."

Judith smiled reassuringly. "Of course you can! You're as fine as any nobly born girl. It's not unheard of for a lady to advance so high by marriage. You're quite capable of it. You taught me everything I know."

Audrey couldn't answer. What could she say? "I'm needed here," she finally said.

Judith stared at her aghast. "You don't mean to tell me you've turned him down because you think I need you? I *do* need you, but not that much, Audrey." Audrey looked almost hurt.

Judith walked away a few steps, anxious to express herself better. "That isn't what I meant. What I'm trying to say is, I would have relied on you, before, allowed you to give everything of yourself to me. But things have changed somehow. I believe I'm stronger now. Look what I have already withstood. I'm ready for whatever the future may bring." She returned to Audrey and laid her graceful hands on her shoulders. "I could never allow you to sacrifice your happiness for me. There has been too much unhappiness already, too many broken hearts.''

Audrey gazed at Judith in admiration and pride. Her little charge had grown up. She was a woman now, and Audrey's work was through. ''Thank you, milady,'' she said gratefully. ''You'll never know—''

Judith clutched her maid to her. ''I know,'' she murmured. ''Truly, I know.''

Chapter 23

"Now, the Johnson daughter is well-favored and would make a good match," Lady Grace Langsforth said. "Her family's lands adjoin ours on the north side. I'm sure we can convince them to include a parcel of it as a dowry."

"That would be a simple matter, considering she's as big as two men and picks her nose," said Errol, delicately patting his thin lips with his napkin. The family meal had just begun in the great hall, and as usual, the favorite topic of conversation was finding a suitable match for Richard, the only hold-out among his brothers as far as marriage was concerned.

"Hush, Errol!" Grace said. "Don't be rude. Another possibility is the little Winston girl. Very docile and well-behaved. She will make a good wife for you, Richard."

"She's nine years old, Mother," said Richard's oldest brother, Horace.

"A betrothal could be arranged," Grace replied primly.

"No," Richard said firmly. He didn't look up from examining the goblet of wine he had barely touched. "I'm not marrying any of them."

"Richard! Don't be impertinent," his mother chastised. "You will marry, and soon. I've allowed you to run wild long enough. It's past time for you to take a decent wife and settle down.''

"Take a well-connected wife, you mean," Richard said drolly, his eyes flicking up to meet his mother's.

His mother didn't understand. "Why, of course a well-connected wife. What other kind is there? And I must choose her for you, of course. Your judgment is horrible. None of us have forgotten the terrible mistake you made over that ill-bred Ashton girl. It was appalling. I don't believe this family will ever live it down."

"Excuse me, milords, miladies," intoned the family butler from the entrance of the great hall. "Lord Richard has a visitor. She will not give her name, and she is most insistent she be allowed to see him immediately. Oh!" The woman in question brushed past him and entered the vast hall. All eyes turned to her.

Audrey had not bothered to wait for her summons. She knew how things worked in great houses, particularly this one, and she also knew she simply had to ignore proper protocol and get to Richard himself as soon as possible, before she was sent away.

"Audrey!" In one motion, Richard leapt over the table. In an instant he was holding her tightly against him. "You came! I can't believe it!" He swung her around joyfully.

"Judith convinced me not to stay with her," she explained quickly, breathless from his welcome. "She said I ought not to sacrifice my own happiness on her account."

"Thank God for Judith," Richard said happily, laying kisses all over Audrey's face.

"Richard! Get your hands off that wench immediately!" Lady Grace cried. "That is no way to behave in my hall!"

Richard ignored her, but he turned to his family at large. "Everyone, I'd like to introduce you to Audrey Higgenbotham, my bride."

"Your bride!" cried Lord Ambrose, Richard's father.

"You heard right," Richard said lightly. "We're going to be married tomorrow."

"Married!" Lady Grace was aghast. "But who is this girl? What family does she come from? What are her connections?"

"Her connections, you ask?" Richard said with a grin. He slapped a hand to his chest. "Right here is the most important connection for a wife of mine to have. She's irrevocably connected to my heart."

"She is cute," murmured Ambrose. "And look at that figure!"

"I know that wench," Horace said. "She was here during that fiasco of Richard's wedding." He turned his back to his wife, Beatrice, and spoke low to his father. "I tried to bed her, but she would have none of me."

"Lady Judith Ashton's maid, that's who she is!" Errol grinned. "You've really stuck your neck out this time, brother."

At this revelation, Grace's face began to darken like a strong winter storm. "I forbid it!" she cried angrily. "A penniless servant? Richard, you go too far!"

Richard ignored her outburst, though her shouting shook the walls. He was still holding Audrey's sweet figure tightly against him, and spoke primarily to her. "Right now, I'm going to take Audrey to my room and welcome her properly." His brothers whooped and whistled merrily. "Then tomorrow, we're going to the parish church in Lankenshire and be married in a simple but meaningful ceremony." He smiled at his family expansively. "You're all invited, by the way."

"This is outrageous!" Lady Grace cried, rising to her feet. "Send that girl away immediately! She's obviously nothing but a fortune hunter. Why, look at her! She has nothing to offer."

Richard looked at her, all right, and the heat of his gaze was palpable in the room. "She has everything to offer me, for I'm nothing without her."

Audrey laid her hand gently on Richard's face. "Ah, dear Richard, that's the most romantic thing I've ever heard you say." Their gazes locked in remembrance of Richard's attempts to play the romantic swain.

He took her hand and kissed the palm. "Because it's true."

"By the Cross, he's brave," Horace said in admiration. "God knows I let Mother force a bride on me." The sentence barely left his lips before his wife, Beatrice, smacked him.

Lady Grace turned to Horace in a fury. "Because if I hadn't, you idiot, you would have done something foolish like this!"

"What's so wrong in it?" said Lord Ambrose at her side. "I'm tired of discussing it, Grace. Brides, dowries, weddings, it's extremely taxing. After all, Eric of Sweden fell in love with a girl selling nuts outside his palace and married her. If a king can marry a nut seller, our fourth son can marry a well-bred lady's maid."

"I will not hear of it!" Grace cried. "I will not allow our esteemed name to be connected with a baseborn wench such as she."

Richard was too busy dropping light, sensuous kisses on Audrey's mouth to hear her.

"I will disown you, Richard," cried his mother furiously. "You will lose every cent! You will be cut off from the great name of Langsforth forever!"

"Dear," Ambrose said, an amused expression on his features. "I truly don't think he cares."

"Come, my sweet. We have more important business elsewhere." Richard took Audrey's hand and led her toward the exit.

"Richard, get back here immediately!" Lady Grace cried.

At the door, Richard turned and looked directly at his mother. "Mother," he said evenly. "I want to say something to you. I've been meaning to say it for a long time."

"Well then, what is it?"

"I love you dearly, Mother."

"Why, Richard, how sweet—"

"Now, butt out."

He swept Audrey off her feet and into his arms and carried her from the room. Behind him, the room was silent for one long heartbeat. Then Horace clapped his hands. "Bravo, Richard! Well said."

His other two brothers joined in the applause, accompanied by their father's chuckling.

Chapter 24

April, 1602

Someone was following him. The sensation that he was being tracked had started several days ago. At first Marcus assumed it was his overactive imagination coupled with a very real fear of discovery. He had just returned to London after spending several months touring the countryside with the Lord Chamberlain's Men, including performances for appreciative students crowded into the courtyards of Oxford and Cambridge.

Marcus was beginning to think he had been woefully careless in deciding to accept the role William Shakespeare had written for him. He had appeared in minor character roles on stage at the Globe without causing the least suspicion.

But now he was acting the title role in *Othello*. He had been willing to take the risk, considered it worth it for the opportunity it presented. Neither he nor William Shakespeare truly expected anyone would recognize him after this long. Marcus Sinclair was dead. But a new actor, Anthony Smith, had been hired by the Lord Chamberlain's Men. He was a superb character actor, appearing on stage as fat merchants, Egyptian prelates and fairy kings.

Unlike the ill-fated Marcus, Anthony sported a full beard and mustache. For this latest role as Othello, he applied makeup that darkened his face so much that he would be convincing as a black-skinned Moor. No one could possibly know who he really was when he was on stage, or rather, who he used to be.

Or so Marcus had believed. But with the eerie sense someone was following him growing stronger day by day, he began seriously to reevaluate his assumptions.

Marcus turned the corner into the narrow, twisting lane where he lived. Anthony lived in a different location from Marcus Sinclair, naturally. He could hardly have kept the same address. He had taken up residence in a Bankside boardinghouse with three other working-class men. Their landlady, an inquisitive widow, was unfortunately overly interested in her boarders, particularly the mysterious Anthony Smith, who managed to evade her questions despite her efforts to draw him out.

Partly thanks to her, Marcus knew his time was almost up. Last evening, after he arrived home, she confirmed his suspicions. She was quick to tell Marcus that a well-attired gentleman who claimed he was a potential boarder had asked questions about who else she let rooms to. One thing led to another and she had told the man almost all there was to know about Anthony, which thankfully wasn't much.

The landlady had apologized for having said so much and wished fervently her talkativeness wasn't going to cause problems for Anthony, even going so far as to ask if he might not be hiding from the law. "You keep so to yourself, Anthony," she had remarked. "Never any trouble from you. Never taking a ladyfriend to your room, or even visiting with male friends, for that matter." Marcus knew her probing was a broad hint to tell more about himself, but he had been as circumspect as always, quickly retiring to his room.

The news of the gentleman visitor disturbed him more than he had thought it might. He knew he was living on borrowed time. But he was drawn to the stage like a moth to the flame. Other than touring with the company, where else could he be but in London? The finest stage productions were in London, and he was too much a professional not to want to ply his craft with the best in the world.

Marcus stopped suddenly in front of an apple vendor's cart. He listened closely, thought he heard footsteps a block behind also stop. But the darkening street was too congested to be certain. Ignoring the apple vendor's sales call, Marcus continued forward, this time turning left down an even narrower alley. A plan was forming in his mind, though he knew it might bring about the end for him as readily as it might remove this threat that dogged his steps.

He slipped around a third corner and paused. At first he heard nothing. Then the now familiar pat of footsteps on the dirt road began to grow closer. He was definitely being followed. In a moment he would know from what quarter this latest threat was coming.

The man passed the alley entrance without seeing Marcus. In an instant, Marcus was upon him. He shoved him against the nearest wall and pressed his knife to the man's throat. "Why are you following me?" he demanded.

The man's eyes, less than six inches from his own, grew wide with fear. And then something else—recognition. Marcus' own eyes were locked to his, fear starting its dread path through his nerves. For a moment the two men were frozen together, each absorbing the knowledge of what this encounter could mean, but neither able to break through the initial shock of recognition.

Marcus released his hold on the man and stepped back. It may not be too late to try to circumvent the coming events if he acted quickly enough. "Excuse me, I thought you were someone else," he began lamely. He quickly turned and began striding down the narrow alley. Only a moment passed before the footsteps began to follow.

"Marcus Sinclair."

Marcus hesitated briefly, then continued walking. He shuddered deeply. The man knew him, as well he might. The one man in all London who held his life in his hands. Was he now to be murdered by the same man twice? Marcus half expected to feel a knife in his back. But he walked on as if he hadn't heard Howard Ashton, continued around the corner into the lane where he lived. The footsteps behind him continued apace, not getting closer or farther away, merely keeping step.

Marcus didn't hesitate in front of his boardinghouse door. He continued onward, for to enter would merely tell Ashton where he lived, if indeed he didn't already know, which was unlikely.

He continued around the next corner, unsure where he was heading, but knowing he had to get to the more populated area of Bankside before he could make a break for it, blend with the crowd. Until then, he merely had to act as if nothing were wrong and pray the man behind him would assume he had made a mistake.

Marcus headed down Maiden Lane. The Globe wasn't far away. Perhaps he should head there. *No, Sinclair, stupid idea.* The theater had been his sanctuary until now. But after today, he wouldn't dare set foot in it.

What was he going to do next? He had no choice but to continue on, away from his past. He couldn't begin to think what he might do after this evening. One step at a time, he told himself. Easy now. *Think.*

Unfortunately, while the street was fairly busy, since it was about suppertime there weren't enough people about to allow him to get lost in the crowd. But if he made a run for it, it would only increase the suspicions of the man trailing him.

He lost the sound of the footsteps following him. Had the man fallen behind? There was too much noise about for him to be certain. Marcus strained for the sound, but it was lost amid the clamor of the carriages, horses and people moving along the thoroughfare.

Marcus saw a gentleman's carriage in front of a door leading to a brothel. It was a familiar sight in Southwark, and one perhaps he could make use of. Marcus decided that as soon as he passed the carriage, he would slip inside the brothel, chancing that the man following wouldn't be able to see where he had gone.

Marcus came abreast of the carriage and was about to turn in the brothel door. Just then, the footsteps behind him pounded hard into the pavement. "Clyde, stop him!" called Howard.

Marcus took one running step and slammed full into the Ashtons' powerful groom. Clyde's massive arms wrapped around him like steel bands. Panting hard, Howard Ashton jogged up to the two. Marcus was struggling and swearing furiously, the groom holding him securely. Marcus was not a small man, but he could not break free of the brawny groom's grip.

"I have him, master," Clyde said. "What do I do with him?"

"Put him in the carriage," Howard said. Marcus heard a victorious note in Ashton's voice and shuddered inwardly. He was once again in the baron's power and had lost his chance to escape. He stopped struggling, preferring to keep his dignity.

Howard slipped into the carriage beside him, his own dagger drawn before him. He held it in two hands, nervously, as if unaccustomed to the weapon or afraid of having to use it.

Marcus settled back into the seat and stared at him, his face stony. He would wait for Howard to speak first, learn the lay of the land.

"It *is* you! I can't believe it! You're alive!" Howard rattled on, inexplicably happy to see him.

Marcus replied laconically, "Am I really?"

"Marcus Sinclair is sitting right here, in my carriage," Howard said in amazement. He quickly reached up and slapped the roof of the carriage. Clyde started off down the street, heading for London Bridge.

"Marcus Sinclair is dead," Marcus said bluntly.

"How did you manage it? I don't understand it. When I saw you at the Globe, I thought you looked much like Sinclair."

"Judith said you hated the theater," Marcus interrupted.

Ashton looked sheepish. "Actually, I have lately found myself there more and more frequently. I saw *Othello* for the third time today. Something in your stance, or your voice, recalled your memory to mind despite the blackness of your face paint. Of course, it's easy when one is thinking of something to see it before you. But then I got to studying the program. Anthony—Marcus. Mark Anthony. It was a code!"

"Not exactly, for it was never intended to be broken."

"But I did it! I saw *Anthony and Cleopatra,* too. Anthony gave up everything, an entire empire, for the woman he loved. It reminded me of you, though another man played that part. Of course, I still wasn't sure it was you, even after seeing

Othello for the third time. When I first grew suspicious, I waited outside the theater and watched for you. You appeared, and I got a better look. The beard threw me a moment, I admit. But then I thought I heard someone call you Marcus.''

That had been something of a problem. Every player who knew him before knew who he really was, of course, and it wasn't easy to break old habits.

"Then I followed you."

"I noticed."

"Several times. I had to be sure, you see, sure it wasn't an old man's imagination. I would go see whatever was playing; then I followed you wherever you went. You never went out to celebrate with your fellow actors, or to the brothels, which I admit impressed me. You spent a lot of time sitting on the riverbank, staring across the Thames at London.''

Marcus crossed his arms in front of himself. This conversation was entirely too personal. He felt as if his privacy had been violated, for his thoughts when he visited the riverbank were of an extremely personal nature. Those were the times when he indulged himself, taking out his memories with Judith, reliving them before once more tucking them away in his heart.

"Then I followed you home."

"And spoke to my landlady," Marcus added.

"Aye. She told me what she could about you, which wasn't much. But the time you took the room at her boardinghouse coincided nicely with your—death."

"You have been most thorough," Marcus commented dryly.

"I was. I had to be sure, you see, had to be sure this all wasn't some figment of an old man's desperate imaginings."

Howard Ashton was inordinately pleased with himself, and it irritated Marcus to no end. Was the man crazy, or simply looking forward to murdering him again? "All right. Let's get this over with. You caught me out."

Howard was brimming with curiosity. "What happened? I had thought you executed; then I learned later you had died in prison. How did you manage to escape entirely?"

"*I* had nothing to do with it. Some friends of mine arranged it."

Howard slapped his thighs. "It's incredible, that's what it

is. And you've been in hiding these three months, right here in London! Unbelievable!''

"Lord Ashton, I have no wish to be rude," Marcus said coolly. "But there is no love lost between us. I know you set me up, and I know why you did it. You wanted me out of the way. So that's where I am. I don't exist anymore, not to your daughter, not even to myself. So if you would be so kind as to allow me to continue as I am, nothing more need be said.''

Howard Ashton eyed him closely. "Aye, you know what really happened that night, don't you? I learned that later. Tell me how you knew.''

"I overheard you and Mowbray discussing your—arrangement—at Mowbray's wedding festival.''

"As far back as that! Why, you could have blackmailed me yourself for a small fortune.''

Marcus ignored that remark. "I was angry with both of you for making Judith into a pawn in your power games," he said bitterly. "So I didn't hesitate to help Richard free her. I knew she would be safe as part of the Earl of Langsforth's household. But I knew Mowbray was not the kind to let you get away without payment of some sort. I knew you were as rich as Croesus and could afford to pay him off.''

"Aye, I suppose that's true. Marrying Judith to him seemed the easiest way to satisfy him." He glanced at Marcus, who was glaring at him. "I admit now it was a selfish thing to do, so you needn't say anything. Pray, continue. How did you know the rest?''

"That night, Kennington let slip a remark about how he was taking care of me while you were dealing with Lord Mowbray. It wasn't difficult to piece together the rest.''

"But you never told a soul that I was the one who killed Mowbray. Why? It meant your own life!''

"You know the answer already, or you should by now," Marcus said bitterly.

"Judith," Howard said in amazement.

"I was not going to be the man to steal her father from her. She loves you very much.''

"Yet I didn't hesitate to steal her lover from her," he said thoughtfully.

"As you say," Marcus said grimly.

Ashton sighed heavily. "That kind of love—it must be rare."

"I wouldn't know."

"Yet it continues?" Ashton asked carefully, eyeing his captive.

Intense pain flashed briefly across Marcus' face, then disappeared behind a mask. It lasted but a moment, yet it told Howard all he needed to know. He smiled slowly, savoring a thought, a wish that had been merely a daydream. What was to prevent it from coming to pass? "I've got you now. You can't get away from me this time. It will be awkward, a bit. A little explaining to do at Court, but it can be done. There's no reason it can't. Of course, you may have to keep your new name, or people will wonder. And you must quit this acting business. A shame, as you are quite good. You can always dabble as some nobles do, I suppose, putting on your own spectacles for your guests. And there's patronage, of course. Lord knows, there will be sufficient funds. The London house—that can be part of it, along with its one thousand pounds a year household budget from my estates. There's the matter of the title, but that can skip a generation. The children—the first boy, of course, will inherit it."

Marcus was no longer listening. The man was muttering about some financial matters that made little sense to him. He was still tense from this extremely awkward encounter, his thoughts concentrated on the best way to escape.

Where he was being taken was still a mystery. Any moment the carriage would probably be driven into a dark alley, where he would be pulled from the carriage and beaten or stabbed to death. If only Lord Ashton didn't look so positively pleased at the prospect of sending him to his death a second time.

". . . that's what matters in a husband for Judith. Strength of character. I've always believed that was the true key to nobility in a man, regardless of his origins," Lord Ashton continued.

Marcus barely heard him. The carriage had long ago crossed the vast London Bridge and was now thundering up Bishopsgate Street. Marcus found himself looking for Judith's house, as he always did when he passed by here—which wasn't often, for he usually made an effort to avoid this neighborhood. There was always the fear he would run into someone who would recognize him. Besides, seeing the house where he had last made love to her, and memory of the pain he had inflicted on her, hurt too much.

But now, Marcus' gaze gravitated toward the tall, stately home set off the street, and he imagined the woman who used to live there, before she married and moved away with her perfectly suitable, nobly born husband.

"... fine, strapping sons, I'm sure," Howard was saying. "They say country stock is hardy, and considering how well you've withstood what I've put you through, I'd say that's true."

Marcus remembered well what this man had put him through. A ruthless beating, which his knees still reminded him of when he overtaxed himself. Followed by a severe fever that almost claimed his life. An arrest, a brutal lashing in prison, a mock trial, a death sentence. And worst of all, being forced to give up the only woman he had ever loved, ever would love, each day living with the knowledge that she was married to another man. What more torture could the man beside him devise?

"I wish you would finish this business," Marcus said tightly.

"I'm trying to, man, I'm trying to."

There it was. Marcus was headed for his death, once again. Marcus knew Howard was guilty of murder, making the actor very dangerous to him. Howard would not hesitate to remove the threat Marcus presented, particularly when he should have been dead already.

Marcus' gut tightened at the prospect. Since Shakespeare revived him, he had known he was living on borrowed time. The clock had just stopped ticking. Marcus pondered Judith, wanting suddenly to know all about her, what she was doing, where she was living, what turn her life had taken.

"Is she happy?" Marcus asked quietly.

Howard looked surprised by the question. "What do you think?"

"I hoped she might be, with her new husband."

"There *is* no husband—yet. Haven't you been hearing what I've been telling you? Judith refused to marry any man, any *living* man, that is. And I haven't the heart to force her. I couldn't do that after the pain I caused her."

Marcus stared at him in disbelief. Was that compassion he was hearing? But then, he had always known the man cared for his daughter, in his own way.

His gaze turned once again to the Ashton mansion. The carriage slowed and turned into the drive. So she still lived here with her father.

Howard slapped the carriage roof again. "Pull up here, Clyde."

Clyde did as bid, stopping the horses in the center of the drive. Howard turned to Marcus. "Well, here we are."

"Aye, here we are," Marcus echoed, in false imitation of the man's disgusting joviality.

"You don't appear very excited."

"Excited? I try not to appear excited at the prospect of my own death," Marcus said wryly, his eye on the sharp dagger that was still pointed toward him.

"Death?" Howard looked confused. Then he followed Marcus' eyes. His hand had relaxed on the blade, but he hadn't yet put it away. "Oh, this! So sorry." He slipped it back into his scabbard. "Well, you can get out now. I'm going uptown for a drink. I feel the urge to celebrate, and I imagine you don't need me around the rest of the evening."

Marcus was thoroughly lost. Had Judith's father gone mad? He made absolutely no sense. Before he left the carriage, thinking angrily of the long walk home Howard's bizarre actions were forcing him to undertake, he decided to attempt once more to figure out what all this was about. "All right, enough is enough. Why did you bring me here?"

Howard looked surprised by the question. "Goodness man, haven't you got ears?"

"Of course, but—"

"Haven't you heard what I've been saying?"

"I hear perfectly, but—"

"Goddammit, Marcus Sinclair. I want you to marry my daughter!"

Marcus simply stared, certain he hadn't heard the man right. He glanced at Howard with suspicion. "Perhaps I don't hear perfectly after all. I thought I heard you say you want me to marry . . ."

"My daughter, Judith. You remember her. Slender, blond—"

Marcus scowled at him. It was hardly a time for jokes.

"You do still love her, don't you?" Howard asked pointedly.

"Do you have to insult me by asking me that?" Marcus said disparagingly.

"No, I'm sure I don't. So, why are you sitting in here with me, when you could be up there with her?" Howard gestured toward the second-story window, a window Marcus knew very well from experience led to Judith's bedchamber.

"You're inviting me to visit her chamber?"

"Aye, why not? Tomorrow we'll make it legal. But you have to promise me one thing."

"And that is?" Here it came, Marcus thought. This was all a bloody poor joke, and now the punchline was about to be delivered, with himself as the laughingstock.

"Tell her I sent you," Howard said gently. "She'll understand."

Dazed by the events, Marcus stumbled out of the carriage. He stood there in the drive while Howard Ashton's carriage rolled back to the road and turned left toward town. Marcus lifted his gaze toward the balcony and the window beyond, lit by a soft golden glow.

Judith sat near the balcony, allowing the cool spring air to caress her skin through a partly open door. A cittern nestled in her lap. Now and then she plucked out the strains of a song heard only once, a lifetime ago, but never forgotten. She cradled the instrument in her arms and began once more to re-create the heart-stirring music, imagining the golden springtime when a man sang to her of love, when she was young enough to believe that dreams came true.

She tried to discipline herself not to indulge her memories too frequently. But when she did, she lost herself fully inside them. She started to hum along with her uncertain music, wishing fervently that she could remember all the words. "Come away, come, sweet love," she sang softly. A nightingale flew

by, adding its own trilling note to her composition. "Come
away."

> Come away, come, sweet love,
> The golden morning wastes:
> While the Sun from his sphere
> His fiery arrows casts,
> Making all the shadows fly,
> Playing, staying, in the grove;
> To entertain the stealth of love.

Judith froze, her hands stilling on the strings as the voice
floated up to her from below her balcony. Someone knew her
song, the song Marcus had written for her.

The voice continued singing, its deep, rich voice making her
heart soar, it was so like Marcus' voice.

> Thither, sweet love, let us hie
> Flying, dying in desire,
> Winged with sweet hopes and heavenly fire.
> Come away, come, sweet love.

Judith rose slowly to her feet, the cittern falling forgotten to
the floor. She stepped onto the balcony into the caressing
warmth of the spring evening. "Who's there?" she called
uncertainly. She went to the edge and looked down, but saw
no one. "Who is singing?" she asked again, disconcerted.

"Judith, it's me."

The voice was with her on the balcony. It poured over her
like divine nectar. Gradually, so as not to disturb the spirit—
for what else could it be?—she began to turn around.

He stepped from a shadow cast by the house and stood a
mere five feet from her, looking for all the world as if he were
alive. Judith fell to her knees and clasped her hands. "Spirit,
why have you come?" she asked in awe. "I should be afraid,
but I'm not. You are the true likeness of Marcus, and I could
never fear him."

Marcus moved in front of her. He slipped his hands under her arms and lifted her firmly to her feet. "I'm real, Judith. Let me show you." He pulled her into his arms and settled his mouth on hers, coming home to where he belonged.

Judith was stunned by the reality of his kiss. She barely had time to enjoy it before she suddenly realized he was *alive!* She pulled back and gazed up at him in amazement. She lifted her hand to his cheek, her fingertips playing along the unfamiliar thick black beard. But his eyes—it was Marcus, her Marcus, and he was alive! Judith buried herself in his arms again. She wrapped her arms tightly around him, afraid she would lose him to the night if she let go.

But her senses told her a different tale. She reveled in the reality of his hard physique against her own body, the sweet hint of his own male scent. He was surely no specter, but warm, real and very much alive. Her heart pounded with exhilaration. It was impossible, but he was real, real! "Marcus! Oh, Marcus, I can't believe it!" she gasped, tears springing up behind her eyes.

"Judith, darling, I can scarce believe it myself," Marcus said, his breath teasing the tendrils about her face. "A short time ago, I would have sworn I was dead."

Judith pulled back and searched his magnificent gray eyes. "But you *were* dead—weren't you? And now you're alive! I'm afraid to question it, afraid you'll disappear back from whence you came." A joyous laugh bubbled to the surface and spilled out into the night air. "Afraid I'll wake up! Oh, Marcus." Judith caressed his face, exploring each of his features, relearning the knowledge of him under her fingertips.

Marcus stroked her back, kissed her face, whispered words of love and longing so moving Judith had never imagined she would ever hear the like.

"How can this be? Or have I completely lost my mind?"

"Not unless we're both mad," Marcus said with a chuckle.

Marcus explained how he had been drugged into a false death and smuggled out of prison. His explanation naturally led to describing where he had been since prison, how he had been living merely a few miles away in another neighborhood.

Judith's initial shock at seeing him appear before her had

passed. As she absorbed what he said, a new emotion welled up—irritation. "Marcus Sinclair, you were living a few miles from here and you didn't bother to tell me? But why?"

"How could I tell you, Judith? How? Your father—"

Judith's eyes widened. "Oh, my God, my father! Quickly, come inside or he may see you when he returns." She pulled him toward the balcony doors leading to her room. Marcus complied, a smile teasing the corners of his mouth.

Judith closed the doors and locked them tight, then drew the drapes to block any possibility of someone from the street seeing into her room. "I have no idea when he may return. He's become obsessed with some pursuit lately, though I can't fathom what it is. He's been acting strangely. But enough about him." Clasping her hands together, she began to pace. "We have to make plans. Tomorrow we'll run away. Or should we leave tonight? Oh, I can't think! It's all so sudden, I—"

"Judith." Marcus settled his hands on her shoulders, stilling her. "Do you truly love me enough to run away with me?"

Judith looked into his eyes. "You know I do. I have for a long time. The day of your arrest—nay, that evening at Lord Chamberlain's, during the revelries. I saw what our love meant, and I knew where I belonged, for all time. Even though you were determined to convince me otherwise."

"Do you understand why I tried to convince you it was all a lie between us?"

"Aye, I do. You thought you weren't good enough for me. And that, Marcus Sinclair, is ridiculous."

"What about the hardship? You saw where I lived, my poor apartment. Could you live with me under those conditions, without your maids, your gowns, your jewels, your feather mattress? Do you realize what my daily life is like?"

"Marcus! I'm amazed at you. You did not hesitate to sacrifice your very life for my happiness—or what you thought would make me happy. If you truly think I'm so selfish I can't give up a few paltry possessions to be with you, why, why, it just makes me furious." She gazed up at him, her luminous eyes full of joy. "Except I'm too happy to be furious."

Marcus absorbed her commitment, reveled in it. "What about your father? I know he's more than a paltry possession to you."

"I love my father, Marcus. I would not enjoy hurting him. But I love you more." Her eyes were alight with a fire of independence Marcus had never seen before. "I've learned through all this that I cannot allow him to make of me what I'm not. I cannot spend the rest of my life the dutiful daughter, particularly when my father does not understand his own obligation to me. I cannot allow anyone to use me as a possession. I simply refuse. I belong with you, Marcus, and no other man will ever lay claim to me."

Marcus grinned broadly. He caressed her cheek tenderly. This was what he had longed to hear her say. "Truly?"

"Truly."

"I'm glad. For you realize he's responsible for this."

Judith hugged him tightly, fervently wishing she could make all the pain of the past disappear. "I know, darling. Oh, I know. He caused everything. I'm so sorry, I—"

"That's not what I mean," Marcus interrupted pleasantly, holding her shoulders and locking eyes with hers. "Despite all my attempts at concealment, Howard Ashton found me and brought me here tonight. If you can believe it, he actually suggested I spend the night with you, and plans that we shall be married on the morrow. He was emphatic that I tell you it was he. For once, I'm quite happy to comply with his wishes."

Was there no end to the revelations this night would bring? Judith knew then her happiness was unbounded. Not only had Marcus returned to her, so had her father. He had done the impossible. He had restored Marcus to her. In that instant, she forgave him everything. "Aye. I understand completely."

And Marcus—she knew now he had been testing her commitment, her independence, her willingness to be his alone. She was ready to become an actor's wife, a commoner. But her father's blessing meant Marcus' station in life would be changing, not hers. He would be elevated into the gentry, and the great House of Dunsforth would endure. Judith smiled to herself wryly. As if it mattered! All that truly mattered was that they would finally be together.

"Then, I suppose there's only one thing left for me to do," Marcus said sagely.